STOLEN
IDENTITY

STOLEN IDENTITY

—————— a novel ——————

VIANN PRESTWICH

Covenant Communications, Inc.

Covenant

Cover image © 2004 by Comstock Images

Cover design copyrighted 2004 by Covenant Communications, Inc.

Published by Covenant Communications, Inc.
American Fork, Utah

Printed in Canada
First Printing: August 2004

10 09 08 07 06 05 04   10 9 8 7 6 5 4 3 2 1

ISBN 1-59156-583-9

To Chris Bryant

Acknowledgments

My appreciation to Journey of Hope, an organization that supports and educates those who have mentally ill friends and family members. Also special thanks to those who work at Valley Mental Health. Their often unrewarded efforts provide an enormous service to the entire community.

PROLOGUE

Michael faced the gun with a mixture of shock and acceptance. He'd had a feeling about this man all along—but hadn't anticipated the ends he might go to to get what he wanted. *There are witnesses . . . He wouldn't dare shoot!* This was the last thought Michael had before his body slammed into the pavement.

Several minutes passed before he could open his eyes. He tried to focus on the red rock surrounding him. His left ankle ached, his head throbbed with each heartbeat, sweat mingled with blood. Was there a bullet wound, or were his injuries only from the fall? Michael couldn't tell.

He closed his eyes against the mocking rays and tried to numb himself to the pain. When had he taught himself to be numb? When had he learned to hide his crying? The sun burned his face as he tried to picture himself sobbing as Laura had done, her tanned cheeks striped with ribbons of salt, her beautiful face contorted, ugly.

In an attempt to stay conscious, the twenty-four-year-old shuffled through his memory and pulled forward childhood images, trying to find times he had cried. When had he lost control, abandoned his tight hold, and surrendered his stoic stare? After a childhood of numbing himself to emotion, he felt anguish now. Could it be he felt the pain so acutely because of the last few years of happiness?

What had Gail told Laura? *"You find happiness in the responsibilities God gives you."* He really had found happiness. Every responsibility had brought happiness, until now. Now he had miserably failed the two people he had promised to protect. As his blood soaked into dry ground, he found he still couldn't move. He was too tired and too beaten to do anything more than move back in time and remember.

CHAPTER 1

As the brightness of the morning faded out the streetlights, Michael closely watched his mother stack coffee cups onto a tray. She'd told him to wear his new clothes. Did that mean he started school today? Should he start walking past the warehouses, across the park, and to that big brick building? If he didn't go now would he be late? Shouldn't he leave before Dad came in and stopped him? Without speaking to the anxious child, the slender woman pushed through swinging doors and greeted the first customer of the morning.

Michael followed his mother to the front of the restaurant. Slowly circling each table, he carefully placed spoons onto large white napkins.

"Cute kid," said a trucker who had just sat down for breakfast.

"Thank you," said the young mother. Then Michael overheard what he'd wanted to know all morning. "He's five and will start kindergarten today."

Michael's expression never changed. He carefully arranged silverware, but his small hands trembled as he dreamed of running across the playground with a group of boys. Michael hoped the boys would be his friends. He would let them have the swing and even offer to push the swing if someone would just be his friend.

The only other child Michael knew was his little sister, Stephanie. She would sleep at home until their father decided she was ready to work.

Last week, Michael's mother had left right after the lunch rush and taken Michael to the store. She bought him five new shirts and three pairs of jeans. Then they had stopped at the large brick building surrounded by grass and swings.

Without holding his hand, Michael's mother had marched through the double doors and stopped at a table. A woman was handing out registration sheets. "Fill in the student's name, his parents' names, and any other children living in the household," the women said quickly.

As his mother took the forms and dropped into a vacant chair, Michael said each of the names to himself. *The student is me, Michael Ryan Ross.* Michael watched his mother's hand quickly print the letters. *My dad is Joseph Ross. My mom is Shannon Ross. My sister is Stephanie.* The young boy looked down the long hall and wondered which room would be his. He never dared ask.

Michael liked kindergarten. He enjoyed racing across the playground and playing tag. He knew all his classmates by their first and last names. He pushed them in the swings, and often someone offered to push him. At three o'clock he hurried home where his mother would be taking a nap before going back to work the supper crowd. Michael and Stephanie would sit on the large couch, their legs jutting straight out in front of them. Michael carefully pulled papers from his backpack and spread them onto Stephanie's knees.

"*C* and *S* sort of sound the same," explained Michael, solemnly pointing to a paper he had carefully colored earlier that day. "So it's easy to get *C* and *S* mixed up. Brandon Lewis spelled "cat" with a *K*."

Stephanie would look appreciatively at the *C* and *S* papers while Michael dug in his backpack for a hand puppet to show her.

In first grade, however, Michael learned he had to limit his friendships. One fall day, he ran all the way from school. Dodging the garbage spilling from the ever-present trash cans, he'd thundered up the boardwalk and slammed open the screen door into the unlit living room. The shades were closed as they always were. The house was dark, dusty from the dirt lot outside.

"Hey, Mom! Mom?" he yelled.

"What?" mumbled his mother, digging a work smock out of the laundry basket. She threw her seven-year-old son a T-shirt from the basket. "You better change. Your dad wants us there earlier. He thinks you should start coming straight to the shop without stopping here."

Ignoring any discussion of his father, the young boy unbuttoned his school shirt and then tried to calmly ask his mother for permission to do something he'd never done before.

"Could I, please, go to Jacob's house on Saturday when the shop's closed? Jacob told me I could come. He wants to be my friend."

"You're not going anywhere!" his mother snapped.

"But, Jacob said I could," Michael protested, surprising even himself at his emotions. He had never been in a friend's home.

"Next thing you know, some punk-face kid will be wanting to come here." Wearily, she pushed thick, dark hair back from large eyes.

"He can. I don't care," Michael said. "We'll be quiet."

"And do what?" His mother scowled, "Play in your bedroom? 'Yes, friend, this is my room. It used to be a bathroom, but we don't have water anymore since the pipes broke. So they made it a bedroom for me.'"

The anger that rained down on Michael's life had seldom come from his mother. Typically she ignored everything but her children's most basic needs. Her energies were spent meeting her husband's demands. And this day was similar to all the other days. She had put in six hours of waiting tables, had a two-hour break to clean house, rush to the Laundromat, and nap, and now she was going back for another five hours of work. Shannon Ross felt burdened by her son's request to have a normal childhood. She also felt a self-loathing for not having the strength to demand a better life. At that moment she lost control and became incensed at some unseen enemy.

"You're a stupid nuisance. Maybe you ought to go and see that most people don't live in a house without water. That in some families everyone has a bed to sleep on. That some fathers treat their wives and children like family and not like . . ."

She gripped Michael by the arm and pulled him through the small house, pointing to things the boy was so familiar with he hadn't thought of them as strange. The tour included the refrigerator on the porch, the kitchen table stacked with folded laundry, his sister's room without a door.

"Don't cause trouble for me or anyone else by bringing kids over here," she warned him, her anger softening. "You don't need to tell them any of our problems. Just be polite and don't think anyone would want to come here if they knew how we lived."

For the first time Michael recognized things to be ashamed of. He noticed that his clothes hung off pipes running along his bedroom wall. At one time this space had been a second bathroom. Sometime before his memory, the sink had been torn out and a mattress had replaced the tub. The only window in this small room was over his head. Often he'd crawl on the rickety dresser and look through the dirty pane. One Sunday morning when no one had to go to work, he'd pushed the wooden frame open and leaned out. The sun turned distant buildings into jewels. The horizon rose to blue mountains Michael wished he could explore.

"What are you doing?" his father had asked from the doorway.

Startled, Michael jerked back into the room and bumped his head. "Looking out," he said, feeling scared.

"At what?" Joseph asked.

"I'm trying to see where I'm not," he answered carefully.

The father laughed humorlessly. "Trying to see where you're not? Well, this is where you are. Get used to it, kid. You're not even considered an adult for another twelve years. You're mine until then. Now go help your mother. She's got all your dirty clothes to take to the Laundromat."

Michael jumped from the dresser and almost made it through the door before his father swatted him.

As long as Michael could remember, they had made weekly trips to the Laundromat. There wasn't enough water at the house for laundry or baths. He could remember his mother begging his father, "Please, can't we fix the lines? Please, honey. They are getting too old to bathe in a sink at the restaurant." For a while she had taken Stephanie and Michael to live with their grandma. Michael had loved it there. There were baths in a deep tub, meals around a table, good-night kisses. But then his father had called, and they'd gone back to the small white house on the edge of town.

In their house now, meals were never eaten around the kitchen table. On the rare occasion they ate at home, plates were handed out in front of the TV. The dishes were haphazardly stacked in the sink to await a barrelful of water that would be hauled from the restaurant. This water was only used for the toilet and dishes, never showers or laundry.

Less than a hundred yards from the railroad tracks, the restaurant shared the block with the UPS docking station. Trucks that serviced the Las Vegas, Nevada, area provided constant noise for the family business. Warehouses and large parking lots stretched for nearly a mile before fanning out to tiny houses on randomly placed lots. One of these lots held the Ross family home. Past the homes and across a neglected park sat Michael's school. Other children left school together, crossed the park, and called each other best friends. Michael figured he would never have a best friend. He never went to Jacob's or anyone else's house to play.

Despite his lack of friends, he loved a desk all his own and clean paper and sharp pencils. He loved learning to write neatly on that paper and slowly penciling his feelings into a journal. He loved his teacher, and he loved to have happy stickers placed on his assignments when he did his best.

He carefully carried each paper home and tucked them neatly under his mattress. No one saw the schoolwork. He knew instinctively that no one wanted to. His mother's advice for succeeding in school had been a lecture about saying "yes, ma'am" and "no, sir," like she'd taught him to do with the customers at the restaurant. His father's only references to school were veiled threats about what would happen to any child of his who caused trouble.

"Don't you cause any trouble," his mother had echoed later. "You show them you've got manners and show them that we're proper. You don't need to tell them any of our problems. You just show them your manners."

He'd shown them his manners for over four years now, calling his teachers "ma'am" and "sir" and thanking them for every attention. Understandably the teachers liked him. Understandably some of the other boys didn't. One day, that was made clear to him.

"You're teacher's pet," a boy called out as Michael exited the schoolhouse.

"Mikey is a sissy teacher's pet," they sang to him as he walked past. Surprise, instant fear, and hurt tightened his stomach.

"Am not!" he turned and yelled.

"Oh look, the baby's mad," the smaller of the three boys teased. "The baby's mad."

"Don't get all worked up," challenged the leader. "You'll get a rash where it hurts."

"Leave me alone!" shouted Michael as he turned away and headed toward his father's restaurant.

"The baby is a scaredy cat."

"You need the teacher to save you," taunted another.

"I'm not scared!" screamed Michael. "Not of you or nobody." Striking out blindly, he dove into the three boys. His fists flew randomly. He could hear laughter as they dodged his ill-directed blows. He screamed again and ran toward the three, who easily stepped aside.

The bigger of the boys pushed Michael from behind, and he fell hard onto the gravel road. Spitting rocks and dirt, he sprang to his feet and faced his enemies calmer and more self-possessed than seemed possible of a boy who just seconds ago had been in a screaming rage. Pain was something this boy recognized. The jolt to the ground had given him the presence of mind to defend himself, if not adequately, at least respectably.

The three boys' voices rang out as Michael tried to fight. His feet spread wide in a wrestler's stance, and it took the boys several attempts to pull him down. All three fell to the gravel road, and their leader topped the pile, pummeling the outnumbered youngster. For a while they looked like a tower of boys, then the two fell to the sides and the oldest and biggest of the three rose to plop down again on Michael's stomach. Feet pinned by the two other boys, the attacked boy forced himself not to feel the pain in his stomach and face.

"Stop it!" yelled a female voice from Michael's right. "Leave him alone." Relief filled Michael, but then more embarrassment. He *did* need a teacher to save him.

The largest boy rose slowly. Finding that his companions had already escaped, he grabbed his sweatshirt from the road and ducked behind a line of cars.

Michael's fourth-grade teacher looked concerned as she approached. He was one of her favorites with his polite manners and quick mind. Yet there was something tragic in this small boy's life. She had tried to reach behind the clean, shabby exterior, but had always faced a polite wall.

"You okay?" the teacher said softly as she stooped to help him up. Michael nodded and attempted to tuck his shirt into worn corduroy pants.

"Who were those boys?" she prodded.

"I don't know," mumbled Michael. "I gotta go."

"Wait, honey. I'll get something, and we'll wash the blood off your eye."

Michael didn't answer. He turned and walked out of the school lot, one hand clutching his stomach where he had been kicked, the other hand nursing his swelling jaw.

Slowly the small boy trudged up the hill toward his father's restaurant. Around three years had passed since Michael had dreamed of spending Saturday afternoon playing at a friend's house. He knew this was not the first fight he would face, but he hoped it would be the worst.

Although it was the end of October, the sun was still warm, and Michael could feel the blood drying on his face. Hoping not to meet any classmates, he made a detour through the park and ducked into a dirty public restroom to wash his face and hands. Even with this precaution, the blood on his clothes and the swelling around his eye would be incriminating.

Not wanting to arrive, yet scared of being late, Michael hurried the five remaining blocks to the restaurant. He had planned to enter through the back door and escape as much attention as possible. However, a delivery truck blocked the alley and the back door. Blindly, almost by instinct, he went around to the front and pushed open the heavy glass door.

The air-conditioned room made him shiver in his wet clothes. Hurrying to reach the kitchen, he wove between half-empty tables and stepped behind the counter.

"Whoa, son," his father said as Michael tried to pass. "What's happened to you?"

Rather than answer, Michael stared at his father's white apron and tried to count grease spots where the fabric stretched tight over a small stomach bulge. The boy didn't answer even when his father put an arm around his shoulder and bent to eye level.

"What kind of nonsense have you gotten into?" the balding man continued. His voice was soft, and each man at the counter chuckled to see this loving father talk to his small, wayward son.

The boy still refused to reply. The listeners were amused at the father-and-son exchange. These men liked the shop's proprietor. He listened to stories about their families, and he amused them with stories of his own. He was congenial and they considered him a friend. Not that they knew him well. They did not know where he lived or even where he was from, but the atmosphere was friendly and he or his wife always served them and then stopped to chat.

"Okay, son," the man said kindly. "Get yourself something to eat and I'll be back to help you clean up. Then we'll talk."

Michael shrugged the heavy hand off his shoulder and headed for the door that led to the kitchen.

He could hear his father talking to the men. Laughing, they conjured up possible reasons for his fight.

"Poor boy. I don't know. I've done what I can. Tried to teach him to get along. Maybe if we'd had another son. Maybe he needed a brother to play with. I've got to spend more time with him. Maybe . . ." His father's voice droned on, speaking confidentially to the men who waited patiently for him to finish so they could tell their stories.

"You should have told him what happened," Stephanie whispered as she skillfully skinned an onion. "You'd sooner he heard in front of someone than have to tell him back here. He's not in a very good mood," continued his seven-year-old ally.

The two of them worked almost mindlessly, without hesitation or emotion. They had done these respective jobs every day since they could hold a knife and reach the sink with the help of a stool. Even as they cut, sliced, and cleaned as if all were well, they could sense impending doom. There was a gathering storm, brewing unobserved to even the people seated in front of it. The storm was hidden behind a calm exterior, a convincing smile, and an agreeable laugh.

The counters had been scrubbed, and each plastic container in the cold walk-in fridge had been refilled. The floor was swept and supplies for the next day set out in readiness when the kitchen door opened with a bang. Both children whirled and got a glimpse of the dining room's empty interior. Stephanie grabbed a large, white cloth and industrially began to clean already-spotless surfaces.

Michael, trying hard not to be intimidated, stood against the back wall as far from his father as possible. The nine-year-old refused to allow his eyes to falter as they stared at the man leaning comfortably against the doorjamb.

"Did you cry when they whipped you?" his father asked across the room.

Michael shook his small head, squinting his dark eyes and drawing his lips in a tight line—a learned expression of toughness.

"You'll learn better than to come in here embarrassing me in front of the whole world, bleeding like a sissy, getting in fights you can't win."

Not one muscle changed on the young face as he appeared to listen to the man who so recently had convinced four intelligent men that he was a model father and companion.

As a child, Michael hated his father's kicks and jabs. Punches hurt, but he now felt the worst had always been the verbal lashings. Joseph Ross knew what each child valued most, and that was what he took.

Several months after the fight, Michael's dad found the carefully preserved school papers. He'd come into the living room where they were all mindlessly watching a horror movie, too tired to go to bed. Standing in his underwear, Michael's dad had one by one thrown the sheets into the air. "Look at this, Mikey's got little smiley faces on all these papers."

Horrified, Michael watched his father thumb through the stack of assignments. His father tossed two of the school papers into the air. "Very good." "Nice effort." His voice was mocking.

With only the light from the TV, the boy watched as his father carefully read each teacher's comments. "Very pleased with your effort." Taking a corner between thumb and forefinger, his father tossed the page into the air. The white paper fluttered to the ground and landed against Michael's knee. Paralyzed, Michael didn't move. His mom and sister remained unsure of the scene's significance. "You have great potential," the man read, and sent another page flying. "Very sensitive," he read from an English essay in which Michael had described a thunderstorm. The boy's father tossed this directly into the writer's face.

Michael's mind went numb. The papers danced like falling leaves for another minute, and then Joseph laughed at his son and went to bed.

After his sister slept, Michael slowly gathered the sheets and read each comment. Carefully stacking the papers, he rolled them into a tight cylinder and jammed them into the side of a full trash can. He never brought another paper to that house, and it would be years before he would be called sensitive again.

CHAPTER 2

Laura Keeyes started school the same year her family moved into their house on the Washington side of the Columbia River. She and her two older brothers had roamed the large empty rooms, hiding in spacious closets and crawling under the large honeysuckle bushes bordering the lawn. They'd marveled at how close the river was, but were warned to never go down the lane and across the street unless someone was with them. The river was no place for children to play without an adult, they were told.

With her parents occupied unpacking boxes, Laura had skipped quickly down the gravel path and slipped among the bushes along the river's edge. She trailed sticks against the current and threw leaves into the flowing water.

Ignoring her mother's frantic calls, Laura sat in the tall grasses and decided she'd sneak to the river every day, even if her parents didn't want her to.

An hour later, Laura was found. The spanking was mild. The lecture about swift currents and drowning was severe.

"You hate me!" Laura told them. "You don't want me to have any fun."

"We love you," said her father, "and we want you alive."

She didn't go back to the river alone. In time she understood why.

Like Michael, Laura loved school. She loved her desk and shiny new pencils, but mostly she loved her friends. She often brought several friends up the lane to her own home. All of them got off the bus together and ate snacks at the spotless kitchen table.

Laura's mom seldom minded. She melted cheese over tortilla chips and poured grape juice into plastic cups while listening to school stories much too jumbled in the telling to make more than the vaguest of sense.

At 5:48 P.M., Laura often ran outside and listened for the drone of the commuter plane. Her father would be piloting the plane with commuters from Seattle. If his load was light and there hadn't been much turbulence, he would dip his wings as he passed over the house. Laura waved frantically and knew her father was on his way home.

When job offers from larger airlines had been discussed, Laura always listened intently to her father and mother's conversation. More hours, more money—and more travel and less time at home.

"I can't, Mandy," her father would always conclude. "I have this new Church calling. I need to be to church. Changing jobs would require flying three out of four Sundays."

Often on a summer's evening, the family would follow the Lewis and Clark Highway to the bird refuge. Laura would get as close to the shallow shore as she could and wait impatiently for the large carp to swim close. The fishes' mouths would open wide, and she'd throw bread at them. One evening, a small girl only a few years older than Laura came and silently watched as Laura tossed small pieces of crackers at the greedy fish. The water would churn and bubble as the carp struggled for the food. Once the crumbs disappeared, the water would again settle into a smooth current rippling over the shiny fins. Laura quietly handed the girl a cracker. Without breaking it, the other child awkwardly tossed it toward the river. At the same moment a woman's voice shrieked, "Get over here, you brat!"

Laura jerked around, almost falling into the shallow water. The other girl turned slowly and started toward the picnic area as a woman rushed toward them. Laura watched as the angry mother grabbed the girl's skinny upper arm. The fingers pinched hard into the soft flesh, and Laura could see bruises from previous lectures. "Don't be wandering off," the woman snarled, "or we'll just leave you. You want to be left? Would serve you right." The mother marched her daughter up the bank. Laura thought about the girl all the way home.

"Why was her mom so mean?" Laura asked.

"Maybe she doesn't know better." Laura's father was reluctant to discuss the incident.

"They should have left her," Laura said. "She could have come home with us."

"You can't just take someone else's child," her mother replied.

"Why not? They weren't nice to her. She could have been my sister."

"We can't interfere," insisted Laura's mother. "We don't know all the story."

"Why does she have to have a mean mom?"

"Honey, I know it doesn't seem fair."

Laura worried about the little girl for a long time, often plotting ways to kidnap the unhappy child. Laura decided she would smuggle the girl home, conceal her in the closet, and the two would play secret games in the evening. Laura even saved money and bought an extra doll. Finally, though, as the years passed, Laura believed her mother. There was nothing they could do for the little girl with bruises.

* * *

White shirts and ties were not typical dress for the run-down restaurant. Of course, neither were name tags and clean-shaven chins. *These guys are too young, too clean, and too happy to belong here,* thought Michael. He sent his sister out to wait on them and then continued to stack a new shipment of supplies. He carefully slid the boxes of vodka and scotch behind gallon jars of pickles. The shop had no liquor license and only certain customers paid extra for the restaurant's special blend of alcohol and coffee.

"They're missionaries," said Stephanie when she reentered the back room. "And they say there's a prophet living in Salt Lake City. They're nuts, but they're cute. You think they're celibate?"

Michael didn't comment. He heaved a hundred-pound bag of onions and left to place it in cold storage. When he came back, he could hear Stephanie through the kitchen doors, flirtatiously asking the missionaries if they were like priests. The two young men didn't seem to understand her implications.

"No, we're not like priests. We don't do this forever. We preach the gospel for two years," said one skinny, short-haired boy, "then we go back home and attend school, or work, or whatever."

"And then you can date and stuff?" Stephanie asked pointedly.

The faces of both boys went red. The taller, darker of the two mumbled something and then cleared his throat and looked directly at Stephanie. "Yes," he said clearly. "We'll go home, get married, and have a family. But right now we're out telling people that families can be eternal. That you can be sealed together forever as a family and live together in heaven."

Stephanie laughed a bitter, sad laugh. "That, good buddy," she said, "sounds like the *opposite* of heaven to me. I've prayed for death so many times just to rid myself of this family. Now you tell me I'll have them on the other side?"

A tenderness surged through Michael as he saw the pain his sister bore. He stepped through the kitchen door and took her arm.

"Hey, maybe they got a plan where we don't have to take everyone. I wouldn't mind being with you."

Stephanie smiled, the first real smile he'd seen in a long time.

"You got that plan?" she asked the boys.

"We do," one said quietly, and he began telling the brother and sister about the plan of salvation.

Michael knew they had a few minutes to spare; as Michael and Stephanie got older, their father had started a baking business. This meant he came to work very early. After delivering his cinnamon rolls to diners around Las Vegas, he went back home to bed. His wife managed breakfast and lunch at the restaurant. The two teenagers came in after school and their mother went home. Michael and Stephanie worked alone until their dad came back for the small supper crowd and closed the shop himself. Some of his friends would stay late to watch movies. His two children relished the time he was gone. On this day they enjoyed it more than usual.

Customers trickled in, and Michael and Stephanie filled orders and then went back to hear the two young men.

Stephanie was the first to notice it was five o'clock. "Get out of here. Dad's coming. He'd kill us if he saw us talking to you," she suddenly interrupted.

So urgent were her pleas that the men thrust a book with gold letters at them and got ready to leave.

"We'll come back," one said.

"No!" Michael said.

"Never," reiterated Stephanie. "Dad would kill us."

"You call us then," said the skinny missionary, digging in his backpack.

"Yeah, yeah," said Stephanie, hurrying them out the door.

The two young men pushed pamphlets at Michael. "Our phone number is on the back."

"Go," said Stephanie. "Just go." The young girl spun into the back room and attacked a pile of pans. Her brother cleaned dirty tables.

"Been busy?" asked Joseph when he came in ten minutes later and saw tables without supper setups and empty napkin holders. He sneered at the cash register tape and then bellowed, "What have you been doing?" He raised one hand in a threatening gesture but didn't strike. He hadn't hit anyone since Michael had hit him back almost two years earlier. Lately their father had resorted only to emotional punishment. He started his emotional assault later that evening after the restaurant closed. Two men had poured themselves heavily laced cups of coffee and were settled comfortably in front of a TV pulled from the office. One was Stewart, a regular after-hours customer. His shallow complexion suggested a diet void of much nutrition. Michael once wondered how a man so skinny could appear so soft and flabby.

The men carried on conversation that was repulsive to Michael, and his father directed a few cruel comments at his offspring as they cleaned up. But this night, neither Stephanie nor Michael were concerned with their father's insults. They were both thinking of a Christ who could love them, of a book that had warmed Michael as he held it, and of two innocent boys who spoke of a God who heard prayers—a God who loved.

The walk home was colder than usual since they were late. Michael's backpack felt heavy with the incriminating evidence it held.

"Dad will kill you if he finds that book."

"He won't find it."

"Michael, he goes through our rooms. He knows everything."

"I'm leaving soon. I graduate in three months and then I'm leaving."

"He'll make you come back," Stephanie said wearily.

Michael had left once before, but the police had picked him up. He'd told them his father had hit him. A social worker came to the house. His mother had said things had been "tense" lately, but that things were better. His father had apologized, acting as if this was the first time he'd ever lost his temper, and he was, outwardly, extremely remorseful. The social worker filed a report. But there were no records of any injuries to either child. Immunizations were always up-to-date. They had good grades and no scars. Nothing ever happened.

"You could leave too," Michael urged Stephanie, coming out of the bitter memory. "Just come when I do. I'll be eighteen. He can't make me come back." Michael suddenly liked the idea of taking Stephanie on the trip he'd been determined to make since his father had caught him kneeling on his dresser and gazing at the distant mountains.

"Where?"

"I haven't decided yet."

"You don't know where you're going. You haven't got any money to go with, Michael. Sounds like a plan for failure."

"I've got some money."

"A whole lot you can save from our twenty dollars a week."

"A little bit from there 'cause sometimes I talk Mom into buying my shoes and telling her I've got extra fees at school, but most of the money I have is from learning to run the till like Dad."

"You've been stealing?" Stephanie stopped and looked at her brother. "Michael, no. He'll catch on."

"No, he won't. I've been taking about thirty dollars a week for over a year. I've got almost two thousand dollars. You can have half if you promise to leave."

"But I'm not eighteen."

"I could send for you in a year. I'll have a place by then."

She took a deep breath and nodded, and all the way home they made plans. The cold stars twinkled. The two siblings' breath was visible in the crisp night air, but Michael felt warmer than he had for a long time. As Stephanie opened the screen door to their home, Michael gently grabbed her wrist for the second time that night. "You can have some of the money, Steph. I'll find a place and a job, and then you can come."

"You promise? You'll send for me?"

"Sure." Michael smiled and swung his backpack down from his shoulders. He could feel where he'd stuffed the Book of Mormon into a side pocket. "Aren't families supposed to be eternal?"

* * *

"Why, Mom?" Laura pleaded pathetically. She had screamed the night before without success. This morning she was trying a new tactic.

"I wish Scott and Curt were here," she whined. "They'd take me."

Her parents remained firm. She couldn't go. "Laura, you spent everything you have."

"I want to go so bad." The senior class had planned a trip down the coast to California, and Laura felt that she could convince her parents if they understood what she'd be missing. "Just lend me the money."

"If you hadn't bought a prom dress and movie tickets, you'd have enough," her father reminded her.

"The boys would lend it to me."

"I don't think either of them is in a position to. Curt can't lend you money from his mission in Scotland, and Scott needs everything he can make to finish school and support his new family. Laura, you have finally got to understand that you can't do everything. You can't have everything you want."

"I don't get *anything*."

"You bought a dress."

"I *needed* that dress."

"No one needs an eight-hundred-dollar prom dress," her father replied.

"You don't understand."

Laura's mom got up from the table. "She did look pretty, though."

"She would have looked just as pretty in something a little less extravagant," Lance told his wife.

"You don't understand," Laura wailed. "*Everyone* is going."

"You made different choices for your money," her father said with a sharp look at his wife. They had discussed this the previous evening and had decided they would not give Laura any more money. He could tell, however, that Mandy was ready to give in to their daughter.

"It's going to be a long summer," Mandy said quietly to her husband.

"I heard that," Laura said, forgetting that today she wasn't going to yell. Her voice rose. "Maybe I'll leave right after graduation. Live with Scott until BYU starts."

"And do what?" her father asked.

"Get a job so I'll have my own money. So I can be my own boss, do anything I want."

Laura had never had much of an "income." When she was twelve and ward members had called asking her to babysit, she'd usually declined.

"The Raymonds have nice children," Laura's mother had said, "and they pay well. Why did you tell them no?"

"That baby drools," Laura had said.

"All six-month-old babies drool."

"No, I think there's a problem there. He sticks his tongue out all the time."

"He's discovering his body parts."

"Ooh, it's gross. That other one, she kept pulling her clothes off. Then she'd get her mom's shoes—shuffle around in them. Just her underwear and her mom's shoes on. When the shoes fell off she'd scream and cry. You'd think even a two-year-old could figure out that those shoes wouldn't stay on. The kid had an attitude."

"And you don't?"

"What do you mean by that?"

"Never mind." Her mother had shaken her head in surrender.

Years after that, a part-time receptionist's job at the airport delivery service had worked well until it interfered with spring-break plans. All of Laura's part-time jobs had interfered with something.

Laura's parents looked at each other and knew that it was now time she got a taste of being her own boss.

The plans were made: After graduation Laura would take her Honda, live with Scott, and get a job. Laura left, not admitting her fears.

* * *

Michael's mom attended his graduation ceremony. She remembered from her own high-school graduation that the extra gold tassel on Michael's graduation cap meant honors. She read and reread his name listed as a scholarship recipient to the University of Nevada, Las Vegas.

Shannon Ross could also understand the school counselor's disapproval and disgust when her graduating son turned down the paid tuition. In a school not known for its academic excellence, the counselor was proud to have found a scholarship for a "boy from an uneducated family." When Michael told the school employee that he had other plans, she criticized and complained about the "nut not falling far from the tree" and how he would end up in a dead-end job. Michael listened vaguely, smiled grimly about the insinuation that he was like his father, and then continued with the plans he'd made the Saturday after seeing the missionaries.

He had been finishing a chemistry assignment in front of the TV when the "Mormon cult" football team from BYU started playing. His father was in the room as well, having closed the restaurant for the day.

All Michael's life his father had hated the "cheating religious fanatics." Today the team was winning a lopsided victory on their home turf. Disgusted, the older Ross left the room to take his traditional Saturday-afternoon nap.

Michael watched as the camera panned around the university and the narrator introduced viewing football fans to Brigham Young University. Manicured lawns, well-dressed coeds, and modern brick buildings faded in and out on the screen.

Michael focused on one thing: a sign which said, "The Church of Jesus Christ of Latter-day Saints." The same words as on the missionaries' name tags. The same name as on the pamphlets and the blue book hidden in his school locker.

"That's the Mormon cult." Michael sat up and grinned. He'd go there. Even if he couldn't get into school, he'd go there.

So on June 3, Michael celebrated his eighteenth birthday by waking his sister and promising her a thousand dollars when she was ready to leave. He'd send her an address soon. He packed a backpack with extra clothes and his book from the Mormons.

The bus station was more than six miles away, but Michael knew he had until 10:00 P.M. before anything headed north, so he walked slowly and finally sat down and wrote his mother a short note.

"We're all victims," he told her. "But not me anymore. I'll write soon." Michael addressed an envelope and thought about his mother. She'd just been too unsure and scared to change things. Then one day, too discouraged.

Alone, Michael headed for Provo—but he'd always felt alone. Now he had a destination.

CHAPTER 3

Laura decided that living with Scott was okay, but her brother kissed his wife too much, and the young married ward had more babies than adults. Often the congregation produced more noise than the speakers.

Her first paycheck was nearly as disappointing as hunting for a job had been. Janitorial positions were plentiful but had severe drawbacks. The shifts started at either 4:00 A.M.—sleep time—or after 7:00 P.M.—social hours. Other job openings weren't as numerous.

"They just don't need managers of your caliber," joked Scott when she described the other positions she'd noticed.

"I could be a secretary. I've interviewed three times and they didn't choose me," Laura ranted. "It's not fair. They picked a senior girl. She's going to graduate and leave. Why would they want her?"

"Maybe she was more qualified," Scott said carefully.

"I got A's all the way through English," Laura's voice was pitched to a childish whine.

"Can you type?"

"I hate typing. It's so slow."

Later that week Laura applied to wait tables, but they all said they wanted experience.

"Like it takes brains to hand out food," she fumed.

Her biggest disappointment was when she went to the Continuing Education Department at BYU and applied to help write and design brochures. "It's a wonderful place," she enthused to her sister-in-law as she described the mock-ups and then the final glossy product. "That's where I really want to work. They're going to make a decision by Friday."

Laura's phone call on Friday was of the "Thank you for applying. We had a lot of qualified applicants and couldn't use everyone" variety.

After spending the weekend sulking, she'd finally accepted a job at campus food services. She started at 10:00 A.M. handing out desserts and flirting with the boys through the lunch hour. After that she scrubbed the pots. Her fingernails split, her back ached, and the steam wilted her hair. She almost quit when she saw the amount of her first paycheck. Taxes weren't a new concept to Laura. Someone had mentioned them in government class. Yet no one had explained to Laura how severe a dent the civic duty would take from her income. Laura could barely afford to pay her brother a small rent, fuel her car, and still buy the leather sandals she'd seen one of the cashiers at food service wearing.

* * *

Michael spent his first night in Provo, Utah, sheltered by an abandoned house in the center of town. After eight hours on the bus, he was glad to be alone. The night was warm for June, and he thought about taking up permanent residence. "The shower is about the same as at home," he laughed to himself. "Yet there's more space."

With a map and helpful instructions from amused college students, Michael found his way to the registrar's office. The woman on the other side of the glass window hid her surprise when he wanted to register, and gently explained that the acceptance deadline had past. "You could sign up for continuing-education classes," she told him, pulling out a catalogue. "Here's a listing of classes. What are you interested in?"

"I don't know."

"What are your hobbies?" she asked.

"Nothing, really." The boy looked young and scared. The self-assurance that helped him successfully escape his home was slowly draining. The realization that he wasn't prepared for this hit him hard.

"What do you like to do in your spare time?" The graying woman was kind.

"I'll look at this," he said and took the magazine.

Michael walked quickly and blindly for a few minutes. Finally he sank to a long bench and looked around. Students confidently moved past. They knew where to go. They belonged here. The scared eighteen-year-old turned and looked at his reflection in a plate-glass window.

His dark hair was shaggy. Not long, but longer than those around him. His clothes were the same as his hair—shabby and shaggy. He'd come this far. Somehow he had to survive in this environment.

A group of young men in white shirts and ties came toward him. Michael sat up straight and tried to find the ones he had met at the restaurant in Las Vegas. Certainly one of them had to be with this group; there weren't that many boys who would dress like that and be missionaries. His two must have come back here. The young men went past without Michael recognizing any of them. He slumped back on his bench.

Finally, he rose and wandered around the campus. He didn't care that others looked at him; he'd become insensitive to his peers years ago. The food court smelled inviting, and he decided to head in that direction.

But when he saw the prices, Michael turned away. He saw ties and white shirts again, and he followed them down a flight of stairs and watched them go into a barber shop. He looked carefully at each face. Not one was familiar, but the hairstyles were similar. Michael took his place in line and had his hair cut missionary style. Afterward, Michael carefully studied what the other males on campus were wearing. Then he prowled around what he assumed was the student center until he found an abandoned *Daily Herald*.

With a pen taken from the registrar's office, Michael circled several job possibilities and then went back to his deserted house and looked through the continuing-education magazine. That night he slept warmly in a sleeping bag he had brought with him.

The next morning, Michael shaved in the restroom at a Maverik station. He caught a bus out to Provo Towne Center and carefully selected a job-interview outfit: pants with creases down the legs, collared shirt, and a pair of shoes like the missionaries wore.

With a city map, he started walking toward the first employment possibility. By 2:00 P.M., the new shoes hurt. Michael limped toward the Oasis House. He'd walked miles and filled out several applications, but with no telephone number and no address, he knew that unless he was hired on the spot, he had no way to get a job.

The closer to the Oasis address Michael got, the more he wondered. *Funny place for a bar in this residential area. And strange that they'd want a morning cook. Still . . .*

The address was a huge old home set back on a large lot. *The place must have been a regular mansion when it was first built,* thought Michael. Large trees shaded a white wraparound porch. Aging brick had been skillfully repaired at the corners and foundation. A sign on the heavy wooden door read, "Oasis House—Welcome."

The man in the lobby had two coats on. His hair hadn't been combed, and both black Keds were untied. His faded jeans barely reached to the top of his large ankles. The white socks were grimy and gray.

"Hi." His greeting was friendly. "Have you ever seen a UFO?" He looked expectantly at Michael.

"No, not recently."

"But you have before? You've seen UFOs?"

Michael looked around. No one else was in the entryway. An oak desk sat on one side with a guest register. Several worn easychairs were pushed against the walls.

"I'm applying for a job," Michael said to the man he now guessed to be in his mid-twenties. The boyish grin looked much younger.

"I'll apply too," he said. "Then we can watch for UFOs together."

Realizing the kid was probably joking or drunk, Michael decided to play along. "You know they only pay us if we spot one," Michael said. "So we might not make much money for a while. Maybe I'd better get another job too. Someone said there was a cooking job here."

"Oh yeah, I always cook. But not today. You know the main dish was veal. You know what veal is? Baby cows. Aliens never steal calves. They usually take the bulls. Pick them right up. Never leave a track. We should go out where there are lots of bulls. We'd see aliens for sure."

"Where's the kitchen?" Michael asked.

"The veal's gone. Everyone else liked it. But not me. What's your name?"

"Michael."

"I'm Connor. Connor Steele."

"Let's go see what they're having for tomorrow."

"Probably fish. It's Friday. You think they got fish in outer space? I bet not."

"I bet you're right. And probably aliens would be really curious about fish. UFO commanders might be in the kitchen right now checking out tomorrow's lunch."

Connor's grin showed beautiful teeth. "Hey . . . yeah."

Stoop shouldered, he ambled off down a wide hall. Michael followed and noticed large rooms through open doors. One was lined with computers being used by people of various ages and genders. Michael could see a woman using a word-processing program. A younger teenager had a game of solitaire opened on the screen.

Another room had large tables occupied by people of various ages and dress. One man was asleep, his head on an open book. He snored softly.

The kitchen was large and modern. Two males were splashing water over large square pans. A pretty, twenty-year-old brunette was industriously scrubbing at a beige countertop.

"Have the aliens taken all our fish yet?" asked Connor.

No one answered him, and he cheerfully started opening large refrigerator doors looking for seafood.

"I'm here about the cooking job." Not knowing whom to speak to, Michael made a general announcement to the room.

A well-manicured yard could be seen through a screen door. Bushes were trimmed back to reveal tilled flower beds where petunias and marigolds were beginning to bloom. At the edge of a sprawling patio was a grouping of picnic tables. At the tables sat several people smoking. Michael watched them for a moment.

"The smoker-joker group," said a man washing dishes. He left the pan he was scrubbing, pushed the door open, and yelled out, "Any of you jokers want to come in and help finish the floors?" A young man in an expensive polo shirt and slacks put out his cigarette and left through a back gate.

"Come on," yelled the apron-clad weightlifter.

A pixielike girl straddled the table bench and looked toward the house. Her shorts were frayed, but diamonds sparkled in her earlobes. "I got group employment at three o'clock. I can only help until then." The other smokers ignored the call for help.

"Come on," the man said, wiping his hands on the white cloth stretched across a well-developed torso. He led Michael into a small office, sat down behind a cluttered desk, and waved to a straight-backed chair.

"I'm Arnie. You want a job?"

"Yes, sir."

"Can you cook?"

"I can cook."

"I need references."

"I have none," Michael paused and then plunged into the first honest explanation he'd given all day. "Sir, I can cook. I can work. I learned to cook and work in my dad's restaurant. I have no references because my dad didn't want me to leave. In fact, I don't even have an address yet. I'll work free for a week. If you don't like me, I'll leave. Try me on a week's trial."

Arnie studied the young man with the new shirt. "That might be a good idea. Can you work in a place like this?"

"What kind of place is this?" Michael was genuinely interested.

"What did you think we were?"

"From the name 'Oasis,' maybe a bar, but I don't think that's right."

Arnie laughed and propped his loafers up on the desk. "A bar's calmer, more predictable than here. 'Course Caleb, one of our clients, thinks we're a bar. Always wanting to know when happy hour is. He's also suggested we have a ladies' night. Let's see . . . What are we? Well, to start with, we're crazy."

Michael remained silent, unsure whether Arnie was joking. But the room was blissfully air-conditioned, and he needed a job.

"Our clients are mentally ill," Arnie clarified.

They are crazy, thought Michael.

"When our clients are stable enough to enter the workforce, we provide a way to ease them into jobs. We have a lot of training here, none of which is paid. For example, a client can come learn to cook in the kitchen. Some clients take orders and wait tables during the meals. Others are cashiers. We have a secondhand and craft store manned by clients. We teach gardening and landscaping skills. Clients do all the house's janitorial and maintenance work under the direction of a coordinator. I coordinate cooking. We have an office pool that teaches computer and secretarial skills.

"When our people have worked here for a while and feel comfortable about going out to work, we have some paid positions in the community that are shared by several workers. So if one client can't be there, the other one can or a backup is also trained. We have coordinators for that too.

"Some people go out on group employment. We take a group to K-Mart twice a week to unload stock and put prices on shoes and toys. Another group passes out fliers every Friday, and one group cleans up after community banquets and ball games.

"Your job would be to help teach cooking skills when we have someone who wants to learn. At the same time, you need to make sure that meals are prepared on time. We feed everyone that comes in. Sometimes we have lots of help, sometimes we have none. The help is sometimes more work than not, but some of our workers are great help and will make good employees. We charge for the meals, fifty cents or a dollar—mostly so we can give someone experience running a cash register and handling money.

"The staff coordinators work the same jobs as the clients. Frankly, with a few exceptions it will take you a while to know who the coordinators are and who is being trained. I cook. Chris does grounds and maintenance. Lorraine runs the store and helps clean. Rhonda runs the office pool, and Dennis supervises educational studies. Katie supervises group employment, and Amber does outside placement. I've filled in for all of them. Ruth is sometimes upstairs, sometimes not. She oversees everything, writes for grants, tries to get donations, helps everywhere. She's incredible. Started this whole thing.

"We cook breakfast and start serving at 7:30 A.M. Mornings are the most unpredictable. We may have ten people to serve or maybe thirty. Lunch is served at 12:30. We always have help for that. Saturdays we just serve brunch at 10:00 A.M. The only suppers we prepare are on holidays for those who have no other place to go.

"I usually work six days a week, and it would be nice to have someone to rotate with. Can you work with people whose reality is not always the same as your own?"

"I worked for my dad."

Arnie paused, but didn't question the new applicant. "Okay, come tomorrow and we'll see how you do. You need to be here by 6:45 A.M. Is that a problem?"

Michael shook his head.

"You okay working this Saturday? You don't have plans?"

Michael smiled for the first time all day. "I thought maybe I'd help Connor watch for UFOs, but we'll do that another time."

Arnie laughed as he stood up. "You should go with him sometime. Connor's a really bright guy when his meds are working. He's on a new prescription, and I think they're kicking in. This week he's only *looking* for UFOs. Last week little green men were talking to him."

"What did they tell him?" Michael asked, his amusement mingling with concern.

"I don't rightly remember," Arnie said, frowning in concentration. "But if they tell you the same thing, then maybe we *do* have visitors from outer space and need to reevaluate Connor's diagnosis."

"Or get *me* diagnosed," Michael said as he reached out to shake Arnie's hand.

Arnie smiled as he watched Michael walk away.

* * *

Michael squeezed past the "Do Not Trespass" sign and crawled into his vacant building. He moved his sleeping bag to a snug basement corner and, finding a broken door, set it on an edge so that no one coming down the stairs could see his living quarters. The basement was comfortably cool after the long walk in the sun, and Michael pushed his rolled sleeping bag against the wall and leaned on it. Eating canned peaches and a peanut-butter sandwich from a sack of groceries he'd bought on the way home, Michael was content with his lodgings and the prospects of a job. He thumped the bag to get it more comfortable and felt the hard paperback. Digging the book out, Michael turned it over in his hands. He'd read all the pamphlets the elders had left him. Several of them had referred to this book. Michael decided it was time to start reading it. *The Book of Mormon: An account written by the Hand of Mormon . . .*

* * *

"My life's just not working out," Laura moaned to Klarissa. The two girls had known each other since they'd started nursery in the same ward. Although they had attended different high schools, girls' camp had always found them together, eagerly discussing how perfect life would be when they could get out of "this Gentile town and attend BYU."

Klarissa knew the most about BYU. Every summer since turning fourteen she had spent a week at one of the youth workshops. Laura didn't remember a lot about the one year she went with Klarissa. That summer she was fourteen and much more homesick than she was willing to admit. The classes were wonderful, she'd told her parents, but Laura only remembered one lecture, and that was because of the pale blond girl who had been in their group.

"You can receive personal revelation," the speaker had said. "Revelation that will make your life and the lives of those around you easier." To prove her point the speaker told a story about a man who was walking home from work. He was a little late, and night was settling fast. He felt impressed to walk home a different way than he normally walked. Along the path there were bushes framed by trees. As he approached the area, he heard a panicked girl's voice and a threatening male. He thought about hurrying past. "I have a family," he had said to himself. "If I got hurt who would care for them? I should mind my own business." But again an impression came to him that he should help the girl. Sprinting into the bushes, the man wrestled with the girl's assailant. Several times the man was nearly overpowered, but finally the attacker ran off and the man wearily turned toward the crying girl. He could see her huddled in a sheltered spot, her face hidden in the dark. Gently, so as not to scare her, the man told her things were okay. "I won't hurt you. You're going to be all right." The girl's crying stopped, and there was silence for a moment. Then the girl said, "Daddy?"

"Wasn't it wonderful that he could receive inspiration to help his daughter?" asked the lecturer.

The pale blond spoke softly, "But everyone is someone's daughter, so it shouldn't matter who he helped."

"But it's really special being helped by your father," Klarissa had said. "Knowing the Lord tells your dad when you're in trouble, that's really a comforting feeling."

"I don't have a father." The blond's voice was still soft.

At the time, Laura had felt an overwhelming empathy for the girl without a father, and she had felt a gratitude for her own father. Now, four years later, she was at BYU again and she clearly remembered the whole scene. She even remembered the empathy and gratitude. Still, she continued to complain.

"I've got to find another place to live. You're lucky to be staying in an apartment with other girls. I don't want to hurt my brother's feelings and move out, but really, Klarissa, the room I'm in is so cramped. I don't feel like I can hang my own stuff up 'cause they've got plans to put the baby in there as soon as I move out. And my job—I can't work with food for four years."

That her brother and food services would be glad to have her gone never occurred to Laura.

CHAPTER 4

Arnie saw that Michael could cook. Even though the young boy's skills were more with sandwiches and single-item entrees, the trainee learned quickly. Arnie, however, was most pleased with Michael's other talents. Michael had convinced Caleb that women liked guys who knew how to make fajitas. Caleb had been helping ever since. Michael's good looks and kind manner in the kitchen immediately attracted three female clients who had previously spent most of their time at the smoker-joker table.

Michael taught one how to hold two eggs in each hand and crack four at a time. He complimented another on how quickly she peeled potatoes, and the third one was thrilled when he invited her to help drain vegetables. "I need someone I can trust," Michael had told her. She'd hurried over, her stocky, unshaved legs protruding from baggy polyester shorts. "Thanks for helping," he told her sincerely. "Hope you come more often." She stayed and scrubbed starch from a large pot.

Even Connor came to help because Michael was willing to discuss whether aliens were really green or if they just wore green space suits.

Michael knew he was treating those around him exactly as his father treated people. *But I'm not a fraud like Dad,* thought Michael. *I really like these people.* He didn't, but he was starting to.

At the end of the week, Arnie asked Michael to fill out employment papers and then instructed the accountant to pay the new cook for the previous week. Michael looked at the check for a long time. He wanted to thank Arnie for what seemed like a generous amount. But mostly he wanted to thank Arnie for saying the rolls were the best they'd ever served. He wanted to thank Arnie for laughing when the power mixer flipped pancake batter on the floor. He wanted to thank Arnie for never once acting like his father. Instead, Michael muttered an almost unintelligible acknowledgment of the payment and left.

On Saturday, Michael learned about Utah garage sales. As he walked the two miles from work to the old building where he'd taken up residence, he passed more people selling their property on their lawns than he'd ever seen in his entire life. He browsed through several driveways full of bud vases, old dressers, and used ski equipment. He quickly decided he didn't need lamps since his apartment had no electricity. Amusing himself, Michael entertained the idea of buying two prints featuring sailboats against a setting sun. *The cracked frames would match my bedroom wall,* he thought cheerfully. Kitchen tables weren't appealing, but an assortment of plastic bowls got him thinking about when he would need to find an apartment. Finally he bought a sleeping bag. Having another one for padding would be luxurious. At the next garage sale Michael splurged and bought a used mountain bike. A woman explained that the bike had been her son's but he was going on a mission and would need a better one for the mission field. Michael had no clue where the field was, but figured it must be in rough terrain if the boy needed a better bike than he'd left.

The same home had an assortment of shirts that apparently weren't appropriate for "the field," and Michael felt the weight of ownership by the time he left. Seventy-five dollars had purchased him a new Coleman sleeping bag, a Raleigh bike, five shirts, and a cereal bowl. He took these home, hung the shirts carefully along a door frame, and unrolled the sleeping bag under his old one.

That afternoon, Michael opened a savings account and rented a safe deposit box to hold the account book and extra cash. He also discovered he didn't have to wash at Maverik. He would need a student card to check out equipment or gym clothes at the PE building, but no one noticed if he just showered and shaved there. He carried shampoo and soap in a plastic bag. Often he'd go to the large library and read about mental illness until dark and then ride back to his abandoned house. Michael was content.

One night he arrived home and found a handwritten note on orange paper tacked next to his sleeping bag. "You are trespassing.

Please vacate the premises or you will be prosecuted for unlawful habitation."

What happened to simple signs like "Please, leave" or "Find another rent-free place to sleep"? Michael thought.

Find another place. Michael planned to do so immediately. He decided to find something tomorrow afternoon, but when he arrived at work that next morning he learned that Katie was sick and there was no one to take the work group to mark shoes at K-Mart. Twelve expectant clients were waiting after lunch, discussing what to do with the money they would earn.

When Michael volunteered to go as supervisor, Arnie and Amber both explained to Michael that he didn't have to take the group. Michael insisted. Most of those congregated had been going for several months. Surely among all of them they could figure out the job.

A van dropped the group off at the back of the large store. Before he drove away, Dennis promised he'd come back for them at six. "Or earlier if you have any problems," he'd said. "I've got several clients studying for the GED, but Amber's in the building, and I could leave if you need me."

"We're fine," Michael had assured him.

Two hours later Michael was sure they were fine. They had been led into a section of K-Mart's storage. Crates with shoe boxes formed a U around the work area.

Netta and Marie, both in their thirties, had lost families in their struggles with manic depression. Now both had been diagnosed and were battling to get themselves back. The two women eagerly began sticking prices onto boxes.

Brennan, a nineteen-year-old, moved slowly and methodically. Brennan never spoke or focused on another person. He did, however, verbally address each box of shoes and recite its contents.

Stan, a tired man in his twenties, stayed close to Michael. His long legs stretched past gray sweats to reveal bony ankles and size 13 running shoes. The worn sweats stretched tightly over a small belly and were kept up by colorful suspenders. After every box of shoes, he would ask, "Is that right? Did I do it right?"

Sad eyes peered out from above fifty-year-old Toby's beard as he willingly accepted Marie's and Netta's instructions. His body was so tired he could hardly carry but one box at a time. He never stopped, but continued to trudge along as if he were slave labor in a coal mine.

Gail, still in the frayed shorts she had worn when Michael had first seen her, carelessly checked boxes before stacking the various sizes in order. Her auburn hair was cut even shorter today, only about an inch long all over her head.

Connor ambitiously priced shoes and was quick to tactfully correct any errors.

Michael felt useful and proud. The shoes were tagged and stacked neatly. He might have to call Dennis early because they were being so efficient. As Michael calculated how much it would cost to buy everyone a congratulatory soda pop, a saleswoman from the pet department rushed back to the workroom.

"Someone needs to stop him!" she cried.

"Who?" Michael asked, scanning the group for anyone doing something socially unacceptable.

"The newt guy. He's taking all the newts." The girl turned to leave. Michael and nearly half the work group hurried after her.

"Who's the newt guy?" Michael asked Stan, who was keeping pace with the bewildered supervisor.

"Seth," he answered.

Michael only vaguely remembered who Seth was: a small thirty-five-year-old child with a shiny mop of blond hair.

As they rushed to the front of the store, Michael tried to remember when he'd seen Seth last.

"He thinks they're his," Gail said as they passed housewares.

"They are," Connor said.

"The store bought them from him," explained Gail. "Seth raises newts to sell at pet stores, but mostly he just raises them."

As the hurrying group neared the pet department, Michael watched as Seth used a net to fish frantically in a large aquarium. Everyone seemed to expect Michael to do something.

"Seth," Michael said in what he hoped was a calm yet forceful voice. "You need to stop."

Seth didn't turn around but expertly scooped up two of what looked to Michael like water lizards and deposited them into a large vase that still had a price sticker on it.

"Seth, stop!"

"They've ruined the nitrogen cycle," Seth said, carefully inspecting the tank for more newts. "They've introduced too many residents in too short a time. I offered them free plants. Did they take them? No! There are dangerously high levels of ammonia in here. Nitrites have become toxic. Murder. That's what's happening here."

Seth moved to the next tank and muttered something about a "bacteria bloom."

The salesgirl looked at Michael and said, "I'm getting the manager."

"Seth," Michael said. "Why are you taking the newts?"

Seth turned over an aquarium castle looking for any unnoticed occupants. Satisfied that he had all the little amphibians, he took his vase and stalked past the returning salesgirl and the manager. They both spoke to him, but Seth ignored them. He left through checkout 12 after paying for the vase but not the newts.

Michael paid the store $3.95 a piece for eleven newts, decided he would not buy anyone pop, and momentarily realized that if he'd been working for his dad he'd have just spent two weeks' wages.

When the van arrived at 6:00 P.M., the group had just barely finished the work. When Dennis asked how things went, Michael shook his head and went to the backseat. Dennis's chuckle and the animated voices of the others assured Michael that the story would be told and retold.

"I'll show you where he lives," offered Gail.

Everyone but Connor, Gail, and Michael had left after returning to the Oasis House. The remaining three were standing outside the dark building, and Michael had asked for the third time if they were sure Seth would be able to carry the newts, water, and vase all the way home.

"We can go see him," Connor said. "It's only a couple miles."

"I only have my bike here," Michael said.

"I have a car," Gail said. "I don't have a license, but I brought the car."

"I've got a license," Connor said.

Prepared now to drive somewhere, they all headed toward the back of the house.

"How'd your car get here?" Michael asked Gail as they stopped in front of a Ford Escort.

"Drove it," she said, handing Connor the keys.

"Without a license?"

"You think maybe I should walk?"

"You could ride a bike like Michael," suggested Connor as he crawled into the driver's seat.

"That would wear out my shorts," Gail said.

Michael started to laugh, then stopped. He didn't know if she was joking or not.

Seth's apartment was three blocks from K-Mart. Connor led the way around the side of an older home.

"I can't remember which door." Connor suddenly sounded frantic, scared.

"Follow the hose," Gail said.

Michael looked down and saw a green garden hose running along the narrow sidewalk. It stretched around the corner, down five wet stairs, through an open door, and onto muddy linoleum. There they saw Seth bent over an aquarium that filled nearly the entire apartment.

"Someone kink that hose a little," Seth greeted them. "I'm getting too much water."

As he walked around, Michael could see this wasn't a regular aquarium. Lights shone from under gravel beds. Filters pumped water from one compartment to another. Newts moved over rocks, plants, moss, and Plexiglas. Small cameras bolted to the corners recorded every movement.

Gail bent next to the largest tank and absentmindedly lit a cigarette.

"Don't smoke in here," snapped Seth. "You'll ruin the newts' environment."

Gail took a long drag and blew the smoke toward Seth.

"Get out of here!" Seth demanded.

"Didn't these swimming lizards use to live in the wild? Like in marshes and streams out in the real world?" Gail asked conversationally.

"You can't smoke in here," said Seth. "Leave."

"First tell me. Aren't there newts in the wild?"

"Yes."

"And they live through forest fires, right?" Gail blew another long trail of smoke before opening the door to flick the cigarette out onto the concrete landing.

"Dang," said Seth. He had dropped to his stomach and was using a hand drill to make a hole in one Plexiglas wall.

Curious, Michael knelt beside him. The garden hose was slowly leaking water into the other side.

"What are you doing?"

"Rather than set up a whole new tank," Seth explained as he carefully turned the drill, "I'm going to use the water from that tank because it already has an established nitrogen cycle. I need a safe tank for the newts I saved today. Here, you do this while I set up a background sheet and get some plants."

Michael lay down next to the newtarium and drilled slowly. He then realized Seth had spent the last two hours adding to the newtarium to give his friends a place to live.

"Does your landlord ever complain about all this water in the basement?" Michael asked as he continued to drill.

"My mom owns the place," Seth said. "She bought it when I started going to Oasis. She rents out the top."

Seth gathered plants from the other section and spread them next to Michael's head in anticipation of water that would eventually flow through the wall.

Michael looked up to watch Seth tape a picture of a river on the outside of the new tank. The drill finally penetrated the Plexiglas, and water sprayed around the drill and into Michael's face and hair.

"You got it through," Seth cheered. Gail giggled. Connor used a paper towel to wipe water from Michael's face. Seth unkinked the garden hose, and they all stood to watch as the new tank filled.

"They'll be okay," Seth said with a sigh of relief. "I'll have to wait a couple weeks until I can get newtcams for that tank. I hope everyone will be patient."

"Newtcams?" Michael asked hesitantly.

"For my website."

"You have a website?" Michael struggled to keep doubt or surprise out of his voice.

"I get two or three hundred hits a day," Seth said proudly. "I'll get more after word gets around that I've got a whole new tank to watch."

Seth led them to the bedroom, and they all stood around a card table that held the latest in computer technology. After logging onto his own website, Seth showed Michael which tank was on the screen. Michael watched the newts move on the monitor, then ran to the other room to see the newts live. He changed cameras and watched a newt in a different tank move slowly over a boulder. Hurrying into the other room, he saw the same newt finish his descent.

Gail lay on the bed and complained about not being able to smoke. Michael ignored her as he read from Seth's website about the difference between newts and salamanders, *Nitrobacter* and *Nitrosomonas*. Connor sat in the only easychair and snored softly.

Late that night, as he pedaled back to his affordable housing, Michael thought about how much he had enjoyed the afternoon and evening. With a twinge of pleasant surprise, he realized that the first friends he'd ever had were mentally ill.

In the cover of darkness, Michael cautiously slid himself and his bike through the locked gate. Nothing looked disturbed. *I'll move tomorrow,* he thought with a nagging fear in the back of his mind. Where to? He'd seen lots of signs. "Now renting for summer. Low rates." But Michael was uncomfortable rooming with other guys. Besides, he didn't want to spend the money.

CHAPTER 5

"Get up!"

Michael was disoriented. The morning's rays blinded him as he stared at the dark silhouettes of two men. Sitting up in his sleeping bag, he rubbed his eyes and squinted into the sun. Alarm shot through Michael. Was he late? He jerked up and grabbed over his head for his watch.

The young policeman reached for his stick. Michael looked at the watch and then realized it was Saturday. He didn't have to be at the Oasis House until nine. He had over an hour. Only then did he acknowledge the two officers standing in his bedroom.

"Stand up," one said. "Slowly."

Michael climbed out of his bag and stood there in his shorts and socks. Connor, Gail, and Michael had left Seth's house too late for him to get a shower at the PE building. His hair still smelled like a well-established nitrogen cycle. Two K-Mart price tags decorated the ankles of one sock.

"You're trespassing. You can't stay here," said one of the silhouettes.

Michael strapped his watch onto his wrist and bent to collect a pair of jeans.

"We warned you once, and now we're required to arrest you."

Michael still could not make out their facial features. "I'm only here in the evening. I'm sorry. I promise to move tonight, but right now I've got to get to the Oasis House. I help with brunch today."

"Oh, the Oasis House?" asked one officer, cautiously moving forward. "You been going there long?" he probed soothingly. "They treat you well? A good place. We'll help you, son, and I'm sure one of the counselors there will help you find a place to live. They'll take care of you."

Michael hesitated as he tucked a T-shirt into his jeans. He smiled slightly to himself and left the shirt hanging sloppily over his belt. Stuffing a comb in his back pocket, Michael set a cap on his disheveled hair.

"We'll help you get there this morning and talk to someone about finding you a place to live."

"I could talk to Arnie," Michael said slowly. "He's my friend."

The police helped load the few possessions scattered around the basement, and they stowed the bike in their car trunk. The uniformed men chatted uncomfortably while Michael sat silently for the ten blocks to where he was to start fixing a meal.

"I need to get to the kitchen." Michael quickly jumped out when they stopped, shouldered his pack, and tried to get the bike. "Thanks for bringing me."

The officers were persistent and helped carry the untidy bundles of sleeping bags and clothes as they followed Michael around to the back. With the early smoker-joker group as an audience, Michael led the two men into the kitchen.

Arnie's concerned look greeted them. He liked Michael, but in the sixty seconds he watched the cops walk the shamed boy to the door, Arnie admitted he knew nothing about him. The boy could be a convicted felon, a sociopath, a kleptomaniac.

With a compassionate hand on Michael's shoulder, the older officer spoke. "Are you Arnie?"

The cook nodded.

"This boy told us he helped you in the kitchen. We found him sleeping in that old mansion waiting for reconstruction on University Avenue. He's been there for several days now. We could tell right away that he maybe wasn't aware of what he was doing, so we brought him down here. Hoped you guys could find him an appropriate placement." The man had whispered the last few sentences, trying to keep the situation confidential as four smoker-jokers appeared at the screen door. They stared with frank curiosity at the policemen and Michael. "Can you handle this, or is there someone more appropriate for us to contact?" The officer's hushed tones drew the eavesdroppers closer.

"I'll notify the appropriate personnel," Arnie said seriously. "We'll get him an appropriate placement."

Weaving through the small group of onlookers, Arnie followed the officers out into the bright summer morning. "Thanks for recognizing this kid needed help and not punishment," he said loud enough for everyone in and out of the kitchen to hear. "We could use more men like you on the force." He sent them off with another hearty thanks and then turned back to the kitchen where Michael was ignoring questions by cracking eggs into the noisy industrial mixer.

The elder cook's relief had turned to amusement. He switched off the mixer, then leaned against a counter and inspected the trespassing criminal. "You want to explain?"

"Just trying to save some money."

"Not the best of facilities in that old trap," Arnie observed, still lounging comfortably. He sniffed. "You smell like a dead fish."

"We went to Seth's place last night," Michael said defensively. "I didn't have time to get a shower."

"Where exactly do you usually shower?"

"At the PE building."

"On campus?" Arnie was surprised. "You just waltz down there to shower?"

"No one ever said anything."

"Is there anything else I should know about?"

"No. Are we going to cook breakfast or not?" Michael's question included the onlookers.

Ignoring the rebuff, one of the eavesdroppers asked, "Now where're you gonna live?"

"You can stay with me," another client said, moving forward.

Michael softened. "Guys, thanks a lot, but I'll be okay."

"There's an old abandoned toolshed two houses down," Arnie said, "but it's kind of a long ride to the showers." He chuckled and went to get meat from the walk-in refrigerator.

Connor rushed toward Michael as soon as he heard about the morning's visit from two policemen. "You can live with me," he offered generously. "We can be roommates."

Michael was touched by all the offers, although not everyone was as generous. Caleb suggested a viaduct where he'd lived for several months, but told him to beware of a guy named Heart. "He's got a heart tattoo, but nothing like a real heart. He can get pretty mean if you sleep in his spot."

Michael worried through most of the afternoon, but never once considered that someone should or would help him find a place to live.

"You want me to show you that toolshed?" Arnie asked after the last mop was hung and the last washcloth thrown into the laundry.

"Arnie, I'm okay."

"I can lend you some money until paychecks come."

"I'm just trying to save."

For the second time that day Arnie thought how little he knew about this boy. "Listen, son, there are lots of rooms for rent right now because it's summer break for most of the students. Rent is less than half of what it will be when school starts again. Go find yourself an apartment. Leave your stuff here." He motioned to the pile of sleeping bags and clothing. "I'll give you a key to the back door. You can come back and get your things when you have a place. You might get a raise by the time fall semester starts and rent goes up."

When Arnie came back with a key, he put a hand on Michael's shoulder. "Son," he said solemnly, "if you came to me right now asking if you could rent a room, I'd charge you an enormous cleaning deposit. Go take a shower, then look for housing." The older man chuckled as he left.

For three hours, Michael knocked on every door with a "For Rent" sign, but because it was Saturday, most places didn't have anyone with the authority to take his deposit.

When Garrett answered the door in torn jeans and a BYU T-shirt, Michael instinctively knew his luck was changing. "Hunter," Garrett yelled, "there's a guy here looking for an apartment." That's when Hunter appeared and offered to let this complete stranger start sleeping in the other room. "My brother's the manager. He won't be back until Monday, but heck, he's had trouble renting this dump. I'm sure you can move in now and then pay up when he gets back."

"You getting ready for your mission?" Garrett asked as he gave Michael a tour. The apartment was upstairs in a ten-year-old four-plex. The building was well maintained, although it showed evidence of many past occupants. A wall was patched where, Garret explained, one young man had vented his anger at being jilted. A window screen was bent where one group had torn it out to throw water balloons at passing coeds.

"My mission . . ." Michael said vaguely, not quite understanding the question and not quite comprehending why they kept referring to this carpeted, newly painted bedroom as substandard living. "Well, I don't know."

"Still having trouble making up your mind, huh?" continued Garrett. "Well, both Hunter and I just got home. He went to Virginia. I went to Denmark. It was great. You'd never regret going."

They showed Michael which cabinets he could have in the kitchen and then invited him to a dance that evening. "There'll be lots of girls."

"Thanks, but I'll just spend the evening moving my stuff in," Michael said as if he had a truckload of boxes to unpack.

As Michael was leaving to get his sleeping bags and shirts, Garret explained that they were the second ward to meet in their building, so church didn't start until 10:30 A.M. Michael tried to understand what a ward was or why they weren't allowed to go to the first one, but hated to ask, so he let it be.

* * *

Laura sat on the crumbling cement steps and looked down the street. She'd slept until noon and then found a note on the counter from Scott and his wife saying they would be gone until evening. She'd watched TV, eaten nothing but junk food, and called three girl-friends. She'd done exactly what she'd always imagined would be so much fun—no responsibilities, no one telling her what to do. Somewhere her subconscious was telling her this wasn't enough. Where was the sense of purpose she had always imagined she would feel going to the Y?

The Friday night dance was fun, she thought. She'd danced her share. "A good dance to go to," she'd agreed with Klarissa. There were lots of returned missionaries, but no one had asked her out. Laura was searching around for something to look forward to. Going to Klarissa's ward the next day would be fun. *I hope I meet someone.* With nothing to do but sit in silence, she vaguely realized she had arrived in Provo with no goals, no purpose.

That guy on the bike has a purpose, Laura thought as she watched him pedal up the street. On the bike's handlebars he balanced something that looked like poorly rolled sleeping bags. On his back was a heavy pack. *He's really cute,* Laura thought as he approached. She squinted as he crossed on the opposite side of the street. Did she know him? His dark hair was almost black with the damp of sweat. Shirts on hangers were attached to the stuffed pack and flew behind him like victorious flags.

Normally Laura would have regarded such an unconventional sight with scorn, but in her current mood she envied his determination. She admired anyone who would pedal under such a load on this hot summer evening. She admired anyone who was determined enough to succeed regardless of how hard the task was, or how stupid he looked, and who was passionate enough to achieve on his own without waiting for someone in the elders quorum to give him a ride. *I'd never do that,* she thought. And for the first time in her life, that thought was not smug.

* * *

Alone in the apartment, Michael peeked into all the kitchen cabinets. He wondered what his roommates ate. One of them liked Cheerios and the other liked generic Froot Loops in the economy bag. Canned soup and peanut butter shared a cupboard with some pancake mix and instant pudding. With a twinge of guilt, he also opened his roommates' closets. Among the jeans and T-shirts were dark suits like the missionaries had worn. Ties dangled from a wooden hanger. Michael was sorry the yard sales had closed for the day; he probably needed a tie for church.

No one said anything about his light-green shirt being open at the collar when he appeared in the kitchen late the next morning. Michael drank some yogurt he'd bought the night before, not wanting to borrow a spoon.

When he noticed Garrett and Hunter gather their scriptures, he went to his room and got the blue book he'd hidden in one of the drawers. The others hadn't said anything about his clothes, but he saw a look pass between them when they saw his book. Michael was unsure why. It was labeled the same as theirs on the binding.

Michael was unprepared for all the young people chattering happily in the church. Not that he had ever been to church before, but he had more or less pictured a robed man greeting them at the door and then delivering a speech. Instead the first speech was given by a beautiful blond girl who flounced to the podium and spoke about being homesick, about knowing Christ was her friend, and about missing her boyfriend back home. A short, redheaded young man with a pitiful beard talked of shaving for school and going into the mission field, and how he was sure it would be the best two years of his life. He sounded uncertain. Two girls behind Michael whispered something about "good riddance."

The Sunday School class immediately started to discuss the D&C. Michael spent several confused moments before he figured out the group was referring to a book he didn't have rather than a medical procedure. A slender brunette slid into the seat beside him, followed by another girl.

"You should have called me, Klarissa. I spent the whole night doing nothing," the girl beside him whispered loudly.

"I guess I just wasn't willing to admit I got stood up."

"Well, call next time."

They were silent for a minute as the teacher discussed something called the degrees of glory. When the class roll was handed to Michael, he wasn't sure where to sign. A small square had been drawn on the bottom of the sheet with the heading "visitors." After hesitating a few seconds, he carefully wrote his name and handed the roll to the girl beside him.

"Where you visiting from?" she asked. She was trying hard to make eye contact.

"The first ward," Michael said to amuse himself.

"Me too," she replied. "But I was going with my brother and sister-in-law, and all the kids are so noisy. You like this one better?"

"Yeah," said a confused Michael.

"Maybe we'll both start coming here. What's your name?"

Michael nodded vaguely about coming to the ward and told her his name. Then she asked what his major was. He shrugged.

"Me neither," she said, "It's so hard to decide what you want to do for the rest of your life." Michael turned to look directly at her for the first time. He liked how her brown hair softly outlined her face. The full lips and dark eyes were pretty, her smile flirtatious. That he liked. The lesson and the girl's chattering were confusing though.

"You going to the fireside tonight?" she asked.

Michael shrugged again, vaguely wondering what religious practice these people did with a fire on hot summer evenings, and trying to catch what degree of glory murderers and apostates obtained.

"The speaker's supposed to be really good," the young woman continued. Michael finally nodded, then turned his attention back to the discussion about celestial, terrestrial, and telestial places spoken of in this D&C. He couldn't figure out how it related to the book he held in his hands.

After the women left for their own meeting, the discussion centered around how practice was going for the BYU football team. Michael stared at his blue book. He watched the others handle their more expensive, thicker versions. At the end of the three hours, Michael just waved to his roommates and walked home while they stood in the foyer and flirted with girls. The brunette from the first ward waved back.

Michael lay on his sleeping-bag-covered bed and watched the ceiling. He felt defeated somehow. His mind reviewed the morning church services. He never did learn what a degree of glory was.

Garrett knocked tentatively on Michael's door.

"Yes," Michael said, jerking to a sitting position.

Garrett cautiously opened the door. "There's a stake fireside tonight. You want to go?"

Steak sounded good, but Michael was even more cautious than Garrett seemed to be.

"What exactly do you do at these firesides?"

"Didn't they have firesides in Las Vegas?" Garrett asked as Hunter appeared behind him.

"I don't know," Michael admitted quietly.

"Weren't you active?"

Michael's irritation reached a peak. *Active?* "Yeah, I worked hard."

"I mean active in the Church."

"I really don't know anything about your church."

"Did you get your Book of Mormon from the missionaries?" Garrett asked.

"Two guys with name tags and white shirts," Michael said. "I rode the bus out here to find out more about it."

"You came here to find out about the Church?"

"Well, they told my sister and me about your beliefs and gave me the book."

A look between Garrett and Hunter made Michael set his face in stone, mentally withdrawing. He was angry at himself for telling them so much, angry at them for invading his space.

"We can tell you about the Church," Hunter said.

"The church I went to this morning was a poor excuse for a worship service," Michael replied coldly.

The returned missionaries saw a golden investigator vanish. "So, you don't want to learn more about the Church?"

Michael wanted to reply in a forceful negative, but then thought about the young woman who had sat next to him in Sunday School. She had tried to be friendly. The memory softened him slightly. "What does your church have to do with this book?" he finally asked as he held up the Book of Mormon.

"What did the missionaries tell you when they gave it to you?" Garrett asked.

"They didn't have much time to talk. My dad wouldn't have let them come back, but they gave me the book. I was curious about it."

"Curious enough to move here," Hunter said. "Have you read it?"

"Yes," Michael said, though he didn't add that he'd used up several flashlight batteries reading in the basement he'd occupied before.

"Did you like it?"

Michael didn't know how to respond. How could he tell them how he'd felt reading? How could he explain to them that he'd felt safer in an abandoned building reading that book than he'd ever felt in his life? How could he explain that his soul had come home every night as he read names he'd never heard of? How could he tell them of his disappointment at church when no one had even talked about the stories in the book or explained how it related to a religion? How could he explain that he felt more love from a book than he ever had from a person?

"I liked it," he said, and the comfort he'd felt reading by flashlight breathed itself into the room. Michael's roommates recognized that feeling and smiled.

Hunter still had his missionary flip charts, and sitting on Michael's garage-sale sleeping bag, the returned missionaries forgot about the girls they were supposed to walk to the fireside. They taught Michael about the Book of Mormon and challenged him to continue reading and to pray. He agreed. In the same sequence they had learned as missionaries, the elders taught Michael about the first gospel principles. Garrett suggested that as Michael learned the truth of what he heard, he'd want to be baptized.

Michael's expression looked suddenly on guard, and immediately Garrett started the third discussion and taught about the apostasy and restoration.

As the time passed, Michael felt a warmth, a calm, and a love from two excited elders who had come home to find their most receptive investigator, one who listened attentively until the doorbell rang.

* * *

Klarissa's ego was injured. First she'd been stood up Saturday night, and then Garrett hadn't walked her and her roommate to the fireside. True, she wasn't all that interested in him. He was a little too short and optimistic for her taste, but still, Laura had been interested in that guy who had come to church with them. So after church, Klarissa had hinted until Hunter and Garrett offered to walk them all to the fireside. They hadn't even shown up.

Laura was disappointed that Michael hadn't come, but Klarissa fumed all the way through the fireside and then decided to get revenge. After the fireside, they stopped at Klarissa's apartment to change into sweats. Wanda volunteered to bring the rope she had used to tie luggage to the top of her Toyota.

The women giggled as they marched down the street and then sobered upon spotting the fourplex. "That's Garrett's car," Klarissa said, "and there's Hunter's. Maybe they're out in the other guy's car."

"He doesn't have a car," Laura said. She saw a bike chained to the railing at the bottom of the stairs, and then remembered the guy she'd seen on a bike. She wondered if they could be the same.

"You sure the other guy has no car?"

"I'm sure." Laura didn't want to explain.

Stealthily they approached the door.

The only witnesses were a rising new moon, an apartment of four girls in a run-down house across the street, a newly engaged couple parked in the alley, and two roommates enjoying the challenge of playing catch in the gathering dark.

The three conspirators quietly wrapped the rope around the doorknob and granny-knotted it into a wad of twists. The nylon cord was then strung to the cast-iron railing. The girls figure-eighted the rope and again wrapped the doorknob, then the railing, and back to the door until the rope was only long enough to make another series of bulky twists that served as a knot.

Counting to three, Klarissa pushed hard on the bell while Wanda and Laura knocked urgently against the door. The three then thundered down the steps and sprinted across the street to hide behind an overgrown lilac hedge. The two ballplayers greeted them with friendly hellos and then watched with interest as someone inside the apartment tried to pull the door inward. Apparently, two unthinking occupants were now putting excessive pressure on the inside doorknob. The aging cast-iron railing gave way and collapsed. The door swung open. Garrett and Hunter stumbled to the floor, smashing one another on the way down.

Klarissa sat on the damp ground. "That'll teach him to stand me up," she said and started giggling again.

"You got a problem," one of the guys with the ball yelled over to the boys.

"Did you see who did this?" yelled Hunter.

"You been making enemies lately?" yelled the ballplayer. "Break any promises to girls? Stand them up or anything like that?"

"Where'd they go?" yelled Garrett.

"Well, now," drawled the informant. "I can't imagine they could have gotten too far."

Klarissa was giggling uncontrollably, and Laura was curious about Michael, so when Klarissa suggested they go apologize, only Wanda dissented. She was concerned that the rope owner had to pay for damages. They debated the merits of each alternative while one of the ballplayers pointed to the girls on the ground.

Garrett and Hunter loped across the street. Michael, unaccustomed to such camaraderie, hesitated and then followed more slowly. He arrived in time to hear the end of Klarissa's explanation. "We didn't really do it. We just came to see why you weren't at the fireside. We knew you were gentlemen and wouldn't have stood us up. Now we know you guys just got tied up."

"The fireside," Garrett hit his head with his open hand. "I totally forgot. We were teaching Michael here the discussions."

"So you're a nonmember, huh?" Klarissa asked.

Michael felt like he had just been accused of a crime.

"Come over," said the enthusiastic Garrett. "There's ice cream in the fridge."

Soon the group was sitting around the apartment living room eating out of mismatched bowls.

Klarissa took a dainty teaspoon of ice cream and turned to Michael. He had withdrawn a little and was sitting on a kitchen chair just inside the dining room. "So you're not a member?" she repeated.

"No." Defensiveness edged Michael's voice.

"He's taking the discussions," Garrett said.

"How do you like them so far?" Laura asked.

Michael didn't understand what "discussions" were. He only knew that for nearly two hours Garrett and Hunter had told him about a loving God who would answer prayers like He answered a fourteen-year-old. Michael had always assumed there was a God, but figured this Supreme Being was an uncaring individual watching with grim amusement the antics of His slightly unintelligent creations. Why a merciful, kind, and just Personage would allow so much suffering confused Michael, but when the two returned missionaries told of Joseph Smith praying, Michael felt that they spoke the truth.

"How did you hear about the Church?" asked Laura.

"Some guys gave me this book."

"Why didn't you just contact a ward in Las Vegas?" Klarissa pressed.

Michael shrugged. He didn't want to say that he didn't understand what a ward was. He didn't want to cheapen his quest by saying that he came partly because his father hated Mormons. All these people were confusing. Michael just wanted to crawl back into his book and get comfort there. That was so simple. Degrees of glory, D&C, Relief Society, priesthood, firesides, and rambling sermons by kids his own age made no sense.

"Where are you working?" Laura asked.

At last here was something he could be proud of. These Christians would appreciate that he was earning a living by helping people become self-supporting again.

As best he could, Michael explained his job and what the Oasis House was.

"You work with crazy people?" Klarissa interrupted.

"They're mentally ill."

"Maybe Garrett or Hunter can help you find a better job."

"It's a good job," Michael said, remembering what he felt was a generous check, remembering the camaraderie he felt working alongside Arnie.

"They really are crazy?" asked Laura. "As in psychotic?"

"They're mentally ill," Michael said again.

"People like that should just get their act together and get moving," said Klarissa with disgust. "Acting depressed and moping around hearing voices. I bet half of that stuff is in their heads."

"I think that's the point," said Garrett, obviously annoyed. "It *is* in their heads. It's a sickness of the brain."

"Well, isn't the first step in self-control controlling your thoughts? God said to control your thoughts. Well, these guys are just people who choose not to," Klarissa argued.

"I don't think they can choose," Michael said calmly.

"Everyone can choose. God gave everyone free agency," Klarissa retorted. "We had a neighbor who sat around all day and didn't do anything. My dad had to mow her lawn because the bishop told him to, but every time my dad finished he would come in and say, 'Sure feels good to do some honest labor. If she would just get a little physical exercise, she'd sure feel better.' That lady wasn't mentally ill. She was just lazy."

Laura had been watching Michael during Klarissa's little speech and saw something happen to his eyes. His face remained pleasant, but his eyes went cold.

Klarissa continued, "We have completely medicalized the concept of bad behavior. Now it's all a disorder and not the person's responsibility." Klarissa's voice was a bit less assured as she felt Michael's disdain.

"You don't think anyone's mental health has a genuine root in some biological malfunction?" Garrett asked.

"No," Klarissa assured them.

Garrett tried several times to slow Klarissa down. Wanda just wanted to go home. Laura wanted to tell Michael she didn't agree with Klarissa, yet she'd never thought about mental illness and didn't want to sound stupid. So she remained quiet the rest of the time, as everyone else debated.

* * *

After the others left, Michael lay on his bed for a long time and thought about his sister, Stephanie. He needed to write her, now that he had an address. Tomorrow on the way home from work, he'd buy paper and envelopes. Mentally, the tired young man composed a letter to his sister. He'd tell her he had a good job at a place that helped the mentally ill. Michael planned to leave out the fact that he cooked, in case his father was intercepting the letters. Also, in case his dad got the letter, Michael decided to tell Stephanie that he had two good-looking roommates who had once been missionaries for the Mormon Church. Stephanie would understand, and his father would be furious. Maybe Michael would even write that he had been going to the Mormon Church and was thinking about joining it.

I'm not, thought Michael. *But I like their Book of Mormon.*

CHAPTER 6

"What's that?" Arnie asked, motioning to the pan Michael was scrubbing.

"Seth's version of a breakfast burrito." Michael's tone was neutral. That was one thing his father had taught him. He never showed hurt or disappointment.

Vaguely, Michael was aware that his irritation didn't come from having to feed nearly double the number that usually attended on Monday morning. He wasn't even really upset that ten clients could have helped cook but all claimed urgent counseling sessions, group employment, education classes, or a chat at the smoker-joker table; no one stayed to help cleanup.

The tired cook was unable to admit even to himself that he was mostly hurt that no one had asked him about the details of his supervising group employment that past Friday afternoon. No one had asked why he'd come to work that next Saturday morning smelling like Seth's newts. No one had even asked if he had found a place to live. And the strangest thing of all was that he cared.

He ignored Arnie leaning against the large sinks and reached for a pot scrubber.

"You're lucky to have Michael," said a female voice Michael didn't recognize.

"Yeah," Arnie agreed.

"You used to be the guy scrubbing pans," the female voice continued. "You ought to treat him better."

"I treat him good. It's you who sends him over to K-Mart to get in trouble."

Michael turned around and recognized Katie, the group-work supervisor who had been ill last Friday. With her was Ruth, the director, who had come down twice before and watched him work. She likes to know her employees, Arnie had informed him.

"I knew that little rascal Seth wouldn't leave those newts alone," Katie said, shaking her head in amusement.

"We're sorry," Ruth said to Michael. "We've tried to turn his obsession into a useful occupation, but once he raises those lizard creatures, he can't leave them be."

"I should have watched," Michael began.

"You're just there to help them, run interference if they need it, or call for backup if anyone gets in trouble, but they're all adults. You can't force them to behave well."

"Connor and Gail went with me to his place to make sure he was okay."

"I know." Ruth smiled. "Seth called me after you left—at my house, at midnight, woke my husband. Some days this job, Arnie . . ." The seasoned worker shook her head. "I need a vacation."

"Or an unlisted number," Arnie said.

"Really," Ruth agreed. She turned back to Michael. "Seth called, said you'd helped get a new tank ready. Said he wouldn't be in to deliver fliers today because the first seventy-two hours after relocation were crucial and he needed to be with the newts. He, however, reassured me that all those slimy creatures would be fine. I was much relieved." She nodded with mock seriousness.

"Have you seen his place?" Michael asked almost shyly.

"No," said Ruth. Katie admitted she hadn't either. "I've been upstairs and logged onto his website, though."

"He really is online?" Arnie asked.

"You can watch his newts live from seven different newtcams," Michael explained.

"Incredible."

"The site also has pages and pages about setting up tanks. Blueprints for tanks, the best plants for a newtarium," Michael said.

"Wish he'd use some of that obsessive energy and get our website set up," commented Arnie.

"Maybe Michael can encourage him," Ruth suggested.

"I don't think so," Arnie said. "Michael's already got a job." He motioned to the stack of pans.

Ruth ignored Arnie. "Really, Michael. Seth likes you. Maybe you'd be the one that could convince him to get the Oasis House website finished. You handled the K-Mart thing really well. I appreciate you."

"If you appreciate him so much," Arnie said, "reimburse him for the newts he paid for."

"We're working on that," Katie said cheerfully.

"It's okay," Michael said.

"No. We'll work something out," said Ruth. "By the way, did you find a place to live? Arnie was worried about you."

"I wasn't worried about him," Arnie complained. "He's a big boy. I figure he can take care of himself."

"I got an apartment," Michael said.

"Any roommates?" asked Ruth.

"Two."

"Good guys?" Ruth asked.

"Yeah, I think so."

"Be sure and spend some time with them. Get to know some other people besides just the ones around here," Ruth suggested. "You hang out here all the time, you lose perspective."

"Leave him alone," grumbled Arnie. "He's a grown-up."

When Michael finally turned back to his dishes, the water was cold. He drained it and filled the sink with warm suds. He cheerfully scrubbed the rest of the pots and started preparation for lunch.

Connor had promised to be back from counseling in time to help fix the veal. Michael mulled over the fact that even though Connor still looked for UFOs, he hadn't mentioned anything about the spacemen having an aversion to veal.

* * *

Seth entered the house just as lunch was over. He reported that his newts were all well with the exception of a small female who had died, weakened by all the excitement and probably too much smoke inhalation. He directed his last comment to Gail, who was perched on a stool in front of the cash register.

After checking on the newtcams, Michael asked Seth about the Oasis House home page. The page had a picture of the house and links dealing with schizophrenia, depression, bipolar disorders, and state mental-health organizations, but nothing about the program at the Oasis House.

"We need to get pictures of us here," Michael said, "and explain what we do."

"I know. I know. I know," Seth repeated over and over. "They keep telling me to. I know. I know. I know. I know. I know. I know I don't get stuff done. I know. I can't figure out some of this stuff."

"I'll help you," Michael said loudly, interrupting Seth's self-deprecating lecture. "I'll help."

"Okay," Seth said. He pulled a disc box from the desk's middle drawer. "Pictures are on here and every department wrote an article."

Michael tentatively took a disc and pushed it into the disc drive. Seth studied the contents, took a big breath, and opened the first file.

A little before seven that evening, Michael started to complain. "We've been up here almost five hours. We don't have to finish today."

Seth ignored him and added another graphic to the job-placement page.

"Everyone else is gone," Michael said. "My eyes hurt. My head hurts, and I'm hungry. Let's finish tomorrow."

Seth stared at the screen and rearranged some icons.

"Seth," Michael said firmly, "your newts need you."

* * *

After work on Tuesday, Laura looked up the address of the Oasis House. She drove slowly past it, wondering what went on inside. She hoped to catch a glimpse of Michael and then chided herself. She didn't even like him. He didn't seem to have a whole lot of social skills. He would hardly talk to her during Sunday School class.

As she drove, Laura continued to list unacceptable qualities about him. He wasn't a member. He wasn't going to the university. He didn't even have a car. What kind of potential did a guy like him have anyway? Laura drove past the Oasis House three times before going home, disappointed that she hadn't seen the boy she certainly wasn't interested in.

* * *

The next morning Michael was telling Arnie about Seth. "He wouldn't quit. Once he got started, he wouldn't stop."

"Get used to it. Obsessive behavior is often associated with those who are mentally ill."

"Like Connor's UFOs?"

"Yes, and Stan's suspenders, Caleb's dog. We see it a lot. Rand was obsessive exactly like Seth, only with hamsters."

Arnie sat down at his desk, taking a rare break. He laughed a little. "Rand loved hamsters. He *loved* them. He played with them and laughed at them. He'd started with one and then complained it was lonely. We convinced him for a while that hamsters liked to be alone, so Rand bought tunnels and running wheels. He named it Fluffy or Blondie or something. At night he'd play with it until he'd fall asleep, then the hamster would roam the apartment and leave droppings or gnaw holes in things.

"After having a taste of freedom, Fluffy didn't really want to stay in the cage. He'd gnaw at the plastic tubes and wiggle out. Rand would reinforce the tubes with packing tape, but nothing worked for long.

"Finally Rand became convinced that Fluffy would stay in better if he had friends, so he bought two more hamsters who immediately had two litters of babies. Within six months he had more than seventy-five hamsters. He spent every bit of money he had on new cages, but he never did figure out he needed to keep the males and females separated.

"There were hamsters everywhere. The smell was bad; the damage was worse. After major threats from the landlord, Rand finally agreed to get rid of them. He put them in two glass aquariums and started driving to pet stores in the valley. One aquarium was supposedly full of females and one of males. I don't rightly know how accurate he was. He'd carry one of the glass aquariums into a pet store and ask the attendant if they wanted to buy some hamsters. He did this most of one morning. The water bottle was dripping. The cage was wet. The hamsters were crawling and messing over each other. Most pet stores didn't even want him in their store. On about the fifteenth stop, he lugged his hamsters up the escalator of the mall and then past several leather and import stores to where a pet store used to be. It was gone. He got so upset—yelled a few things about stupid malls and idiotic people. A security guard told him to get out with his aquarium. Someone else spoke to him. He was so distraught and overwhelmed that he dropped the aquarium right next to a leather-goods store. The glass broke in three places, and hamsters scuttled off in all directions of the mall. Apparently people were screaming and threatening Rand, but he escaped too."

"You're kidding." Michael was appalled.

"Oh no," Arnie laughed.

"You laugh?"

"Actually, I laugh when I think about his female bunch still sitting in the car."

"What did he do with them?" Michael asked.

"Well, he dug around in some trash and found about twenty pop cans that he cut in half. Then he went and bought forty pounds of hamster food. He drove into the canyon to one of the premier golf courses and parked his car outside the fence next to the fifteenth hole. He lined the cans up along the edge of the green and filled each one with water from jugs he had brought. Then he poured the hamster food out, 'On the short grass,' he told me, so the hamsters could find it easier. Rand then let all those pregnant hamsters loose on the green."

Arnie chuckled contagiously. "Can you imagine riding up in a golf cart and finding all those jagged cans of water and scattered food? I find that funnier than the ones he dropped in the mall."

Michael laughed and then asked if the story was really true.

"Heck yes." Arnie rubbed his eyes. "That would be the end of the story, except he got to worrying about the hamsters at the mall. For weeks he obsessed about where they would get water, or what would happen if someone stepped on them. He would beg me to come with him and look for them. His biggest concern wasn't for the 'independent hamsters,' as he called them, but he said there is always one hamster that comes back looking for the security of a cage. He just knew that hamster would walk up to some unsuspecting shopper and get smashed.

"The leather-goods store actually got the brunt of the hamster damage. Apparently those little critters chewed on some fine cowhide and ruined it. One day the leather-goods guy recognized Rand. Not too difficult a task since Rand would stalk around the mall in a winter coat with pockets full of hamster food. He'd hunt for hamsters behind shelves and under clothing racks. He would scatter food in places he felt were good hideouts for his friends. Finally, the one store owner had him arrested. They couldn't think of any legal charges, so Mr. Leatherworks called People for the Ethical Treatment of Animals and tried to get them to press cruelty-to-animal charges. It was a mess." Arnie grinned.

Michael looked at his boss suspiciously.

"No, Rand's for real. Someday you'll meet him. I hope someday he'll be ready to come here and start working toward getting a job. Rand's my brother. He's how I got involved in mental health."

"Where is he now?" Michael asked.

"He lives in a group home. His grasp on reality is pretty limited. If you're going to work here, don't lose sight of the fact that malfunctions of the brain can be tragic for everyone involved. But even then, I've learned we better laugh when we can." Arnie stood up and smiled, patting Michael on the back. "So, anyway, if you buy a leather coat and there's a hamster nest in the pocket, you'd better laugh."

CHAPTER 7

"A guy out in Roosevelt says that a lot of UFOs come out there because of all the mineral deposits. Someday we need to go look there," Connor suggested as he climbed. It was sunset, and Michael and Connor were about halfway up the mountain behind the Utah State Mental Hospital. Michael was surprised that the big man seemed so confident climbing up this narrow trail.

"We could go out to the Uintah Basin and check. Before my mission, my dad and I used to go out and talk to people who said they had seen UFOs."

"You went on a mission?"

"Yeah, to New York. You ever been there in the fall when the leaves turn colors? It's really beautiful."

Michael watched the man move ahead of him as the trail narrowed. The belt around Connor's massive waist had missed a loop. His T-shirt was pulled up to reveal a couple inches of white, fatty flesh. Michael had trouble picturing his shuffling, slow-talking companion in a crisp, white shirt and teaching people in New York City. Michael was growing accustomed to the differences in Connor. Often his language and manner were completely absurd. At other times, Connor seemed exceptionally bright and coherent, quoting statistics and scientific data.

As the trail widened, Michael caught his friend and the two hiked purposefully up the incline. After a moment, Michael asked, "Did you enjoy your mission?"

"At first," Connor said, "but then I started losing it."

"Losing it?" Michael asked.

"I lost touch with reality. I guess I did some really weird things, and finally I completely broke. They sent me home after the first year. I'm better now. I think this new medication is working. It's the third one I've been on. This one is the most expensive, but I think I'll be ready to go back to work. I've been really lucky to have the Oasis House and my parents and everyone help me."

They stopped and looked back over the valley. Lights were beginning to twinkle on. The lake reflected a pink sunset. Cars glimmered along the freeway as stars appeared among the scattered white clouds.

"Pretty, huh?" commented Connor.

"How old were you when you went to New York?" Michael asked.

"Nineteen, like most guys," Connor said. "I attended BYU for a year and then got my call."

"You were at BYU?" Michael had been around long enough now to know that not everyone was accepted to the Church-run university. How had this slow-talking, UFO-believing guy gotten in?

"Actually, I had enough credits to be considered a junior by the time I left. I could have graduated early from high school, but I was playing football, so I went a half day at Timpview High School and then a half day at the university."

"What were you studying?" Michael asked, trying to digest, among everything else, that this guy had played football.

"Electrical engineering. I planned to transfer after I got home from New York to a more advanced program."

"How'd you get interested in that?" Michael asked.

"Did an internship with a company that builds the electronics components for exercise equipment. It was very cool. But I've forgotten a lot of it."

Michael stared at Connor and then decided his mentally ill friend was hallucinating an entire earlier life. What was strange was that it had been an unusually lucid day for Connor. Even his talk of UFOs had been more realistic and based in science. On the way up the hill, Connor had explained to Michael about God having other worlds and that the flying saucers were probably just people from God's other planets checking in on the earth. "'Course, maybe all these UFO sightings can be explained by atmospheric occurrences or come from folks that need a medication adjustment," Connor had explained logically. With such discussion in mind, Michael had agreed the medication was working better, but now with talk of playing ball and taking advanced classes, Michael thought maybe Connor was improving in some areas that dealt with language control yet was imagining life before his illness.

"If we walk along this deer trail we'll cross behind BYU. It's only a couple miles. Then we drop down the hill and we'll be right at my parents' house," Connor said, breaking into Michael's thoughts. "Dad will give us a ride home. That is, if you want to meet my folks." Connor finished his invitation a little uncertainly. "Or we can just go back now."

"No, let's walk," Michael said, wondering if Connor's parents' living on the other side of BYU was just another fantasy. "We could use a long walk."

The trail traversed the hill, and Michael watched the campus below him. He imagined what it would be like to belong in that school.

"We have to go up a little here," Connor said, "and then we drop down onto a road. You can see the house from here. Third one on the left."

The third house on the left was an expansive white home with five pillars in the front and a large privacy fence around a huge lot. When they got there, Connor swung the unlocked door open and yelled, "Hey, anyone home? Mom? Dad?"

Michael followed hesitantly into a large entrance hall. To the right of the double outside doors was a wide staircase leading up to a balcony. On either side of the entryway were what appeared to be two formal living rooms. The one on the right had a hardwood floor and a large grand piano. Several dark-wood and leather chairs surrounded the outside of the room. The living room to the left had soft gold carpeting. The sofas and chairs all had pale gold threads running through elegant white material. Wide arched doorways led to either room. Connor continued through a doorway directly in front of the outside doors. Michael cautiously followed.

"Connor?" A man rose from his leather couch in front of a large entertainment center and embraced the new arrival. "You're looking good," he said enthusiastically and stepped back to get a better look. "Glad you came by. We haven't heard from you in a couple days."

"Where's Mom?" Connor asked, looking around the large family room. Michael could see a kitchen to one side and a patio.

"She had a meeting. Something to do with changes in the extraction program. She should be back in a few minutes. Introduce me to your friend."

"This is Michael. We were out looking for UFOs," explained Connor. "We didn't see any. I told Michael we should go to the Uintah Basin."

"We could do that," his father said agreeably.

Michael felt uncomfortable even after he was invited to sit down. He'd never been in a home this grand. He'd probably never talked to anyone with as much money as this man obviously had. And how could someone like Connor—who flitted in and out of reality—have been raised here?

"You still working with that group at K-Mart?" Connor's father asked after turning the TV off.

"Yeah, usually."

"Great," the man said heartily. "Just great."

"Michael took us last week," Connor said.

"Oh, you're on staff?" Disappointment sounded in his father's voice. "I thought I knew 'most everyone down there."

"Michael's just new," Connor said.

"Son," said the father, "why don't you go to the library and get that book about sightings in the Basin?"

Connor ambled out of the room.

"Is Connor not doing well?" Connor's father wasted no time questioning Michael.

"What?"

"You can talk to me. Even though Connor is of legal age, he signed a release of information for his mother and me."

"Release of information? Sir, I don't know what you mean."

"So you counselors can talk to us." Brother Steele was impatient. "Is Connor not functioning well enough to go places alone?"

"Brother Steele, I really don't know what you're talking about. I just help Arnie in the kitchen. I'm certainly no counselor. Connor wanted to watch for UFOs. He's always been friendly to me. I like him, so I thought I'd come along."

Connor returned. "Dad, I can't find the book."

"Oh, yeah. I guess we left it in your room."

Connor moved toward the stairs and Brother Steele continued. "So you're not monitoring Connor?"

"No, sir. I'm just the new cook in the kitchen. Connor has helped me out a lot in there. I've never heard anyone talk about his therapy and certainly not to me."

"You like him?"

"Yes, sir."

"He used to have lots of friends before his break," the older man reminisced softly. "He was really popular and very bright. He was always on the honor rolls. His energy level was always high. A different person came home from that mission. His illness stole his identity." Brother Steele spoke sadly. "But we love him. We think he's improving. Maybe someday he'll get back some of what he used to have."

Michael didn't know what to say.

As Connor came down the stairs, an energetic, slender woman came through the side door. "Connor," she said excitedly, "if I'd known you were coming, I'd have skipped my meeting. They were just setting next month's extraction goals."

Michael looked at her closely. He associated extractions with dentists. He supposed she could be a dentist.

She was delighted to see her son, happy to meet his friend, and attentive to their plans for a trip to the Uintah Basin. "There are a lot of places to explore out there while you wait for spacecrafts," she said cheerfully.

Michael's hesitation to join the trip was misinterpreted. "You don't have to go," the older man said.

"It's just that we've all been working six days a week. I hate to ask Arnie for a day off when he doesn't get one," Michael explained.

"We'll leave after your work Saturday and be back in time for church on Sunday."

* * *

When Arnie heard about the weekend plans, he insisted Michael leave early. "Come in at nine, get the meal ready, and I'll clean up alone. Tell Brother Steele you can leave by eleven or eleven thirty."

"I wasn't asking for time off," Michael insisted.

"You can do it for me next week," Arnie said.

"I will," Michael assured him and then finished assembling ingredients for Gail, who wanted to learn to make cinnamon rolls. This was a skill Michael had brought to the kitchen. His father's restaurant had made huge sticky rolls that sold for two dollars each, a considerable profit. Clients at the Oasis House often requested them.

The Lincoln Towncar pulled into the Oasis parking lot at 10:00 A.M., and Brother Steele got out. Then Connor's dad came into the house. He took a seat in the dining hall next to two clients whom he addressed by name—Wade and Karma. Wade was severely depressed and wouldn't look at anyone, but he'd talk about his dog. Brother Steele was talking about dogs that morning. He ordered a special from Karma, an elderly client whose personal hygiene often made speaking to her a challenge.

Arnie saw Michael watching. "I don't know how the man dealt with Connor's mental illness when it was first diagnosed. I seldom get to know people and their families until the illness is stabilized. By then both Mr. and Mrs. Steele had decided to help Connor and anyone around him."

Arnie and Michael walked back into the kitchen and started placing large pans of eggs into serving warmers.

"The Oasis House has received several donations from him, and I know he's endorsed some of the grants we've received."

"Is he just nice to me because he wants Connor to have a friend?" Michael asked.

"Probably," Arnie said as he turned to start filling orders.

Maybe that was the case on the day he visited Connor's parents' house, but during the overnight excursion Michael felt genuinely liked. The trip to the Basin started through Provo Canyon and up to Heber. Connor wanted a milk shake from Granny's Drive-In. As they slurped ice cream that was threatening to escape their cups, Brother Steele asked, "Should we show Michael the old Spanish smelters or go out to Josie's Ranch and the Dinosaur National Monument?"

"I've only been to the smelter once," Connor said. He started to get flustered. His hand fluttered in his lap and he kept repeating himself. "Probably I couldn't find them. I don't remember good. I don't know, Dad. I only saw them once or twice. I probably can't remember. I only saw them once."

"Then to the ranch and quarry we'll go," said Brother Steele, interrupting Connor's obsessive worrying.

"I could try and find those old smelters," Connor said sadly, "if you really want to go. I just get lost sometimes, you know." He spoke the last in a whisper.

"I'd sooner see that old box canyon again anyway," remarked his father. "And I bet Michael would too. We'll find the smelters someday when it's not so hot."

Connor felt immediately better. "I remember about the Lost Rhoades Mine, though," he said. Connor turned to speak to Michael. "I can tell you about the lost mines if you want me to. I'm not going to go looking for them, though. There's a curse on them, don't you think, Dad?"

"Could be," his father said. "Right good possibility."

"The mines have a curse on them?" Michael asked Connor.

"Well, the smelters that you can still see are from mines the Spaniards had, but those mines probably didn't produce nearly the amount of gold that the Carre-Shin-Ob mine did. That mine is now called the Lost Rhoades Mine and probably has a curse on it."

"Carre-Shin-Ob?"

"Yeah, the sacred mine of the Ute Indians. The gold that came out of that mine, or maybe a couple of mines, was what was used to cover the angel Moroni."

"They put gold on Moroni?" Michael asked, confused.

"The statue on the Salt Lake Temple. He's covered in thin layers of gold. It's a really hard process that took a lot of gold because there's so much waste."

"Connor's done a lot of reading about where the gold supposedly came from," Brother Steele said. "Parts of the stories must be true, but, like all history, we don't really know what part of the story is authentic and what part is legend."

"I think the story is pretty accurate," Connor said. "Where else could the Saints have gotten the gold? We know there were a lot of gold coins in the valley minted by the Church. No one hauled that much weight up from California."

"Is there a lot of mining done out there now?" Michael asked.

"No commercial gold mining."

"Why not?"

"Because they lost the mines."

"How can you lose mines?" Michael asked, confusion obvious on his face.

"Okay," Connor said. "I'll start at the first."

"Careful," Brother Steele warned Michael. "Connor loves this story. He's given school reports on it and even wrote a letter to Church leaders asking if these mines were where the gold came from."

"What did they answer?" Michael asked.

"The Church historian wrote back and said he would neither deny nor confirm the reports. Now son, tell a brief version so we don't bore Michael too bad, or he won't come again."

Connor started his story with a detailed account of an Indian chief who liked Brigham Young and was willing to show one white person where the tribe got its gold. When this chosen person died, so did the secret of where the mine was.

"Surely someone has gone looking for the mine," Michael said.

"Thousands of people. All the time you hear stories about people finding an opening and then going back and it's gone. Or finding an opening and then getting shot at or breaking a leg or something. Some say that the Indians still know where the mine is and that they're guarding it."

Brother Steele slowed the car as they passed through a small town. Worn buildings lined a wide street. "This is Duchesne. It's thirty miles to Roosevelt and then another thirty to Vernal where we'll spend the night."

"Where are the gold mines supposed to be from here?" Michael asked.

"Probably northwest of Vernal," Connor replied.

"Where's the dinosaur quarry?"

"On the other side of Vernal. We pass it to get to Josie's Ranch," Connor explained. "The ranch is named after Josie Bassett, who built her cabin at the entrance to a box canyon. They say that's where she hid Butch Cassidy's horses."

"Really?" Michael asked.

"Supposedly," Connor nodded.

After inspecting the ranch, the three men returned to Vernal and ate at the motel. Afterward Connor fell asleep as soon as they got to their room.

"The medication saps his energy," Brother Steele explained.

"Today he seemed so . . ." Michael stopped.

"So normal?"

"Yes. Is he really still sick or could he go off the medication?"

"Probably not. He's tried before. You met him when he had been back on for about three weeks. He was stabilizing, but still, well, you know, he was sort of preoccupied with UFOs then. Nothing logical. That's because he tried to go off and got so out of touch with reality. It was all I could do to convince him to take the medication again. He was just starting to get better when you first met him. But the meds have a lot of side effects Connor hates. He can't think as clearly as he once could, he gains weight, he's tired, his energy level is low. He may never have the strength to hold down a full-time job. Sometimes being totally disconnected with reality feels better than all the side effects and the understanding of what you used to be compared to what you are today. That's why some mentally ill people don't want to take medicine. And then for some, the meds are not nearly as successful as for Connor. He's reacted very well."

"This is the best he'll ever be?" Michael asked.

"I used to believe I could buy enough therapy or medication to heal him. Now I know his cure is in the hands of the doctors and the Lord. I just support him and help the best I can. My family can only hope, pray, do our best, and leave it in the hands of the Lord."

"Do you believe God could heal him?" Michael asked tentatively.

"Well, our Father in Heaven is a God of miracles. He can do what He feels is best. Will the Lord provide a miracle for Connor? I don't know." The man looked directly at Michael. "But He's already given me a miracle in my life. The strength I've felt from the Lord is a miracle—the comfort He sends me during the nights when I worry about what Connor's future will be. That comfort has been a miracle. The change in my perspective about other people and how I judge others is a miracle. I used to see things in black and white, right and wrong. I see things differently now. As much as Connor has changed,

I've changed too. Sometimes I feel like Connor had to go through this trial so that I could learn compassion, so that I could learn to be less judgmental."

Except for the loud breathing of the sleeping Connor, there was silence in the room for a long time. Michael thought about what Brother Steele had said. Finally, Connor's father spoke again. "Another thing I've learned is that just when we think there's no hope and we can't go forward, a small miracle happens to let us know our Heavenly Father recognizes our troubles. The Oasis House was an answer to our prayers. And I think you've been an answer too."

"I don't think . . . I don't . . ." Michael mumbled self-consciously.

"No, don't feel embarrassed or obligated to Connor because I said that. It's really helped that you've just been there, acting like you respect him, giving him an opportunity to gain confidence in his own abilities."

Michael took a deep breath. He'd enjoyed the day so much. He wanted this man to be his friend, but he also wanted to understand. "Can I ask you a question?" he asked.

The older man nodded.

"Do you resent that you sent him on a Church mission that caused his mental illness?"

"Michael, the mission didn't cause Connor's illness."

"Arnie told me lots of missionaries come home with mental illness."

"It happens. The stress of a mission might speed up the onset of mental illness, but certain types of mental illness simply manifest themselves at about the age that young men are when they're serving missions."

"What did you think when Connor first came home?"

"First I had to find someone to blame for what had happened, so I was mad at Connor. I thought maybe he'd done something we didn't know about. Then I got mad at his companions because I thought they must not have loved him enough. Next, I accused the mission president of not keeping a close enough watch. Then I wondered, Why us? Why him?"

"You're not mad at God?"

"Some days. But," Brother Steele smiled, "I can't cure Connor, so I really only have two options: I can be bitter, tired, and angry all the time, or I can accept the comfort God gives me while understanding that we all have trials."

The two talked for a long time that evening. Michael lay awake even longer watching car lights splash cold white against the lonely night. *I can be bitter, tired, and angry all the time,* Brother Steele had said, *or I can accept the comfort God gives me.* A calmness crept into the hotel room. *And I can either be bitter, tired, and angry all the time about my father,* Michael realized, *or I can accept the comfort God seems to be giving me.* The car lights became warm beacons in a cozy night as Michael thought about how he would tell Stephanie about this comfort.

The next morning, Connor was dressed first and suggested they drive through Nine Mile Canyon on the way home. "It'll take an extra hour," commented his father.

"Two," Connor replied. "I want to hike up to the Indian petroglyphs."

All agreed. Michael was amazed at the steep red cliffs. The Indian paintings were so easy to spot. After hiking about an hour, they returned to the car and started the three-hour ride home. They arrived at Connor's house and changed into Sunday clothes. Then they hurriedly drove to the church. They slipped into a crowded back pew just as the hymn "Nearer, My God, to Thee" started. And Michael felt nearer to something spiritual as he sat in the chapel between Connor and Conrad Steele.

Unlike at the university ward he had attended with his roommates, these speakers made sense to Michael as they talked about compassion and fast offerings. He loved watching the mothers try to quiet toddlers with small bags of cereal and crackers. He puzzled over how a pink bow stayed stuck on the bald head of an infant girl. He watched in fascination as a little boy crawled under the benches and was hugged by an elderly couple when he popped up in their row.

During Sunday School, Brother Steele lent Michael a leather-bound set of scriptures. He learned that D&C was short for Doctrine and Covenants and that within this book was a code of health called the Word of Wisdom. By priesthood Michael had figured out where the table of contents was and how to watch others to see whether they used the big or little book in their scripture sets.

As Michael and the Steeles ate supper that night, Brother Steele answered Michael's questions about wards, meeting schedules, firesides, and what "FHE" stood for.

As Michael grew more comfortable with the Steeles and their grand home, his questions multiplied. They more fully explained the Word of Wisdom. He found that "standard works" were scriptures and that people went to temples to do work on behalf of the dead. And even though he still didn't completely understand the extraction program, he knew it didn't have anything to do with teeth.

The full-time missionaries arrived during dessert and asked Michael if he'd like to hear more. He decided he ought to hear their version, especially since they seemed to represent the ward he liked best.

Elders Johnson and Glease leaned forward eagerly as they taught an investigator that not only knew the answers, but also seemed to instinctively know what questions were going to be asked.

Michael was slightly amused when he recognized the same topics Hunter and Garrett had taught him. He was also aware that the Steele family—especially Connor—were earnestly listening to concepts they probably knew by heart. With a surge of compassion for his friend, Michael realized that Connor had once worn a dark suit in a stranger's living room and determinedly explained these same concepts. Michael also recognized the now-familiar warmth that settled into his heart.

* * *

At 10:15 Sunday night, Garrett and Hunter were standing at the kitchen counter eating microwave popcorn and discussing where their roommate could be. They stopped both activities when Michael walked in.

Someone muttered "hi" into the awkward silence.

"You had a good weekend?" Garrett asked.

"Yeah." Michael's reply was tentative.

All week they had been carefully considerate of one another, almost to the point of avoidance. Michael hardly ate in the apartment. He left before the other two got up and was often in his room before they came home. He didn't know that roommate etiquette required that he reveal he was leaving for the weekend. He didn't know they wanted him to sit around and discuss girls, pretend to share food, and then go for pizza instead. But mostly, he didn't know that they wanted to continue teaching him about the Church.

"My brother needs you to fill out some papers," Hunter said.

"Oh," Michael said suspiciously. He'd already paid two months' rent and a cleaning deposit to a guy who lived in the bottom apartment.

"Some personal data so we know who to contact in case something happens to you. You know, if you get hurt or something."

Michael turned away. Loneliness pushed into his chest where warmth had so recently been. He shrugged and struggled to produce his usual noncommittal tone. "There's only one person you need to tell if I die. I'll get you her number."

He turned to face them with a wry grin and added, "And you guys can divide up all that really good stuff in my room."

They weren't sure whether to laugh, and Michael went to bed. They didn't offer him any popcorn as he walked away.

* * *

After lunch on Monday, Gail volunteered to wash dishes. Unless pressured, Gail had seldom worked. Her main occupation had been to sit at the smoker-joker table and tell the funniest jokes. Michael gratefully accepted the help and her usually funny personality. But today she fumed through several pans, muttering loudly, "I hate this. I hate this." Her colorful speech continued. She frequently added obscenities that Michael hadn't heard strung together quite so viciously since he'd left home. Trying not to be obvious, Michael watched the pretty, petite girl. Her short hair shone chestnut and, unlike many of the others, seemed always to be freshly washed, cut, and styled. She wore the same earrings and frayed shorts he had seen her wearing his first day, although the T-shirt was different.

"I'll help you," Michael offered as he set two more serving trays next to Gail's sink.

"You can't help!" Gail spun around to face him. "You don't know." She lifted a heavy pot out of the water and flung it at Michael. Greasy water and suds covered his apron and seeped into his jeans.

"I hate this place. I hate you," Gail screamed, and then she cried. She turned back to the sink and pounded clenched fists into the remaining water. Her hair hung limply forward.

Arnie stood to one side until the girl's energy was spent, and then he pulled her toward the side door, talking softly about working things out.

Gail was calm until the side door opened and the heavy smell of cigarette smoke drifted in.

The first explosion had been mild compared to Gail's renewed rage. Somewhere in the slurred ranting, Michael understood that Gail was trying to stop smoking because someone named Autumn had asthma.

"No nicotine patches for Gail, oh no," the girl's voice rose sarcastically. "That's contraindicated to the meds I'm on. But the smoking isn't contraindicated. I'm leaving." Gail jerked toward the door.

Arnie held her firm.

"You need to stay with a support group in a mood like this, Gail. Don't leave. Go upstairs, or I'll go running with you."

"They can't ask me to do this." The girl was crying again. "They can't ask me." She slumped to the floor and laid her head on the hard tile. Arnie sat next to her and talked soothingly. The water she had thrown earlier pooled around them.

Michael and two others cleaned the kitchen around the two figures on the wet floor. Gail's anguish didn't subside. Arnie stayed next to her.

* * *

Tuesday morning no one said anything about Gail, and Michael didn't ask, but he was unsettled when she came in to help wash.

She seemed remote and sullen as she vigorously scrubbed an already-clean pan.

"What else?" she asked, spinning around to catch Michael watching her. "You need anything else done? Like maybe I could mop the floor?"

"No. We're okay." Michael paused before asking. "You okay?"

"Yeah. No. No." Her voice was low. She watched her hands as they twisted and pulled at one another. "No. I'm bipolar. I'm crazy. I want to be well." Tears slid down her high cheekbones. "I want my baby."

Gail appeared to slump, and Michael was scared she'd end up on the floor again. He stepped closer, and Gail fell against him. "They took my baby." She leaned heavily, her anguish as real as the day before.

Michael stood and let her cry. He could feel how small she was, how hard she shook. Rhonda from the office pool arrived and eventually convinced Gail to go upstairs and talk.

Arnie explained later. "She wasn't caring for the baby. Gail went into a manic phase and left Autumn for nearly eighteen hours. Then during her depression, she would forget to feed her."

"How old?" Michael asked.

"Almost a year now. A beautiful little girl."

"But Gail's stable now. It seems to me . . . I mean, could she have the baby back now?"

"I don't know. I don't know if Autumn would be safe or not. Right now they're saying that Gail's smoking is bringing on asthma attacks in the little girl."

"Lots of parents smoke. That's just an excuse."

"Maybe, but right now Autumn probably isn't safe with her."

"Couldn't someone help her? Help so she could get her baby back?"

"Michael, we're our clients' advocates. We fight for their rights and against discrimination. But the baby needs protecting too. We're doing what we can to help Gail. Rhonda's trying to find her temporary placement so she can work into a job. A psychiatrist is trying to regulate her medication, but Gail keeps going off the meds."

"Why does she do that if she wants her daughter back so badly?"

"She enjoys the manic phases."

Michael squinted. "Huh?"

"Manic energy is often much better than the stable, drab feeling meds give her."

"Where's Autumn's father?"

"I don't know. I've never asked. I've heard Gail say he gave her those earrings. I doubt she got them from her folks. They don't have that kind of money."

"Where are her parents? Why don't they keep the baby until Gail gets better?"

"They're struggling," Arnie said. "They don't know what's best for Gail or for their granddaughter. They don't like Gail's smoking, but they've tolerated it until now. However, they're convinced that smoking is hurting both Autumn and Gail, and they won't help Gail get custody until she quits smoking and can at least help with the rearing." He paused, trying to explain why the issue was so difficult for Gail to deal with. "Connor says you've been going to church."

"Yes."

"You know the Mormon Church has the Word of Wisdom?"

Again, Michael nodded. Except for coffee, Michael was pretty much in compliance since the other vices reminded him so much of his father.

"Gail's parents are very active Mormons, so they don't believe in smoking, right? But Gail has convinced herself that smoking relieves some of the symptoms of her illness. So what would you do if you were her parents, or her for that matter?"

For a long moment Michael thought. As with every concept, he had felt peace with the Word of Wisdom. If it was true, there had to be another solution. "There has to be a remedy that's better for everyone involved," he started.

"Probably. I'm sure we could get something that fills her needs without the negative side effects of smoking. But think how hard it is to simply let go of tobacco, then add to that the fact that Gail thinks it's helping her illness—losing that could make her panic even more."

Michael nodded, seeing how complex and difficult the situation was. He knew he couldn't fix it, but that night he prayed like his roommates and the elders had taught him. He included Gail in that prayer.

CHAPTER 8

Motivated by Michael's vague promise to help clean and add onto the newtariums, Seth had been incredibly helpful at the Oasis House. After Gail's whirlwind emotions Monday and Tuesday, Michael found Seth's predictability and single-mindedness comforting. He had spent both Monday and Tuesday evenings in Seth's basement.

Wednesday evening Michael rode up the steep hill to the Steeles' home and listened to the elders take turns telling him about salvation and physical death and redemption from sin. Elder Glease then asked Michael if he was willing to follow the example of Christ by being baptized.

"Someday, I guess," Michael muttered.

"We'll be holding a baptismal service next Saturday. Will you prepare yourself to be baptized on that date?" Elder Johnson asked.

"I—I've got to think about this," Michael stuttered, and then felt he needed to leave. Ever since then, he'd avoided Garrett and Hunter because he felt certain that if he talked religion with them again they'd repeat the invitation to be baptized.

Thursday and Friday nights Michael stayed in the computer lab of the Oasis House long after everyone else had left. He surfed the web looking for possible links to add to the Oasis House site, which Seth had nearly finished. Michael also tried to find information about mental illness and addiction. Late that night, he found the official site of The Church of Jesus Christ of Latter-day Saints. He read the document called "The Family: A Proclamation to the World." He read conference talks and perused a map of the various Church missions. He understood the phrase "mission field" a little better.

By Saturday, fatigue from too many early mornings and late nights had settled heavily onto Michael. He went home after work and fell asleep. As daylight started to fade, he woke up to the sound of girls' laughter mixed with his roommates'. "We made these cookies," said one chipper voice unfamiliar to Michael, "and we can't eat them all." Half awake, he heard girls flirting with Hunter and Garrett in the kitchen. Michael listened carefully at first to see if either of the voices was Klarissa's or Laura's.

The group bantered and talked about majors and the heat and how lucky they were to have cookies.

"Where's your other roommate?" asked another voice, unknown to Michael.

"Who knows?" said Hunter.

"I've heard he's crazy, as in he hasn't turned the corner yet but the blinker's on."

Michael shrugged to himself. He'd been called a lot worse. After knowing those who were truly mentally ill, he wasn't insulted.

"He's okay," Garrett said.

"That's not what I've heard."

"He's okay," Garrett insisted more forcefully, and Michael felt a puzzled kind of gratitude.

"Klarissa says he acts weird. She said he hardly talks."

"He's not exactly Mr. Social," Hunter commented dryly.

Garrett mounted a stronger defense this time. "He moved here because of the Church."

"From what he said the other night," Hunter said, "he doesn't have any other place to go."

"What do you mean?" asked a female voice.

"I don't think he has a family, or at least not one he can go back to."

"Maybe he's running from the law," a third female voice suggested.

"No," Garrett said firmly. "The guy wanted to know about the Church."

"Like a convict before his execution," a female voice suggested.

"No, he wants to know about the Church, mostly about the Book of Mormon. He's read the whole thing. He feels the Spirit. Maybe he's uncomfortable with us. Maybe he thinks *we're* the weird ones. He's probably had bad experiences we can't even imagine. Give him a break."

They were leaving for pizza or something. Michael didn't listen much after that. He was overwhelmed that someone he barely knew had defended him.

* * *

As dusk settled over the valley, Michael walked slowly toward the Oasis House. He knew his roommates were at a dance. They'd come back from pizza while Michael was eating a sandwich in the kitchen. As Hunter busied himself elsewhere, Garrett had invited Michael to go with them.

"No thanks," he said quickly.

"You'll want to go to church tomorrow, though." Garrett stated rather than asked.

"Sure," Michael said.

"Hunter and I have an early-morning PEC meeting," Garrett explained. "Then we were asked to sing in the ward choir. They're starting practices tomorrow right before church. You want to sing?"

Michael shook his head. "Not really. I'll just see you at church."

"I'll have time to run back and walk over with you," Garrett offered.

"I can find it," Michael assured him, still wondering what "PEC" stood for.

Having slept all afternoon, Michael was rested with no place to go. He could check Connor's apartment or Seth's. Walking in the evening air, he wondered what the dances were like. Maybe he should have gone. He could have told Garrett thanks for what he'd said to the girls in the kitchen.

Impulsively Michael turned into the deserted yard of the Oasis House. He looked at the dark windows and felt a strange pang of loneliness. Rows of pink petunias were blooming wildly along the front walk. He saw one small section the sprinklers had missed. As he used a hose to water the dry spot, Michael thought of the blossoms in front of his father's sandwich shop. As a timid kindergarten student, he'd painted a clay pot and stuck a pink petunia in it. The teacher had assured him that his mother would be very pleased with her Mother's Day gift. She'd been pleased. "Thank you," she said. "I'm glad you're my son, too." Her voice was mechanical. She placed the pot on a storage shelf by the back door. Following his teacher's instructions, Michael watered the flower faithfully until mud ran over the top and soaked the particle board beneath.

Michael had seen the broken pot and bright bloom on top of the garbage can. His father had called him "fairy princess" when he'd dug a hole and planted the petunia in the hard dirt by the restaurant's front door.

But at age six he'd known how to defend himself by comparing his father's restaurant to the closest competition. "The Shake Out has flowers," he'd said. Later that week his mother was instructed to plant flowers. Michael had tended them, making sure the soil was damp, the weeds pulled, and the dead blossoms pruned. By the time he was twelve he took money out of the till to buy marigolds to plant.

Later he took classes at the high school and spent an hour a day in the school greenhouse. He had planted tomatoes in sterile potting soil and was encouraged to try new flower varieties. He carried his successes to his father's restaurant and cultivated them in the ever-expanding flower bed. No one in Michael's family had mentioned the flowers, but customers often commented on the profusion of color in the well-tended garden.

Michael wondered if anyone was caring for the blossoms he'd planted this year, or if his absence would be noticed when the plants all drooped and died. He thought about his sister Stephanie. How was she being treated? She'd answered his first letter with the firm warning that Dad had read everything.

> . . . *but thanks for writing. I'm glad you found a place to go. Dad was pretty mad, but he's telling the regulars that you're going to school. He acts like he's paying tuition at some Ivy League school. Are there any of them in Utah? Are you going to go to school? You just said you had a job, but not what it was. I wish I could think of a way to get mail without Dad seeing it. He said if you had anything to do with that Mormon cult you couldn't come back. He wouldn't even serve you, much less let you come back to work. But that's really stupid since we really could use some help around here. I was pretty mad at you when you first left 'cause there was so much to do. But now I'm glad 'cause maybe if your job is as good as you say it is, you can help me come there.*

Don't write back and say you can. Dad would have my hide. I'll just hope—helps me get through the day.

Love,
Stephanie

The day after getting Stephanie's letter, Michael had figured out the time difference and called the shop, hoping his dad had gone home for a rest. Stephanie answered. She was frantic to be off the phone. "He's started showing up earlier, accuses me of stealing from the till."

"Are you?"

"Not now. I tried to save some money like you. I got too scared."

"Call me collect. From a phone booth or something. We'll talk."

"What's your number?"

"Check the caller ID. Does my number show?"

"It's there."

"Copy it down and then erase it from the machine."

"Can I come there? Will you help me leave?"

"I'm saving all my money."

"Promise?"

"Promise."

"I've got to go."

She'd hung up. No one had tried to make a collect call to the apartment. Michael had told his roommates to accept any calls from Stephanie. They'd looked at him speculatively but he'd made no explanations. She still hadn't contacted him.

Lost in his worried thoughts about his sister, Michael mechanically turned the hose off and walked around the side of the large house to water a bed of geraniums that had started to bloom. The place was shadowed, the flowers nearly black in the lost light. A sudden movement and a distinct smell quickly brought him out of his musing. Gail was sitting at the long picnic tables.

She was hunched forward on one of the benches, her left elbow propped on the cool tabletop, her head on her hand. Her other hand held the butt of a cigarette. She sucked hard on the brown filter as Michael walked over.

"Gail?" There was no response. "Gail."

The diamonds in her ears caught a glint of reflected light. Every other aspect of her seemed dark.

A small pile of cigarette butts lay next to her elbow. Again Gail inhaled until there was nothing left but the colored filter. She raised her head and flicked the completely used cigarette in the nearby shrub and picked up another nearly smoked butt. Holding it carefully, she lit it with the flick of a cheap lighter and lay her head back down on her arm. Michael suddenly realized the girl had come here to collect unfinished cigarettes from the smoker-joker table, and he felt slightly sick at the thought.

"Gail," he said, "if you have to smoke, let's go buy you some." Michael cringed as he made the offer. He hadn't been very old when he'd come to loathe cigarettes. Customers had blown smoke in his face as he served their sandwiches. The butts had carelessly been tossed in his flowerbeds. Nevertheless, anything would be better than what Gail was doing.

The girl examined the pile until she found a particularly long butt. She prepared to light it.

"Gail," Michael said more forcefully. "Let's buy you some." He reached over to take the lighter from her slightly shaking hand. She jerked, grasping the cigarette and lighter to her sweatshirt.

"I can't quit. Go away." Her voice was dead. Michael had heard every emotion from this little woman. He'd heard excitement, boredom, complaints, and anguish. Tonight there was no emotion.

"Come on," Michael said, sitting across from her at the picnic table. "I'll take you home."

Gail inhaled deeply and blew smoke slowly. "I can't go home." She was silent for a long time. "They won't want me back if I'm smoking." The cigarette was gone. She tossed it into a large bleeding-heart plant. Gail raised up and poked the pile of butts she had collected.

For a while they just sat there. Michael occasionally asked questions. Gail never answered one, she just talked slowly, long silences between random thoughts. From her rambling, Michael discovered that Gail's parents had told her she couldn't smoke. She had to go regularly to the Oasis House and work toward a full-time job. On Sunday she had to attend church. If Gail met these standards, they would help her get custody of her daughter Autumn, Gail's daughter, and they would help raise the little girl.

"They don't want to," Gail said, her voice still quietly dying. "They always thought I should give her to someone."

"Why? Didn't they want a grandchild?"

"We even chose a family. Before Autumn was born. She needs stability. That's what they say. They say I'm not ready to be a parent. They say someone that is ready should have her." Gail didn't cry, but she started to shiver.

"Come on," Michael stood and went to Gail's side of the table. "Have you got your car?"

"They said I couldn't drive. I've been sleeping too much. They said I wasn't safe. They said I needed exercise. They don't want me back if I'm smoking."

"You hungry?"

"Food, yuck."

"When did you eat last?"

Gail couldn't remember.

"Come on." Michael stood and went to Gail's side of the table. "Let's go home."

"They won't let me in."

Michael didn't question her. He accepted her version of family life. Who was he to doubt that parents could be cruel—or, on the other hand, to question their parenting tactics. They had more experience with Gail than he did. And, he realized, he had no idea what her version of reality was right now anyway.

"Come on."

The shivering girl rose and let Michael lead her around the house and to the sidewalk.

"They won't let me in," she said softly, but offered no resistance as Michael moved her. They walked slowly, like sweethearts. Gail murmured and rambled.

"You taking your meds?" Michael asked her. Although his understanding of the various psychotropic medications was limited, he knew sudden noncompliance with the medication schedule could be dangerous.

"Flat. That's what they call it. A flat effect. I hate the stuff."

"You got any?" Michael had to ask several times before Gail answered.

"I got a weekend's worth from Ruth," Gail said and tapped her purse.

In her large handbag, Michael found a pillbox with seven compartments, two compartments for each day—an A.M. and P.M. slot. He noticed Saturday morning's compartment was empty.

"Let's get you something to eat," Michael said, "and take the rest of your meds."

She was leaning heavily on him as they walked nearly a mile to a restaurant that never closed. As soon as the waitress set menus and water in front of them, Michael dumped three pills from the P.M. slot into his hand and forced them on Gail.

"You okay?"

"Tired," she breathed. "I need to wash my hair."

"It looks fine," Michael reassured her.

"Wakes me up to wash it," explained Gail. "It clears my head to get my hair wet."

Michael suggested she try to eat. Gail cringed as he read from the menu, assuring him she couldn't possibly stand food. Even so, she consumed a hamburger, a shake, and most of Michael's fries. After checking Michael's shake glass and finding it empty, she laid her head down on one arm and closed her eyes.

"You want anything else?" Michael asked.

Her eyes stayed closed. "A cigarette. I really need a cigarette."

"Well, I could . . ." Michael started uncomfortably.

"No. No. I'm not going to. I'm back on meds. I think they're kicking in. I'm going to make it. I'm going to get my little girl back." Gail sat up. "You should see her. She's so sweet."

"Where is she?"

"Alice and Keith have her. They're okay. I mean, I chose them a long time ago. They have a little four-year-old boy they adopted. They'd take Autumn, but she's mine."

For the next two hours Gail talked about her daughter. She told Michael how pretty Autumn was and how good, and how their temperaments were "just alike." She talked about a lot of other things, and slept sometimes between talking. Michael just listened and rested himself. They left the restaurant and started walking back toward campus as the sun rose. Gail walked very slowly, and Michael wondered if he'd make it to church.

"If I washed my hair, I'd be awake enough to go see her."

"You can use my place," Michael said, taking her arm and steering her across the street. Then he asked, "What's PEC?"

"One of many acronyms Mormons use," Gail said, making her way to the only sofa the apartment had to offer. She lay down and closed her eyes. "I used to know what it stood for. It's a meeting of the ward leaders, I think. You going to join the Church?"

"No. I don't know," Michael said. "I went last week. I told them I'd go this week."

"Good," Gail said. "You go and I'll take a nap. See you in three hours."

She curled fetal-like on the sofa. Michael unzipped one of his sleeping bags and pulled the warm flannel over her. She sighed, "I just need a nap."

As he left to take a brief nap in his own room, she mumbled something about him taking some heat because she was in his apartment.

Probably, he thought. He'd been warned not to get too involved with the clients. That the heat might come from his roommates never occurred to him.

* * *

"Hello," Laura said brightly when she spotted Michael standing between Garrett and Hunter. The foyer was crowded as the college-ward members mingled in front of the chapel doors. The first ward was being subjected to a long-winded speaker and was late dismissing.

Moving closer to the three roommates, Laura continued, "You still hanging out at Looney Toon Acres?"

Michael looked uncomfortable standing between Garrett and Hunter, but his voice was firm. While his hands awkwardly palmed his blue Book of Mormon, his eyes were hard, fixed, and determined. Laura knew she'd said the wrong thing.

"I still work at the Oasis House," Michael said mildly.

"Cured any of the crazies yet?" Klarissa spoke from beside Laura.

Michael looked at Laura and Klarissa. The two returned mission-aries flanking him moved instinctively closer. They might not under-stand him, but they knew how to care for an investigator.

Before anyone could think of a way to relieve the tension, Michael's stony face broke into a convincing smile. He spoke in a friendly tone. "Ladies," he said, "we haven't cured many, but don't worry." He winked. "We'll always have room when you need us." Turning, he worked his way through the crowd coming out the double doors. His roommates followed. Hunter scowled, but Garrett grinned delightedly.

"He acts so superior. He's got a long way to go before he'll be ready for baptism," Klarissa hissed in Laura's ear. She then spent most of the meeting alternating between ridiculing Michael and deciding what kind of cookies they should make to take to which guys. She'd take some to Hunter and Garrett, but she certainly didn't want Michael to think they were meant for him.

Laura spent the meeting ignoring Klarissa and trying to decide where to live. She'd planned to move in with Klarissa as soon as Wanda had left after summer school. Even to herself, though, Laura refused to acknowledge why she'd suddenly changed her mind. She had to find another apartment, though, and she wanted to stay in the same ward.

After the meetings when Klarissa asked Laura if she had any chocolate chips and butter, the correct answer would have been no. Technically, none of the food at her brother and sister-in-law's was hers. She didn't buy it, she only ate it, and she only ate it four or five times a week, and only sometimes did she take butter, sugar, and chocolate chips to make cookies. Her consumption was insignifi-cant—at least from her point of view.

Today Laura didn't even want to go to Klarissa and Wanda's apart-ment to make cookies. She considered staying with Scott and Jamie, but really the two were nauseating. The young couple spoke directly to the unborn baby. They asked the unresponsive child what he wanted for supper, what music he wanted to listen to, and if he would please make his arrival at a convenient time. All the talking wouldn't have been so bad if the couple hadn't spent so much time rubbing Jamie's stomach. Laura couldn't stand that.

So, rather than listen to the parents-to-be, Laura went home and collected cookie ingredients. She decided she'd figure out a way to get some of these cookies to Michael. En route to Klarissa's apartment, Laura once again drove the indirect path to peer at the windows of Michael's apartment. She smiled as she passed. *No,* she thought, *I'll do better than take him cookies.*

* * *

During the opening hymn, Michael had thought little of Laura's and Klarissa's behavior in the foyer. Instead, he worried about Gail. At the end of the three-hour block of services, Michael hurried back to the apartment. His two roommates, encouraged by Michael's ability to locate scriptures and answer questions about the Atonement, scurried after him.

"Would you like to hear more discussions about the Church?" Garrett asked the slightly distracted investigator.

"Yeah, sure," Michael said as all three men marched briskly toward home.

"We probably should call the elders to come teach you," continued Garrett, "rather than us giving the discussions."

"No," Michael said, slowing to face them. "You guys just teach me."

Hunter was only slightly skeptical. Garrett was buoyant. Michael was just fearful that the elders they called would be the ones he'd been listening to at Connor's.

They walked the last block in silence and waited while Hunter unlocked the door. The sound they heard, in what should have been a vacant apartment, was water running in the bathroom. The boys had just enough time to recognize this when the water was turned off. "Who the heck is in there?" Hunter asked.

"Probably Gail," Michael said, glad she had the energy to get up.

"Gail?" asked Hunter not at all pleasantly. "Gail who?"

"Gail . . . uh," Michael said thoughtfully. "I guess I don't know her last name."

"She's in my bathroom," Hunter said, "and you don't know her last name?"

The three stared at the bathroom door listening to the movements of someone looking through the cabinets.

"What's she doing here?" Hunter demanded.

"Probably washing her hair," Michael speculated. "She was really tired when I left. Washing her hair helps her wake up."

"Oh, great," Hunter said. They heard the sound of Hunter's hair-dryer through the closed door.

The bathroom door opened and Gail stepped out. Her hair was wet. The dryer still whirred behind her.

She nodded slightly to the boys and said, "Your turn," then slipped around the corner.

"She's using my towel!" Hunter accused unpleasantly as he yanked the blow-dryer plug from the wall.

"I should have told her which one was mine," Michael said.

Hunter's language then deteriorated.

Garrett told him to stop.

"I won't stop!" he yelled. "I had roommates like this before my mission. I don't have to tolerate some Gentile dragging girls over here. I served the Lord. I did what I was supposed to. I deserve better than this."

Gail came back around the corner, Hunter's towel slung over her shoulder. As she pulled one of Michael's combs through her hair, she spoke to Hunter. "Get your self-righteous butt down off that Rameumpton. You RMs think the only thing standing between you and celestial glory is marriage. You might think your calling and election is made sure, but in the charity department, he's way ahead," she said with a nod toward Michael.

She draped the towel over Hunter's right shoulder, plucked her shoes from the floor in the hallway, crossed the living room, and opened the outside door to let in a conduit of sun. Michael followed her into the bright afternoon.

They walked toward campus for several minutes before Michael spoke. "I have no idea what you just told them," he said.

Gail grinned and sat down on the curb to put her shoes on.

"You feel better?" Michael asked.

"I haven't crashed."

"Are you going to?"

"I'm back on my meds, so maybe not." She stood up. "I'm going this way," she said, motioning toward the Provo Temple.

They walked up to campus and past the MTC. Rather than climb the hill to where Connor's folks lived, the two wound their way through streets confusing to Michael. Finally, Gail turned onto the front walk of a small brick home. She knocked and a young woman answered the door. She welcomed Gail and warily eyed Michael.

Gail stepped into the bright living room without making introductions. The room was tidy except for a few scattered toys. A man sat in an easychair reading the Sunday comics to a little boy too young to understand the humor.

"Gail," the man said, "your parents have been looking for you." He laid the comics down and sat forward. The little boy reached for the newspaper and toppled off the chair in a playful fall controlled by his father.

"Hi!" the child waved to Gail. "Hi," he said to Michael. "You know who Snoopy is?" Instinctively Michael knelt to the boy's level and listened as the enthusiastic child described Snoopy's comic-strip camping trip with Woodstock and his friends.

In the background Michael could hear the couple explain to Gail about having made a promise to her parents. "We told them we'd call if we saw you."

"Autumn asleep?" Gail asked as the man went to the phone.

"She'll be awake anytime," the woman explained.

Still kneeling, Michael watched the two women. Gail appeared on the defensive and the other woman seemed tense.

"See this?" the little boy pointed to the comic strip. "It's a food dish for a dog. I don't have a dog."

"Do you want a dog?" Michael asked.

"Not a junkyard dog."

"A junkyard dog?"

"They bite," the boy explained. He looked down and spent a solemn moment thinking of biting dogs. Then, as though flipping an internal switch, he grinned and held up three fingers. "I used to be three. I had a birthday. Now I'm four. I am, huh, Mom?"

"Yes," the woman said, moving toward them. Gail stayed in the middle of the living room to watch down the hall.

"Gail," the woman began, "you haven't introduced me to your friend." She paused slightly and then did the introductions herself. "I'm Alice Sargent."

"Michael Ross."

A baby's voice called, "Mama, Mama."

"I'll get her." Gail smiled. "She must have heard me out here," she said over her shoulder as she hurried down the hall.

The man came back from the kitchen and exchanged a look with Alice.

Gail didn't immediately return. Alice invited Michael to sit down and then formally introduced him to Shane, who took up residency beside Michael on the couch. Carefully the boy spread the comics open on his legs. They all sat for a moment listening to the kind of sounds a mother makes to a child she loves. Then Keith Sargent introduced himself.

"You're a friend of Gail's?" he asked.

"Yes, sir."

"How long have you two known each other?"

"A few weeks." Michael's answers were short until he realized what an awkward position the couple was in. "I met Gail when I started working at the Oasis House."

Alice and her husband visibly relaxed.

"She's not doing so well?" Alice asked.

"She's struggling." Michael knew his answers sounded like he was a counselor or something and understood Gail's situation. He didn't.

Mother and daughter came down the hall. The one-year-old was riding on one of Gail's hips. Her tousled hair was a deeper brown than Gail's, and a bow was still tied into the wavy locks. Her cheeks were pink from sleep. Gail was kissing one of those cheeks, hugging the girl to her in an attempt to savor the feeling. Michael smiled. The joy and light on Gail's face gave him the first hope that she could get well. The little girl was beautiful, the mother shining.

"This is Autumn," Gail said, kissing the baby again and hugging her tight.

Autumn leaned away from Gail to reach toward Alice. "Mama." Gail pulled her back. The child grunted unappreciatively and pushed away with both feet and hands. "Mama," she insisted, again reaching for Alice.

Gail lowered the child into Alice's lap, where the toddler smiled and snuggled close into the familiar warmth of her caregiver. The weariness of the night before seemed to return to Gail's face as Autumn put a thumb in her mouth and relaxed against Alice, who smiled softly and cuddled back.

Keith had moved to talk quietly with Gail. Over Shane's chatter about Garfield and Odie, Michael could hear Keith explain that he had called Gail's parents, who were on their way, and that everyone had been worried about her.

Does he really care? Michael wondered. *Is the concern in Keith's voice genuine or is it like the concern Dad uses as a prop?*

"We went camping," Shane said, pointing to a tent in the *Beetle Bailey* strip. "Me and Dad slept in a tent in a sleeping bag. My bag was big."

"Did your mom go?"

"No," Shane said. "She had to stay so Gail could visit Autumn. Do you have a tent?"

"No," Michael said just as someone knocked at the door.

If Keith was a good actor, then Gail's parents were even better. Their concern was etched into gray hair and worried eyes. Michael hoped this concern was genuine too—he felt like it was as he watched them. They smiled briefly when introduced to Michael. They stiffly hugged their daughter—parents trying to parent an adult who had needed help last night but hadn't gone to them. Their love for Autumn seemed deep, but they never encouraged Gail to take the little girl from Alice.

Michael was glad to escape. He'd enjoyed Shane, but he certainly didn't want to discuss Gail with her parents. He was confused about what would be best for her beautiful baby. Politely he had excused himself, exited the house, and then hurried around the first corner so no one would notice him walking and come to offer a ride. Pausing slightly, Michael looked toward the mountains. He was within a mile of the Steele home.

The steep climb to the large house made Michael sweat, but he wanted to clear his head from the complications of dealing with mental illness. Michael seldom thought of Connor as mentally ill anymore. Connor was still heavy and was often fatigued, but his thinking seemed normal. Several of the staff at the Oasis House had warned Michael not to be disappointed if Connor relapsed. A situation could occur that caused excess stress, or medications that had worked well for a while could sometimes suddenly become ineffective, they had explained.

The Steele house was vacant, as Michael knew it would be. The family had gone to visit someone in a city called Bountiful. Michael hurried along the path that surrounded the mountain above the campus, enjoying the pull on his muscles. He headed downhill just past the mental hospital, slowing his steps so he wouldn't get to the apartment before his roommates had left for the fireside.

The apartment wasn't empty. Garrett was sitting at the kitchen table with the Bible and another book open in front of him. Michael groaned inwardly upon seeing him, but smiled casually. "Hi," he said.

Garrett turned his chair to face his roommate. "Hi," he returned. There was a short pause. "You want some ice cream? I can't really concentrate on Leviticus anymore."

Michael had wanted a sandwich, but he agreed to share choco-late-swirl ice cream with Garrett.

"Hunter went to the fireside, but I decided to catch up on my Bible-as-Lit class."

Michael put a spoonful of ice cream in his mouth.

"He's a really decent guy," Garrett continued. "He's been a good roommate."

Michael swallowed. "Yeah, I can see that. Really understanding sort."

Garrett grinned at the sarcasm. "That girl must have needed a place. Is she one of the . . . uh . . . people you have at your job?"

Michael nodded.

"Is she okay now?"

"She's with her folks." There was another long pause as they both ate ice cream.

"Hunter is a little sensitive to even the appearance of evil. I think it's because when he was on his mission, his dad left his mom. The lady was a family friend who had just always been around. His dad had given her rides and taken her to help her buy a car. Innocent things like that. Hunter liked her and everything. Then one day his dad left the family and moved in with the other lady. Anyone would have hated that. Having your dad leave while you were serving a mission would be pretty upsetting."

"Not to me," Michael said grimly. "I'd give anything for my dad to leave the family."

"Not really," said Garrett automatically.

"Really."

Garrett looked at his roommate. "That bad?"

"No. I mean, you live through it." Michael felt uncomfortable with the sudden sympathy he heard in his roommate's voice.

They ate ice cream and talked. Not easily, but Garrett made an effort to understand Michael without intruding. They talked about Gail's smoking, about how early Michael had to get up, about Garrett's college classes, about BYU housing rules, and about whether there was enough bread to make sandwiches.

During their second bowl of ice cream, accompanied by a ham sandwich, Michael told Garrett about meeting the missionaries, hiding the Book of Mormon, watching the football game on TV, and coming to Utah.

"You left without telling anyone?"

"Stephanie knew."

"Your girlfriend?"

"My sister."

"Where'd you live before you moved in here?"

Michael was trying to decide if he should explain, when Hunter suddenly returned. Irritation showed plainly on his face as he studied the two men lounging comfortably among dishes and opened jars of mayo and mustard.

"Should I lock up?" he asked irritably, "or is someone else coming to spend the night?"

"Lock up," Michael said as he finished his sandwich. "I'll make Gail her own key if she needs it."

Garrett grinned.

Michael's voice continued, pleasantly addressing Hunter. "You want a sandwich? Garrett's ham, my bread. You're more than welcome."

"No."

"Okay." Michael opened the fridge and started to clear the table. "Thanks for the ice cream," he told Garrett. "Next week, I'll buy." He finished setting dirty dishes in the sink and then announced he hadn't gotten much sleep the night before and was going to bed. As he left the room, he turned back to Hunter. "Look. I'm sorry. I didn't know about the rules—I'm still learning. But, just so you know, Gail didn't spend the night. She just napped on the couch during church." Then he went to bed before Hunter could respond. He figured he'd work it out later.

* * *

Michael answered the door the next Tuesday evening. He was holding an open Book of Mormon and was wearing only faded jeans.

Laura stuttered under his direct gaze. "I—I just came by to see you and say I'm . . . uh . . . sorry about what I said on Sunday."

Michael didn't pretend not to know what she was talking about.

"I didn't really mean it," continued Laura self-consciously. "I just. I don't know. I just . . ." she stopped.

Michael smiled a little. "I figured you just didn't know what to say, and so instead of keeping quiet, you said something stupid."

For a moment Laura was offended, then she laughed. "You don't ever say anything stupid?" she asked flirtatiously. Now she was on familiar ground.

"Lots of times, but only because I'm stupid, not because I can't think of anything to say."

"You're not stupid," Laura said seriously.

"About some things," Michael said matter-of-factly.

Laura looked down awkwardly, caught herself staring at his bare chest, and fixed her gaze back on his face. Now she felt stupid.

"Your roommates home?" she finally asked.

"No, I'm sorry," Michael said. "They have night classes. You can come back later."

"No. I wanted to see you."

Now Michael felt awkward.

"I really just wanted to apologize." There was another long pause. Laura had spent the two days since Sunday practicing the clever repartee she would engage in when she came to see him. Nothing she was saying was clever. "I don't believe what Klarissa says about people and why they're crazy."

"She seems to feel her view represents the majority," Michael commented.

"I don't know," Laura said. "I never thought about mental illness before. Did you? Before you came here to work, I mean?"

Michael grinned. His tense face transformed. Laura watched it and took a shaky breath. "No, I guess I didn't," he admitted.

"To prove I'm truly sorry," Laura launched into an excerpt of her prepared speech, "I'll buy you pizza."

"Well, I . . ."

But she flew into the rest of her reasons, and he finally let himself be convinced, leaving her long enough to pull on a shirt and make sure there was money in his wallet. She drove them to the Brick Oven. He hated being driven, but he decided he enjoyed sitting across from Laura, feeling like one of the college crowd in the noisy, fragrant restaurant.

He also enjoyed sitting close to Laura in the small car on the way home and hearing her chatter.

Garrett saw Michael get out of Laura's car and began quizzing him about his date as soon as he entered the apartment.

"It wasn't a date," Michael insisted, and he told both Garrett and Hunter about Laura's invitation. He didn't tell them how he'd never ordered pizza in a restaurant, but he did admit that she was kind of cute and he'd had fun.

"You going to ask her out?" Garrett pressured.

Michael shrugged with a tense, don't-bother-me look on his face until he realized he enjoyed the rapport. He grinned at them. The two boys sighed a little in relief and grinned back.

Laura didn't tell anyone where she'd been.

CHAPTER 9

"I don't think it would work out," Michael said as politely as he could.

"That's fine," Brother Steele said. "You certainly don't have to."

"Why wouldn't it work out?" Connor asked, his disappointment apparent. "Dane and I had it all figured out. We'd pack a lunch."

The missionaries had just left the Steele home after giving Michael the last discussion. They had once again asked him if he would be baptized, the same question Garrett and Hunter had asked the previous Sunday when they had given Michael the last discussion. Michael had put them both off, but in the last month he had decided he really did want to get baptized. He just didn't know who should baptize him.

His thoughts strayed back in an attempt to decide, and in his preoccupation, he forgot the invitation completely. It had been a month since Gail had napped in Michael's apartment—probably the best month of Michael's life. When the supervisors from the Oasis House had heard what Michael did with Gail, they hadn't approved; however, they admitted he had proven his commitment with several of the clients. Since then he'd been invited to several staff meetings to discuss the needs of specific clients, including how case managers could help deal with emergencies and what other help was available.

As far as life in his apartment went, Garrett treated him like a friend and Hunter was amiable. Michael had even attended a couple of firesides. One weekend Connor had come to see Michael's apartment just as the three roommates were getting ready to leave for Michael's first dance. They invited Connor, and Michael watched closely as Connor danced and talked with a young woman who remembered him from high school. He wondered if she knew what her old classmate had been through.

Garrett had talked Michael into going to Lagoon with the ward. Never having gone to an amusement park, Michael was surprised by how much fun he had and how many girls tried to sit next to him on the various rides. Those same girls had previously asked him to dance at his first dance. At the time they'd done so because Garrett asked them to help his "investigator" feel at home, but at Lagoon they shared cotton candy with the "investigator" because they wanted to. Laura was among those who wanted to, but she just waved and asked if he was having fun. He was.

Another Saturday, Connor and his older brother, Dane, taught Michael to water-ski. That day Michael thought he caught a glimpse of what Connor was before his breakdown. Despite a lack of practice, Connor got his heavy, white body up on skis right away, and he tenaciously hung on for several minutes before exhaustion forced him to let go of the rope and slowly sink up to his life jacket.

Michael's debut was nearly as triumphant. The brothers tutored him well, lined up the boat, and dragged their student to his feet. Michael grinned and concentrated on moving out of the boat's wake. Once he got into smooth water, though, he relaxed too much and let his shoulders get ahead of his feet. For several seconds he flew above the water, still gripping the handle. Even after his body was submerged, he didn't let go of the rope, and water surged into his open mouth and eyes. He struggled to breathe. The boat slowed and the life jacket pulled him into an upright position. The Steele brothers didn't laugh until they could see Michael was unharmed, then they howled in unison. Dane slapped the boat rail and laughed that if Michael needed a drink, he could have had a soda pop. And Connor added that if they were going to troll for fish, they'd find smaller bait.

"We'd better try some fundamentals again," Dane said. "Let go of the rope when water starts beating you in the face."

"I know." Michael grinned.

"He knows," Connor said. "He's just got a bad case of separation anxiety. Doesn't want us to leave him."

"You've been seeing too many shrinks," Michael informed him. "Let me try it again."

"Maybe *you* need the shrink," Connor laughed. "You're suicidal."

They didn't leave the lake until late evening. Connor napped while Michael awkwardly tried to thank Dane for teaching him to ski. "I've never really done this kind of stuff before," he said.

"You don't owe us anything," Dane said simply. "We owe you."

Now the ski trip had been two weeks ago, and Michael had been hoping for another invitation. Suddenly he remembered that Brother Steele was talking. In fact, here was that waterskiing invitation and he was turning it down. Michael was uncomfortable and he got even more so as Connor talked. "We'll invite your roommates. They can bring a couple of girls. I was going to invite Karma. You could ask Gail or that girl that took you to pizza. The elders can't water-ski, but they said they'd come by for an evening picnic. We have it all planned. We have it all planned." Connor began repeating things, making sure Michael understood. "We'll invite your roommates. They'll come. You can invite Gail or the girl you went to pizza with. Your roommates can come."

The roommates would like to come, Michael knew. The Sunday morning after he'd skied with Dane and Connor, he'd gingerly limped into the kitchen, muscles sore, skin burned. "Where you been?" Garrett asked jokingly. "A fish fry?"

"Waterskiing," Michael said.

"Looking at you, maybe I'm glad I didn't get an invitation," Garrett laughed.

"My first time," Michael said. "Connor invited me."

"Tell him to take us next time," Garrett had said.

Michael apologized to the Steeles. "Probably not this weekend."

"Why?" Connor sounded tired.

"He's got his reasons," said Brother Steele. He also sounded tired.

"Why?" Connor's hand twitched restlessly against the outside of his leg. He got up and walked distractedly toward the kitchen. "Why?" he softly asked the empty room. "Why?"

"It's hard to mix professional and personal life, huh?" Brother Steele suggested quietly to Michael.

"It's not that," Michael shook his head.

"Embarrassed?" Brother Steele's voice was low, a little scornful, and sad.

It was the sadness that helped Michael decide. He just didn't know how to start. "Brother Steele, I should have told you long ago." Brother Steele looked at him the same way Arnie had when the police brought him to work.

"I'm not as smart as you think I am," Michael continued. "The missionaries ask questions, and I get them right because my roommates have been teaching me the discussions too. I haven't told them that I meet with the missionaries up here, and I haven't told you, because, I guess, I like hearing it twice. I understand things better. When I first started, I didn't think it would matter because I wasn't planning on getting baptized, but now . . ." his voice trailed off.

Connor came back in the room and was motionless except for his hand hitting his leg. "What are you talking about?" he asked.

"My roommates have both been missionaries. When they found out that I wasn't a Mormon, they started teaching me the same lessons the elders here have been teaching me." Michael grinned ruefully. "I'm not as smart as the elders think I am. I've heard most of this twice."

"And if we went waterskiing, everyone would find out?" Brother Steele smiled as he made the connection.

"You're not angry?"

"Angry? Oh no. Just so grateful to find someone who likes this religion so much he wants to hear about it twice."

"You think my roommates will feel that way?"

"I guarantee it," Brother Steele said. He felt a surge of love and pride for the boy sitting opposite him.

"So maybe we ought to get you baptized this weekend rather than go skiing," Connor said. He was more excited than he had been about a skiing trip.

* * *

Connor would baptize him. He'd cried when Michael asked. "You sure?" he kept asking. "You sure?"

Michael asked Garrett to confirm him a member of the Church, and the missionaries agreed to be witnesses. He'd gone back to his apartment and waited for his roommates to come home from their night class. They were, as Brother Steele had said, pleased that Michael had listened twice. Even though it was after ten o'clock, Garrett had insisted on calling the bishop to schedule the font. The bishop didn't admit not knowing who Michael was, but rather assured them that the entire bishopric was certainly happy he was to become a member.

That weekend the room with the baptismal font was crowded. The elders quorum president had taken it upon himself to walk through the ward knocking on apartment doors and telling ward members about the baptism. Girls who had asked Michael to dance felt they'd helped him accept the gospel. They came to the Saturday-afternoon ceremony and formed clusters in summer pastels and bare legs. Girls who had rode the Tilt-a-Whirl with him secretly hoped for a date. Returned missionaries reminisced about golden converts.

Both Brother and Sister Steele were present. Dane had come in his own car, but walked over to sit next to his parents. Arnie sat next to Katie and Ruth in the back. His expression had been unreadable when Connor had used breakfast at the Oasis House to announce Michael's baptism. When Ruth heard, she'd rushed from her office and hugged Michael.

Laura watched him rise from the water. Something caught deep in her chest, and she held her breath as she saw him regain his footing and hug Connor. His face, which had often seemed to her sulky and usually unreadable, glowed. His smile spread uninhibited.

Afterward, Connor invited everyone to an open house in Michael's honor. That he could be the reason for such a gathering had never occurred to Michael. He felt truly and completely happy. Later that night he wrote to Stephanie and told her how people visited, laughed, flirted, ate, and congratulated him. He told her about a comfort he felt in his inner core—a relaxed feeling that gave him energy to do right, a stillness to replace the anger, a peace that abolished the habitual defensiveness. He told her about their brother, Jesus Christ, who cared about them and who would send a comfort to them, in the form of the Holy Ghost.

On a new page he talked about Gail, how she had come in a dress, how she had mingled with the guests, how beautiful she had looked, and how she had shook hands with Garrett and Hunter, calling them "elders," and saying she hoped they would set a good example for their new-member roommate. *They didn't even recognize her at first*, he wrote.

He ended his letter by telling Stephanie that he knew that Joseph Smith was a prophet.

You feel good just reading the Book of Mormon. There really is a man on the earth today who is a prophet. I'm glad I got baptized. I know what I did was right.

The letter was never sent of course. Michael felt that none of the night's spirit, none of the evening's tranquility, would endure once that letter entered his old home. His dad's mockery would rob the words of anything elevating. Michael reverently folded the sheets and slipped them inside the journal Connor had given him as a baptismal present. Then, on another sheet, he wrote a short note wishing Stephanie a happy seventeenth birthday. In a year, he promised himself, he would go back to get her.

* * *

I love you, Laura wrote her parents. *I'm grateful to you for all you've done for me.*

Laura's mother read the e-mail out loud to her husband when he came in from the airport. Her parents' eyes met. This was a different Laura.

"I had a pretty good week," Mandy Keeyes read from her daughter's e-mail. "I decided to declare a major. You know I wanted that job at Continuing Ed." Laura had complained vehemently about being "passed over for some girl." Her brother Scott had confided that Laura had only thought she had a chance because it was a friendly interviewer. "I read the job description," Scott had explained to his parents. "She was not qualified."

Laura's letter glossed over her previous disappointment and told about her conversation with "a friend." "Well, I was talking to this friend the other day. He said I should get qualified so I can get the job when the other girl that got it graduates."

"Are you following this?" Mandy asked her husband.

"Just barely."

The letter continued to tell about the lost job. "It's a cool place where they design and print all the brochures for the school. Things like youth leadership conferences, football camps, etc. He said in two years I could be ready to step into the girl's job. So I registered for a couple graphics classes and a computer graphics class."

"I'd like to know what kind of job inspired this dedication," commented Mandy Keeyes.

"I'd like to know what kind of *boy* inspired this," Lance suggested.

"What do you mean?"

"Keep reading."

"We had a ward computer date on Saturday. Everyone was supposed to fill out a questionnaire, and then the computer found our perfect dates. Klarissa is on the activities committee and she was in charge with some guy who is way too old for college. *He* needs a date. Anyway, I was helping and we had to change some of the computer matches 'cause someone brought this stupid program and it was putting all the wrong people together. Technology just can't deal with matters of the heart. It matched up younger guys with older girls. Some of the couples it matched had girls taller than the boys. We fixed it, and then I said I'd go out with one guy in the ward because I didn't know if anyone else would want him.

"Klarissa can't stand him. He's not going to school right now. He's just working. I think he plans to go sometime soon. He just got baptized, and he's from Las Vegas. He doesn't know a lot about the Church, but his roommates said he read the Book of Mormon before he even took the discussions.

"He's not way tall, but he's taller than me. So that was okay. And he's kind of quiet, so you think he's shy, but when he does talk he doesn't talk shy. In fact he says some blunt things, so that's why he and Klarissa don't get along.

"It was fun. We all went up to that ski resort Robert Redford owns, Sundance, and had supper in the lodge. My date doesn't own a car so we went with his roommates and their dates. I sat in front and he sat in back, but that was okay. I mean, I just went with him to fellowship him in the ward."

Mandy looked up from the computer screen. "She's fellowshipping a guy who doesn't own a car?"

Lance grinned. "Keep reading."

Mandy shook her head and read, "Anyway, I've decided to not live with Klarissa. We're still friends and all, but I think it would work best if we didn't share an apartment. So I'm looking for an opening somewhere in the ward. I've kind of gotten so I like the ward, you know? I'll let you know.

"I'm excited about school starting so I can get qualified. Your loving daughter, Laura."

"Can you believe it?" Mandy asked. "Less than three months and she's chosen a vocation, volunteered to fellowship, dumped Klarissa as a role model, and decided she loves us. Send BYU a check next time they ask for donations."

"If you're rewarding influence, send the money to the boy."

"What boy?"

"The boy she spent the whole letter talking about. Probably starting with the 'I love you.'"

Mandy Keeyes looked doubtful.

"The one who doesn't talk much but who says valuable things when he does talk. The one who told her to get qualified."

"You think that was the same guy?"

Lance nodded.

"You think Laura's that smitten?"

Lance smiled. "She's already chosen him over her friend."

Mandy's brow wrinkled questioningly.

"She's got to stay in that ward but doesn't plan on living with Klarissa," he hinted.

There was a long silence as the sun filtered into the clean kitchen. Memories of Laura filtered in with the sun. Mandy reminded her husband of one night when their youngest child had brought in her leather-bound copy of the Book of Mormon. "I'm done. Finished. Read the whole thing." Laura had dropped the book triumphantly on the table. "Pretty fast, huh?"

After congratulating her, Lance had suggested something vague about pondering the word rather than just reading for speed.

"I had to hurry. Anyone not done by tomorrow's seminary class can't have banana splits."

Mandy smiled at the memory. "It's amazing she was ever accepted into the Y," she commented, shaking her head at the circumstances Laura was now in.

"High ACTs."

"You're *sure* it's all the same boy?"

Lance nodded.

"He'd better be a good guy," Mandy said. "She's had lots of crushes. This may pass."

"I always told the kids to marry someone better than themselves." Lance thought fondly about his little girl.

"This guy wasn't raised in the Church," Mandy pointed out.

"No one offered him a banana split to read the Book of Mormon," Lance countered.

CHAPTER 10

"You going to get registered?" Ruth sat down across from Michael. He'd been idly flipping through college catalogues stored in the office-procedures room. Summer term had just ended and the campus was swarming with people attending BYU Education Week. In two weeks fall semester would start, rent would go up, and Michael would be one of the few nonstudents in his ward.

"It's too late to register," Michael answered.

"You probably could get into some night classes," commented Ruth. "Not at BYU, but maybe you could start something at UVSC."

"Where?"

"Utah Valley State College. It's up in Orem."

"It's sort of expensive."

"Not as expensive as not going."

"I don't know what I'd study."

Ruth picked up a catalogue. "What are you interested in? What do you like to do?" she asked.

Michael had been thinking about what he wanted to do. "I like working here. I guess I could get a degree in counseling or something."

"Oh, please don't."

The boy looked at her with surprise and then embarrassment. She had been so pleasant to him. He'd assumed she'd want him to stay. The older woman smiled. "The last thing we need is another counselor," she said, thumbing through a fall course list from UVSC. "Counselors are a dime a dozen. What we really need is someone who can work with our clients. Someone who can offer them jobs. Michael," she continued, "you have a very calming personality, yet you're bright and pick up on things quickly. I would hate to lose you, but what we really need are people with skills, people with businesses, people who would be willing to use Gail as a secretary. Someone who would be willing to use Connor on a part-time basis. Someone who could tolerate Seth. Someone that was successful enough to pay his employees."

"What kind of businesses?" Michael asked.

"If we had someone like you who owned a catering business, for example. There was a gentleman in the Salt Lake area that catered. He did educational conferences—furnished the breakfast bar, a mid-morning break, and lunch. Most of his workers were mentally ill. Sometimes he lost business because an employee would act *inappropriately*." Michael and Ruth both grinned. At the Oasis House, the word *inappropriate* was used to describe a wide range of behavior—anything from burping during pizza night to sacrificing a frozen bone-in ham on an altar built in Abrahamic fashion.

Ruth continued, "Brother Miller used his catering service to do a lot of ward picnics, and often members would hire him for their corporate jobs. He was good at what he did, and often people were grateful that he hired people who needed jobs."

"I could learn catering." Michael sounded less than enthusiastic.

"No, Michael. I wasn't suggesting you do that. I just was giving an example. We need store managers, advertising consultants, restaurant managers, any number of people who will work with our clients. Or you could stay here and work, but I can't imagine you sitting all day listening like a counselor. You like movement too much."

"You know what I used to think about doing when I was in high school?" Michael started timidly. He wasn't in the habit of sharing dreams.

But Ruth was easy to talk to, and she gave him her full attention.

"I thought about being a landscape architect."

Ruth smiled and nodded, encouraging him to continue.

"I like drafting—took all the classes I could on computer-aided drafting. And I really liked the horticulture classes. I used to draw up all these landscape designs . . ." His voice trailed off as he saw the improbability of him ever owning a business. "But I could maybe mow lawns for people."

"Let's hope you work here for a long, long time," Ruth said. "In the meantime, why don't we see about registering you in a few classes headed for a degree as a landscape engineer?"

"I probably couldn't."

"You probably could," Ruth said firmly and pulled out an application and scholarship form for UVSC.

"A scholarship?" Michael laughed.

"Who knows?"

* * *

Michael had turned down her help with a scholarship. Instead he'd enrolled in some online classes through UVSC.

"Look," he'd said, explaining his favorite one. "Really, it's just what I want. *Residential Landscape Design: landscaping with an urban horticulture emphasis*. It has sections on landscape design, estate gardening, and greenhouse management."

"You're so close," Ruth said. "Why don't you just go up and take a couple classes with other students?" The woman's hidden agenda was that Michael experience a little more of the conventional side of Utah than was represented by the Oasis House.

"I'd need a car to get up there."

"Well, buy a little used car."

"No. I couldn't right now."

"Don't you have a license?"

Michael smiled at her concern. "Actually, I do have a license. I never really used it to drive a car. I drove our delivery van in Vegas, though."

"So your driving record's good?"

"Never had a ticket."

"Don't you want a car?"

"Someday."

"And when that someday comes, you'll explain to me why today isn't the right time?"

"Yeah." Michael smiled. He felt support from Ruth because she didn't pry. It felt like she trusted him to make wise choices. He wasn't ready to talk about saving money for Stephanie, especially after the last phone call.

Just last week, Michael had dialed the restaurant's number. He'd hesitated on each number, finally hitting the last three with quick resolve. Two rings buzzed heavily before the phone was answered by a vaguely familiar male voice. Michael paused. He couldn't hang up. "Is Stephanie there?" he asked.

"May I ask who's calling?"

The voice sounded more familiar—his dad's favorite movie partner. Stewart's pale eyes in his pasty face had probably already seen the number and recognized the caller's voice. Michael couldn't hang up or lie.

"Tell Stephanie Michael wants to talk to her."

She'd been angry when she'd answered. "Why are you calling?"

"Is that Stewart? Why's he answering the phone?"

"He comes in. Helps in the afternoon."

Michael couldn't imagine those long, white, feminine hands doing any work. "He works the grill?"

"No. He runs the till and answers the phone."

Michael could picture that. "Bet he does some creative cashiering," Michael said bitterly.

"Not any worse than the last guy."

"Who else has worked there?" Michael asked.

"Just you."

Michael's guilt hit suddenly and hard. He'd never thought he'd been a thief; he was just surviving.

"I've got to go." Stephanie's voice was cold.

"I'm worried about you. You shouldn't be in there with that guy."

"You left. What are we supposed to do, close down? Make the place self-serve?"

"I'm saving money so I can come get you."

"So no cult leader's talked you out of your stolen stash?"

"What?"

"Forget it. I've got to go."

"Wait."

"I don't think so."

"Stephanie, call me from school. Call collect. Tomorrow." Michael spoke rapidly, knowing she really probably had to go or risk abuse. "I'll be here all afternoon. We can talk without someone listening."

Stephanie hesitated, then hung up the phone.

The numbness he had always forced himself to feel during times of disappointment had crept through him, only to be beaten back by guilt over two thousand stolen dollars.

Stephanie didn't call. Michael spent most of the afternoon staring at the phone and feeling sick in the core that had felt peaceful since his baptism.

Had Stewart been listening? Is that why his sister had sounded so angry? Was she angry at him? Why had he left knowing what she would have to endure without him? What happened to Stephanie after he called? Did she hate him? Had she told his dad about his own creative cashiering? *Was* it stealing? Had he repented? He'd been baptized, but he'd never thought to repent of theft. Had he really done something wrong?

"Father in Heaven," he began.

* * *

Laura moved a week before her brother Scott brought his wife and new son home from the hospital. The baby's face was red and lizardlike. His fists, the ones Scott claimed had uncommon strength, were scaly and scabbed—also like a lizard. The infant had no identifiable chin and either squinted or slept. Whatever hair he had remained hidden under a knit cap designed to "help the baby maintain his body temperature." That's what the overprotective parents had emphatically told Laura when she had tried to be polite, pushing the cap back and asking about the hair.

Scott's pride was palpable. He carried his bundle like a fragile treasure. Cautiously, the first-time father moved through the apartment like he was avoiding land mines. He often stopped to wink at Laura, as if to imply she was next. Laura just rolled her eyes.

* * *

Michael had planned to move when school started and rent went up; however, Garrett's warmth and Hunter's begrudging respect were starting to feel like home. The ward members all recognized the new convert and cheerfully greeted him.

Michael became a regular in the Oasis House office-procedure room. He'd finish cleanup, then make his way to a computer. His mere presence in the computer lab boosted attendance, so he helped clients, learned about more computer programs, and did homework assignments for his online classes.

When he saw his grades, Michael felt like he was back in elementary school and his teacher had stuck a star on his paper. He didn't know that Arnie checked that first grade and then reported the ninety-six percent to Ruth. Brother Steele asked openly how things were going and listened intently when Michael hesitated about signing up for another class.

"It's kind of expensive," he said

"You're earning plenty."

"I'm saving for a couple things."

No one mentioned money or college for the rest of the evening, but just as Connor announced that he'd better get home or he'd fall asleep, Brother Steele started a new conversation.

"When Connor's mom and I joined the Church, we found paying tithing a hard thing to do. Money had always been our barometer of success.

"When Connor was ten, one of the elders who baptized our family spent a weekend with us. He crossed his legs during priesthood meeting, and I noticed he had a hole in the bottom of his shoe. As far as I could tell, it was the same hole on the same pair of shoes that he had started wearing out when he'd taught us over two years earlier. I looked at his shoe, and I looked at his face, and I knew I had more money than him, and still I wasn't as successful as he was. That next week, I not only paid a full tithing, but I opened an account for Connor's mission. Within six months we had deposited enough to support him out in the field." He paused. "You know Connor didn't stay out two years. There's still enough money in there. It still needs to support someone."

Michael smiled, but didn't know what to say. On the way home, Connor was tired. He puffed as they walked. His psychiatrist had told him that physical exercise might help his mood swings. So they walked. Michael was tired; he would have liked a ride. Connor didn't have to get up to cook breakfast.

"Tell your dad I'm okay for money. I don't need help with tuition," Michael said when they'd come over a rise and were striding down an easy slope.

"He wasn't offering you tuition money," Connor said between gasps. "He was offering to support you on a mission."

For a long time Michael didn't speak. As he walked beside Connor, he pictured an Elder Ross in a dark suit and a new white shirt. This confident elder was carrying scriptures down a strange road in a strange town. The same elder was sitting in a living room telling a father about why Jesus Christ died. Michael felt a warmth in the cool October air, a joy, a comfort, a desire. Then he remembered Stephanie. He needed to take care of her. The thought took him away from the familiar street in Provo, Utah, distracting him from the topic at hand.

Stephanie had never tried to contact Michael. Finally he'd phoned her at the school where he'd had to beg the counselor to let him talk to her.

She had just sounded tired and hurried. She'd call, she promised, but she hadn't, so Michael had called a month later. This time the counselor had said that unless this was a family emergency, she was unable to accord her the privilege of taking an outside call.

Connor looked over at Michael as they stopped at an intersection to wait for a car. "I hope you let dad do it," he said, pulling Michael from his thoughts.

Michael hesitated. "I doubt I can go on a mission." The car went past and still Connor watched Michael.

"There's no reason you can't. You'll be qualified a year from your baptism date."

"I've kind of made another commitment for about that time."

"Your sister?"

Michael was surprised. "How'd you know?"

Connor checked traffic and started across the street. He was still winded and his gait was slower than ever. "Hey," he said taking a big breath. "I'm actually pretty smart for a crazy guy."

They were nearly to Connor's apartment before either spoke again. "I promised Stephanie I'd come get her—help her leave, but she makes no attempt to contact me." Michael paused. "I think maybe she's in trouble. Maybe I should go back. Maybe I shouldn't have left her there."

"Maybe just pray for her." Connor returned.

Anger surged through Michael, surprising him. "Pray? That's it? Prayer can't penetrate that evil place she lives in. You don't have a clue. You have rich parents who treat you like a human being. You can't possibly know what it's like to . . ." Michael's voice trailed off. He saw Connor's heavy cheeks, the roll of fat just above his belt. He saw his friend's hands tremble, a side effect of the meds he was taking. A picture of Connor next to a football trophy flashed in Michael's memory. "Running Back—Most Yardage Gained in a Season."

"Prayers work two ways. They help you understand where you can go, and they help you accept where you are," Connor said softly. "Eventually the answers do come."

"Like they've come for you?" Michael said bitterly, although all his anger had dissipated somewhat.

"Sometimes it doesn't work out like we want it to. We don't know how or when our prayers will be answered, but we still have to pray."

Connor opened the door to his apartment and sat heavily on the couch, while Michael stood in the doorway. The irony of asking advice from a mentally ill person was not lost on Michael, but he trusted Connor. "Would you have to repent of stealing if you took a loaf of bread because you were starving?" he asked.

Connor didn't answer. He closed his eyes and his breathing deepened. Michael went over and forced him to his feet. He supported his best friend across the kitchen and down the short hall into Connor's darkened bedroom.

He eased Connor down onto the bed and asked if he was okay. Connor tried to push his right shoe off with his left foot. Michael leaned over and pulled both shoes off and Connor rolled over and curled up in sleep.

Before leaving, Michael threw a blanket over Connor and then looked around the room. An entertainment center stood in one corner covered with picture frames, empty grocery sacks, pistachio shells, and a disorganized array of books. There was no TV. Connor had told Michael about a time when he would get reality and TV confused, often acting on the assumption that the media portrayal was accurate.

"It was especially difficult when I was on my John Wayne kick," Connor had explained. "I really identified with John. Had a hat. Wanted a gun."

"But now you're stable. TV would be okay," Michael had suggested.

Connor had shaken his head. Sometimes you had to give up a lot to be your best self, he'd explained.

Michael left the apartment. He walked home trying to justify having taken two thousand dollars from his father's till.

CHAPTER 11

Laura was angry when she jammed the small car into reverse. Her three roommates had been waiting nearly half an hour while she argued with her parents on the phone. The three girls cast sidelong glances at one another as Laura rolled through a stop sign on their way up Provo Canyon.

Tara and Lydia, two sisters, sat in the backseat. Tara was a freshman at BYU majoring in chemistry. Lydia had just returned from a mission in Brazil. After coming home, she had quickly boxed up clothing that had been stored for her during her mission and sent it to a family in her last area. She worked nights as a waitress and days as a part-time payroll secretary for a company that made and boxed laundry soap. Hopefully she would soon have money enough to pay tuition at UVSC. As daughters of a part-time school bus driver, part-time farmer from Blackfoot, Idaho, they both felt Laura was more than a little spoiled when she called her parents for money.

In the front seat sat Sonny, a happy girl with Korean parents. Her mother sent her jars of kimchi, which she cheerfully offered to share. Sonny winked at the sisters in the backseat, took a deep breath, and then asked, "Are you upset, Laura? Do you need to talk about it?"

"They don't give me any credit. I swear, what more do they want? I'm studying like a dog. I've worked ever since I got here—in not the greatest of circumstances, I might add. I need a better computer. Every other graphics student has one. They refuse to buy me one. Actually, I think it's mostly my dad. Mom would probably help me, but Dad won't."

"Insidious form of abuse," mumbled Lydia so only Tara could hear.

"Shocking," Tara agreed quietly.

"They expect me to save enough money from this pathetic job to pay for it," Laura continued.

"Saving money, how absurd," Lydia said to her backseat audience. "And they call themselves parents."

"Shocking," Tara replied.

"I wanted to quit my job so I can concentrate on school. I know they help Scott with money."

"Don't they pay your rent and tuition?" Sonny asked, bracing herself against a curve taken much too quickly.

"It's not exactly like they're paying all that much for rent. There are tons of other places more expensive. I could have chosen them. You've got to admit we live in the slums."

"The drive-by shootings do interfere with my sleep," Lydia whispered. "And those ladies on the corner." She shook her head.

"Shocking," Tara said. The three girls didn't know why Laura had chosen their neighborhood rather than some of the more upscale places, nor did they know the reason Laura had been so eager to go to the Saturday snow party that the activities committee was sponsoring. However, the word "slum" gave Lydia material for several miles.

"The slum rats are the worst." She nodded at Tara. "'Course, I don't think we should destroy them *all*. You never know when the soup kitchen will run out of meat."

Tara made a face.

"I really hate banging on the pipes for a little heat. The worst parts, of course, are the pitiful cry of hungry babies, the smell of boiled cabbage, the wail of sirens, and the drug pushers on every corner."

Sonny wanted to listen to Lydia, but instead let Laura vent about an injustice Laura probably knew in her heart was actually just. "They think I'm not really going to use a computer or appreciate it if they buy one. Heck, everyone has a computer. Even I had one at home."

"Why don't you just get that one?" Sonny asked.

"It wouldn't work for what I want. I really need one that will run these graphics programs. They don't understand."

Laura loved her design classes. She loved the creativity and color, the whole design process—except for the details. One professor had told her she was talented, but until she was ready to proof twice, she'd never remain employed.

Laura pulled off the main highway into a turnout packed with cars belonging to members of the second ward, and parked behind a truck with a snowmobile trailer. Skimming the crowd, Laura looked for Michael. She'd gone to his apartment on Thursday and invited all three roommates. "It's apparently an unusually deep snowpack for this early in the year. The activities committee wants to take advantage of it," she'd tempted him. Michael had hedged about his ability to get Saturday off.

"I'll talk to your boss," Laura had threatened playfully. "We need you guys there."

"You ever been snowmobiling?" Garrett had asked Michael.

"No."

"Then you have to come," Laura insisted. "It'll be a cultural experience."

The whole time she spoke, Laura was unaware of the emotions that flickered behind Michael's guarded eyes. He had tried not to watch her too closely, but he found her hands fascinating. They waved to emphasize every point. Twice one of the small palms had rested briefly on his arm as she encouraged him to come. Still, Michael made no promises except to ask Arnie to trade Saturdays. When she left, it occurred to him that if he'd held out longer, she might have touched him again. *Pathetic*, he'd thought. *I'm pathetic.*

After parking her car, Laura finally spotted Michael standing next to a snowmobile where Hunter was giving him instructions on how to drive the Arctic Cat.

Forgetting her computer problems, Laura waved at him as he climbed onto the cold seat. "That's that new convert I told you about," she told her roommates. They watched him cautiously urging the machine up a worn trail.

Laura missed his return. She was sliding down a steep incline on an inner tube. The sophomore she was riding with had asked her out twice in the past and apparently considered her company at this activity a date as well. Unaware of the date she was on, Laura excused herself when she saw Michael. He stood by the propane stoves wrapping cold hands around a Styrofoam cup. "You having fun?" she asked.

He looked up in surprise and pleasure. "Yeah," he said, burning his tongue on the hot liquid. Within five minutes Laura had convinced an already-willing Michael to go with her back up the trail. When a machine became available, Laura climbed on and Michael slowly settled himself as far behind her as he could get, but when Laura gunned the machine forward, he could feel the warmth of her back against his chest. He wrapped his arms as loosely around her waist as possible. He could feel her sway under his thin gloves.

"That your car?" someone asked as the couple returned and pulled in among the other snowmobilers.

Laura nodded.

"You gotta move it so we can back the trailer around."

"Here, take the keys," Laura told Michael. "Move it for me. I want a warm drink. I'm freezing." She pulled off a glove and dug into an inside pocket of her snowsuit. As Michael reached to take them from her, he felt her hand's warmth against his icy fingers.

As Michael pulled Laura's small car forward, he thought about how much he had wanted to stay on that snowmobile with her. For several minutes he stared unseeing at the snow-covered landscape and felt again how warm her hand had been when he'd taken her keys. Why did he keep watching for this one girl? She'd been nice, but she'd probably laugh if he ever asked her out. Where would he take her? What would Laura think of Stephanie? They had nothing in common. What if she'd already noticed he liked her? Maybe he should just avoid her.

After returning the keys, he did avoid her the rest of the day. He tried to avoid her the next day in church, but as Hunter and Michael left priesthood meeting, Laura bounced over with her roommate Tara and asked if he'd had fun the day before. He had.

"You like winter sports?"

He did.

"Have you tried skiing?"

He hadn't.

"You should."

Maybe someday, he thought.

"Have you seen the lights on Temple Square?"

He hadn't.

"You should."

Maybe someday.

"We should go next Saturday," Hunter spoke from beside Michael. Michael tried not to let the surprise register on his face. Hunter was suggesting they go somewhere? Garrett was the one who usually did the inviting. "Why don't you girls come and we'll go?" Hunter asked. The invitation included Tara. *She would be Hunter's type,* Michael thought.

If they left Provo around three the next Saturday afternoon, they'd arrive in Salt Lake in time to see the lights come on and could tour the grounds before the weekend crowds started. That was Hunter's proposal.

"We should leave by about two so we have time to see all the Nativities on the Main Street Plaza," Tara suggested. "They have luminaries and floating lights in the fountains. It's awesome."

"You're not done with work by two, are you?" Laura asked Michael.

"Saturdays are my early day." Not completely unwillingly, Michael was being swept into this outing. Next Saturday at two, they all agreed, and Michael spent the week looking forward to going. He would avoid Laura later.

By 1:50 P.M. the next Saturday, Michael had showered so he wouldn't smell like grill grease, combed his short hair, and put on a clean shirt, idly wishing, for the first time, that he had something casual and new. Hunter was emptying trash and transferring textbooks to the bedroom so that the girls wouldn't think they were complete slobs. Garrett was lounging on the sagging sofa reading an English assignment and complaining that no one had invited him anywhere and that he'd probably end up a bachelor with straight A's. The anticipated knock at the door wasn't from Laura and Tara, though. It was Gail and her little girl Autumn.

"Hi, guys," she said as she swept in with the well-blanketed Autumn on her hip. Gail looked pretty. She had wool pants and a bright Christmas sweater under an oversized coat. Autumn's sweater was a smaller version of Gail's and emphasized the mother-daughter resemblances.

"Hi, Gail." Michael's greeting was cheerful and kind, but he wanted Gail to leave. Laura would arrive any moment, so his greeting wasn't completely genuine, and for an instant he felt like his father. The gut-wrenching self-hatred for being fake made him even more pleasant.

"What's up?" he asked Gail enthusiastically as he leaned toward Autumn and shook her hand softly. The little girl eyed him appreciatively.

"I've got Autumn for the whole evening," Gail said. "Wondered if you wanted to go to the mall with me. Show her the Christmas lights."

Irritation rippled through Michael. *Why did Gail have to need help tonight?* He'd spent all week nervously anticipating an evening with Laura. "Your hands are cold," he told Autumn, holding her little fingers. None of the irritation showed in his voice. "Your cheeks are too." He rubbed the little pink face. Then he felt slightly guilty and began thinking of how to solve the problem.

Hunter was about to solve it by telling Gail that Michael had plans when the doorbell rang; Laura and Tara pushed through the unlocked door. Introductions were made, and Laura said she thought they had met at Michael's baptism. Garrett and Hunter didn't explain when and where *they* had first met Gail. Everyone said how cute Autumn was.

"We're going to Temple Square to see the lights," Garrett finally announced, throwing his textbook on the end table Hunter had just cleared. "You want to come?"

"I won't be intruding?" Gail's hesitance showed slightly around the edges of her question, and Michael's hypocrisy vanished. He wasn't his dad when he said, "Heck no. Three guys. Three girls. Like group dating."

"And Autumn?" Gail's vulnerability was more apparent.

"She's with me," Garrett said. "I've got to get my shoes." He left as Michael tried to silently thank him.

"I have to call," Gail said, looking around for a phone, "if I take her very far." She set the child on the floor and then stepped into the kitchen where the phone hung. Autumn swayed briefly and then sank in a pile of blankets.

Laura and Tara looked at each other. They could hear Gail speaking softly into the phone. "You've met Michael. Yeah, from Oasis House. Just to see the lights. I'm sure. Of course. I'm fine. I won't let her starve.

I've got a diaper bag." She finally called for Michael. "She wants to speak to you."

Michael took the receiver and listened for a moment. "I promise," he said several times and then listened. He promised again and then hung up.

"She told you how to use the car seat, huh?" Gail said.

"Yeah."

"And what she eats?"

"Yeah."

"And to be careful?"

"Yeah."

"You'd think Autumn was *her* kid," Gail mumbled as she lifted the toddler from the floor.

They carefully hooked the car seat into Garrett's old Mercury Sable station wagon. Hunter drove because Garrett said he wanted to sit by Autumn in the middle seat, which left the two jump seats in the back for Michael and Laura. There was no way for them to sit that didn't force them into close contact. He was embarrassed for a while, but then Michael gave up and enjoyed the drive.

"There's no power in this car. I thought it had a bigger engine," Hunter complained as they started.

"Plenty of power," countered Garrett. "Really good engine. It's the transmission that's shot. Slips a lot. That's why I got the car."

"Is this car safe?" Michael asked, remembering his conversation with Alice about Gail and Autumn.

"Hope so," Garrett said as he played with Autumn.

They arrived safely, parked in underground mall parking, and then walked from the neon commercial lights to the quiet lights of the Nativity. The group wandered slowly through the Christmas experience. The music was soft. The people spoke in hushed voices. Twice Michael resisted an urge to reach for Laura's hand. Finally, he asked to carry Autumn, enjoying her weight, the lights that reflected in her wide-eyed wonder, her tired head starting to rest on his shoulder. She whined for her mommy. Gail took her from Michael. The little girl whined twice more for her mother and then was finally content with Gail. Not long after, Gail said she had to find something for the little girl to eat.

They chose a Denny's close to Temple Square so they wouldn't have to drive too much in traffic. "That transmission scares me," Hunter said as they settled into a booth. "What if it gives out?"

"It will," Garrett said confidently.

"Not tonight I hope." Hunter shook his head at his roommate.

"We always drove clunker cars," Gail said as she spooned soup into Autumn's mouth. "It was like a family tradition to drive out to my grandparents and break down. My sisters hated it. I thought it was kind of cool. Alone on the deserted road out by Delta in the middle of the night while Dad walked to find help."

"Every year?" Hunter asked.

"No," Gail said, laughing and digging into the diaper bag for a bottle. "Happened twice though. We loved Christmas at my grandma's. She spoiled us rotten."

"You have two sisters?" Garrett asked.

"And two brothers. Five of us."

"Are any of the others . . . ?" Hunter started to ask about her siblings.

"Crazy?" Gail finished for him. "Nope, just me."

Laura and Tara looked awkwardly at one another. They hadn't known for sure if Gail was an Oasis House client or if she worked there.

"Our Christmas tradition," Garrett spoke into the silence, "was to line the sidewalks with luminarias. You know those candles in a bag? My brothers and I were like pyromaniacs. We saved candles and bags all year—big bags and big candles, little bags and little candles. It was great."

"Our family tradition was to spend the whole week before Christmas complaining about having to work at the school bus garage," Tara explained. "My dad always volunteered us to clean the buses over Christmas vacation. We got paid, but we complained."

For an hour they discussed family celebrations. Michael listened intently as Laura told how her mom had always gotten her and her brothers matching pajamas for Christmas Eve and matching clothes for the holiday church services. "If I had a green dress, Mom had a green dress and the boys had green ties. She got pictures of us in our matching outfits. She said it helped us feel like a family unit, connected forever."

"Did it work?" Michael asked, sincerely curious.

Laura thought for a while. "I don't know. What did your family do for Christmas?" Laura asked him.

"The restaurant my family owned was situated in an industrial part of Las Vegas." Michael hands lay quietly on the table. He chose his words carefully. "We served a lot of delivery people, short-haul truckers, freight officers, people like that. Those kinds of people are a lot busier during Christmastime, so they eat out more and keep later hours. We kept the shop open longer to accommodate them. So mostly we worked."

"But you closed on Christmas Day?" Laura asked, almost stated.

"Officially, yes," Michael replied blankly. "But Dad fed some people who didn't have anywhere else to go."

"That was nice," Tara said.

Michael didn't say anything. He didn't explain why these men didn't spend time with family. He didn't explain about drinking and foul movies and tiresome manipulation. His face betrayed nothing, but Laura felt something was unsaid.

On the way home, Gail fell asleep as quickly as Autumn did, both of them leaning against the car seat. Garrett gave occasional suggestions to Hunter about how to drive a car losing its transmission. Laura and Michael stretched cramped legs across the spare tire and talked about Christmas lights and classes and computers. Laura told Michael about trying to save money for a computer.

And so for the next several weeks, he would often ask how much she'd saved. He applauded every dollar, and Laura wouldn't have taken a computer from her parents if they'd offered it. Even her roommates noticed an ambition previously lacking, though they had no idea that it was Michael's quiet encouragement that motivated Laura.

But that night, in the darkened car, they talked softly, their shoulders touching as the gears jerked into place. When they reached the apartments, Michael transferred Autumn's car seat to Gail's car, then helped Gail into the passenger seat. "I can drive," she muttered.

"I'll take you home," Michael had said.

"She okay?" Garrett asked, motioning to the slumped form.

"I think so," Michael said. "Some medications cause a lot of fatigue."

Garrett offered to follow Michael and give him a ride back. Michael declined. The other girls waved, and Hunter and Garrett began walking them to their apartment.

The light was on when Michael pulled into Alice and Keith's driveway. He saw a curtain move as he unstrapped the seat. The front door opened before he knocked.

"She's asleep," he said as Alice reached for the baby. "Gail is too."

"Is she okay?"

Michael didn't know which "she" Alice was asking about, so he told her that Autumn had been a good baby and Gail was just tired. He was going to drive Gail home now. With the two foster parents watching, Michael climbed back into the driver's seat, started the car, and drove around the first corner. He pulled to the side of the street and gently shook Gail. "Where do you live?" he asked.

She woke enough to give him instructions to the other side of Provo. He led her up the cracked walk of her parents' home and handed her car keys to her mother, who was attempting to appear unconcerned. "We had fun, but Gail got tired on the way home," he explained.

"Her new meds," the mother said, leading Gail toward a bedroom. "Thank you," she said over her shoulder.

Michael closed the door and started walking. When he rounded the first corner, he stopped to check his watch. *Only ten thirty,* he thought. *I should be home by midnight.*

* * *

Michael spent December twenty-fourth shopping, his first Christmas shopping ever. He hadn't bought presents before, so shopping didn't occur to him, but when Garrett and Hunter stuck a bow on a large box of cereal and a gallon of milk for him, the lone Christmas-break occupant of the apartment got to thinking others might give him something. His two roommates had signed their names on a folded piece of notebook paper. Scrawled along the top was, "Merry Christmas. This is so you won't starve while we're gone."

Until that night, Christmas had been construction-paper Santa Clauses assembled at school and presents the teachers helped him make for his mom that sometimes he didn't give to her. During his elementary school days, Christmas had been a few wrapped toys under a white plastic tree. When Michael and Stephanie were older, no one bothered setting up the plastic tree. Presents consisted of needed clothing items stacked next to the TV.

This Christmas was different. There were lights and food and thoughtful presents. After breakfast with the Steeles, Michael opened presents with the family. Dane gave him sunglasses "for next year's waterskiing trip." Connor gave him four ties, all of them red because "red means you're serious about your message." Brother and Sister Steele had carefully wrapped a leather-bound set of scriptures and two white shirts. The group graciously accepted his gifts of scented candles and gourmet chocolate.

Mostly, there was the Christmas story—a small baby held by a poor, tired mother, and angels singing to humble shepherds; but for the first time the birth of this Child had a personal meaning for Michael.

Midmorning on Christmas Day, Michael went to the Oasis House and cooked an afternoon meal for four clients with nowhere to go. He'd volunteered when he saw Ruth fixing a tree and making sure there were gifts underneath. There were also presents for him under that tree. Gail had left him a package of white T-shirts and a picture of her daughter. Michael grinned. The T-shirts must have been to replace one she'd apparently taken the Sunday she'd napped at his place. Ruth had wrapped up a scholarship application with letters of reference from several staff members. After reading them, Michael decided he'd like to have himself working for him. There were three Christmas cards from Oasis House clients. Technically, one was a Halloween card with a black witch and two ghosts, but the thought was still seasonal. "To my lifesaver," was written on another envelope in a very feminine, unfamiliar hand. Michael studied it for a moment. The expensive card inside extended Christmas greetings. The same feminine scrawl expressed thanks for giving them back their husband and father. "He never came home until he found someone he trusted. Thank you, Arnie's wife and family, Kitty, Jessica, Josh, and Katrina." Michael reread the message aloud. He knew Arnie had a wife and three children. He hadn't known that he, Michael, meant anything to them.

That night Michael cleaned up the small meal, walked two Christmas "guests" home, and then moved along the cold street back to his apartment. Most of the windows were dark, the occupants gone for the holidays. He wondered what Stephanie was doing. He knew she'd had less warmth in her Christmas than he had. Alone in his apartment, Michael looked around. His new white shirts gleamed from the closet where he had carefully hung them, reverently draping the new ties around the collars. His leather scriptures sat on the desk near his bed. A plate of fudge and a tin of cheese popcorn were there, too, left at his door by some unknown elves. He thought of the people who cared for him. He sat motionless and felt blessed, loved. But he also felt lonely, sad, and extremely tired because this was the first Christmas he'd truly experienced compassion from others. Because warmth had touched this holiday, the past ones felt colder. Stephanie's situation appeared increasingly more dismal. Alone, Michael refused to cry.

CHAPTER 12

Stephanie continued to ignore Michael's calls. By late spring, he was so concerned about her he bought a plane ticket to Las Vegas. A couple of days later he was flying home, praying that his sister was all right. Every muscle tensed during the flight. Even his chest felt tight.

When the plane landed and he and the other passengers were given leave to exit the plane, he was the first one off. He stopped at the first car rental agency he saw and rented a small sedan. Michael drove into the parking lot of his dad's restaurant. He noticed it looked older, more run-down. *Has it always been this way?* he wondered. His flower beds out front were now just packed dirt bordered by a few hardy weeds. He parked and slowly climbed out of the car and made his way to the front door.

The little boy in him hesitated a long time before pushing the door open. He didn't know how to time this meeting; he didn't know who worked when, so he'd opted for the typically slow time before supper. Stephanie looked up when he pushed the plate-glass door open. She froze in midmotion, her arm extended to drop silverware into its designated slot. Michael could see the bony protrusion of her wrist. Her arm was only slightly thicker at the biceps.

"You idiot," she said, shaking her head. "You actually came." Her tone was almost affectionate, unlike the phone calls during which she had only been angry, tired, or accusing.

"You alone?" He motioned toward the kitchen, ignoring two men drinking coffee in a corner booth.

"Mom's in the back. Dad's making deliveries. He'll be glad to see you."

"I'll bet."

"Oh no, he will. He's lost a lot of life since you left. No one to beat up."

"You need to leave too," Michael said.

"I am."

Michael smiled. "All right!"

"I'm going with Carl . . ." Stephanie's voice trailed off and they both looked up as their mother came from the kitchen.

Out of habit, her eyes scanned the tables for new customers or diners needing service. Then her gaze rested on Michael. In all his memories his mother was nothing but a silent shadow that had been beaten back if she tried to get in the light. To the customers she was vivacious, cheerful, and friendly. But she was scared and silent when the kitchen door swung shut behind her. She did not have her own voice; she'd lost it to ridicule. Today, however, her eyes softened at the sight of her strong, good-looking son who stood straight and looked untouched by his father's abuse.

"Well, lookie here," they heard as Joseph Ross came through the front door. He glanced at the two customers just getting ready to leave and checked the sarcasm in his voice. As the men left, Joseph called out a hearty farewell and then turned his attention to his son, but for the first time in his life, Michael didn't watch his father. He'd spent so many years refusing to divert his eyes that he'd never seen his mother. As his father cursed, insulted, and talked about not giving handouts to thieves, Michael saw his mother's eyes do something. They seemed to glaze over and look inward. She glanced up in alarm as Michael moved toward her, but relaxed when he smiled.

Michael finally turned his attention to his father as the man's nasty tirade mentioned the conditions upon which Michael could stay.

"I'm not here to stay," Michael said as he pulled a handful of cash from his pocket. "I'm paying this back. Not that you deserve it. But stealing from a thief is still stealing." He laid the money on the counter next to the till. "Two thousand, sixty dollars."

"You took a whole lot more than that you ungrateful . . ."

"No," Michael said firmly. "That's how much I took. I've paid my debt, and I've come to tell Mom and Stephanie that they can come stay with me. I've got a place." He hadn't really planned to invite them both, but it would be worth it to see Hunter's reaction when *two* women moved in. He looked at his mother and sister. "I've got enough to buy plane tickets for you both."

Joseph laughed. "You're going to take my girls? You and whose army?"

Michael continued to watch his mother, who now watched back. He thought he could see a spark of pride at his rebellion and a glimmer of envy. She smiled slowly and walked the short distance between them. Standing close she said, "Thank you." The words "I'm proud of you" were never vocalized, but Michael felt them for the first time.

"I'll stay here and help your father," she continued. "Take Stephanie though."

"Stephanie's staying here where she belongs," Joseph bellowed. "She's still a child. She'll do as I say."

"Stephanie, you can come with me," Michael said.

The girl's affectionate look had disappeared.

"I'm staying," she said.

"Get out!" Joseph said to Michael and pointed to the door. "Get out."

"Are you sure?" Michael asked both his mother and sister. They nodded.

Michael awkwardly put an arm around his mother and promised to write. She patted his shoulder and said she hoped he would.

Stephanie led the way to the front door of the restaurant and stepped out into the spring sun with Michael as their father yelled in the background.

"My birthday's in three months," she said.

"Then you'll come?" Michael asked eagerly.

"No," she said. "I'm going with Carl."

"Who?"

"He used to make deliveries here. Now he's got a good job at one of the casinos on the Strip. But he still comes in, usually while Dad's gone in the afternoon. Carl promised to help me find a job and a place to live. Mom doesn't even know."

"And you trust some guy you met here? He could just be feeding you a line. What do you know about him?" Michael asked.

"You trusted those missionaries. What did you know about them?"

"I know a lot now," Michael began.

"I don't want to hear about them," Stephanie said, waving one hand to stop Michael. "Carl says they're a cult."

"They're not," Michael protested. "Remember what the missionaries said when—"

"Yeah, I remember." Stephanie faced her brother. "I remember you left. You walked out on me. You think you had it bad. You don't even know what it's like being a girl in that house."

"I'm sorry."

"You should be." Stephanie turned toward the restaurant. "I gotta get back. I've still got another eighty-nine days with Dad."

Michael put a hand on her elbow to stop her. "Come to Utah with me."

"No." She left him standing in the parking lot.

Have faith, he told himself quickly, before the fear and discouragement could sink in. *My prayers can penetrate the evil. Something good will happen.*

For her birthday he sent Stephanie a card and two hundred dollars. As he dropped the blue envelope in the mailbox, he said a short prayer that no one—especially their father—would steal the money.

Three weeks later Michael opened the mailbox to find a letter from Stephanie. Sitting on the top step leading into his apartment, Michael read how grateful Stephanie was for the money. *Dad said it should go to him, but he didn't take it. I needed it since I left the next day. Carl came and picked me up. I think Mom felt bad, but you never know what Mom's thinking. Dad was surprised. Got really mad. You know the routine.*

Michael did.

I don't work with food anymore, she bragged. *I count money for the same casino that Carl works for. Isn't that great?*

No, Michael thought. *That's not great. You could come here. Go to school. Learn to laugh because things are funny, not just because a customer expects you to.* Michael wanted his sister to have a dress and a testimony and roommates that used rope to tie boys' apartment doors shut. *But she got the money,* he decided. *That prayer was answered.* He would continue praying.

* * *

The Sunday after Stephanie's birthday, the bishop called Michael into his office and suggested the time had come for Michael to fill out his mission papers. Michael shook his head regretfully and explained he couldn't possibly go on a mission.

"You're old enough. You've been a member a year," the bishop said briskly. "I've even received a letter from a man who promises to support you financially."

Michael smiled, "Brother Steele."

"Are you worthy?"

"I'm not sure," Michael stuttered.

Flipping open his temple-recommend book, the bishop asked Michael all the questions written there.

"You're worthy," he concluded afterward.

"Not really," Michael said. "Sometimes I feel like a fraud even going to church. I don't know that I have the right to tell other people how to live."

The bishop quit shuffling papers, and guilt seeped through him as he realized how little time he had given the young man who sat before him. He had asked Michael to attend the temple preparation class, and the elders quorum president had made certain Michael attended a couple of temple trips to do baptisms for the dead, but no one had sat down and heard Michael's personal concerns.

The bishop now took that time. After an hour of speaking with Michael, the bishop finally said, "The Lord needs you. He will care for you. You have communication skills that will serve you well. You have developed strength from your trials. That strength can ensure your success. When you come home, you will no longer feel like a fraud."

"I promised my sister I'd help her if she ever needed me," Michael said.

There was a long pause, then the bishop looked Michael in the eyes and said, "I feel impressed to tell you that she won't accept your help for the next two years even if you're here."

* * *

The entire Steele family attended when Michael spoke in his ward for the first and last time. They confirmed their willingness to fund his mission when they bought his suits and luggage and took him to the MTC.

Brother and Sister Steele wrote. They called Michael "son" and were just as devoted as they would have been if he had been their son. They wrote when Connor was readmitted to the state mental hospital. His medication had quit working, and he'd started seeing UFOs again. His parents were sure his new medication would work better. The birthday present Michael received had all three of their names on it. They wrote when Connor was released from the hospital and had moved home. He'd be better soon and they were sure he'd find another job. The family sent Michael care packages, a Christmas box, and even remembered the anniversary of his baptism. He called them at Christmas.

Gail wrote him, sometimes every month, sometimes every week, sometimes every day, depending on what manic stage she was in. If the letters were once a month they were long and sad. In them Gail talked seriously about placing her child for adoption because she didn't have the energy to care for the active little girl. When Gail's letters came every day, she didn't mention Autumn. These letters rambled about everything around her—Oasis House, jobs, weather, and food. When the letters came once a week, Gail was going to make it. She would get a better apartment, keep her present job, and make a safe home for her daughter.

Seth sent updates on the newt colony, including blueprints of a new newtarium and, later, pictures of the finished product.

Arnie wrote about once a month with news of the Oasis House. He resisted begging Michael to come back, but did mention every time one of the new cooks left, unable to deal with the confusion. Ruth wrote and said that Arnie sure needed him.

Laura wrote occasionally, "as a friend." She told that to anyone who suggested she was writing a missionary. "He's just a friend," she'd remind dates. Her letters sometimes required four or five drafts.

Hunter wrote a couple of times a year, first about his new wife, then about their new baby. Garrett wrote more often about wanting a wife and needing some kids.

Every companion complained that Elder Ross got more mail than any of them. Michael tried to answer every letter but was particularly careful to write Stephanie. These were short letters that avoided preaching, but still conveyed the joys of Church membership. He talked about his companions and what interesting cooks they were. He tried to joke about carrying groceries home on a bike. Often he described the little kids he met. Racing ten-year-olds around the church parking lot during the Cub Scout bike rodeo was good for a half page. *When I have a son,* Michael wrote, *I'm going to teach him to at least let the elders win one race.*

Being the speaker at a Young Women early-morning devotional gave Michael an opportunity to describe for Stephanie how the girls had hiked from their camp cabins wrapped in sleeping bags and eating potato chips. This letter included as much of a sermon as Michael dared about the peacefulness of the Holy Ghost.

Stephanie waited a year before she answered her brother. She was still working at the casino, she said. She didn't make as much money as Carl wanted her to.

"Thanks for your letters," Stephanie wrote. "Carl doesn't like what you're doing, so maybe you can send my mail to the casino address for a while."

Michael read the last line several times. Was Carl as controlling as their father had been?

On Mother's Day, Michael dialed his home number. Knowing that his dad was probably listening, he wished his mother a happy Mother's Day.

"Are you ever coming back?" she timidly asked.

"I'll come visit," he said, moved by the sadness in her voice.

Unlike other missionaries, Michael didn't mind basement apartments without much light. He couldn't understand the preoccupation some elders had for their surroundings. He didn't view long walks on cold evenings or sweltering bike rides as punishment. Life for him had always meant battling something, but for the first time in his life the battles often brought victories. Victories so warm and soul-satisfying that Michael's face softened into a perpetual smile.

Never once did he want this experience to end—until one fall day three weeks before his release date. Stephanie's second letter was even shorter than the first.

Don't write any more until you hear from me. Carl doesn't want me to have this baby. I've got to take care of it. I'm leaving for a while.

Love, Stephanie

Without speaking to his companion, Michael picked up the apartment phone and dialed the mission office.

"Church of Jesus Christ of Latter-day Saints, New Jersey Cherry Hill Mission. May I help you?"

"May I speak to President Scott?" Michael asked.

"He's busy right now," the elder replied.

"It's an emergency." His voice was impatient as he avoided the questioning look of his own companion.

When the president finally answered, Michael was blunt.

"This is Elder Ross. I just got a letter from my sister. I think she's planning to get an abortion. May I call her?"

"Immediately," was the mission president's one-word reply.

Finding Stephanie's phone number was not easy. Eventually, Michael and his companion went to a member's home and used a people-search on the Internet. Carl answered the phone on the first ring. He was apparently expecting another call and wasn't happy to be talking to Stephanie's brother.

"Oh, it's you, Preacher Boy," he snarled. "Stephanie had some things to take care of. She'll be back when she's finished."

"Is there a number I can call her at?" Michael asked politely.

If Carl knew a number or a location he wouldn't tell. Michael had the impression the man didn't know.

That night, when the mission president called to ask if things were okay, Michael didn't know what to say. He felt sick.

"Do you need to go home?" President Scott asked.

"I wouldn't know where to find her," Michael admitted. His voice cracked with emotion.

CHAPTER 13

Michael had been right. Stephanie had planned to find an abortion clinic. Carl had told her there were plenty listed in any phone book, and from his wallet quickly counted out a thousand dollars.

"That should be enough." He had lifted one of Stephanie's hands and forced her to take the cash.

Staring vaguely at the money, Stephanie heard Carl's Impala roar to life outside their apartment. Soon he would be at the casino calling out that he had change for gamblers. "Change, change." He wore a blue silk shirt that he hated, and he flirted with old ladies as he miscounted their change and told them they looked lucky. The first-timers believed this handsome, dark-haired young man as he directed them to slots that seemed to pay better. "Don't tell anyone I told you about these, okay?" He would pat their arm, smile familiarly, and slip the money he'd fleeced them out of into a front pocket. Cocky, big, drunk men were his favorite. With them he acted humble, subservient. They never suspected he stole a share of their money.

The casino's soft-money count room where Stephanie worked actually paid a higher wage than Carl's job, but Stephanie never took any extra. "All that money you guys count and you can't think of any way to get some of it?" Carl often remarked.

Flipping open a heavy phone book, Stephanie leaned both elbows on the kitchen table and stared at the ads. She grimly admired whomever it was that manipulated the alphabetized index in such a way that to find abortion listings, she had to scan past adoption agencies. Finally abortion ads stretched down the page.

Stephanie imagined the phone call. The clipped voice would explain the cost and ask what method was to be employed for payment. An appointment would be made for the procedure. A woman with a clipboard would call her name and she would walk through rooms reeking of disinfectant, then lie down and the problem would be solved.

Carl would be happy. Stephanie's eyes went back to the top of the page—*Adoption.* An agency's name was written in feminine script. "Call and talk. See if we can help." More than anything Stephanie wanted to talk. She dialed the number.

Ann's hello was warm. Stephanie hesitated; Ann waited. Ann knew how hard this call could be.

"I'm pregnant," Stephanie finally said.

"Do you need help?" Ann pulled a notepad toward her on the cluttered desk.

"Maybe. I'm probably okay."

"If you want to meet, we could talk."

"I'm in Las Vegas," Stephanie said. "I'm not sure where I'm calling."

"We're in Utah," Ann said calmly. "You could catch the bus, and I'll meet you at the station."

Stephanie thought of Michael. He'd be back in Utah soon. Provo, Utah, was the city he'd been in. Stephanie thought of her brother's last letter. He had ripped a pair of pants racing Cub Scouts on their bikes.

"How far from Provo are you?" Stephanie asked.

"About thirty miles north," Ann said.

Stephanie looked at the thousand dollars sitting on the table.

"I'm not sure what to do," Stephanie spoke pleadingly.

Ann waited silently as she twirled a pen in her fingers. The forty-year-old mother of three knew her role was to be a calm supporter of whatever decision the girl at the other end of the line made. Ann took a deep breath and expelled it silently.

"I'm not sure what to do." Stephanie's voice verged on a whine.

"The choice is always up to you. If you need time to think, we can provide a place."

"You know where I could live up there?"

"I have a place you could stay for a while. But I must tell you that we *are* an adoption agency. You must decide if that is an option for you." Ann didn't explain that Stephanie's living expenses would be passed on to any adoptive family, and if Stephanie didn't place the baby, then her expenses would still be passed on to an adoptive family. These families might pay for two or three girls who changed their minds at the last minute. Legally the girls could change their minds even after living rent-free for several months. The uncertainty in Stephanie's voice signaled to Ann a possible hike in adoption fees for a family who finally did receive a child.

But Stephanie came. Ann met her at the bus stop. The two went straight to a condo where an unmarried nurse named Cassie had a room available. The nurse was plump, optimistic, and kind. The fridge was crowded with fresh vegetables, fat-free milk, and ready-to-bake crescent rolls. Cassie told Stephanie to eat anything she wanted but not to make long-distance calls without using a calling card. The mothers-to-be room had a large bed with a coverlet that matched the flowered curtains and an overstuffed chair the same color as the flower petals. A copy of the Book of Mormon lay on the nightstand.

* * *

For months after returning from his mission, Michael ignored Laura—not really ignored her; he had checked the latest address on one of her letters to him in the mission field and rode his bike past the complex into which she'd moved. However, he never called her. He wondered whether she'd really want to see him. Just in case, he rented a room a block from her apartment.

He did call Stephanie's number, however. Carl was even ruder this time and spent most of the short conversation insinuating that Michael knew where she was.

"I don't," Michael assured him, "but when she gets back, could you have her call me? I'll give you my number."

"You back in Utah, Preacher Boy?" Carl asked.

Confused and concerned, Michael hung up and called his dad's restaurant. He hadn't talked to his mother since May. He needed to tell her he was back, and maybe she would know something about Stephanie.

"What do you want?" his dad asked after recognizing Michael's voice.

"I'm back from my mission," Michael said. "Wanted to see how things were."

Joseph snorted, "You're real concerned about us all?"

"Is Mom there?" he asked.

"She's busy."

With effort, Michael kept his voice neutral. "May I talk to her for a minute?"

When Shannon finally picked up the phone, she thanked her son for calling. How was he doing? She was glad he was going to school. She didn't know where Stephanie was. Stephanie never phoned. When was Michael going to come visit?

"I just started going to school," Michael explained, "and I'm working. But I'll try. I'll call you again soon. If you need anything let me know, okay?" Michael could hear his father in the background saying that Shannon's minute was up. "If you hear from Stephanie, tell her I'm trying to find her," Michael said quickly. He heard his father yell, "Get off the phone, woman!"

"You jerk," Michael said as he banged his own phone down. *He hasn't changed,* Michael thought angrily. *Why is he like that?*

Out of habit, Michael started to say a silent prayer for Stephanie and his mother, but his anger stopped him. He'd prayed so many times, and things just seemed to be getting even more complicated.

Laura didn't know about the complications in Michael's life. All she knew was that he was back and still riding that stupid yard-sale bike he'd stored in the Steeles' garage. She'd seen him riding it to the Oasis House. Reed, her boyfriend of several months, had a brand-new Volkswagen convertible he'd driven clear from California. Reed was on an accelerated track to graduate with an MBA, and she'd be his advertising consultant. *Reed is more my kind of guy,* Laura thought as she wondered whether Michael was going to go to BYU or continue his studies at UVSC. But Michael hadn't called or stopped by since he'd returned. He hadn't even hinted at any interest in her. She was the one who saw him at stake conference and suggested they try pizza again, "Just for old times. I'd love to hear about your mission." Of course her boyfriend wouldn't care—Michael was just a friend.

Reed's taller, Laura thought after Michael agreed to meet her the next night.

They talked for a long time. Laura told him she had been getting experience with summer internships and would be ready to graduate in the spring with her bachelor's. He congratulated her. Feeling confident, Laura told him about getting her job with the Continuing Education department. "It's the job I wanted when I first came here. Remember you told me to get qualified?"

Michael did remember. He remembered how pretty she had been, but how whiny he'd thought her, how spoiled and soft she'd seemed. No strength. She seemed stronger now, maybe even prettier. Not so much posturing.

"You like the job as much as you thought you would?" he asked.

"Well, not at first. It was hard. Every design I made someone made a billion changes to. We have to send everything to so many department heads for approval. They all make a change or addition. I used to get mad. Now I'm getting used to it." Laura laughed a little at herself. She ate a breadstick and then wiped buttery fingers on a napkin. "I guess I thought everyone would just look at my work, applaud, tell me how wonderful I was, and then hang it on the refrigerator like my mom did."

Laura talked about her computer and how she was saving for an upgrade. She told him about designing the most beautiful brochure. "It was the most expensive job I've been allowed to do. It was for a Holy Land tour offered to people who make big donations to the university. The paper was expensive; the pictures were the best—everything quality. I spent hours working on it. I must admit the design was good—award winning, honestly. They were going to enter it in a design contest. Then someone noticed that the registration form was black with white lettering. Visually appealing, but unless these rich folks have a white pencil handy, there's no way we could have read the applications."

Laura had never told Reed about her mistake. She had been too embarrassed after having imagined awards and prizes, imagined how she would phone her folks and modestly admit she had won a design contest. Somehow, she didn't mind telling Michael.

She also revealed to Michael her secret dream to design web pages. "I don't know. I just really like design, especially on the computer."

"If you ever want to volunteer, call the Oasis House," Michael told her seriously. "Our website hasn't been updated since Seth went to work full-time nearly a year ago."

"You don't have someone paid to do it?" Laura asked.

"It's hard to get the money to pay someone to do all the things that need to be done. Usually a client has the skills. Right now we don't have anyone, although we have people volunteer all the time."

"Why?"

"Because they know Oasis House provides a service that no other place does."

Michael told her how, except for Arnie and Ruth, the Oasis House staff had completely changed. The clients hadn't changed nearly as quickly. Seth worked in a pet store dispensing more advice than most customers wanted. Gail had just completed a course to become a legal secretary.

"How is Gail?" Laura asked tentatively, wondering how big a part she played in Michael's homecoming. "Did they finally let her have her daughter?"

Michael hesitated before telling Laura about Gail and Autumn. The experience had left him slightly confused.

"About a month ago," Michael told Laura, "Gail announced that the judge had given her custody. She danced around the kitchen in the Oasis House, and kissed us all. Told the guys at the smoker-joker table she was never coming out there again. I went over and helped her wallpaper a room in her apartment and bought a Mickey Mouse lamp. She sold her diamond earrings and used the money to pay the deposit on the apartment. She got a dresser and painted it white and then spent hours with little plastic . . . what do you call them . . . uh, stencils, putting rosebuds and leaves all over."

"How old is Autumn now?" Laura asked, fascinated with Michael and the story. She'd never seen this man talk so animatedly, never seen his face so open. She watched his hand turn the moist drinking glass and then mimic painting flowers.

"She was two when I left, so she's like four now. She talks and talks. She asks about the flowers outside and then wants to know what we're eating before we answer about the flowers. I don't know how she learns anything, but she does. She knows a lot of the flowers by name, petunias and marigolds and things. She's smart and pretty. Gosh, she's cute. She looks a lot like her mother."

Laura felt a knot of something she couldn't explain when Michael described the mother's and daughter's beauty.

"On the day Gail was supposed to get Autumn, we planned an afternoon party. Made a cake. Hung a few balloons. We all waited around. She never came and never came. Pretty soon most everyone had wandered off or gone to their jobs.

"Arnie and I finally drove to Gail's apartment to see if everything was okay. No one answered when we knocked, and I finally just went in." Michael had trouble describing the scene. He'd called out her name. He could see a bike, and three blue balls. A doll Michael had never seen sat in a kid-sized rocking chair. Both had obviously just been purchased. Michael called again, "Gail, you home?" and pushed the door open a little wider. Gail was curled in one corner of the couch staring numbly at him.

"Gail?" Michael had worked with mental illness long enough now to speak calmly even when alarmed. He'd exchanged a look with Arnie and the two of them had moved toward her. "Gail, you okay?"

She nodded.

"I didn't get her." She looked up at Michael. "I couldn't."

"Why?"

"She loves the backyard," Gail said. The young mother hadn't been crying when the two men came in, but now she started. "Love isn't enough. You know that, don't you? I asked them to adopt her. They wanted to anyway. Love isn't enough. She needed more than love."

The tears had started to slip unheeded down Gail's cheeks. "I don't know why I'm crying," she said. "I know it's right. I feel calmer now than I have since she was born. Love isn't enough. Keith carries her around. They have supper together. She should stay there. Do you know she kisses Keith on the cheek? Autumn needs a father. I gave her one." Gail smiled. "I'm glad I did," she said, then laid her head back on the arm of the sofa and cried.

Michael remembered the scene and then looked at Laura. He'd been silent a long time. "She decided Autumn needed a father and a mother. She left her little girl there." He didn't tell how Gail had come to the Oasis House with a big carton of cigarettes and had thrown the carton onto the table. "Someone convince me not to smoke these," she'd said.

"Was she pressured into giving up the baby?" Laura asked incredulously. "They can't do that to her. It was her child. She was the mother."

"Yes," Michael said slowly. "She was the mother, but she made the decision without any pressure. She realized how much more they could give her—a father, a big brother, a temple sealing. All Gail had to offer was an apartment and day care."

"You think she was right?" Laura was doubtful.

Michael didn't hesitate. "She was right."

"But Gail loved her daughter."

"But now Autumn will get love *and* all the rest."

"You don't think her real mother can love her more than someone who just adopted her?"

Michael thought of his mother and her inability to love if her husband didn't approve. He thought of his father, a man who controlled but never loved. Michael thought of shopping for a mission suit with Brother Steele, how Connor's dad had put his arm on Michael's shoulder and told the store clerk, "My boy here needs the best missionary suit you've got." Michael had protested but had liked the way everyone had assumed he was Brother Steele's son.

"No," Michael told Laura. "Parental love doesn't require the DNA to match."

"So you think that Autumn is better off?"

"It would have been hard for Autumn to spend that many years with a family and then be moved. Kids bond. Breaking that bond is not always detrimental, but a series of caregivers compromises a child's ability to develop neurologically."

"And you learned about this child psychology where—in Childhood Development class?" Laura laughed at Michael's serious speech.

"Yes," Michael said. "I started it this semester."

"Really?" Laura had avoided child-development classes.

Michael nodded. Next semester he was planning to take a success-in-marriage class. He knew that his role models were not adequate as examples of parents or spouses, and more than anything Michael craved a successful family.

"You took it at BYU?" Laura asked, when what she really wanted to ask was why he'd take such a class.

"No, at UVSC."

Laura felt Michael withdraw and struggled to lighten her tone. "When are you going to transfer to the Y?" she teased.

"Probably never."

This time Laura did ask why.

He shrugged. "It's a really good program."

"There's more prestige in graduating from a private university," Laura said.

"I don't need prestige. I need to know how to be a landscape architect."

Laura cringed. His tone was reprimanding

"Well, I just thought it would be easier to get to BYU since you don't drive. You know, since you only have the bike." Laura motioned outside where he'd chained his bike to a pole.

"I take the shuttle from the Oasis House."

Actually, he drove the shuttle. Ruth had made the arrangements, determined that Michael would quit taking all his courses online and experience some normal college life. He got paid for his driving and had a scholarship. The shuttle, however, left at two and got back at nine. Michael worked long days; Ruth worried about that. Michael didn't tell Laura about having a chauffeur's license. They soon left the restaurant.

Michael didn't tell Laura a lot of things he would have liked to confide in someone. He didn't tell her about Stephanie's disappearance. He didn't tell her about his constant concern that no one was caring for his sister.

CHAPTER 14

Michael would have worried less if he had known that Stephanie was spending the most peaceful six months of her life. She rested each night under a clean comforter. She sat in a warm kitchen nook each morning to eat yogurt sprinkled with cereal. The adoption agency found her a job working at the Sears mail-order department two blocks from the condos. She received kind prenatal care from a doctor who often commended her for her unselfish act of placing her baby for adoption.

Christmas was celebrated more warmly than Stephanie ever remembered. She attended Ann's ward supper, where children in bathrobes and sheets solemnly told of a King born in a stable. Ann's husband and three teenagers were comfortable with Stephanie; she wasn't the first birth mother they'd entertained. They gave her presents: gloves, bath salts, a bulky coat to fight the winter chill, and a calling card.

There were only two people she considered calling: Michael and Carl. She knew Carl's number. She wasn't sure how she could even find Michael.

Stephanie enjoyed flipping through files of potential families for her baby. She read how the couples planned to discipline and about their extended families. Stephanie felt so content thinking of this growing child having one of these homes. Her child would be raised in happiness. Somewhere out there in the world, she was going to have a successful child. Maybe in eighteen years she would take Carl and they'd meet this child grown to adulthood. By then Carl and she would be successful. Stephanie imagined a tender meeting with a grown child.

She finally chose a couple in their late twenties. The wife taught school; the husband repaired hospital equipment.

Ann asked Stephanie if she wanted to meet the couple. This was a safe step since nothing would go wrong with this adoption; Ann's previous hesitations about Stephanie were gone. Here was a woman determined to place. The expectant mother declined a meeting but thought the parents-to-be should have time to prepare. Ann called them, told them there was a mother who wanted them to raise her baby. The woman cried, but through her tears she quickly made plans to clear out a home office for a nursery.

Heavy at thirty-seven weeks, Stephanie liked herself more than she ever had before. Instead of walking to work and watching for signs of spring, she'd now take a few weeks off to give birth. They'd offered to let her go back to the catalogue outlet after she delivered. She was tempted, but Carl needed her. Buoyed with her success, Stephanie took her new calling card, walked to a nearby pay phone, and at one o'clock sharp, called Carl. He'd be readying himself to go to work, preening in the mirror, tucking in his blue silk shirt, and plastering back his hair. He'd been angry with her, but he'd be worried now. She was sure of it.

"Where are you?" he exploded. A little of Stephanie wilted.

"In Utah."

"With your brother?"

"No, I'm by myself."

"So when are you coming back?"

"You didn't want me as long as I had the baby."

"You didn't keep it," he snarled. "Don't tell me you have a baby."

"Not yet. But when I do, I've found a family that wants to adopt him."

"Him? I'm having a son? You're not peddling him off to strangers. I don't want my son raised by strangers. How much are they paying you?"

"Nothing. You can't sell babies."

"Well, you can't just give my kid to strangers either. Why didn't you take care of this when I told you to? You took off, left me alone, and now look how complicated you've made things. I'm working my tail off. Vern and I could use some help."

"Who's Vern?" Stephanie asked.

"He manages these apartments," Carl explained proudly. "But him and me, we got a side business that's going to make us rich. You could help."

After he castigated her again for leaving and not doing what he told her to, his voice softened. "I've missed you, and honey, I really could use you. If we're to have any future together, you've got to be willing to do your part. I've got to go. Vern wants me to drop some things off before I go to work. Get it worked out and then get back here."

Stephanie walked home. She shouldn't have called. What had she been thinking? She'd just felt so good about things and wanted to share her feelings with someone. Now she didn't know what to do. He didn't want the baby. He didn't want someone else to have it. She couldn't abort now. Probably she never had the nerve to abort, but after feeling him move, after recognizing his little hand in the ultrasound, after hearing the heart swoosh against hers—she couldn't have done it.

Stephanie unlocked the condo door. Cassie was chopping chicken into a green salad. She put a slice in her mouth and then smiled. "You're looking tired. Sit down. You doing okay?"

"Fine," Stephanie said vaguely.

"Nevertheless, you need to sit down. That BYU channel runs devotionals in a few minutes." For several weeks Stephanie had come home after work and watched TV. Her favorite programming had turned out to be the devotional and conference reruns that BYU television played. She'd started watching them to understand more what Michael believed. Now she watched them because she felt a peace from the speakers' words.

Stephanie took the remote and the salad when Cassie handed them to her. "You need to rest up," Cassie said. "Just a couple more weeks. Does the doctor think you'll be about on schedule?"

"Yes," Stephanie said without making eye contact. She pointed the remote at the TV and then sat numbly watching a blank screen.

"You okay?" Cassie asked again.

Stephanie nodded dully.

"Ann was coming over tonight to help you fill out final papers for placement. You want me to call and tell her you're too tired? Put it off for a couple days?"

"No." Stephanie wasn't even sure what she'd just said no to. She'd been with kind, understanding people too long. She had forgotten how Carl could twist everything. No matter what decision she made now, it would be wrong. She'd felt so right an hour ago. Now nothing was right.

When Ann walked into the room she could feel trouble. Cassie shrugged in answer to Ann's questioning look. Stephanie still stared at a blank TV.

"You okay?" Ann sat next to the silent girl.

Stephanie's nod was slight.

"You want to talk?"

"What else have we got to fill out?"

"A few legal forms. We've typed up all the ancestral and medical history. We need to update a few legal things."

"Haven't I filled out enough forms?"

A Stephanie the two women didn't know emerged. Upon first meeting, Stephanie had been scared and sad. Slowly, she had accepted adoption. Lately, she'd seemed comforted and at peace. Now she was bitter, complaining that she'd told them the height, weight, and medical problems of each of her known relatives. She'd written her unborn child a letter, and she'd bought an expensive wooden keepsake box to give him as a token of her love. What more did they want?

"You've left most of the birth father's information blank."

Stephanie said nothing.

"If you don't know who the father is, we just write that."

"I know the father," Stephanie answered angrily. Some part of her was hurt that they'd think she didn't know the father. "I know him," she said more slowly.

"You're not now, or have ever been married to him?" Ann asked, even though Stephanie had already answered these questions. Husbands had a lot more legal rights than unmarried partners. Ann didn't want any surprise spouses showing up during the adoption process.

"No." Stephanie leaned forward. Her large stomach pressed against the coffee table. "Why?"

"In Utah, unmarried fathers have to take steps to demonstrate parenthood. If he does not protest placement . . ."

"He's already protested," Stephanie said, standing up and placing the untouched salad on the table. "He doesn't want the baby given to someone," Stephanie said sadly. "He'd be really mad." Stephanie ignored everything else Ann tried to explain to her. Instead she went to her bedroom and quickly closed the door.

The next day, she collected her paycheck and took a bus south. When it reached Provo, she got off. She carried her one suitcase until she found a run-down motel that rented by the week.

* * *

Laura continued to date Reed for several weeks after her lunch with Michael, but the California native didn't seem as perfect as he had before. *How stupid to buy a convertible if you live in a snowy climate,* Laura thought during one cold ride. She was irritated when he told her that he was five inches taller than the average height for men. "Who cares?" Laura had snapped. "I don't think height matters."

Sometime that same week they'd discovered several things they didn't agree on. Laura wished he'd stop smoothing her hair all the time, patting the top of her head, and readjusting her bangs. At first it had seemed like a caress, but now it felt like an intrusion on her space.

"Let's be friends. We're not right for each other," was how the conversation started one night. Then Laura called to tell her parents that she'd broken up with Reed. Reed e-mailed his parents to explain how he was having second thoughts about Laura and how he'd be more careful before he got serious again.

A week later, Laura called Michael and asked if the Oasis House still needed someone to update the website. Michael's roommates teased him about another girl chasing him. He'd been to more than his share of preference dances. With friendly persuasion from his roommates, he'd even asked out a couple of girls. Although he was flattered that the girls liked him, he wasn't flattered enough to pursue any of them. *Certainly,* he assured himself, *I'm not interested in Laura either, but she could benefit from helping someone whose life isn't as charmed as her own.* They decided to meet Saturday after lunch cleanup. It took some time to make the website look just right. Ruth even suggested some rather time-consuming improvements and smiled at Laura's willingness.

For several weeks Michael and Laura spent Saturday afternoons updating the Oasis House website, then they spent Saturday evenings walking around campus, going to the student movies, or eating a late supper in the apartment where the fewest roommates were home. Often they'd balance plates on their knees as they sat on the couch and watched TV, companionably fighting over the remote control. Every time Michael attempted to change channels, Laura would grab his hand. He liked the way she moved closer. She liked the feel of his warm hand. He changed channels a lot.

Michael was reluctant to ask Arnie for a Saturday off in the spring, although he was sure Arnie would take the shift since Michael had been working Saturdays several weeks in a row. What Michael didn't want was the teasing he was sure would come with the request.

"I don't mind," Arnie said, throwing a load of white aprons into the laundry basket. "But Laura, well, can she handle the website without you?" The staff liked Laura. She regularly ate with the clients. Anyone who needed help in the office-procedure room often asked Laura.

"She won't be in either."

"What?" Arnie asked. "What kind of volunteers are we getting lately? They come for four or five months regular and then one day they have something better to do?"

"Her parents are flying in Saturday morning."

"Okay, that excuses her. What's your excuse?" Arnie grinned.

Michael smiled back. He didn't have to give Arnie any excuses, but Arnie and Ruth were a big part of his life. "Laura's dad has just retired and bought a small plane. He's flying it out here. Offered to take us up."

"Meeting the folks now? Must be serious." The two men had locked the kitchen and were standing in the entryway. Michael was getting ready to drive the shuttle up to UVSC.

"No," Michael said not very convincingly. "I just want the airplane ride."

"You ought to think seriously about her. You could do a lot worse."

"The problem is," Michael said, "she could do a lot better." He nodded at his boss, pulled keys from his pocket, and stepped outside to greet the shuttle riders like a man without self-doubts.

Saturday morning Lance Keeyes' personal plane landed at the small airport west of Provo where Laura had driven Michael to meet her parents. Mandy and Lance Keeyes smiled in response to Michael's polite greeting. Laura chattered nervously to cover the silence she anticipated until she realized Michael and her father were having a quiet conversation about Starvation Reservoir and the High Uintahs.

Michael, in the copilot's seat, was fascinated by his view of the mountains. The plane bounced through turbulence as the Uintah Mountains made way for the red butte of the Uintah Basin. Michael pointed out the town of Roosevelt, recognizing the oil refinery puffing smoke into the air. Lance was interested in Michael's previous trips to the northeast corner of Utah.

From his copilot's seat, Michael told them about the dinosaur quarry, but Mandy refused to let them land and rent a car to tour the area. "Laura and I planned a trip to the mall," she informed the two men who were picking out modern oil rigs where ancient bones could be found.

Lance banked the small plane back toward Provo, suggesting that he'd really like it if someday he could come back and they could all explore the area.

Michael didn't talk about Connor's UFOs, but he did mention the mines that may have produced the gold for the angel Moroni on the Salt Lake Temple. The pilot listened with interest and Laura strained to hear over the engine. Mandy said she didn't believe in an Indian mine that got lost. Lance suggested that the gold had to come from somewhere. As the two women sat back, tired of struggling to hear, Lance continued to ask Michael questions, and the two men discussed a range of topics from land terrain to gold plating to Indian reservations to what the communication between pilot and control tower meant. The flight back was soon over. After they had landed and were walking across the tarmac, Laura's father decided to treat them to lunch.

They drove to a restaurant close to the airport and ordered light lunches in an empty diner.

"You're from Las Vegas?" Mandy asked Michael politely.

"Yes," Michael said. He had been comfortable riding in the air where he could talk with Laura's father, but now, sitting across the table from Laura's parents, Laura close to his side, he felt uneasy—like he was being evaluated. Despite his inner uneasiness, he only appeared reserved and a little unapproachable.

"There's a lot to do in a town like Vegas," Mandy commented almost accusingly. Michael had been told the same thing at least once a week since arriving in Provo.

"We lived a long way from the Strip," Michael said. "Sometimes I made deliveries there in the early morning, but I don't think I ever saw it at night."

"What did you deliver?" asked Mandy.

"Sticky buns," Michael said, smiling faintly. "My dad made these cinnamon rolls with a sticky sugar-and-pecan bottom. For a long time we had contracts with several places to make and deliver them every morning."

"Your folks own a bakery?" Lance was curious.

"They run a small restaurant in the industrial section of Clark County," Michael explained. "The rolls were our specialty."

Laura watched the young man's face. He betrayed nothing of the aversion he felt toward home. The bits she knew about his childhood distressed her, yet his face remained dispassionate.

"They're kind of the salt of the earth?" Lance suggested as the waitress served their sandwiches.

"The salt that's lost its savor," Michael returned. His tone didn't invite more discussion. The group gratefully turned their attention to the food.

"Do you have any brothers or sisters?" Lance asked.

"One sister." Michael didn't mean for his answers to be so stiff.

"Does she still live in Nevada?"

"I'm not sure," Michael said uncomfortably.

No one spoke for a few minutes.

"Isn't there a pretty big university in Las Vegas?" Mandy asked, falling back on what appeared to be a safer subject.

"Probably not as big as BYU," Michael said. "When I toured their campus as a senior I think they had about 24,000 students. It may be bigger now."

"Did you ever have any plans to attend college in Vegas?" Lance asked.

"I had a scholarship to UNLV," Michael said.

Laura looked closer at the boy next to her. She hadn't known about a scholarship.

"But you left so you could come to BYU," Mandy said with the first approval her voice had registered during the entire interview.

Laura stiffened. She knew Michael would say he wasn't attending the Y, a fact Laura hadn't burdened her folks with.

Michael was irritated when he felt her stiffen, but decided to be kind. "I really didn't want to attend school at UNLV. But mostly I came to Utah to learn about the Church."

They laughed a little about how he'd learned more than he'd expected, and then briefly discussed his mission. No one asked how his family had accepted his Church membership.

Somewhere before dessert, Lance started to ask questions about Hoover Dam. "Have you ever seen it?" Lance asked.

"On field trips."

"Ever see it from the air?" Lance asked.

"Can't say that I have." Michael grinned.

"While the women shop, let's fly down there," Lance proposed. Michael looked unsure. Lance ignored the response and promised Laura that he'd have Michael back by dark. "We'll meet you ladies at the airport."

"Exactly what time?" Mandy asked, not certain she liked her husband's familiarity with Michael.

"About ten."

"That's really late for Michael," Laura teased.

"Just be sure you take him straight home." Lance smiled.

"I'm sure she will." Mandy wasn't smiling. She still wasn't smiling later that day when she told Laura to be careful about spending too much time with any one person. "I know you've known him since he joined the Church and you feel protective toward him. And Michael is, I'm sure, a good guy. But getting involved with someone like him could be complicated."

"What do you mean?" Laura felt annoyed.

"There are always problems when a boy comes from a background such as his."

"What do you know about his background?" Laura faced her mother.

"I know he wasn't raised like you. He didn't learn some of the basics that we've tried to instill in our children." Mandy started to warm to her topic.

"Maybe he learned some things I didn't. Like how to not judge people."

Mandy hadn't wanted to ruin the day with an argument, so at that comment she remained silent and bought her daughter a new coat.

Laura knew enough about her mother to know that the silence didn't mean agreement. Laura also knew enough about her mother to know that she could probably ask for new gloves to match the coat.

In the meantime, Michael and Lance flew over I-15 past Provo, Beaver, Cedar City, and St. George. Fascinated, Michael watched the land below them and discussed geology with Lance.

They refueled in Las Vegas after Michael pointed vaguely toward where his home had been. As the two headed toward the dam, Michael explained to Lance that what most people thought of as Las Vegas was really a bunch of unincorporated towns.

"There's Enterprise, Spring Valley, Whitney, Winchester. I think most of the Strip is actually in Paradise," Michael explained, drawing upon conversations he'd heard as he'd poured coffee and delivered sticky buns.

The two men found Hoover Dam and then followed Lake Mead's shoreline before turning north and flying home. A disgruntled wife greeted Lance when they landed twenty minutes late.

As Laura dropped her parents off at a hotel, Lance invited Michael to eat lunch with them before they flew out the next day. He declined, much to Mandy's relief, saying he had meetings tomorrow. As they headed to Michael's apartment, Laura listened to him talk about watching houseboats out on Lake Mead. She wished he'd kiss her good night. He got out, told her he'd really enjoyed talking with her father, and then waved good-bye.

CHAPTER 15

"You seen Michael's car?" Connor asked Laura when she stepped into the office-procedures room.

"I'll show it to you," a new client offered, rising slowly from her chair. "Then you have to help me on my assignment."

Ever since Michael had driven the car over on Thursday, everyone had wanted to tell Laura about it.

"Did you tell your girlfriend?" Seth had wanted to know upon seeing the car. Without waiting for an answer, he'd asked Michael to haul a load of Plexiglas. "I got some newts that need a bit more room. We could put the glass in the back if we rig the hatch open."

"I don't have a girlfriend," Michael had said.

"Oh man, not this again," Connor had retorted. Then they'd all gone for a ride. Michael drove, then Connor.

"You bought a car?" Laura addressed Michael. She was surprised. She'd gotten used to his frugal ways and felt a sense of disappointment that he was becoming more like everyone else.

"And he got a good deal, too," Connor said. Laura smiled as he spoke. She liked Connor, and today his speech suggested he was doing well. She listened to his description of the car while she noted Michael's discomfort with all the attention.

"An almost-new Honda," Connor said. "I'll bet the first hundred thousand miles were all city miles. And after that it seems to have proven itself to be a mighty fine off-road vehicle. The cracks in the seats match nicely those in the windshield."

"I got the windshield fixed," Michael muttered.

"With an almost-new windshield from the junkyard."

"It's a salvage yard."

"And those scratches from the wreck, why they haven't begun to rust at all, what with the primer smeared all over them."

"Sounds attractive," Laura said.

"And it has special features," Connor nodded. "The front light shorts out when the right blinker is activated, and if it stalls in an intersection, all you have to do is get out, open the hood, blow out the fuel lines, and the engine starts running again. If it doesn't, the bald tires make pushing very easy."

"We only had to push once," Michael said. "And that's 'cause Gail flooded it."

Laura's pleasure diminished a little when she heard that Gail had already driven Michael's new car.

"When Michael had the correct change in his pocket to pay for this marvelous vehicle, we knew it was meant to be," Connor finished.

"What convinced you to buy a car?" Laura asked.

"I've quit driving the shuttle."

"Why?" Laura asked.

"I've got night meetings. One of the guys in our ward got married. They gave me his calling."

"Elders quorum presidency," Connor reported. "No staying out late on Saturday nights now. Michael has early morning meetings on Sunday."

"We don't stay out late Saturday," Michael said.

"Well you should."

"Is Ruth upset that she has to find someone else for the shuttle?" Laura asked.

"No." Michael grinned remembering Ruth's response.

"A car?" Ruth had said in mock exasperation. "The boy bought a car. Arnie, did you hear that? I've tried to get some sort of normalcy in that kid's life ever since he came here. 'Associate with your ward,' I told him. 'Don't work so hard. Go to a real campus.' All it took was a Church calling. He buys a car and starts socializing with his neighbors."

"You shouldn't have worried. Don't you Mormons believe in leaving it in the Lord's hands?" Arnie had badgered her.

"Well, the Lord could have done this earlier. I mean, come on. He's just started being a kid, and he'll be getting married soon."

Michael had interrupted their conversation. "I'm not looking to get married soon."

"Oh please," Ruth said. "Of course you need to get married. You know, Laura would be a great wife. You need some kids. You'll be great with kids. Don't be putting that off."

This time Arnie interrupted. "Leave him alone. Let the Lord work on the marriage and the kid thing, too."

"You think the Lord can?" Ruth had turned to Arnie.

"Of course. That's probably an easy one for Him."

"So you have faith. You know, don't you Arnie, that faith is the first principle of—"

Arnie interrupted again. "I've had the discussions, Ruth."

"I guess two miracles in one day was too much to ask for."

"Maybe next week," Arnie said.

"What day?" Ruth asked.

* * *

Curly brown hair surrounded the round face. Newborn eyes didn't completely focus. Small legs stretched tentatively and then curled back into the white gown. A clenched fist found its way to the tiny mouth. The little boy sucked noisily. A nurse leaned over the small crib and picked up the seven pounds of healthy infant. "You're a handsome little man," she cooed softly. "A precious little bundle." The woman carried the child to the new mother. "Honey," she said softly. "You awake?"

The woman in bed hesitated and then turned to face the intrusion. "What?"

"I just thought you'd want to hold your baby now."

"Is he okay?" the woman asked suspiciously.

"He's wonderful. He's healthy. He's bright and he's beautiful," the nurse said. "But he's hungry. He'd probably nurse."

"I don't want to nurse him. Find him a bottle or something."

Nervously, the older woman tried to tactfully explain. "Well, honey, formula does cost a lot. And," she finished lamely, "sometimes breast-feeding provides a bonding experience."

Without looking at her child, Stephanie closed her eyes. She kept seeing Carl. He'd be so mad now if he knew she'd given birth. If Mom knew about this new baby, she would want to help, but Dad would probably be as mad as Carl. *If Mom wanted to help me, she'd have to do it against Dad's wishes.* For a sickening moment Stephanie recognized the similarities between her baby's father and her own.

"Is there someone I can call for you?" The nurse spoke kindly.

Stephanie opened tired eyes and looked up. "Could you help me find my brother?"

* * *

Michael was easy to find. As soon as Stephanie described her brother's job with the mentally ill, several hospital staffers named the Oasis House. Michael had just started to make lunch when he was called to answer the phone.

"It's my sister," Michael told Arnie and Connor, who had waited impatiently in the kitchen. "I haven't known where she was since her last letter to me on my mission. She's right here in Provo. She just had a baby. I can't believe it. I've worried about her all this time and she's right here."

"Is she by herself?" Connor asked.

"I don't think the father wanted the baby."

"Does she have a place to go?"

"I don't know," Michael admitted.

"You're living in student-approved housing, so you can't have her stay with you," Connor mused.

"I was made aware of that rule." Michael smiled, remembering Gail.

"My roommate would probably think he was having hallucinations if a baby showed up," Connor said. "Mom probably wouldn't mind a baby, but they're gone for the weekend. Gail's got a spare bedroom in her place. Might do her some good to have it filled for a while. I'll find a place for your sister in case she needs it."

"You're the best friend I ever had," Michael said.

"That would be me," Connor agreed.

"Get out of here," Arnie told Michael. "We can handle lunch."

As Michael left the kitchen, Connor called a final farewell. "Good luck. I'll tell Laura why you're not here."

Great, thought Michael. *That will impress her.*

* * *

Michael rushed to the hospital in his sputtering little car. A pink-smocked woman directed him to the maternity ward, and he stuck his head into six rooms before recognizing Stephanie's dark hair on a white pillow.

"Steph," Michael called softly, moving toward her bed. "Steph?"

Stephanie watched him come. He was the best-looking boy she had ever seen.

"Fancy meeting you here," she said.

"You okay?" he asked. At those words, she smiled at the long-forgotten familiarity of his voice. They began talking. She explained how she had left to have an abortion and found the adoption agency instead. She talked about the condo where she had stayed and her job.

A blanketed bundle lay in a crib on the other side of Stephanie's bed.

"Is that your baby?" Michael asked, pointing awkwardly.

"Go look at him," Stephanie said.

Standing over the crib, Michael watched the motionless face of his nephew. The baby was so still that Michael rested one hand on the blankets to see if he was breathing. The form wiggled. It was a sudden movement that included his whole body and rearranged his face. A bit of heaven did seem to have trailed to earth with this newborn.

Michael suddenly felt hungry to hold a child. He longed to feel the warm weight of a baby and to stare into brown eyes that matched Laura's. Scolding himself for having such unrealistic dreams, Michael stood for a long moment with his hand on the soft blanket.

"Have you chosen a family to adopt him?" Michael asked as he felt an overwhelming surge of love toward the child.

"I can't," Stephanie said.

Michael carefully chose his words. He said he understood that it would be hard to give up a baby; then he tried to explain how Gail had tried to raise her baby but had decided love wasn't enough and that babies need a mom and a dad.

Stephanie closed her eyes as her brother talked.

"You don't understand," she finally said. "Carl would never sign the papers."

"So what are you going to do?"

"I guess I'll call him," she said wearily. "I'll go back, but can I stay with you for a few days? You always said I could."

"Yes," Michael said. "That shouldn't be a problem," he lied.

By the time Michael reentered the Oasis House, Connor had called Gail at her work.

"I don't care if she stays," Gail had told Connor, "but Michael will have to come after work. I don't want to be alone with a new mother. I haven't done a baby in a long time, and I wasn't too good the first time."

When Laura heard Michael come into the Oasis House, she came down from the office-procedures room where she was helping two clients study for their GED.

"I can borrow a crib from my brother," she offered. "He'll need it back this fall when they have number three, but it's available all summer. Do you need blankets or anything?"

Michael hadn't thought about supplies. He was suddenly flustered. "I don't know. What do babies need?" he said, almost panicking.

"You're pathetic," Laura laughed. "I doubt I'll ever be anyone's choice for mother of the year, but I've been around my brother's kids long enough to know we're going to need diapers, blankets, and a pacifier. That is a necessity. When all else fails, stick that thing in the kid's mouth."

She promised to take the crib over to Gail's first thing in the morning.

That night Michael checked the Internet for information on how to care for newborns. By the time he arrived at the hospital the next morning, he had bought not only four styles of pacifiers, but had a full bag of lotions, rubbing alcohol, cotton swabs, diapers, mild soap, four soft washcloths, and a hooded towel. He also bought a carrier that doubled as a car seat until the baby was twenty pounds.

Stephanie was hurrying to get herself checked out. The adoption agency had helped her secure some state aid to pay for the delivery, but she wasn't covered for another day. If she didn't leave by eleven, she'd be charged. A nurse insisted that all first-time mothers watch a video about caring for newborns. But Stephanie refused. So, while his sister showered, Michael viewed the educational film featuring demonstrations on how to care for the umbilical cord and proper burping techniques. He was pleased to note that he had purchased all the right supplies.

Michael had never heard Gail laugh quite so freely as she did when he carried the baby into her apartment that Saturday afternoon. Laura and Gail were in the extra bedroom trying to assemble the crib. Laura was sitting against the wall holding the fourth side of the structure in place.

"Hurry," Laura begged, "I can't hold on any longer."

"You sure you brought the right doohickeys for this crib?" Gail asked. "This thing isn't long enough."

"Hit it," Laura suggested as she balanced the wood panel against her knees.

"Now the two holes don't match," Gail said. "You have to lower your piece."

"What are you doing?" Michael asked.

His voice startled both girls, and the railing slipped and slid down to hit Laura's shins.

"Ouch!" she yelled.

"That's gotta hurt," Gail said, looking down at the girl imprisoned behind crib slats.

"You okay?" Michael asked, carefully placing the baby on the bed. He hurried over and pulled the back side of the crib up.

"No." Laura stood and slid from behind the half-assembled bed. "That's a cook's job. You finish."

Michael introduced his sister, who had sat on the bed next to her sleeping baby.

"You can stay here as long as you want," Gail said. "Michael can stay too."

"Thank you," Stephanie said wearily. Last night she had told the nurses to feed the baby and not wake her up. Still, she hadn't slept much. What would Carl do when she came back with a child?

The baby stirred.

"He'll need to be fed," Stephanie said. "The nurse said he should eat another two ounces about now."

Michael put his sister to bed and told her he'd care for the baby until she was rested.

"Cute kid," Laura said when Michael carried the infant to the small kitchen. She wanted to say he looked like a lizard, but didn't want Stephanie to hear. Parents were often irritated when their offspring were compared to reptiles. Watching Michael and how he kept smoothing the blankets, she knew such a comparison would probably irritate him too.

"He looks like Yoda," Gail said, seemingly unconcerned that Stephanie would hear.

"Yoda?" Michael said irritably.

"Yeah, like on *Star Wars*," Gail replied, pulling the knit hat off his little head.

"Don't, he'll lose his body heat," Michael said, replacing the blue hat.

"My brother was big on maintaining body heat too," Laura confided to Gail. "Must be a guy thing."

"I just want to know if he has hair," Gail said conversationally to Laura.

"He doesn't look like Yoda," Michael defended his nephew.

Gail pulled the hat back off. "You're right. Without the hat he looks like a newt."

* * *

The girls spent another two hours giving helpful advice as Michael fed, burped, and changed the newborn.

"You got the milk warm enough?" Gail asked.

"You'll burn him if it's too hot," Laura warned.

They laughed together at Michael's exasperated look.

"You can't burp him if you don't hold him up straighter," Gail advised. "The air travels up."

"Don't hit him hard," counseled Laura.

"Put the diaper on tight or you'll get leaks," Gail warned.

"Don't make it so tight it hurts," Laura countered.

Michael rolled his eyes.

"Just trying to help," Laura giggled as she patted him on the back. "But in my expert opinion," her voice softened and her hand lingered on his shoulder, "you're doing great."

Soon after, Laura left to help decorate for a ward supper. Gail agreed to watch the new mother and baby while Michael ran to the grocery store.

"I'll buy your groceries while Stephanie's here," Michael told her.

"That's a good deal," Gail said and gave him a few suggestions. "I only like white bread. Wheat bread is healthy, but with all these toxic meds I'm taking to destroy my liver, I don't bother with healthy. Buy me some soft, white bread, two heads of lettuce, brownie mix—every new mother needs brownies—and no cigarettes please."

Stephanie came gingerly through the doors as Gail finished her list.

"He's always offering me cigarettes," Gail told Stephanie. "I have to continually remind him not to."

Michael rolled his eyes and wrote a list, adding supplies for Stephanie. He checked the baby, asked Stephanie if she was okay, and then left.

Stephanie settled carefully onto the opposite side of the couch from her son. Gail put her feet up in an ugly brown chair that didn't match the couch but was comfortable and big enough to sit cross-legged in. For a while the two women watched the baby breathe.

"How did you meet Michael?" Stephanie asked, wondering if her brother ever dated anyone.

Gail told about the Oasis House and how Michael had helped her when she was starting a manic phase.

"Are you well now?" Stephanie asked, watching the girl for any unusual twitches.

"I'm stable right now," Gail said. "I'm working full-time, I go to church, and I have a calling, but I see a psychiatrist every month to check on my meds. I'm supposed to go talk to a counselor, too, but instead I just go to the Oasis House every week. The staff there knows me pretty well. They're good for a reality check."

"A reality check?" Stephanie asked.

"They tell you if you're acting crazy, because when you're acting crazy you don't know you're acting crazy," Gail explained. "You should see your brother. Michael's always really calm when other people aren't."

"We were trained that way," Stephanie explained. "Our business relied on repeat customers. It didn't matter what we felt—we were required to treat them so they'd want to come back."

"What happened if you didn't?" Gail asked.

"You don't want to know," Stephanie answered, "but Dad got even. Never in front of anyone. He'd lose his cool later."

"I've never seen Michael mad," Gail said.

"I have a couple times," Stephanie said, "but he didn't want to act like Dad, so he tried never to show his anger. He hid it a lot, but it's there. Michael left home because he wanted to be different. Now he's more like you all than like us. He belongs here." Stephanie looked sad. "I don't. I never will. I've never had Michael's strength. I'm just not that good."

"Whoa, lady. People here aren't any better than folks other places. Oh, some of them try harder cause of the Church and all, but people are still people. You've got a right to be anywhere you want to be," Gail lectured. "You don't even know what I've done, and they still let me walk right into church."

The baby stirred in his sleep and pushed the blanket away from one small ear. Stephanie reached toward the infant but didn't touch him. "But now I've got him. Carl is his father. I have to go back."

"But Carl didn't want a baby," Gail said bluntly, thinking Stephanie needed a little reality check of her own. "He's not going to suddenly change his mind."

"He will," Stephanie said defensively. "He'll eventually learn to love his own son."

* * *

On Sunday, Laura brought over a frozen pan of lasagna, and garlic bread in a foil bag.

"It's a charming Mormon custom." Gail set the table as she talked to Stephanie. "Women bring casseroles to new mothers. Usually," Gail raised her voice to ensure that she interrupted Michael and Laura's conversation, "the casserole is homemade. What's this about Laura? This was your one chance to impress Michael with your kitchen skills and you buy a box of preservatives?"

"I checked the expiration date on the bread," Laura defended herself.

"I'm impressed," Gail replied. "Your bread will always be squishy. I like squishy bread."

As they ate the lasagna and garlic bread, Gail suggested that Stephanie ought to name her baby. "We had a dog once. No one could think of a name so we just kept saying, 'Where's the dog? Go get the dog.' Soon the name got shortened to Dog. We called him Dog until he died. Except for Dad, who called him Mouse," she said.

"Why would your dad call him Mouse?" Michael asked, knowing Gail's sense of humor must have been similar to her father's.

"Because he thought Dog was a stupid name."

Laura laughed. Michael grinned at Gail. Stephanie watched them all and wished she belonged there.

"This kid's going to end up being called Baby if you don't think of a name," Gail warned. "And don't let your brother influence you. Late at night I heard him calling the poor kid Yoda."

"I didn't call him Yoda," Michael complained placidly.

"You wanted to."

"Don't listen to Gail," Michael instructed his sister. "She's crazy."

"Just part of the time," Gail said.

"I think I'll name him Ryan." Stephanie spoke for the first time. "Ryan is Michael's middle name."

Each evening Michael cared for Ryan. He sterilized bottles, washed clothes, talked to his sister, and then fell asleep on the couch. Every couple hours he got up, fed the little boy milk at just the right temperature, held him up straight to burp him, and then they both fell asleep in the big brown chair.

Each morning, Gail shook the chair to wake him for work, and then she spent five minutes berating him for doing what Stephanie should be doing.

"It's her baby. She needs to care for him. You're not always going to be here."

"I'm not here during the day," Michael protested. "She cares for him then."

In reality, Stephanie only cared for her baby some mornings. Often Laura stopped in and fed the child. She held him and talked to Stephanie about the two boys they had in common, Michael and Ryan. Often she would lift Ryan's fingers and examine miniature nails that already needed to be clipped. She would stretch out his little legs that, when released, curled themselves back into the same tucked position they must have been in before birth. She was charmed by the baby's presence, and once she even admitted to herself that she wished the little boy were hers and Michael's.

"How long have you known Michael?" Stephanie asked Laura one morning.

"Since right after he moved here, before he went on his mission, even before he joined the Church."

"Was he different back then?" Stephanie asked, watching the other girl hold Ryan.

Laura looked out the window to where sun bounced off the Wasatch Mountains. "Yes and no. He's a lot more open now. Smiles more. But he always seemed to have a lot of commitment to what he decided to do and didn't care what people thought. A lot more resolve than most people."

"He's always been strong," Stephanie agreed. "Stronger than I'll ever be."

CHAPTER 16

Two weeks after the birth of her son, Stephanie dialed the restaurant's number. Her mother answered the phone.

Typically, Shannon had only two facial expressions, cheerful for the customers and unreadable for the family. As she held the phone to her ear, the facial expression softened like it had when she watched Michael return to the restaurant and pay back two thousand dollars. Her husband saw this expression and stopped to watch his wife.

"Come back. You can work here," Shannon said into the phone. "I'll help you."

"Michael's not allowed in this place until we come to an understanding," bellowed Joseph.

For the first time in years Shannon ignored her husband. "I can pick you up. In the morning? The bus comes in at 5:20?"

"He can't just come back," Joseph roared after his wife hung up the phone. "Not until—"

"It wasn't Michael," Shannon interrupted. "That was Stephanie. She's coming home. She has a baby."

* * *

"You're going back?" Michael faced Stephanie.

"Tonight on the eleven o'clock bus."

"You can't just go back," Michael pleaded, shaking his head slightly. "We'll figure things out. You can't go back there."

Stephanie had planned this moment alone with her brother to explain her reasons for leaving. Michael couldn't keep buying everything.

Gail needed to get a paying roommate. Carl needed to meet his son. She could work in Vegas.

"And who's going to take care of Ryan?" Michael asked irritably.

"Mom already offered to help babysit."

"You called her?"

"Yes."

"So you want him to be raised in the restaurant just like we were?" Michael asked. "Do you want that? I'll help you here."

"Carl can take care of us," Stephanie explained impatiently. "He said he had a second job that was paying more than the casino."

"He's stealing something." Michael's words were tinged with the first anger Stephanie had heard in years.

"You don't know him," Stephanie retorted.

"He sent you off for an abortion, and you think he'll care about a baby? I don't think so." Michael's words were bitter, and his voice rose. "And you think Dad is suddenly going to become grandfather of the year?"

"Excuse me," Stephanie's voice was embittered. "Aren't you the guy that works with the mentally ill? Don't you believe in helping people change?" Both fists were clenched as she faced her brother.

"I don't think that has anything to do with this." Michael stood back against the bedroom door where the baby lay in the borrowed crib. "Mental illness has a biological component. Dad chose to be an arrogant—"

"Maybe he doesn't know better," Stephanie interrupted. "Maybe he needs help. Maybe I needed help and you left me."

"I came back," Michael protested.

"You're so dumb." Stephanie was suddenly furious. "You think you had it bad. You don't even know what it was like being a girl in that house. You left. At first I thought you were brave. Then I got mad."

Michael looked closely at his sister. "I'm sorry."

"You should be," Stephanie said as a single tear rolled down each check.

"I came back to get you as soon as I could."

"It was too late." Stephanie pushed hair back from her eyes.

"I'm sorry. I couldn't stay," Michael said apologetically, moving slightly toward her.

"Why? Because you would have gone crazy? Tell me our family isn't mentally ill."

"Mental illness isn't a choice. It's a sickness. Mom and Dad made decisions," Michael insisted. "There's nothing organically wrong with their brains."

"How can you be so sure? How can you try to rehabilitate the mentally ill and not recognize it in your own family?" Stephanie was angry.

"So you're saying we just need to feel sorry for them and try to help them?" Michael met Stephanie's anger with his own fury.

"No," Stephanie yelled, standing up. "Yes."

Michael's anger was gone. There was a wry humor in his next question. "You think a pill would have helped Dad?"

"Not Dad, but maybe Mom."

"You think?"

"Well, there are drugs for social anxiety disorder. A counselor at school sent me to a shrink that prescribed several different ones. Carl sent me to a doctor once who had me try medication for depression. Then they gave me some for anger. I've seen them all. One of them might have helped Mom."

"Did they work for you?" Michael asked kindly.

"Maybe," Stephanie said. "Maybe, I don't know. Does medication work for your people?"

"For some people yes, for some no. But it's hard to explain. Some mental illness is a result of chemical, organic malfunctions. Some behavior problems are due to environment. Some dysfunctions are a combination of both chemical and environmental effects."

"How do you tell the difference?" Stephanie asked. "You don't know which Dad is. How do you tell when people are organically sick or when they're just choosing to live outside of society's standards?"

"Sometimes it's obvious," Michael said. "The rest of the time, I don't know. I think I know which Dad was, though—acting all normal for other people, and in private an abusive—" Michael cut himself off before losing control.

The siblings looked at one another, drained and tired. "Why are you going back to what even you admit is outside of society's standards?" Michael asked, frustrated.

"Because Carl knows who I am. He knows I'm white trash. Would Laura love you if she knew?" Stephanie smiled slightly at the blush that crept up Michael's face. "I've seen her watching you. I've seen you watching her. But you know, if she ever found out what Dad is really like, would she quit coming over here?"

"I'm not like Dad," Michael protested, although he had constantly asked himself the same question.

"We're all a product of where we came from," Stephanie said.

"I came from a Father in Heaven."

"Yeah? Well it's your non-heavenly father people are going to compare you to."

"It doesn't matter what people think," Michael insisted. "I got away from it all. You can too. Carl's a criminal."

"You spent a year stealing from your family to finance your getaway. If Carl is stealing a little bit so that he and I can get out, you have no right to criticize."

"I paid it back. I've changed."

"I know you've changed," Stephanie said, suddenly defeated. "But I can't change. I just don't have your strength. I'll never belong here."

Michael followed his sister into the bedroom where she pulled the one small suitcase she owned out of the closet.

"We do have a Father in Heaven who loves us," Michael began.

"I hope you're right," Stephanie said, opening a dresser drawer.

"Can I at least drive you home?"

"In your car?" Stephanie laughed. "No thanks. I wasn't sure we'd make it out of the hospital parking lot in that thing."

"I could borrow one."

"I'll be okay," Stephanie said with more confidence than she felt.

That night at the bus station Michael bought Stephanie's bus ticket and then returned to where she was sitting on a bench. On the floor next to her were her small suitcase and a large suitcase of baby supplies Michael had insisted on buying. Ryan was nestled in his carrier.

"He'll probably need to be fed at least once before you get to Vegas."

"I'll be okay," Stephanie said. "Laura taught me everything I need to know. She'll be a good mom, Michael, even if she can't cook."

"She can cook."

"For your sake I hope so." Stephanie hit her brother lightly in the stomach.

"We're just good friends," Michael protested.

"Yeah, right."

As the mildly cold air filtered through the station and passengers milled around waiting for the bus, Michael stared at the little boy. All semester, Michael had been one of the few males in his child-development class. He had listened carefully to each developmental stage and had noted everything he could do to help his future children. He was determined he'd rock each one and read to them nightly. He'd not only break the abuse pattern, but he'd be a good father.

He thought back to the fear he'd felt before the child-development class. "I'm afraid I'll resort to the way my father acted," Michael had told his mission president in their final interview. The president had encouraged the young elder to prepare carefully to be a father. "The gospel can change your way of thinking," President Scott had promised.

Now Michael felt hungry to hold this child again. Would anyone read to this little boy? Would they talk to him?

Ryan moved to arch his neck in a stretch. The little boy had gained two pounds. His skin was no longer wrinkled. The little arms reached upward, miniature hands clenched into small fists. One knuckle rubbed against long lashes that framed brown eyes. Michael watched in fascination as his nephew woke up. The little boy stared solemnly in Michael's direction, the brown eyes wide, the smooth cheeks framed with fine, nearly black curls. A sudden constriction in the back of Michael's throat prevented him from talking.

"Take care of yourself," he finally said as he hugged Stephanie good-bye. "Call me."

"Take care of yourself," he repeated to an unhearing Ryan as the bus pulled away. For a long time Michael stared at the empty spot where the bus had disappeared. Finally he turned and rubbed his eyes to stop the tears.

* * *

Hobble Creek Canyon was well marked on the map, and Michael was certain he could find the ward's picnic area. Laura had volunteered to bring the map and help him. The other members of the elders quorum presidency were all bringing dates, and Michael was glad he was with Laura. He loved her. He'd known that since Stephanie left three weeks ago.

Every time Stephanie called she asked about Laura. Were they getting married? Well, had he at least asked her on a real date? Well, get busy, she always said.

This maybe qualified as a date, but Michael didn't believe he qualified for a girl like Laura. He figured she knew that too. She just liked hanging around because she liked all the people at the Oasis House. He didn't understand why she didn't find other boys to date, but Michael thought she came to the Oasis House on weekdays now because she was bored. School was out for her. She was still working about twenty hours at Continuing Ed, but that ended the last day of the month.

"You looking for work?" he asked her as he drove her car up the canyon.

"Yes. No. I don't know. The last couple summers I've helped with the conferences. You know, all the brochures and stuff for Especially for Youth, football camps, soccer camps—stuff like that. As the kids start to arrive there are always last-minute changes, and we print up daily fliers with information. I contact directors, get changes, take them to the office, make fliers, and then take everything back down to the directors. It's a lot of running around, but it's pretty fun. There's some discussion about keeping me for the summer to do that job since I'm trained. 'Course, it doesn't start for two weeks and would be completed at the end of the summer when BYU Education Week finishes."

"Don't you want something more permanent?"

"Yes, but I'm not going to find anything here. There are too many people that graduate and want to stay. I interviewed with a couple companies at the employment office. A company in Portland offered to fly me to their home office for an interview." She laughed. "I'd be booked on my dad's competitor."

"Well, that would be nice, wouldn't it, to go back home?"

"I don't know," Laura said. No one spoke for a moment. Their easy relationship increasingly had these strained slumps whenever the future was discussed. Neither of them was willing to ask if they were going to be in one another's future.

"Well," Michael said in an uncharacteristic mumble. "You better stop hanging around with me and date some potential spouses." He tried to sound lighthearted. His stomach felt like lead. She was the only girl he could imagine wanting to marry.

"But then you'd have to train another map reader," Laura said a bit too brightly.

Michael couldn't think of an answer. The silence was too long.

"You *could* just keep me around," Laura said more seriously. "Unless you don't like how I read maps."

They drove through the flickering light of sun filtering through new leaves. "I don't know that you'd want to be my personal map reader," Michael said.

"And why not?" Laura questioned.

"You're ashamed of my car."

"No, I'm . . ." Her voice trailed off. They both knew she was. At the same time that she was proud of him and his indifference to others' opinions, she couldn't be unconcerned about others' opinions herself. Even today she had insisted that they drive her car. Usually they did. Most nights after working on the website, they'd ride out to the lake, tour Temple Square, shop at the mall, look for deer in the canyons, or take Connor out to the Uintah Basin—always in her car.

The awkward silence ended when they pulled into the parking lot. Laura helped unload buns and juice—Michael's assignment as a member of the elders quorum presidency. They hardly spoke to one another for the rest of the evening. During the ride home Laura asked about Stephanie and Ryan.

They were fine, he thought. He hoped they were fine. Stephanie had said to tell Laura hi.

"Tell her 'hi' from me," Laura said, "and to give Ryan a kiss."

Two weeks later neither one of them had made much progress in dating other people. Laura was out of work and spent most of the afternoons helping in the Oasis office-procedures room, then she helped Michael.

As an intern project, he'd accepted a job designing and land-scaping around a new office complex. His work was free, but the owners were supposed to pay two "co-workers" from the Oasis House. Three workers had shown up the first week, but they dropped out one by one; for one the sun was too hot, one had a relapse, one was doing much better and found another job.

"I'll come help," Laura had said one afternoon as Michael asked the smoker-joker table which one of them wanted to make extra money. For two weeks she dug holes to plant new shrubs and learned what erosion control was on slopes that led into parking lots. Michael dug trenches for irrigation lines. Laura learned how to add drip lines and hook up emitters with various flow rates.

She was kneeling in mud, watching water ooze from a seep hose, when she looked up and saw Michael watching her.

"What's the matter?" she asked. "It's not in right?"

"It's fine," Michael said.

"Then what are you looking at?"

"You're gorgeous," he said honestly. "I was looking at how pretty you are."

"Well, thank you," she said slightly flustered, not because she hadn't been told before, but because from Michael it mattered more.

After they loaded extra hoses in the hatchback of Michael's car, they walked back to check on the water pressure. As they stepped carefully through the flower beds, Laura looped her arm through Michael's. She'd taken his arm on several occasions, but for the first time he reached over and held her hand.

"Thanks for helping," he said.

"You're welcome." Laura leaned her head on his shoulder. Together they stared at the newly planted flower bed, but neither of them was thinking about irrigation systems.

CHAPTER 17

"I got my summer job," Laura said Friday afternoon with a lot less exuberance than an unemployed graduate should feel about securing work. "I start Monday."

"You don't look good," Michael said.

"I think I'm tired or something."

"I've got lots of help today—don't come with us. If you sleep well tonight you'll feel like going waterskiing."

Laura nodded and stayed home. She did feel better the next morning, a little bit anyway. She'd accepted Connor's invitation enthusiastically as she had the other times he'd invited her. Laura arrived midafternoon, just after Michael. Dane and his new wife were driving the boat. Gail had come out with a boyfriend.

Laura's side started hurting in earnest as they packed to leave the lake.

"Must have pulled something," she said as she dragged toward her car.

Late Sunday evening, Michael finished with meetings and hurried to Laura's apartment. Laura was in bed. Her roommates were contemplating calling a doctor. Michael didn't bother with the phone.

"Do you want to take my car or yours to the hospital?" he asked her.

"Mine," she answered automatically. With one hand she clutched her side. "No, yours," she altered quickly. "Yours will be okay. I like yours," she said, trying to laugh.

They took his. It was closest.

Two hours later the third doctor to examine Laura finally approached Michael. "Your wife has acute appendicitis. We need to operate."

Michael didn't bother to correct the doctor; instead he called Laura's parents. They arranged to fly to Provo. Michael didn't offer to pick them up since he didn't plan to leave the hospital. As a surgery staff assembled, there was enough time for Michael to call the elders quorum president. When he arrived with the consecrated oil, the president refused to give the blessing. "You know her better. You do it," he told Michael.

Her hair was moist, her eyes closed, the pain medication taking effect. Michael had done this before several times in the mission field. He'd said words not his own, uttered promises of healing. He'd trembled at the strength of priesthood power. Today he promised her returning health, but something else filled his heart during the blessing; there was future and eternities and love, not just brotherly. There was fear and excitement and joy.

After the blessing, he paused to make sense of it all as the nurse piggybacked another relaxant through an IV.

"She did well," the doctor told Michael an hour later. "Her appendix had almost ruptured. It's a good thing you brought her in."

"She was hardly even sick yesterday."

"These things usually go quite fast. But major surgery takes a toll on the body's system, so you'll need to take care of your wife, okay?"

Michael nodded.

"But she's doing really well. Do you have any questions?"

Michael shook his head this time.

"I'll be by to see her in the morning. They'll call me if there are any complications. You try to get some sleep."

Laura's parents arrived as Laura was pushed out of recovery. She held their hands and asked where Michael was. When the young man stepped forward, she dropped her parents' hands and reached for him. As nurses adjusted the bed, he told Laura's parents almost everything that the doctor had said during the post-op conversation. Mandy and Lance thanked him profusely for bringing their girl in. He said it wasn't a problem, and they all watched the IV drip. For several awkward moments no one spoke. They thanked him again. He apologized for not picking them up at the airport. All of them searched for something to say. They said they'd had no trouble renting a car. He said he was sorry he hadn't brought her in yesterday when she'd first said her side hurt. "We thought she'd hurt herself waterskiing."

"Does she water-ski?" Lance smiled at the boy who he felt would soon be his son-in-law.

"She's pretty good," Michael said, glancing at Lance before looking back to Laura's slightly sunburned face.

"She never wanted her feet hanging where she couldn't see what was going to touch them," Mandy said, remembering other attempts at waterskiing with Laura. "She hated moss and slimy plants."

"Things change," Lance commented, taking note of Michael's worn suit pants, the clean white shirt, his impermeable face.

With no excuse to stay, Michael said good-bye.

"We'll see you tomorrow," Lance suggested. "I'm sure Laura will want to say thanks."

Michael left the room but not the hospital. Staying as close to Laura as he could, he wandered to a waiting lounge and sat in an uncomfortable chair where he watched the dark parking lot and thought about Laura being called his wife. Could he be worthy of someone like Laura?

"Do you believe in Christ?" one of his companions had once asked an investigator.

"I do," the old man responded, "but I'm not like you Church members. I've been pretty bad."

"Do you believe Christ?" Michael had asked.

"I feel He's there," the man said, gnarled hands pulling at a gray beard.

"But do you believe what He says? Do you believe His influence can make you a different person?" The old man had become a different person. Michael had watched even the lines in the old, etched face soften and relax. *Do you believe Christ?* Michael asked himself as dawn crawled over the mountains.

With the dawn came thoughts of his responsibilities. He rose from his chair and walked down the hall to check on Laura. She was asleep. So were her parents. He whispered an "I'll see you later," and headed off to the parking lot. He quickly found his car and sped off toward his apartment. He parked and ran up the stairs. With little time to spare, Michael stopped to change clothes and then went directly to work.

* * *

"They're giving my job to someone else," Laura announced when Michael entered the hospital room. It was almost six o'clock in the evening. Supper had been served, and Lance was surprised Michael had taken so long.

"I'm sorry," Michael said. He felt almost as much panic as she displayed.

"I called Continuing Ed and told them I wasn't supposed to work for a while, and they called back this afternoon and said they'd have to give the job to someone else."

"Listen, honey," Laura's mother said, "your dad and I should help you pack and we'll fly you home. You can rest for as long as you need to and then look for work."

"I graduated, Mom," Laura said irritably. "I can't just go home." She directed her next words to Michael. "Did you bring me flowers?" Laura motioned to an expensive arrangement Michael had just set on the end table.

"They're from Connor's family."

"I didn't think they were from you. Not something that pricey."

"Well, in a way, I did spring for some pretty expensive foliage. The arrangement Seth and Gail made for you is down in my car. The hospital staff wouldn't let me bring it up. It might have bugs since it wasn't straight from a greenhouse. Actually," Michael glanced self-consciously at Laura's parents, "they were picked directly from the starts I just planted in my landscaping project."

"Isn't that called deadheading? Don't you do that to help them produce more blossoms later?"

"Uh, yeah," Michael said, surprised at how much she'd learned working with him. "But usually we pull only the dying blossoms off, and we don't do it until after the shock of replanting has worn off."

"But it didn't kill them."

"No."

"Then you owe me a bouquet."

Her father shook his head slightly. They would do just fine as a married couple.

"What have you been doing all day? It's six."

"Actually, I had a test this afternoon."

"And that was more important?" Laura was only partly joking.

"No," Michael said, "but I also checked on a couple freelance jobs for you."

"Really?"

He told her about the greenhouse having extra stock and needing someone to update their web pages. "Also the office complex where I'm landscaping has just started a website. I just asked them. They said you could come in, and they'd talk to you when you were feeling better."

Lance looked even closer. This boy, insecure as he seemed to be about relationships, was aggressive about some things.

Michael left soon after the conversation about jobs. He'd been thirty-six hours without sleep. Mandy stayed for two more days helping Laura move back to her apartment, stocking the shelves with extra food, wishing the girl would come home, but knowing that in some form Laura had loved this boy since that first e-mail three or so years ago. Mandy was going to have to accept him. A reception on the lawn would be nice; the future mother-in-law started planning.

Neither place really wanted to pay Laura for help on their web pages. She'd allowed Michael to drive her and then gone into the offices by herself. The nursery wished they had funds but they didn't. The manager at the new office complexes knew more about Internet advertising than Laura did. Or at least that's what he implied in a lengthy description of his many accomplishments. His long-winded bragging in the cold, air-conditioned office left an already-weak Laura dizzy and incapable of focusing. She slowly descended the steps to where Michael was pulling tiny weeds from the flower beds he had recently planted.

They didn't talk much as he drove to her apartment. Discouraged, she admitted that maybe she needed to go home. She'd have to beg her dad for enough money to pay next month's rent.

With one hand on her forearm to help her up the stairs, he leaned slightly up and kissed her. For a moment neither moved.

"Sorry," Michael finally said.

"Why?" Laura looked down at his dark, windblown hair. He looked away.

"You need to quit hanging around with me anyway." Michael looked up at her.

"Why?"

"You could do better."

"I don't think so."

"You could."

"I don't think so."

Michael kissed her again. The kiss lasted long enough that Laura didn't care about the noise that his old car made or that she didn't have a job. That night he asked her to marry him. Later she would joke about having to hang around, unemployed and broke, to get him to ask her. Later she would tell how she grass-stained her best jeans hauling sod so he'd figure out that she would be a good investment. Later still, she would tell how she chased him. But that night she just said yes.

* * *

Work had become boring, and Carl was taking more risks in pilfering small amounts of cash. He had figured this lady was easy prey. Her pink T-shirt was pulled tight. Her pudgy hands cradled a cup of chips. Tired eyes gazed wonderingly into Carl's face as she asked for help. He shorted her fifteen dollars. She squealed loudly. He quickly recounted, making the fifteen appear. She threatened to contact the management, then grew interested in a twenty-one table where she plopped heavily, waiting for the dealer to acknowledge her.

Disgusted, Carl realized he'd earned nothing but his wages all day. Stephanie wasn't making much more. Driving deliveries for her dad had seemed like a reasonable plan since they wouldn't have to pay a babysitter. Lately, however, the situation made Carl resentful.

Good old Joe kept wanting more and more hours from his daughter, and that kid was awake more and more. The baby was okay when Stephanie had first moved back. He slept a lot, and by putting him in his carrier as far away from the bedroom as possible, they'd trained him not to cry at night. Carl even liked showing people the boy. But now the kid was never asleep. That was Stephanie's fault. She let him nap in the truck, then he was awake when Carl needed quiet.

One night the boy had been particularly irritating. Carl had not gotten off work until after midnight. Then he'd stopped by Vern's place to show him some possible numbers for what Vern liked to call their "cost-sharing" scheme. By the time Carl stumbled to his own apartment, his eyes ached. The gray of dawn was starting to melt the night darkness when Carl found his bed. Stephanie would be leaving soon to make deliveries.

Sleep didn't come. From the other room came an irregular pounding. Carl charged across the hall to where Ryan lay on a blanket on the floor kicking both feet directly up in the air and then allowing them to land with a thump. The child would smile to himself and then repeat the feat.

"Stop it!" Carl yelled and scooped him up. Plopping the child into the nearby carrier, Carl hooked the straps around his little shoulders and then pulled the buckle up tight.

"Why'd you put him in here?" Carl hollered when Stephanie came into the room. "Put him in the kitchen."

"He's too big for the carrier," Stephanie protested.

"He stays in it until he can learn to lay still."

Two days later Carl threw a shoe because Ryan was fussing for a bottle. The heel struck the little boy on the cheek. Luckily, Stephanie realized, Ryan cried only a moment. If he'd cried longer, Carl would have thrown the other shoe.

If it weren't for Vern, Carl would have sent Stephanie and the baby away months ago. Vern had told Carl that babies were a nuisance, but that Stephanie could eventually be very helpful in their operation.

"She's not very brave," Carl had warned him.

"Well, you're not methodical enough," Vern had said. "We could use a little more caution around here. I think I know just the job for her."

CHAPTER 18

Laura pushed back the small carton of milk she had been drinking from and looked around the Oasis cafeteria. It was Saturday afternoon and they were alone. The sounds from the kitchen had faded. She'd expected to meet her fiancé for lunch and finish making wedding plans. Instead Michael wanted her to go look at a house.

"It's got three bedrooms and a large kitchen and dining room. It's lots bigger than what most newly married couples live in," Michael was explaining.

"But we'd be living with Seth?" Laura asked for the second time.

"Not living *with* him. He lives in the basement. We have the whole upstairs."

"What would we have to do?" Laura asked. "Watch Seth's newts?"

"No," Michael explained. "We wouldn't have to do anything really. Seth's mom just said that if I'd keep an eye on her son, she'd let us live in the main floor of the house."

"Gail says it smells like newts."

"It's free housing just for checking in on Seth. It would make his mother feel good knowing someone who understands him was living above him. She's rented it to people that complained."

"And probably for good reasons," Laura suggested. But reluctantly, she agreed to look at the home.

"The last couple left over a month ago," Seth said when they stopped at his basement apartment for a key.

"Why?" Laura wanted to know. "Why did they leave?"

"I don't know," Seth muttered. "The wife said she didn't want me getting any bright ideas about putting one of my cameras upstairs."

"What camera?" Laura asked nervously.

"Like the ones I use to keep my newts online."

"Why would she think you would?"

"She was paranoid."

"You wouldn't put a camera upstairs," Laura said.

"I don't even have a cord long enough," Seth said, nonplussed.

"Michael," Laura said, taking his arm and pulling him back up the cement steps. "He's got cameras."

"He's not going to put a camera upstairs." Michael dismissed the idea as they stepped onto the large front porch.

Michael was pleased with the floor plan. Large windows looked out onto the street. New carpet spread across the living room and met the new linoleum of a dining room and kitchen. Although compact, the master bedroom had large closets. There were two smaller bedrooms. Laura wasn't nearly as excited about the place as Michael was.

"It's like an oven in here," she commented as the two wandered onto the back porch. "Is there any air-conditioning?"

"I doubt it," Michael said, looking into a laundry room that was equipped with a washer and dryer.

"I don't want to live here," Laura said.

"What's wrong with it?"

Laura moved back to the large window. "It's an old place, no air-conditioning. Feel how hot the sun is coming through this window," she complained.

"Think how warm it will be in the winter," Michael said. "And I can't even smell Seth's newts."

"Maybe not today. He's probably got his windows closed," Laura said. "Michael, this just isn't how I planned to live when I got married."

"What do you want?"

"Dad offered to pay our rent until we got settled. He'd want to."

"We don't need to ask your dad for help. I've even got some money saved. But if we spend it all going through school, it could be years before we can start a business. So I just thought if we lived here now we could save."

"Excuse me. I've worked my way through school. If you'll remember, I didn't exactly start with cushy employment."

Michael didn't want to say more. Her first job in food services was an easy stint compared to working for his dad. Michael didn't like her at that moment. She just seemed spoiled.

"I have a degree. I don't have to live in a place like this."

"Then marry someone else." Michael's voice never rose. He lightly tossed her the keys and left.

Laura stood for a long time waiting for him to come back and apologize. She waited for him to understand that she'd been hoping for a place with other married couples. She was not willing to babysit someone whose main occupation was raising floating lizards.

Michael didn't come back.

Left alone, Laura looked around the living room. *I'm not following him,* she thought. Laura sat on a bar stool and watched through the large picture window, certain her fiancé would return. Utah Lake glistened in the distance. Cars wove along the distant freeway. A motorcyclist turned the corner closest to the house. Laura could see the road climb toward campus.

Immediately below her she saw Michael start down the sidewalk. He passed her car, never looking back. His stride was sure—measured and quick but not angry. Laura liked the way his arms swung. She liked the way his jeans fit and the neat way his shirt tucked into a beltless waist. She knew girls watched him. *I'll have to go to him,* Laura thought in sudden surprise. *He won't come back.*

Even as she became angry that he left, even as she slammed the door and marched down the steep stairs to return the keys to Seth, she felt a sense of pride in Michael's firmness. There was comfort in his strength, his resolve. That pride and comfort diminished within the hour, and Laura spent two angry days seething. She called him a chauvinist. She assured her roommates that he'd better learn now what he could expect. But Laura missed him so much that by Friday she'd decided to go to the Oasis House the next morning. He came to her instead. She was sitting on the concrete steps leading to her apartment. The sun was a brilliant ball against his back. The two watched each other in the orange evening. Michael spoke first.

"I love you."

"Oh, thank you." Laura rose to meet him. "You understand then."

Michael backed up one pace and spoke again. "I love you. But it's not enough."

Laura's smile faded. She watched his dark hair turn burnt orange in the sun. "We're too different. From two different worlds."

"Because I won't live above a newt colony?"

"No, because even if I convinced you to, you'd resent that you lowered yourself to my standards. See, you don't really like my car."

"What?" Laura felt a pang.

How could he explain that his doubts weren't because of the house? His doubts were because she felt better than the lifestyle he wanted.

"Laura, I'm sorry. The way I introduced the idea was wrong. The whole way I insisted was wrong," Michael told her. "You had the right to object and complain. But I guess we're so far apart, I don't think we can ever get together. We were raised so differently. I never step in the shower without being grateful for indoor plumbing. Laura, there is no way I can make you understand. Just please accept that we're different. Too different in too many ways."

There was a long pause.

"You think I'm spoiled," she said.

"We're different."

"I'm spoiled and you're not."

"There's more to it than that."

"Please explain it to me."

"Why? Nothing will change." Michael hurt after two days of limbo. He'd traced so much of what made him angry. "Laura, you want so much more than I do. I'm grateful for running water. You want brass faucets."

"I don't," she protested. "At least, not while you're in school."

"Honey." The endearment slipped out as he looked at her. Her shoulders were bony, sticking through the light T-shirt. Her cheekbones seemed strained. For a moment she looked as vulnerable as Stephanie. "You'll always be disappointed in where my sights are set. We all want more than our parents. But see, I've already got more than they have."

"I know you guys were poor, Michael."

"Laura, we didn't make a lot of money, but that wasn't the problem. We lived without dignity. The way our father treated us stripped us of dignity. We didn't have water at our house. I think Dad did that because bathing at the restaurant stripped us of our dignity. Just like how you'd feel if Seth really did put cameras in your bathroom."

Laura shuddered.

"I'd like to have a family and a big house to put them in. I'd like each kid to have new shoes and be able to play baseball. You certainly need some of those things just to ensure that you can compete in this society. For a long time, I thought that if I had those things I would have friends, that I would have confidence. When I came here and joined the Church, I realized that houses and clothes and cars don't give you confidence—they give you status. Certainly Connor's folks have status, but their confidence comes from inside. My parents could have been even poorer and still given us a belief and hope in ourselves. Dad refused to allow us a an identity beyond his control. That's why Stephanie ran back to a man just like her father. That's what she felt she deserved. I want to suceed," Michael said softly, "but if doing so robs you of who you are, I'm no better than my he is."

Thinking about his father suddenly made Michael anxious. He didn't want to keep talking. Leaving Laura would be easier than explaining how his mission had helped him understand that everyone had gifts, including himself, but that he was still fearful that someday he'd become controlling like his father.

"I want to succeed," Michael said softly, "but if doing so strips you of what you want, I'm no better than my father."

Finally, he told her that if he forced her to live in a certain house, he would be manipulating her like his father had him. He couldn't do that. Love wasn't enough. They had to have common goals. His goal was to save enough money to start a business. He didn't blame her for not having that goal. Laura listened. They talked. The sun was gone. The night was chilly. Laura listened. She asked questions. She tried to understand.

"I'm cold," Laura finally said, hoping he would hold her. He didn't. He said he'd leave.

"Michael?" Laura asked. "It's not over with us?"

"If I forced you to live anywhere, I'd be as bad as my father. If you don't want to try every available situation, I won't be able to relate to your mind-set of deserving more."

"Can't we go to a neutral location, start over?"

"I've thought about that, but our attitudes would still be the same."

"Can we pray?"

He smiled into the dark. "That's what Connor recommends."

"You told him about . . . ?"

"No. When he's rational, prayer is always Connor's answer. He's right. Lately though, I haven't been getting through."

There was no touch in their good-bye.

* * *

Laura called her dad, and he flew to Provo. She met him at the airport with a suitcase. "I just want to go home." The first day with her parents she was silent.

"Are we choosing dresses or not?" Laura's mom finally asked the second morning. Laura had fasted the day before. She picked at eggs she was hungry for, but felt nauseated eating.

"Maybe. I don't know."

"You guys broke up? You plan on telling us?"

"Do you think I'm spoiled?" Her parents looked at one another. "You do, don't you? Michael does too."

"Don't worry about him," Lance said. "Go back, find someone like Reed to marry."

Mandy looked in surprise at her husband. They knew Reed was spoiled. The two of them had discussed it several times when Laura was assuring them that he was perfect. Laura, however, knew what her father was telling her. Everything she hated about Reed was her.

Later that afternoon, Laura asked if they could all go to the refuge. She hadn't been there in a long time. The air was still when they arrived. Laura wandered toward the river's edge. Large sucker fish rose to the surface as Laura threw bits of crackers. The water churned with their frantic efforts to grab the morsels from one another.

"I wonder what happened to that little girl," Laura said.

"You grew up," Lance said.

"No. Remember the girl with the mean mom? I wanted to take her home. I wonder where she is now. I wonder what she's like."

"She probably grew up to be just like her mother," Mandy suggested. "That's all she knew."

"Maybe she didn't," Laura said, defending the grown image of a little girl. "Maybe she got away."

There was a long silence as a cloud covered the sun. The breeze felt chilly. Preferring to find out if there was to be a wedding or not, Mandy tried to dismiss the long-forgotten girl. "She might have run away. She would have ended up on the street. Probably earning a living in an incredibly demeaning fashion."

"Or she got a good job, found a place to live, and is going to school to become an architect." Laura's voice was angry. "She could have." Defiantly, she looked at her mother.

"I suppose," Mandy said warily, not wanting to anger the girl who had spent the first day home barely uttering a word. "That would take a lot of strength."

"To do what?" Laura snapped.

"To change," said the confused mother. "Most people continue to do the things they saw their role models do as they grew up."

"So that's why I act spoiled?" Laura asked, her voice calmer now.

Her mother could say nothing. Her surprise now turned to shock. Lance watched the fish and smiled.

"I don't think it means I have to be spoiled forever. Isn't that the whole gospel message, to repent and change?" Laura rose and started back to the car. Her parents followed. "However," she said over her shoulder, "I think I'll quit being spoiled right after you and Dad buy me a wedding dress. Something simple, straight lines. How about the place over in Vancouver? They have lots of dresses. We could go tomorrow."

* * *

"I trust you to change from how you were raised. I expect you to trust me, too." That's what Laura told Michael over the phone that night. "You take those child-development and family-relations classes to help you be a better family guy. What am I going to do to be unspoiled? I'll live over the swimming lizards. Tell Seth I'll kill him if I ever find a camera in my bathroom."

Michael was in love. He wanted to believe her, so he did. Laura was excited about free rent. They'd budget. She'd find work. Things would be wonderful. They set a date. They planned the wedding. Finally, Michael said they had to hang up. This was an expensive phone bill for an unspoiled girl.

"I bought a wedding dress, and I chose a tuxedo for you," Laura told Michael the next night. "You'll look gorgeous. It's got a dark purple cummerbund. We'll have flowers the same color. They're going to ship the tux to a Salt Lake branch. When I come back, we'll go let you try it on."

He didn't want a tuxedo. He didn't want to get dressed up and parade around. She didn't understand. "So I shouldn't wear a wedding dress?"

"No," he said. "A wedding dress is appropriate attire."

"So's a tuxedo."

"So's a suit. I could buy a new suit for what it will cost to rent this tuxedo."

"We're renting six."

"Six?"

"Yours, Connor's, Connor's dad's, my dad's, and both my brothers'."

"Let's not," Michael begged.

"So what do you want? We go to city hall in our jeans, get hitched, eat supper at Burger King, honeymoon in a tent up Provo Canyon?"

He tried to explain. "I don't mind feeding my friends at an open house. I just don't want to show off for them."

"Isn't a wedding dress showing off?"

"Well, I want to see you in a wedding dress." His voice was soft. She forgave him a lot right then.

"I want to see you in a tuxedo."

"So we'll go to Salt Lake, try it on. You can see me, then I'll buy a new suit."

Laura didn't agree. Michael went to bed late and stared into the darkness. *Okay*, he decided, *I'll wear a tuxedo with a purple cummerbund if that's what she wants.* He didn't, though. When he called Laura the next night, she'd changed her mind. To be more precise, her father had changed her way of thinking.

"He doesn't want a tuxedo," Laura had complained to her parents at breakfast. "He said for the same amount of money he could buy a new suit."

"I like that boy better all the time," Lance said as he buttered a piece of toast.

Laura stopped, juice midway to her lips. What a pleasant idea that her father and Michael would be friends.

"You just don't want to wear a tuxedo," Mandy said to her husband.

Lance stood preparing to leave. "That night at the hospital, I thought that boy looked good in church clothes. There are a lot of church meetings in his future. He'll be needing a good dark suit."

"Can I help you pick out your new suit?" Laura asked her fiancé that evening.

He smiled into the phone. "I love you."

Another three days and Laura was coming back. Michael was glad. Every plane reminded him she'd be flying in.

A wedding in the Portland Temple, an open house in Vancouver, an open house in the Steele home, and more gifts than their house could hold. A three-day vacation at a condo on the beach, compliments of his new in-laws. In that last few weeks, Michael felt he had more joy than his soul could hold.

He'd sent an announcement and a long letter to Stephanie. She'd written her congratulations and told them to come visit.

CHAPTER 19

Laura's dream was so vivid, she was glad to wake up. Two hours later, she dozed off just as Michael rolled over and turned off the alarm. She heard him singing in the shower and shaving before coming back to wake her. This morning he rubbed her back and pushed the hair from her forehead. "Honey? You got a job interview today?"

"Yeah, at eight o'clock sharp. I'm going to get up," she said stretching and settling more comfortably in the covers. As he leaned over to kiss her, she looked up. "Um . . . never mind. Have a good day."

He was in a hurry. "Okay." He kissed her again. "Bye."

She heard him leave. He ran down the porch stairs. The footsteps turned around, and she heard him run back.

"Laura, you okay?"

"I had a dream about Ryan. He was riding around and around Las Vegas in this car seat that was too small for him. He was staring at me out the window. Do you think he's okay?"

Michael didn't think he was. "I hope so. Laura, you don't need to go to that interview. Stop worrying about getting a job. You haven't really taken much of a break since your surgery. Why don't you just keep freelancing for a while?"

"Michael, that was almost eight months ago. I'm okay."

"You really have been great, you know."

Laura knew she had. She liked not having to pay rent. She liked seeing how much of Michael's paycheck she could save. With a money manager program on the computer, she had made a pie chart of their expenditures. Her goal was to earn enough money freelancing to pay for all the food.

"It makes my job easier," she told Michael one night, "if you eat two meals at the Oasis House." She added a few more figures and then suggested that she would start coming in for lunch.

Still, she was proud of the money she made. She worked for a kid's singing group called Musical Express that wanted a website and fliers. A family movie theater that played only G-rated films wanted a newsletter. A retired businessman selling wooden ducks he'd carved wanted to be linked to other carving sites. A student sidelining in windshield repair wanted fliers. Two horticulture majors installing drip systems in small gardens wanted websites and fliers.

When she found out how much money Michael had in savings she was astonished. "We really might be able to start a business when you graduate," she'd said in awe.

"Maybe." Her husband had nodded. "You can thank Brother Steele. He paid for my mission."

Michael was still eyeing her with concern. He could feel her dissatisfaction. "We can move," he tentatively said.

"No." She sat up, then hesitated. "You were right. This is working out well. I just hate it when . . ." She paused and looked up.

Michael waited.

"It bugs me when Stephanie calls." Now that she'd said it, Laura continued speaking quickly. "I've been thinking a lot about having kids. Maybe because there are so many in our ward. It drives me crazy what Stephanie says about Ryan. I asked a mother in Relief Society how old her son was. The kid was a month younger than Ryan. He crawls all over the place. He's really annoying. Comes over and drools on my feet. But when I talked to Stephanie on the phone the other night, she said Ryan has only rolled over a couple times."

Michael lowered himself to the bed and absently rubbed her arm.

"I can't stand thinking of how they're treating Ryan," Laura began.

They talked for a while until Michael had to leave.

"Maybe I'll call Stephanie today," Laura finished.

"What are you going to tell her?"

Laura pushed him off the bed and stood up. "I don't know. Tell her to let the poor kid out of his car seat." She kissed him on the neck. "Go to work."

Michael opened the door and then turned as she headed to the bathroom. "Take a nap," he suggested.

Instead of Laura placing a phone call to her sister-in-law, it was Stephanie who called later that afternoon.

"Dad had a heart attack," Stephanie said. Her voice was detached. "He wants to see Michael."

"Is he okay?" Laura asked, trying to remember which classes Michael had that day.

"I don't know." Stephanie's voice was lifeless. "He's not dead."

Laura agreed to have Michael call as soon as he came home. "How's Ryan?" Laura asked as Stephanie prepared to hang up.

"He's hungry right now," Stephanie complained, "and I'm cooking by myself tonight. There's no one to cover for Dad. Tell Michael even if he doesn't want to see Dad, Mom could use some support."

* * *

Michael's face was neutral as Laura repeated her conversation with Stephanie. He held the phone a long time before dialing the restaurant. They would just be cleaning up from the supper crowd.

"I wasn't there," Stephanie told Michael. "I finished the day's deliveries. When I came back, Stewart was in there. Dad had called him."

"Have you been to the hospital to see him?"

"Yeah. First thing he said was that I was supposed to call you."

"Why?"

"Maybe we need you."

Michael didn't know what to say. "He's not going to die, is he?"

"He might. Apparently he's not a good candidate for surgery."

"He won't die. He's too stubborn," Michael said. "How are you doing? How's Ryan?"

"We're fine," she said automatically. "You promised to come see Mom."

"I will."

"Come now. Bring Laura. Please? You could at least see Dad. He's mellowed some. Don't you Mormons believe in deathbed repentance?"

Michael laughed. "I'm certainly going to try it for sins I've got at the end."

After he hung up, he discussed the situation with his wife. Laura wanted to go. She was certain her dad could get them plane tickets so Michael wouldn't have to miss too many classes. "Family can fly for Dad's price. It'll be cheaper than driving," Laura explained. Arnie would cover for a few days at the Oasis House, she pointed out, and wasn't Connor stable right now and helping out? Yes. Everything was under control. Everything but Michael's emotions.

* * *

Rubbing his burning eyes, Michael looked out over the plane's wing. The horizon was edged with gold from a rising sun. His uncertainty about seeing his dad had made him forget the beauty in which he'd be descending.

Utah's mountains were rugged and massive. These wide spaces were old and familiar. Laura sat silently. Michael hadn't spoken either. He had listened to the engine and wondered why he was going back. He knew, though. He wanted to make certain he wasn't his father. He wanted to encourage Stephanie to leave again. Ryan deserved better. Should he have brought Laura? How would she feel about his dad? The plane landed too soon. His legs protested the cramped position. His emotions weren't ready to move.

"You look good," Michael told Stephanie as they met in the airport lobby. He meant it. She was well dressed. Her hair was shorter, crisp, and clean. The man with her was slender. His hair was long and dark. The tank top revealed an upper-arm tattoo. Michael didn't stare. There was no welcome in the man's eyes. On his hip was a nine-month-old Ryan. The little boy's eyes were dark brown and sober. He watched closely as Michael softly touched one of his hands. They were plump now.

"He's adorable," Laura caressed one smooth cheek. "You are so cute," she murmured. "I fed you when you were only two days old." The little boy made no response.

Stephanie introduced Carl to her brother and Laura. They all said how glad they were to finally meet. Michael knew the man wasn't glad. Quickly, the group found their way to the black Ford Expedition.

"You like our new rig?" Carl asked. "Just got her from the lot last week."

"Very nice," Michael said overenthusiastically, and he wondered how someone who made change at a casino could afford such a car.

Laura was obviously thinking the same thing as she climbed in the backseat and ran her hand over the leather interior.

"He'll have to sit between you," Carl said as he dumped Ryan into the backseat.

"Don't you have a car seat?" Michael was irritated.

"Yes," Stephanie answered, quickly glancing at Carl. "It's in the shop's delivery truck. I take him with me in the mornings and make all Dad's runs."

"She does the work of two at that shop," Carl said as he climbed into the driver's seat. He started the engine and waited for Laura and Michael to settle on either side of the baby. "Make sure that kid sits still."

Stephanie sat rigid in the front seat. Her eyes were unresponsive. His sister's actions were familiar to Michael. Carl's tone was even more familiar. Feeling sick, Michael glanced at Laura, who had already started talking softly to Ryan.

"We'll drop your luggage off at our apartment," Carl said, "and then take you over to see your dad."

"No, that's okay," Michael started to protest. "We planned on getting a hotel."

"No, it's fine," Carl said.

"We don't want to be a bother," Laura said, glancing at her husband.

Michael felt like he was spinning. He vaguely recognized his surroundings, noticed changes—improvements in some areas, continued deterioration in other places. Laura quietly played peekaboo with a totally unresponsive Ryan.

They drove to Stephanie and Carl's place. The two-story apartments had the living room and kitchen on one floor with a long stairway leading to bedrooms on the upper floor. The lawns were well kept. Eight separate complexes surrounded a grassy quad.

"We're going to get a bigger place someday," Carl said, leading them to the living room. "But for now this is home."

Carl watched as Michael examined the furnishings. A soft, brown leather couch and a matching love seat faced a big-screen TV. Brass lamps sat on glass end tables. Double doors led out to a covered patio.

"Very nice," Michael said as he watched Laura carry Ryan into the kitchen and ask Stephanie if the little boy needed food.

"I'll show you your room," Carl said. "We can take your luggage up."

The upstairs was just as well furnished. Both bedrooms had king-sized beds. A walk-in closet and private bath denoted which was the master suite.

"Where's Ryan's crib?" Michael asked, looking around.

"We decided he didn't need one," Carl said. "Stephanie usually just puts him on that bed. But tonight he can sleep in his carrier."

"Don't you worry that he'll roll off?" Michael asked, looking at the high bed.

"No, he's okay. He doesn't move around much." Impatiently, Carl dismissed Ryan as an uninteresting topic of conversation. "This thing with your dad has been hard on Stephanie."

"His heart attack?"

"Yeah. I had just convinced her to get a different job, and now he'll use this to keep her there. Did you know he's got at least a dozen new customers out on the Strip? It takes her nearly four hours to make deliveries. She starts at about six in the morning. When she gets back to the restaurant, your dad leaves and your mom and Stephanie serve the lunch crowd. That needs to stop."

"Why does she do it?" Michael asked.

"Because he makes her feel guilty, and because she can keep Ryan with her while she works."

"She takes Ryan that early in the morning?"

"He just rides around with her in the truck and then stays in the office in the back of the restaurant."

Michael felt sick at the idea of little Ryan being raised in a playpen behind a closed door.

Several minutes passed before Michael realized Carl was explaining how much more Stephanie could make at a different job.

"I'm not going to put up with this much longer. Heart attack or no heart attack, Stephanie shouldn't be working for them."

"Why does she?" Michael asked.

"I don't know." Carl was angry. "She could get a job taking orders for a department store. She did that kind of stuff in Utah. Vern helped us get this apartment. He can help her get a job."

"It looks like you make enough to support you both," Michael said, looking at the bed's heavy oak headboard. "Maybe she could just stay home and take care of Ryan for a while."

"No." Carl's irritation surfaced. "I could use her help to get us established. We don't want to live in an apartment forever. Ought to have a lawn the kid can run around in."

"He just needs space to crawl in right now." Michael spoke in friendly tones, but he had never been more insincere.

"You know, he's a cute kid and all," Carl said generously. "I think I'll really like having a son when he's older, when he can move around and take care of himself, but right now he's really dragging Stephanie down."

Michael's friendly tone had an edge. "He'll never be able to move around if he's always in a car seat."

"My point exactly," Carl applauded Michael. "She needs to get another job. I'm telling you, and you can tell her dear daddy and mommy, that I'm not going to tolerate this arrangement much longer. I don't care if the old man is sick. He can hire someone besides Stephanie."

When the two men returned to the kitchen, Laura was holding Ryan on her lap and spooning yogurt into his mouth.

"I never have time to feed him anything but a bottle," Stephanie said. "Sometimes Mom feeds him stuff while he's at the restaurant."

"He likes it," Laura said as Ryan used his tongue to try to suck the yogurt off the spoon.

Michael wanted to cry for Stephanie and for Ryan, but instead he asked, "How's Dad now?"

"They let him go home," Stephanie said, still watching as Laura reached for a napkin to wipe both herself and the child. "We should probably go see him."

"He's home?" Michael felt nauseated. He'd expected to see his father in a sterile hospital setting. That was why he'd hurried to come. Certainly he didn't want to take Laura out to that house, but Stephanie called home and told her mother that Michael had arrived and that they'd be over as soon as Ryan fell asleep.

"What did she say?" Michael asked his sister.

"That your father will be expecting you," Stephanie imitated their mother's emotionless voice.

Unexpectedly Carl became charismatic. "This might be a strain on all of us going over there," he said kindly. "Let's go out to supper afterward. Something to cheer us all up." He gently took Laura's purse from her hand and set it next to the couch. "You won't need that. I'll treat."

Michael suddenly offered Laura as a babysitter for Ryan. Maybe this way, he figured, he could avoid having her meet his dad. But Stephanie countered that the next-door neighbor was willing to watch Ryan so that Laura could meet her in-laws.

"I'd like to meet your parents," Laura said, irritated that Michael hadn't consulted her. "But we can take Ryan."

"Leave him here. Remember the car seat's in the delivery van. He's better off here," Carl mandated and started for the parking lot, placing a call on his cell phone as he walked. "Hey Vern, we're leaving."

Laura waited as Stephanie took Ryan and his carrier to the neighbor's. "We won't be long," Stephanie said, placing Ryan next to the woman's chair. The older woman nodded, barely taking her eyes from a talk show that featured parents finding children after years of separation. A heavy woman in stretch pants was apologizing to a bearded son for not being there when he needed her.

"You don't want your father to meet me?" Laura asked Michael as Carl drove two miles across town.

"I'm not sure I want you to meet my father," Michael admitted, finally smiling at her. She didn't smile back.

Except for an old Bronco parked out front, the house looked deserted. The boardwalk hadn't kept back the wild vegetation. The small plot of grass that Michael had once mowed was overrun by weeds.

The four hesitated at the door. Carl leaned around Stephanie and impatiently knocked.

"It's open." The voice was weak, but it was still Michael's father's.

On this warm, sunny day, Joseph sat in gloom. The curtains were drawn. Dim light came from the kitchen. His father lay in an old recliner. The man looked sick. His thin legs stretched out under an old cotton blanket. His shirt was unbuttoned to reveal gray hair on a sunken chest. His arms seemed bony, his hair thinner, but the smile was the same, enchanting and seemingly earnest. Laura saw Michael's smile in his father's. Michael saw hypocrisy. No one hugged. Even after Shannon came from the kitchen carrying a coffee mug and an uncertain expression, no one hugged.

"Introduce me to your beautiful wife," Joseph commanded his son. "I certainly see why you stay in Utah. She is a fine specimen."

His son cringed.

For a long while Laura listened to double-edged conversation. Some of the talk was about Joseph's health being better than "that old man you guys call a prophet. I'm younger than him." Some of the conversation was about how lucky he was that Stephanie had come back to help him.

"Couldn't count on my son," was the last bit of the conversation she heard before Laura finally turned and escaped under the pretense of getting to know her mother-in-law. On her way out, she saw Shannon hunched on what looked like a kitchen chair placed near the doorway. Michael's mother didn't seem to be following the conversation.

CHAPTER 20

There was sunshine, and weird-shaped bugs crawled up the tree, bugs Laura had never seen before. A hot breeze came from a direction that blew her dark hair irritatingly into her eyes. Some kids were playing hide-and-seek. All five of the young players would run and hide behind the same tree. The smallest boy could barely talk. He continued to yell, "Wait!" as he chased the others from tree to tree. Once the group was hidden, the youngest would suddenly feel compassion for the left-out seeker. Completely unaware of the game's objective, he'd jump from behind the tree and wave to the other child. "Come on," he'd yell. "Come on."

Laura knew Michael was there before he spoke.

"We used to walk past this park every day. The schools are a few blocks that way." Laura turned to see where he motioned. "The restaurant is farther that way."

"You never came through here?"

"Sometimes to use the restrooms."

The littlest hide-and-seek player had just lost his friends. He was standing in a clearing, bewilderment etched into his young face. He'd looked behind all the trees and the restrooms. He'd called, "Wait. Where are you?" and no one had answered. He then knew he'd been betrayed, abandoned. Desolation replaced his bewilderment. The three-year-old scanned the park one last time, checked once again for his companions, then slumped in the middle of the grassy opening, buried his head between dirty tennis shoes, and cried. Laura cried with him. Michael reached to comfort her and then dropped his hand. His mixed-up family had caused her grief.

"Why go clear around over there? Why not take the short route through the park?" Laura asked. She knew the answer. Why had it been so bad for him? Why hadn't he told her?

"We avoided places other kids might be hanging out." Her husband's voice was bland and emotionless.

"Why didn't you tell me?"

"I told you we were poor. I told you my father was abusive."

"No, you didn't. You didn't tell me you were that poor. You didn't tell me you had no friends. You didn't tell me your mom was so scared. You didn't tell me he was abusive like . . . like that."

The little boy had stopped crying and had crawled over to a tree where he huddled close to its trunk. The roots swelling from the ground enveloped him. His companions had reappeared, chasing each other through the evergreens. He watched them listlessly. They ignored him.

"Shouldn't someone be watching those kids?" Laura asked angrily.

"It's a poor neighborhood."

"Poor people can't be nice to their kids?"

"Sometimes it's not a priority."

"Well, it's not exactly a priority for Carl and Stephanie, and they don't appear poor," Laura's voice rose slightly. "He works in a casino. Exactly what does he do? I'm thinking he's got a business on the side that he doesn't pay taxes for."

"I don't know, hon." Light filtered through green leaves. Michael's face was bathed in warmth. So often that face had been warm, peaceful, kind. So often it had been stoic or expressionless. Laura had never seen today's look—exhausted and sad, bewildered and lonely. There was no smile.

"You smile just like him."

"Who?" Michael asked.

"Your dad."

Michael smiled then, a tired smile. "We smile for different reasons," he said.

"Not always," Laura said. "Sometimes you smile to get what you want."

"When?"

"At work. You're always nice to people even when they irritate you."

"Isn't that a good thing?"

"Only if your motivation isn't to manipulate them so you have enough power to eventually hurt them. That's the power your dad has. He's charming, but he only turns the charm on to manipulate."

Michael nodded, looking over Laura's shoulder. He saw that the little boy had sat down against another tree.

"That's what you worried about doing to me when I didn't want to move into Seth's house."

For a long moment the newlyweds watched each other. Laura turned first and watched the park.

"That's what's going to happen to Ryan," she said, nodding to where the little boy had laid his head against the rough trunk of a tree. He was crying softly. Laura quietly approached his still form. She bent to ask him where his home was. Startled, he sat up and scrambled backward around the tree.

"Are you lost?" Laura asked again softly.

"Leave my brother alone!" A lanky eight-year-old girl bounded toward Laura, followed by a motley gang. "Leave my brother alone."

"I thought he was by himself," Laura tried to defend herself against the onslaught.

Unceremoniously the youngest child was yanked into the group. As they all marched toward the street, Laura could hear a lecture about "stranger danger." That somehow relieved her, and they began walking back.

Stephanie and Carl were waiting at the car. No one spoke on the drive to the apartment. When the group walked into the neighbor's apartment, Ryan was banging one foot against his too-small carrier. He stopped when he saw them. The neighbor lady was snoozing softly in her chair. Michael picked up the carrier and they all walked back to Carl and Stephanie's apartment.

Carl never mentioned the earlier promise of treating them to a meal. That night they ate frozen pizza. When Carl turned on the large TV, Michael got up and took Ryan out of his carrier.

"Doesn't he ever cry?" Laura asked Stephanie as they watched Michael lay him on the carpet.

"He used to, but Carl said you have to ignore it or they get spoiled."

Michael spoke softly to the little boy. "Want to learn to crawl? You think that would be fun?"

Ryan rocked up on his stomach and then kicked. Michael tried to lift him to his knees by balancing one knee under the infant's round stomach and then reaching for the other knee. The first positioned leg would slide out straight behind the newly diapered behind. "Maybe not quite yet," Michael said as Carl ignored them and watched a reality-show rerun.

The next morning, Carl slept until nine thirty and then left with his colleague, Vern, for an important meeting. Stephanie had been gone since five. She had explained the night before that she was going to help set up for breakfast. Sticky-bun deliveries had been cancelled for the time being, but she felt she should go in to help Shannon with the morning crowd. No, she didn't need Michael's help, she said. They had a new cook coming in. She'd need to train him. Mom would be in to wait tables.

Laura had asked if she could please borrow Carl's car and take Ryan shopping at the mall. She would love to have a chance to buy him some things Stephanie hadn't had time to get. Laura was cheerful as she made the suggestion. No one but Michael noticed her eyes were still swollen from her cry in the park and subsequent tears she'd shed later that night.

Without discussing how much they could afford to spend, Laura first picked an expensive car seat and plunked it into the cart right behind where Ryan was sitting.

"He shouldn't be riding around in that huge SUV without a car seat. He doesn't even crawl," Laura hissed. "Stephanie says that Carl will be glad when Ryan's more independent. How's the poor little guy going to learn to do anything?" She held a bright-red T-shirt up in front of Ryan. "Oh, you'll look beautiful in that," her voiced cooed and then turned angry again. "If someone locked you up in a car seat and then a carrier and then a playpen, how would you learn to crawl? Are they stupid?" She looked at her husband, who had been unusually quiet since returning from his parents'.

"They're not stupid," he said, and rubbed the little boy's head.

They bought clothes, shoes, small spoons, and spill-proof juice cups. The bill was over two hundred dollars. They bought apple juice and taught Ryan how to drink from one of the new cups. Riding on one of Michael's hips, the little boy savored this new taste.

The young couple wandered aimlessly through the colorful corridors of the mall.

They passed a high-priced store where leather goods were bolted to the racks. Michael paused and looked at the jackets. He remembered Rand's hamsters running free in a mall someplace in Utah. The storeowner, an uptight man in leather pants, was approaching them. He quickly appraised the two young adults. He took special note of Laura's BYU T-shirt. His eyebrows rose slightly as he observed the sticky juice droplets that Ryan kept dripping onto Michael's shoulder. Michael looked at the man's leather vest. Cow horns were stitched across the front. "May I help you?" the shopkeeper intoned condescendingly.

"Do you have any problems with rodents?" Michael asked. "Have you seen any hamsters?"

He's gone crazy, Laura thought frantically.

"No," the man in the leather said, glancing around for security.

"No rodents, huh?" Michael said, his smile insincere. "Well, if you do find any you might want to spread some fruit around or a few sunflower seeds in the corners. Keep any loose hamsters from chewing on the merchandise. Good luck."

He's lost it, thought Laura as she followed him through the mall. *He'll become a client now at Oasis House.* The couple walked past several stores before Michael stopped and stared unseeingly at a gun display.

"There are a lot of hypocrites around," Michael finally said. "Selling animal skins, then using an organization that fights for animal rights when it's convenient. And I'm the biggest hypocrite of all. I taught love for two years. I believe in forgiveness and compassion, but I'm still angry at my dad. I hate him for making Stephanie feel she has to come back. And now I'm starting to hate Carl for being like my dad."

Laura still didn't understand the animal-rights reference, but she knew he wasn't crazy.

"Stephanie went back, just like a freed animal to its cage," Michael said. "She was scared of freedom."

Ryan appeared sleepy as they loaded packages into Carl's Expedition. Michael set him on the backseat, and the little boy immediately dropped his cup.

"Carl won't like juice on his carpet," Laura commented as she reached under the front seat where the plastic container had rolled. Her voice dropped to a horrified whisper. "Michael, it's a gun." Gingerly she slid the shiny pistol out from under the driver's seat and let it lie on the car floor. Neither of them spoke for a long moment. "Do you think Stephanie knows?" Laura finally asked.

"I think I'll ask her," Michael said, retrieving the cup and sliding the gun back into its hiding place.

* * *

In the early afternoon, the only customers inside the small diner were drinking coffee. Michael spoke to his mom as she scrubbed the grill. Laura was impressed with the organized although run-down feel of the small restaurant. She listened to the mother and son talk about business and suppliers and customers long gone, and customers that still occupied booths for hours each day.

Stephanie came over with a bottle for Ryan. He reached for the food before settling comfortably back into Laura's arms.

"He likes you," Stephanie said.

"He remembers me from when he was first born, don't you, big boy?"

While Michael and Stephanie unloaded freight, Laura visited with her mother-in-law. The older woman was charming, almost relaxed, as she told Laura about how as a young kid Michael had planted flowers out front. Laura told her mother-in-law about Michael's landscape designs, the flowers and shrubs he'd installed. She made the job sound like Michael had a regular business and the workers were not Oasis House clients. The mother stopped her supper-prep work to listen intently.

"Is that what he's always done in Provo?"

Laura told about him training people to cook.

"People like him, huh?" Shannon said.

"A lot."

"They always liked his dad, too."

Laura stiffened. "He's not like his dad," she said too abruptly.

For a long time Shannon thought about her son. "They are different," she conceded. "Michael only smiled when he wanted to. His dad smiles when he wants something."

The restaurant was ready for the night crowd when Michael and Stephanie returned to the dining room.

"We've got to go, Mom," Michael said, "but I want both you and Stephanie to know you can come stay with Laura and me anytime. We're living in a house right now and we have two extra rooms."

"I can't leave your dad," Shannon said softly. "Especially not now."

"I know, but the offer always stands." Michael put an arm around his mother and turned slightly to face Stephanie. "If you ever feel you're not safe or Ryan isn't safe, I'll come get you. I can drive down and pick you up in less than six hours."

"If you can get here that fast, you must have bought a new car," Stephanie tried to joke.

"He can drive mine," Laura said, holding Ryan and trying not to cry.

"You wouldn't care?" Stephanie asked Laura. "You guys are still honeymooners."

"No," Laura said, picturing the small handgun on the black carpet.

"Then take him with you," Stephanie said without moving and without ceremony. "He needs to be with you."

"What would Carl say?" Michael asked.

"It was his idea. Last night he said that Ryan might be better somewhere else for a while, at least until Dad's back to work." Stephanie was decisive. "I didn't think you'd want him, but until he's older he'd probably be safer with you." Stephanie's harsh exterior began to crack. For a moment, Michael really saw her—scared, uncertain, brashly questioning the missionaries. "He can't even crawl," she finished. "Keep him until things settle down." She started to cry. "He . . . he likes you."

"We'll take care of him," Michael said.

Stephanie went to the office and got a ripped diaper bag. She filled bottles with milk and quickly stuffed them into the bag.

"Give Grandma a hug," Stephanie told the little boy, directing him at Shannon. She touched him tenderly on the cheek, turned quickly, and brushed one tear from her own cheek. "Let's go. You'll want to check in early with a kid."

They loaded suitcases in the back of the SUV. At the airport Stephanie pulled up to the unloading area and said she needed to get back and help her mother.

"Bye," she said softly as Laura lifted Ryan out and Michael gathered the luggage. "He likes you," she said again and then drove off. The dark vehicle was immediately lost in airport traffic.

* * *

"Michael, what have we done?" Laura said as they checked in at the airport counter.

"He's being neglected, Laura. We couldn't leave him there."

"Maybe we should have called an agency that deals with protecting children."

"She wasn't going to take him to an agency. He's better off with us than some foster parents."

"Did you tell her about the gun?" Laura asked as they found their gate.

"She knew." Michael moved to a chair in the waiting area and sat down. He placed Ryan on his lap so they faced each other. "Carl told her he needed it so he could protect her."

As he spoke they got their seat assignments and were told that Ryan would have to remain in one of their laps. Minutes later they heard the call to board.

"Where's he going to sleep?" Laura asked once they were settled. "Who's going to care for him while I'm working? Michael, think. He isn't a puppy."

"Hi, big guy," Michael said, avoiding Laura's question. "You're going to like staying with us." Solemn eyes studied Michael. Soon the flight personnel told passengers it was time to take off.

Ryan never moved during the short flight. He reached greedily for a bottle when they got to their house. After feeding the little boy and building him a makeshift bed on the floor, Laura was even more disturbed. "Michael, I can't take care of a baby full-time."

"If you don't want to, we'll call social services." Michael held his breath. He didn't want Ryan to leave.

"No, that would be wrong. He knows us. We're his family. But honey, I'm scared. I can't care for a baby. I'm not exactly qualified to even babysit a kid," Laura said, thinking of her past experiences with children.

"You did great when he was a newborn."

A short time later, Ryan watched them from his pile of pillows on the floor. He kicked slowly at a blanket and watched it move. He giggled faintly and then rubbed one tired eye with the back of his chubby hand. Michael picked up the boy and sat in an easychair. Almost instinctively the little hand clasped onto Michael's thumb, pulling the arm closer around. The large eyes studied Michael for another minute and then sagged quietly in sleep. From the table Laura looked up from a brochure she was proofing and watched the two. *He's not like his father,* she thought suddenly.

Hours later she said, "Michael, do you think Stephanie can ever learn to care for him?" Ryan was asleep, and the new caregivers had just gone to bed.

"I don't know."

"What if she doesn't?"

"I don't know." Michael put an arm lazily along her waist and kissed her randomly at the top of her head. "Love you, good night."

For several minutes Laura considered pushing his arm away, ensuring that he woke up and listened to her. She wanted to make certain that Michael knew the problems. Unless she got help, Stephanie wasn't going to change. Carl didn't think he needed help. They couldn't just take someone else's child. She liked Ryan. She wished that social services had some parenting classes for Stephanie. Laura thought for a long time before falling asleep.

Two days later the couple bought a bag of toys and spread them around the living room and encouraged Ryan to come to them. Laura's freelance work slowed down. She found no new jobs; instead she and Ryan became frequent visitors at the Oasis House.

"I guess it is a good thing we have free rent," Laura said one night as she watched Michael teach Ryan to drink from a glass. "Now that I'm not working as much, we wouldn't be saving any money at all if we weren't living here."

Ryan grinned as Michael tilted the cup and poured water into his mouth. Next the water ran down his chin. "His brain's improving," Michael said. "That's as important as saving money."

Laura agreed. She felt a deep sense of pride in Ryan's improvements. He smiled more. He was vocalizing more.

"Time to crawl," Laura told Ryan one morning as the two lay on the newly vacuumed carpet. Laura pulled Ryan's little knees into a kneeling position. Confused, the ten-month-old looked at the floor four inches below. He rocked on his knees and smiled to himself. With a burst of energy and experimentation, he pushed off with his knees. His body lunged forward, and his nose plowed into the carpet.

For a while, Ryan lay facedown on the floor. He whimpered twice and then seemed to be contemplating what he'd done wrong. Slowly he dragged one knee into a crawling position, and then the other. His little diapered end stuck up in the air as he thought. Slowly he rose up on both hands. This time he lifted a hand and looked at it. Laura could see his concentration. The small hand waved out in front of his little face, and then he placed it carefully in front of him. Just as studiously he raised the other hand, examined it, and placed it out in front of him. He was spread awkwardly. Slowly he slid a lone knee forward, and then the other. *Ryan just crawled,* Laura thought. Fascinated, she watched as Ryan lifted a small hand high in the air and then deliberately placed it in front of him. This time he only moved one hand before sliding a knee and falling forward, pinning his right arm under himself. Stunned that his attempt hadn't been as successful, Ryan lay for a moment, then flipped to his back, caught sight of Laura watching him, and began to kick and laugh.

"You're cute," Laura said, spontaneously scooping the boy up and hugging him tightly. "I love you," she whispered quietly as ache and foreboding seeped through her chest.

Two weeks later the couple bought a used crib.

"There," Michael said after assembling the wooden sides. "Your own bed." He positioned the slightly ripped mattress, and Laura spread out sheets with yellow bears printed on one side.

"Here you go," Michael said, lifting Ryan and placing him in the middle. "You'll like this."

He didn't. Trained not to cry, the small child uttered no sound, but sat in the middle of the crib careful not to touch the barred sides. Tears rolled down his cheeks as he fearfully examined his surroundings. He reached for Michael, his scared eyes pleading to be taken out.

They dismantled the crib that same night. The boy contentedly fell asleep on the small mattress stuck into a corner of his room.

A few weeks later, Ryan slept late. Laura used the time to clean and look through some of the weddings gifts that were stacked neatly in the spare bedroom. There were Pyrex bowls and large bath towels. In one box there were two glass goblets and a bottle of sparkling cider. The attached note suggested the couple use them to celebrate their six-month anniversary. Laura shook her head. They'd just gotten Ryan on their six-month anniversary. The day had slipped by without either of them noticing.

Ryan woke and she fed him. She washed his face and then lowered him to the newly vacuumed floor. "I'll find you something to play with," Laura told him. A stuffed animal got a lukewarm reception from the little boy, a ball escaped under the couch, and blocks were thrown randomly around the room. After that he spent several minutes examining a new broom. He lifted one end and watched in fascination how the other end moved. The bristles were also intriguing. He rubbed them slowly with one finger, then patted at the edge with an open palm. He leaned over with baby flexibility and placed his cheek along the dusty edge. Shaking her head at his choice of plaything, Laura sat down at the computer and concentrated on proofing a brochure for a model train display.

Ryan was so quiet she'd forgotten about him by the time she wandered into the kitchen for a drink. "What are you doing?" Laura was suddenly angry. Her new dish towels, matching wedding-gift sets, were spread across the linoleum. "Stop it. Do you have to make a mess?" Just that morning, she'd carefully folded these wedding gifts and arranged them in a drawer. A blue plaid set was now draped over the little boy's head. A mauve washcloth was clutched in a small hand.

Ryan never looked up at Laura. Seemingly in slow motion, he scooted to his bedroom and climbed on his mattress where he clutched a worn blanket. Something happened inside Laura then. She saw a bruised little girl called stupid and yanked into the car. She saw a dark-haired boy turn from his mother, withdraw from his father, learn to ignore taunts and rejections. She saw Ryan and knew the adult pain he would face.

"I'm sorry," she told the immobile child, guilty tears running down her cheeks. He turned from her as she approached. "I'm sorry," she said again softly. Laura picked up the dishcloths and stuffed them in a drawer. For many weeks they would remind her of Ryan's retreat.

When Michael arrived home that evening, Laura and Ryan were sitting together on the couch watching a rerun of *Home Improvement*. The little boy was gumming a graham cracker. Using one of her new wedding dishcloths, Laura was frequently wiping wet, brown crumbs from the toddler's clenched fists and chin. They both looked up as the door opened. Michael studied the two for a moment, then smiled, a face-transforming smile.

CHAPTER 21

Experienced as he was at ignoring others' opinions, Michael hardly even noticed the variety of viewpoints concerning the addition of Ryan to their newlywed life. Laura, however, knew everyone's bias and avoided those who openly disapproved. That required dodging her visiting teachers, three clients, the Relief Society president, and a thirty-year-old single student who said Laura was too young and hadn't been married long enough to be raising a child. The bishop, a retired auto dealer and grandfather, felt they were earning a heavenly reward.

Ruth, ever vigilant with regard to Michael, was concerned the child would compel the already overly mature boy to an earlier middle age. Arnie disagreed, suggesting this was the Lord's way for Michael to learn the compassion and love that had been absent from his own home.

"You quote scripture and LDS doctrine every time it's convenient for you," Ruth snarled mildly.

Gail, Laura felt certain, approved of this arrangement. For all her brashness, Gail had enjoyed Ryan as an infant and was obviously glad that he was now receiving good care. Gail had watched Ryan several times when the couple had needed a babysitter. If Gail was at the Oasis House and Laura came with Ryan, Gail was always the first to take him, find him something to eat, buy him a toy from the second-hand store, and then play with him in the backyard or in the front hall. Connor was a little ill at ease with the child, scared to pick him up or talk too loudly in his presence, but he often brought toy cars and offered them to Ryan with a little lesson on colors. "This is blue," Connor would say. "The last car I gave you was red."

Ryan nodded gravely as he reached for the car Connor offered.

"He's really smart," Connor said.

Laura agreed. Every day he became more mobile, and she encouraged his explorations. She would put a cracker at one end of the couch and stand Ryan on the floor at the other end. Keeping his hands flat on the cushions, Ryan would walk along the couch until he got the food.

When he heard Laura go into the laundry room, he'd sprint on all fours to follow her. Carefully he'd pull himself up against the washer. With pudgy hands pressed against the white sides for support, he'd lean his head against the vibrating machine and solemnly contemplate the sound. Often, Laura heard him hum the washer noise to himself.

Their second Christmas together, Michael and Laura decided not to travel. They bought a tall tree and hauled it across the porch, placing it in front of the window. They carefully decorated it with glass bulbs, but Ryan broke the first bulb before the last one was put on. Gradually they moved all the ornaments to the top half of the tree and decided that top-heavy decorating had a beauty all its own. Laura's mother had sent the glass balls after lamenting that she wouldn't see her daughter.

"Your dad's doing some holiday shuttles," she had told Laura over the phone. "He says he doesn't like being completely retired. We'd come if we could. You're certainly welcome to come here." Laura had thought about it, but instinctively knew that her mother would resent sharing Christmas with Ryan.

Santa Claus brought a train set and a Hot Wheels racetrack. Michael played with them while Ryan jabbed at the Styrofoam packaging, and Laura took a nap.

They ate Christmas supper at the Oasis House where clients had left more presents for Ryan than for Michael. In the evening they drove to the Steeles' home, and Ryan watched closely as Dane's oldest son ran a remote-control car into the furniture.

On New Year's Eve, Gail announced she was keeping Ryan with her. She was spending the night with Autumn and her family and wanted Ryan to come. The young couple left their little boy, danced on campus, kissed at midnight, and ate breakfast at 12:30 A.M. Ryan was asleep when they stopped at the snug brick home. He was happily lying next to Autumn in a double bed. The pair left him and spent their first night alone in ten months.

* * *

The day Joseph stepped back into the restaurant was the day Stephanie went to work in a clothing store. Carl had insisted that Vern knew someone who would give her a job and that this would be better than working for her father.

Other than telling her to make her own decisions, Michael didn't know what to tell Stephanie about her job change. He hated Carl dictating what Stephanie should do, but he also hated to see Stephanie still working for their father. "You have a right to decide where you'll work," Michael told her. But after the awkward silence they talked only about their mother.

"She's lonelier than ever," Stephanie told Michael on the phone that night. "Dad's hired a couple of waitresses and two cooks. He enjoys being the boss. Mom doesn't have to work so much, but she doesn't know what else to do."

From then on, Michael called his mother at least once a week. He told her about Ryan and about his classes. She waited for his calls.

Carl seldom asked about Ryan. "We may need him someday," Carl had said five months after Ryan had left. Stephanie hadn't understood what Carl was talking about. A few months later she still was unsure what part Ryan could play in their "cost-sharing" venture, but she knew why Carl and Vern had chosen her job. She knew what they did with the numbers Carl got out of purses and wallets he stole at the casino. She knew why they wanted her to write down social security numbers and names when people applied for credit cards.

Carl had been thrilled when she'd first started working as a saleswoman at the clothing store. He had been even happier when he found out that women often tried on clothes and left their purses unattended.

"I don't even need the cards," Carl explained to her over and over again. "Just hurry and copy down the information. I'll make you a form so you know what information we need. You don't think *I* paid for all this," he said, motioning to the new patio furniture. "These, my darling, are compliments of Jamie Lowry, also known as Jamie Lawson. I got her wallet out of her coat pocket when she went to cash in her chips. Isn't it a great system?"

Stephanie didn't feel great. She'd written down some of those numbers, convinced that after a few more dollars, a few more pieces of furniture, and one more new car, Carl would be satisfied. He wasn't. After a time it seemed he never would be. For Carl, the game was an addiction.

* * *

Winter had waved a vague farewell as spring peeked into the bleak March weekend. Several visitors had congregated at the Steele home. Brother Steele was watching twenty-two-month-old Ryan line small race cars along the leather sofa. Brother and Sister Steele put aside anything they were doing when Connor or his friends arrived. Connor had started to pace back and forth.

Brother Steele looked at Michael. "Everything okay with my son?"

Michael shrugged. "I thought so. He seemed fine this afternoon."

Gail overheard. "He doesn't like my shorts."

I don't much like them myself, Laura thought, admiring the petite girl, her well-formed athletic legs sticking out from under a winter coat and frayed Levi shorts. Laura spoke kindly. "Why wouldn't he like your shorts?"

"Thinks I'm relapsing when I wear them," she answered loudly.

"It's the only time you wear them," Connor said from the kitchen. "It concerns me."

"Well, it concerns me when you watch too many movies."

"Are you watching movies?" Sister Steele asked.

"No, I don't need a med change. My counselor says I'm doing fine. Gail needs to check with a counselor."

"Michael needs the counselor," Gail said suddenly, with force. Michael looked interested. "You're playing house with that kid," she said. "When the mother comes back, what are you going to do?"

"We . . . I don't know."

His answer made her more upset. "How can you play with him and love him and get him to love you and then just hand him back over to her? The poor kid. How can you do that? If you weren't going to be committed to him, you shouldn't have taken him." Gail was nearly yelling.

Michael and Laura looked at one another. "We'll always be in his life. Even if he goes back, we'll visit," Laura retorted, feeling a surge of defensiveness. Gail should respect and appreciate the sacrifice it had been to quit work and take care of Ryan. "Stephanie couldn't take care of him right now. She needed us to help her."

"Don't compare yourself to Autumn's parents," Gail said nastily. "*They* thought about my little girl's future. They made me come visit Autumn, insisted on it. They kept me in her life so she'd be bonded to me in case I did take her back. They showed true love. You're just playing."

Ryan had run to Michael at Gail's first sign of anger. He buried his head in fear of the raised voices.

"If he goes back to her, he'll be going to a complete stranger. Do something to protect that kid. If you don't want him permanently, you have no right to let him sit in some limbo where he'll probably just end up hurt."

"Carl has refused to consider adoption," Laura said.

"We haven't talked to him in a long time," Michael said. He'd worried about this issue too.

"Then do," Gail demanded.

"I don't know," Laura said uncertainly. "There could be a lot of complications."

"All responsibilities come with complications. You find happiness in the responsibilities God gives you. You'll miss out on the happiness if you're scared of the complications," Gail said pointedly to Laura.

"What do you mean?"

"Maybe Ryan is your responsibility. Did you ever think of that?" Gail asked.

"No, I just, I just . . ." She looked pleadingly at Michael. How could she explain that she loved Ryan and she couldn't imagine him leaving, but that she also couldn't imagine raising him as a teenager?

"You know what Alice said when she adopted my baby?" Gail's voice was even deeper than usual. "They had her sealed. I went and waited outside the temple." For a long time Gail was silent. Everyone waited.

"She was pretty. Alice hugged her. Keith was all in white. Autumn was in white. Alice said that the Lord gave them Autumn to raise and that parenting meant helping an individual through whatever problems that person has. She hopes Autumn doesn't get sick. Statistically she only has a one in ten chance of becoming bipolar like me, but Alice said if she does, then they will deal with it. Alice said she knows that Autumn found her way into their home because of God's will. And she says she finds great happiness in this knowledge, so she's willing to take the responsibilities associated with Autumn. Maybe Ryan is your responsibility. And if he is, you have to be like Alice and love what's given you.

"And now, I think I am relapsing. I don't think these meds are working again, and so I'm going home tonight to see my mom. Because even when I hated her and even when I didn't know she was trying to help, she was loving me and doing her best. That's what moms are for. And I wish she didn't have to help me." Gail started to sob.

Michael waited for Connor to comfort her, but Connor didn't; he stood behind the couch and cried too. Michael moved to Gail and hugged her.

Laura gathered Ryan up and blinked tears back into her burning eyes. She thought two things: she wished Gail's mother didn't have to be burdened tonight, and she was incredibly proud of Michael.

Later that night, Gail's mother welcomed her daughter home. "It'll be okay," she said wearily, tired not only because she'd been asleep but also tired with the anticipation of what might be ahead. Connor promised to visit soon. "Not if you're watching John Wayne," Gail snapped.

CHAPTER 22

"How long has he been running a fever?" the emergency-room intake nurse asked when Laura showed up at nearly midnight.

"I don't know, a couple of days."

The nurse regarded her with unveiled contempt. "Has the fever been this high for the last couple days?"

"About 103 or 104, I think." Laura was too exhausted to understand the woman's scorn.

"And you just barely decided to bring him in? Who is your son's regular doctor?"

"I don't know. He's not . . . He doesn't have a regular doctor."

"Does he have any allergies?"

"I don't think so. He eats everything."

"Allergies to medications. Has he ever had any reactions while on medications?"

"I don't know."

The nurse looked up with near anger.

Finally Laura explained, "He's not my son. I'm just caring for him."

The woman, now filling out forms, was more kind. "You have authorization to give him medical attention?" she asked.

"Yes," Laura lied.

"Does he have insurance?"

"I'll write a check."

"Most people don't have that much in their bank account." The nurse was trying to be considerate now. "The state can help the mother pay some of these bills."

"I'll tell her," Laura said tiredly.

"Well," the medical professional said, suddenly practical, "right now let's get the little guy some help and worry about everything else later."

Laura was sent to wait with Ryan on the black padded chairs. A TV was showing reruns on Nickelodeon. Laura shifted her legs uncomfortably. They ached dully along the calf muscles. *It's fatigue,* she thought. Ryan's weight had caused one arm to go completely numb. Her other hand stroked his hot face. The long lashes rose wearily, and she could see listless eyes staring up at her. "You're okay, little man," Laura said softly. "We're getting you some help." An ambulance rolled up to the emergency entrance, and four attendants rushed out to assist. Laura knew she was selfish when she wished the emergency patient would leave so that someone would come to help her and Ryan.

The nurses who x-rayed the small child were kind and gentle. They commented on his long eyelashes and his weak smile. They noticed that he didn't cry when they sat him on a small seat and raised his arms to pin them over his head with a chest wrap to x-ray his lungs. Laura didn't explain that Ryan never cried. She didn't explain that she wasn't his mother. She didn't explain why she was there without her husband.

The doctor verified that Ryan had rapid-onset pneumonia and ordered a series of shots. Laura waited until almost 2:00 A.M. before the shots were administered, one in each leg. Finally she wrapped Ryan up and left.

At home she put Ryan on Michael's side of the bed and then, removing only her shoes, crawled in with him. With one hand on his forehead to monitor the fever, they both fell asleep.

"I wrote a check," Laura told Michael when he returned from a weekend campout with some clients from the Oasis House. "They wanted to know if I had permission to get him medical assistance. I lied, Michael. I said yes."

"It's okay," Michael reassured her. "It's okay."

"Michael." Laura was almost panicky. "What if something else happens? We can't keep paying. Do you know how much that cost?" She began to pace the room. Each time she passed Ryan's room, she looked in at his sleeping form. "We need to get him on our insurance. But does he have to legally be our son?"

"I don't know." Michael almost began to feel the same helpless anxiety that Laura was demonstrating.

"Let's adopt him now." When she said the words, a change came into the room. Both of them felt it, and Laura started to cry. "I think we're supposed to." A month earlier when Gail had demanded they take action, Laura had resisted. Tonight the feeling was different.

"He should be our son," Michael said, surprised at the feeling of warmth that had just washed over him.

They talked for a long time. "I'll tell Gail next times she comes," Laura said. "She'll be happy." Gail had stopped by several times in the last few weeks to play with Ryan, ignoring Laura.

"How's she doing?" Michael asked. "She hasn't been by Oasis."

"She seems broken. Twice her mom's called to make sure she was here and hadn't wandered somewhere."

Michael shook his head sadly. Then he looked into Ryan's room and smiled. The young couple stood at the door to the child's bedroom and decided to ask Brother Steele's help in finding an adoption attorney. Fear and excitement prevented either of them from sitting down.

"Maybe Carl won't let us." Laura had finally said what they were both fearing.

"We'll pray about it." Michael picked the boy up and put him in bed between him and his wife. Ryan squirmed to get comfortable, turned at an angle, took up more than his share of the bed, and then slept deeply.

"How was your campout?" Laura asked.

"Everyone was stable," Michael remarked. "It was pretty relaxing. People were in bed by nine. I did a lot of thinking about my dad."

Michael was quiet for so long that Laura was almost asleep before she shook herself awake and asked, "And you decided what?"

Michael put an arm across Ryan and rubbed his wife's forehead. "I didn't decide anything about Dad. I don't know how many of his actions he's accountable for, or if he's been misled all his life. I don't know if he sees reality or if he has a mental problem. I don't know any of that, but for the first time I could think about it."

Michael paused and they both listened to Ryan's breathing. "For the first time in my life, I could think about my father and not feel hate. I've never been able to think about him because of the loathing

I had for his actions. But last night I thought about Dad, and the bitterness was gone."

"That's good," Laura said, not sure she still didn't have feelings of disgust for her father-in-law.

"It took a lot of energy to hate him," Michael said.

* * *

After work the next afternoon, Stephanie didn't drive straight to the apartment. She wondered who financed the car she was driving. Weeks ago she'd figured out that the "cost-sharing" the men were doing and expected her to be a part of was not as simple as the money Michael had taken from the till. *You're so stupid,* she had told herself over and over.

Stephanie continued to drive east, winding higher away from the Strip. The Mormon temple rose above her. For a long moment she stared at it until someone behind her honked, insinuating that she'd sat too long after the light had turned green.

"Sealed to one another as a family forever. That's what they do in temples," she reminded herself softly. Stephanie had remembered that from the devotional talks. Ann, from the adoption agency, had explained the same things about Mormons when Stephanie had chosen a Mormon family. The family's life history had mentioned their desire to be sealed.

"Members of The Church of Jesus Christ of Latter-day Saints have a strong belief in life after death and that families are still a unit in the eternities. These sealings also provide a unity and blessing here on earth," Ann had explained. "Blessings to help families be closer and stronger."

"They believe that?" Stephanie remembered asking.

"They do," Ann had said.

Turning into a subdivision a few blocks from the temple, Stephanie gazed at it. A peace ran through her, the same relaxation that she'd felt watching BYU devotionals while pregnant with Ryan. "Sealed as a family." Stephanie had wanted that for her baby. She'd wanted her little son to be loved eternally by someone who wanted him eternally.

She reflected on Michael's call that morning. "We need to talk," he'd begun.

"Is Ryan okay?"

"He's fine, but he was sick," Michael had told her.

"He's sick?" Stephanie asked, alarmed.

"No. He's fine now," Michael reassured her. Then he explained to her about Ryan's hospital visit and no insurance and wanting to make certain they could always care for him. He told her about bonding and how they'd all learned to love each other and how they wanted to make this arrangement permanent. They'd like her permission. They wanted her to sign a form releasing custody to them.

Her brother loved her son, of that Stephanie was certain. That was the only thing she was certain of. That's what she wanted for her son, a father who would love him. "I'll sign a release," Stephanie said abruptly.

Michael slowly released the air that had been trapped in his chest. "Will Carl?"

"I'll talk to him. I'll make him," Stephanie said. "Laura told me Ryan was running."

"A lot. He bounces up the sidewalk. He refuses to hold our hands going upstairs."

"Does Laura want to . . . does she really want this too?" Stephanie couldn't say *adoption.* It sounded so final.

"Yes."

Stephanie had said she needed to leave for work. Michael was sure she was hiding tears. "Thank you," he had said softly.

Above her the temple shimmered. How could she convince Carl to give the little boy a chance? Carl liked to control things. He wouldn't want Ryan's placement out of his control. Stephanie pictured Michael picking up the child for the first time. She pictured Michael's excitement when he'd told her that Ryan could crawl. "He's really smart," Michael had told her. Carl should have been the proud father.

Why did I come back to him? Why did I ever contact him? Help me! Stephanie prayed to the serenity that seemed to surround the temple. *What can I do now?*

A screen door slammed shut. Stephanie's head jerked toward the sound. Directly to the right of where her car was parked, a sidewalk led to a white brick home where a small boy stood on the top step. The outside lights bathed his slight figure in the gathering heat of evening. The boy waved a friendly one-handed greeting when he saw Stephanie. His other hand clutched the stick of a red Popsicle. Melting juice was oozing down his tanned fist. A similar shade of red outlined his lips.

Does your father love you? Stephanie asked him silently. Sliding from the stick, a chunk of melting Popsicle dropped on the second step. The boy watched the red stain spread on the concrete. "Dad," he yelled cheerfully, using his sticky hand to open the front door. " Can I have a yellow one now?"

Discouraged, Stephanie looked again at the lighted spires. Carl wouldn't tolerate sticky door handles.

Together forever, that's what the Mormon Church preached. *Even if Ryan comes back,* Stephanie thought, tears sneaking out from unblinking eyes, *we're going to be caught and then they'll take him.* Carl was getting so careless. Vern and Carl constantly told each other how smart they were, and they were beginning to believe each other, but Stephanie could see that eventually—probably sooner than later—they would all be caught. She knew that if she went and got Ryan now, his time with them would be limited. They wouldn't have him forever. Forever was an impossibility. Having him just for now was even improbable. Tears slid slowly down Stephanie's cheeks. There was only one way to get Carl to approve this adoption.

* * *

The distance between deciding to adopt and accomplishing the deed was too long, too tedious, and too complicated, Laura decided. The attorney that Brother Steele had suggested they go to told them that they were required by law to have a home study even if it were an adoption "among kin."

Laura was looking at the list of requirements she had picked up from social services. "You still need to write an autobiography," Laura told Michael.

"Haven't you written one?" Michael asked, watching the computer print out his assignment for a night class.

"I have. You haven't."

"Do we both have to?"

"Only if you want to be the father."

"Oh, joy," Michael said. "That'll be great reading."

"We need to go be fingerprinted, and we have to have 'a declaration that applicants are not cohabiting in a relationship that is not a legal marriage and in compliance with Section 78-30-9(3)(a and b).'"

"What does that mean?" Michael asked.

"I think we need a marriage license."

"Didn't we get one of those once?" Michael shoved the newly printed sheets into a backpack.

"We need to verify our health and financial status."

"Is that all?"

"No."

"I'll look at the list when I get home. I've got to go." He kissed Laura and turned to Ryan, who had suddenly sprung into action. The child jumped from his play spot on the floor and darted to the coat closet. "Wait, Daddy, wait." The boy was frantically digging around the bottom of the closet for his shoes. He grabbed them and tried to simultaneously jam them on the wrong feet. "Wait. Don't go."

Laura looked at Michael and cheered. "Definitely age-appropriate behavior. He is *not* delayed," Laura said as she bent to help the boy with his shoes. "You can't go with Michael, but we'll go to the store."

"He really is pretty smart," Laura told Michael later that night as they climbed into bed. "We're working on colors right now, you know."

In detail Laura told Michael how the little boy had padded into her room that morning.

"Time a get up," Ryan had said, patting a cold hand on her cheeks. "Time a get up." His voice had been soft. She could feel his breath as he'd leaned over to peer into her face. Without opening her eyes, Laura had begged Ryan to go back to bed.

"Please, let me sleep."

"Night-night gone." Ryan's voice was serious. He looked out the large windows at the sun. "Night-night gone."

Laura had smiled and squinted at him. Ryan's face crinkled in excitement, and he did a happy dance when he saw she was awake. "Time a eat pancakes," he said happily. "Time a eat red pancakes."

Laura had grinned at the "red."

She'd been putting food coloring in the batter, trying to teach Ryan his colors. He didn't know his colors yet, but she knew he paid more attention when the pancakes were red.

"Okay," she'd said, throwing back the covers. "We'll make red pancakes."

"Yessss!" said Ryan, clinching one small fist, a gesture he had learned from Michael. "Red pancakes. Yesss."

"No one will be able to call him delayed," Laura concluded.

"I'm glad," Michael said, rearranging his pillow and reaching an arm over Laura. "For his sake, I hope he can keep up with the rest of the kids. But if he can't, I'd still love him the same and help him more."

"He's not delayed," Laura stated firmly.

"He could have disabilities that won't show up until he's been in school for a while," Michael cautioned.

"God wouldn't do that to me," Laura said, only half joking.

"He might." Michael was serious. "Would it matter to you?"

"I don't think we have to worry about that," Laura said. "I read to him every day. I take him to new places. He knows all those little kids' songs. We're working on the alphabet. He's going to be way smart."

"And if he's not?" Michael cautioned.

"He will be." Laura yawned. "Good night."

Michael hoped Laura was right. For Laura's sake.

CHAPTER 23

"You're going to adopt him?" Laura's mother was sitting at the kitchen table as pale sunset streamed through the window, bathing Laura and Ryan.

Mandy watched her daughter spoon peaches directly onto the high-chair tray. Laura cut the peach sections into smaller pieces and then handed the little boy a fork. He jabbed industriously at the fruit, finally spearing a piece. He awkwardly angled the fork to meet his mouth and then chewed quietly. Unsuccessful in his next couple of attempts to connect fork with peach, he reached with a hand and scooped up a piece to eat. The peaches disappeared sometimes via the fork, sometimes through a grubby fist.

Lance got a dishcloth and wiped Ryan's face. The little boy turned slightly to watch Laura. "It's okay, honey," Laura reassured him. "He's one of the good guys." She turned to her dad. "Give him a banana. Cut it up some," she suggested.

"I'm your new grandpa," Lance said, cutting the banana into circles.

"You're really going to do it?" the reluctant grandmother asked again. Laura's parents had flown in an hour earlier. They'd come just to see Ryan. Michael had run to class after picking them up from the airport.

"Mom, don't you think we should?" Laura asked.

"I'm concerned about you. Have you thought through the problems this may cause? Wouldn't he be confused that his aunt is his real mother?" She paused. These were the questions she hadn't dared ask when her son-in-law was there. Something about how his answers were so definite made arguing with him impossible.

"We'll seal him to us and he'll be ours," Laura answered. It was what Michael would have said.

Mandy persisted. "Are you sure you'll love him as much as you do your other kids?"

"That's stupid, Mom." But she had wondered, wondered a lot.

"Carrying a baby is the ultimate form of giving," said her mother. "That's when you really start caring."

"That's crazy," Lance said, slightly perturbed. "That means that because you carried them, you love the kids more than I do. Come on, buddy," Lance said, lifting Ryan out of the highchair. "You'll be no problem for me to love."

Laura gave him a grateful smile. She moved closer and murmured to the boy while working his hands through the sleeves of his T-shirt. She pulled the shirt over his head. "This is your new grandpa. You'll love him. He'll teach you to fly." Laura handed the boy to her father. Adeptly she reached into a lower cabinet for a spray bottle and sprayed pretreatment on the little shirt before throwing it into a laundry basket.

Mandy had to admit her daughter was efficient. *She's developed strengths I never knew she had,* the older woman thought.

When Michael arrived home from class, Laura left a content Ryan playing with his new grandfather while she warmed a bowl of potato soup for her husband. He ate as she rehearsed the conversation she'd had with her mother. "I think she wonders if she'll ever feel like he's one of her grandkids."

Michael didn't spout platitudes about how Mandy would eventually learn to love Ryan. Michael knew people sometimes didn't. "Do you feel like he's meant to be our son?" Michael asked.

"That night I did, when you came home from camping. I felt like the Lord was telling us Ryan was to be our son. Maybe I felt that way because I wanted to."

"Maybe," Michael agreed. "If he's supposed to live with us, we'll get him, and," Michael quoted Gail, "'we'll take whatever complications and happiness come with him.'"

* * *

After introducing herself as a state-certified social worker, Kathy MacKenzie entered the spotless living room and looked around carefully. She sniffed twice and then looked again.

Michael welcomed her. Laura told Ryan to say hi. The social worker ignored them and sniffed one more time. She walked to the kitchen and peered at the freshly scrubbed sink. She sniffed again.

Laura knew what the social worker was smelling and mentally berated herself for not burning a candle to cover the distinct fragrance Seth always produced when he cleaned out an old newt tank. Early that morning their downstairs neighbor had hauled Plexiglas out on the back lawn and sprayed it with a hose. It was out there now drying in the sun.

"Would you like to see the bedrooms?" Michael asked, ignoring the strange breathing pattern of their guest.

"Certainly," she said, slightly perplexed that the obviously clean house smelled like brine shrimp. Ryan lifted his arms for Michael to carry him, and they trooped around the small house.

"Our bathroom," Laura said unnecessarily as Kathy examined the shower curtain for mold.

Laura exchanged looks with Michael as they followed their inspector to Ryan's bedroom. The mattress was neatly made up in one corner. A small plastic table they had bought at a garage sale was in the other corner. A box of large blocks and a bookcase were under the window.

"Does he always sleep on the floor?" the woman asked, looking over her reading glasses.

Interrupting each other, Michael and Laura explained about Ryan's distaste for cribs.

"He's old enough for a small bed," Kathy said.

"We'll get him a bed," Michael said quickly.

Kathy led the way back to the kitchen and sat down at the table. She pushed aside the plastic tablecloth and brushed a hand quickly over the wooden tabletop. Convinced there were no crumbs, she flipped open a brown folder.

"I certainly admire you for your kind heart and your willingness to share your life with those that are the most needy," she began in a singsong fashion that indicated she had started hundreds of interviews with the same words.

"We would be the fortunate ones to have Ryan live in our home," Laura said.

Michael smiled at her and adjusted Ryan more comfortably on the chair beside them.

"Well, I'm not sure you're aware of the problems you would face with this boy," Kathy started.

"He's with us now," Michael said. "We're doing fine."

"Yes, you think that now, but he's not very old. As he gets older, there will be many situations and adjustments that haven't presented themselves. As indicated by your file, you are actually the uncle."

"Yes."

"And the boy lived with both his parents for several months, is that correct?"

"Yes."

"You are, as of this time, not the boy's legal guardian?"

"No."

"You do understand that a situation such as this ofttimes results in placing yourself in unforeseen predicaments for which there is seldom a positive resolution. What if the child were to have health issues or become physically needy? Insurance for an adopted child is mandatory."

Michael explained that his work provided insurance.

Kathy waved aside his explanation. She flipped through the folder another time. "Financial statements, health verifications, criminal background," she muttered. "Except for the behavioral assessment that I am obligated to compile, your file is fundamentally complete. In my assessment I will indicate that the picture window in your living room was installed before the present standards which requires safety glass in all windows less than twelve inches off the ground. I would also have to indicate that there appear to be unsafe articles strewn around the backyard. Additionally, this house is on a fairly busy street and is not adequately fenced to protect a child."

"Lots of kids are being raised on this street in homes built about the same time," Laura reasoned.

Michael put a hand on her arm.

Kathy continued. "Also in my assessment I would have to indicate that you've been married less than two years. We do not promote adoption for couples who have only just recently established a partnership."

"This is a special case," Michael suggested.

"I am aware of the peculiarities of this situation and will note such in my recommendations, but first, I want to be assured that this child is available for adoption."

"I talked to my sister," Michael said, bewildered. "She wants Ryan to have a permanent home."

"Stephanie couldn't care for him, and Carl didn't want him around," Laura said.

"I think those are rash statements," Kathy addressed Laura. "This little boy's mother may not have the skills to parent him now, but she could be taught appropriate ways to assume her role as mother. We can encourage her to take some parenting classes."

"Parenting classes?" Laura scoffed, even though at one time that had been her own solution.

"They have helped many people," commented Kathy.

"Ma'am, Stephanie wants us to take her baby." Michael leaned slightly forward. He forced one hand to relax on Ryan's knee. "Why are we talking about Stephanie taking parenting classes? We've been taking care of Ryan for over a year. Can't you just help us get the legal requirements completed for adoption?"

"But I think all of that is premature until we get written consent from both the mother and father."

"Do they both have to sign?" Laura asked.

"In the state of Utah, a biological father of a child born out of wedlock does not have to consent to adoption unless he has established a right to consent."

"What does that mean in English?" Laura asked, irritated.

"It means that since the baby lived with him, the father has probably established a right to consent. Before I continue my assessment, I would like assurance that this father will consent."

"I'll call Stephanie again tonight," Michael said.

Kathy said she was glad to meet them and would send them a brochure of classes that might help them more fully understand the emotional struggles faced within the adoption situation.

As they walked with her to the front porch, Kathy sniffed one last time. "Is it not remarkable how specific wind currents result in a lake odor this far removed from the source?"

Laura and Michael looked at each other casually and agreed.

CHAPTER 24

"No," Stephanie said.

"What do you mean, no?" Carl asked.

"I'm not going to change jobs."

Stephanie's determination surprised Carl, impressed him slightly, but irritated him a lot more. "And why not?" His voice was louder now.

Vern and Carl were suggesting she get a part-time job cleaning hotel rooms.

"People leave all sorts of information in their suitcases," Carl said. "Don't they, Vern?"

"I'm not doing it," Stephanie said again. "It would eventually get traced back to me."

"No, it wouldn't," Vern kept telling her, and he explained carefully all the precautions he would use to ensure her safety.

"We're careful," Carl bragged. "We hold the identities for a while so the first date of our using it won't appear for several months. Then often it's years before anyone knows they have helped to finance our needs. Works the best if we set up the new identity several states away. No one sends the bills to the real person; they send them to the fake address we set up."

"I'm not changing jobs," Stephanie insisted.

"Get a load of you," Carl sneered. "Buy you a few new clothes and see that your hair gets styled and you suddenly think you're hot stuff."

"Stop now," Stephanie begged. "You have enough. You guys are going to get caught."

"If we get caught, so do you," Carl said cruelly.

Stephanie got up and walked to the bedroom. She thought about leaving. Leaving would solve the problem of dealing with Michael and Carl when the inevitable confrontation occurred over Ryan's future. She could just disappear. She could go get Ryan. He was her son. Then the two of them could disappear. Of course, there was no place to go. Even her dad no longer needed her. Stephanie felt too miserable to cry.

"I'm sorry," Carl said almost sincerely when he opened the bedroom door a few minutes later. Stephanie could see Vern hesitate as he let himself out the apartment door. "Really, I'm sorry, honey," Carl said louder this time. "We need you, and I love you. You can't leave. We don't have to make any decisions about changing jobs right now. We'll talk. You and I can work anything out. What can I do to prove I'm just trying to make you happy?"

"You can sign papers so that Michael and Laura can adopt Ryan." Stephanie raised her chin a little defiantly. The small gesture made her feel stronger than she had since living in Utah.

Carl scowled. "When he's older I think we'll want him back."

"I've talked to Michael. They have all the paperwork done to adopt him. We need to sign consent forms."

"Didn't you hear me?" Carl said. "I think I want him back."

Stephanie forced herself to stay calm as she told him that she didn't want her son to come back. "I talked to Michael again last night. They're working with a woman name Kathy MacKenzie. I have her phone number." Stephanie pulled a pad off the bedside stand and pointed to the name and number. "I told Michael we would both sign consent forms. We're supposed to call this phone number, and they'll tell us what to do."

Carl's laugh was scornful. "Are you stupid? I'm not signing some consent form. Why would you ever tell your brother I would?"

With slightly shaky hands, Stephanie held the pad out to him. "This is the best thing for Ryan. What you and Vern are doing is illegal. You could go to jail. What would Ryan do then? Let him have a home. Let him have a normal family."

"You'll go to jail when I do," Carl sneered.

"If you don't sign," Stephanie took a big breath before continuing, "I'll tell the police what you've been doing."

Nothing had prepared Carl for Stephanie's threat. Several seconds passed before he responded. He called Stephanie names. He threatened her. He assured her that she'd rot in a cell before he did.

Finally, he reached over and grabbed the pad with the phone number. "You know," he said, "I think it's about time we taught your good brother a lesson."

* * *

Laura drove quickly to the Oasis House and burst into the kitchen. Michael was layering lasagna noodles into a pan while two clients opened cans of sauce.

"There's no money." Her voice fell slightly short of a scream. "I checked our account to pay the attorney. There's no money. Our account closed two days ago." Laura started to sob.

Ruth came from the lunchroom. Arnie came from the stockroom. The crying had sounded like a client in breakdown. "Where's Ryan?" Michael asked.

"In the car. I didn't want to upset him."

Michael looked at Ruth who quietly left to get the boy.

The husband asked questions. He stayed calm. He comforted his wife.

Ruth returned with Ryan, who ran to Michael with an unopened sucker he'd gotten from the bank.

"See," he said.

"I see," Michael said, a lump forming in his throat.

The little family of three went back to the bank where they waited for nearly two hours to talk to the right person. Ryan fell asleep still holding his green sucker. The bank official explained that gaining access to this type of account required an assortment of data. He listed the information needed and asked what source could possibly have contained such details.

"Have you had any break-ins at your home where someone could have gotten personal information?"

"I don't think so," Michael said.

The men questioned them about their credit card. He asked how much the credit limit was on their card. They told him that the balance was zero.

"No," he told them after punching some keys on the computer. "You owe more than ten thousand dollars." The man scanned the papers on his desk. "There's not much I can do right now. The Federal Trade Commission is responsible for receiving and processing complaints from people who believe they may be victims of identity theft. They can provide you information."

Michael transferred Ryan to Laura's arms and then wrote down the information given him. Ryan woke up and slid off Laura's lap. He tugged hard on Michael's hand. He was tired of offices. He was hungry. Laura hadn't played with him at all.

In stunned silence they wandered out of the bank and drove home.

"What now?" Michael muttered as they parked in front of their house. Kathy MacKenzie was on their porch sniffing the air.

"Still smells a little like the lake," she said by way of greeting.

"I can't smell anything," Laura said irritably.

"It's faint," Kathy said, kindly bending over to shake Ryan's hand. "How you doing little guy?"

"I wanted to come by and tell you that we have been in communication with Ryan's parents. Carl called me a couple days ago. I've been unusually detained by unforeseen emergencies. I only just now found time to come over. I didn't want to communicate this over the phone."

"What?" Laura said even more irritably.

"Carl is very grateful to you for caring for his son. Nevertheless, he feels it was a mistake that they have not come to get the boy sooner. Certainly neither he nor Stephanie has any intentions of making this placement permanent."

"What?" Laura yelled. "They were neglecting him. You can't just let him go back. Who will watch him?"

Ryan moved to hide behind Michael.

"You need to calm yourself," Kathy said. "I think you're causing undue stress on the boy. I'll let you pull yourselves together and be back in the morning to discuss Ryan's relocation. As soon as I hear from the parents, I'll let you know exactly when the exchange needs to take place."

"He's barely two years old," Laura argued. "All he will understand is strangers came and got him. He'll suffer . . . what's it called, Michael?"

"Attachment disorder." Michael reached around and picked Ryan up.

"If he's not returned, he'll suffer feelings of abandonment later." Kathy's voice continued her professional critique. "I am sorry, but you prolonged this episode when you didn't acknowledge the need for rehabilitation. Trained personnel could have interceded and gotten aid for the mother." Laura was so angry that she couldn't respond, so Kathy finally left with an apologetic shrug.

* * *

"We've got to go to Utah," Carl told Vern that evening. "Apparently the good folks that are caring for my son have run into some financial difficulties."

"Well, I'll be," Vern said. "That's a pity. A nice young couple like that."

"You took money from them," Stephanie said incredulously. "From my own brother?"

"Didn't take a dime from them," Carl said.

"Did take a couple numbers out of Laura's purse one day," Vern bragged. "The woman was carrying a social security card, bank card, credit card, her bank statement, and a statement from their credit union. We even happened to know Michael's mother's maiden name. We professionals like that kind of information." Vern did an awkward little jig across the carpet.

"You did take their money," Stephanie said.

"No, I sold a bit of information to an esteemed colleague in Minnesota. There's no way they'll ever trace Michael's problems to me."

"Why them?" she asked, tears burning her eyes red. "They've loved him, cared for him. They're good . . ." Stephanie lost her voice and her vigor. She pictured the young couple, Ryan with them. She saw Ryan with a Popsicle waving to cars outside a real house. "If you ruin Michael and Laura, I'll make certain you don't get Ryan."

"He's my son," Carl said.

"Give him a family," Stephanie whispered.

The men ignored her. They discussed how much safer it was to sell numbers rather than setting up fake accounts. Vern cautioned Carl.

"You've got to slow down, man. Pace yourself. Watch your expenditures. You don't want to leave a trail. You'll get caught."

"Easy for you to say," Carl said. "I got a family to support."

"You're not really planning on getting that boy are you?" Vern wanted to know. "Just go see him. We'll do a little business while we're there. Start a few accounts. Why complicate things with a kid?"

"He's just a little kid. He should have learned to feed himself by now. We'll find a babysitter. I think I want my kid. Play ball with him. Teach him stuff."

"More power to you," Vern sighed. "But keep him out of my way."

Carl came over and knelt by the mother of his child. "Honey," he said, softly rubbing a gentle hand up her arm. "We'll use the money for the kid. We'll move as soon as a bigger apartment is available. The kid can have his own room. You'd like that, huh?"

"His name is Ryan," Stephanie said. "Ryan."

"Okay. Ryan. He'll have a room. We'll be happy, honey. You and me and the kid."

"When are we going to go get him?" Stephanie asked.

Carl hesitated. "I told the woman I'd pick him up day after tomorrow. Vern needs to spend a couple of hours in Utah, then we'll pick the kid up."

"You don't know the town. I should go." But she didn't really want to go. She didn't want to face Michael or Laura.

"I've got an address."

"He probably doesn't remember you. He'll be scared."

"So he toughens up," Carl said with a shrug. His voice only showed some of the irritation he felt. Carl watched Stephanie, hoping she would make no more unreasonable threats. Instead she went to bed and fell asleep, making her own plans.

* * *

Carl was cheerful as he prepared to leave the next morning. "Go buy the kid some toys," he said to the silent woman as he pulled out a stack of credit cards, sorted through them, and handed her a VISA Gold.

"It's got a five-thousand-dollar credit line," he said playfully. "Will that be enough?"

Stephanie took the card without speaking. Disgusted, Carl shoved two cards into his own wallet and dropped the rest into an empty coffee can. He concealed the can on a top shelf in the kitchen.

"We'll see you tomorrow," he said. Stephanie waved, smiling weakly. Happy with that show of surrender, Carl came back, kissed her, and said they'd be a real family when he came back with the kid.

Stephanie watched from the door as Vern got in the passenger side of the new Buick and drove away. Stephanie returned to the bedroom. Methodically she packed, knowing exactly what she'd take— one suitcase, a small one. Then, a little more ill prepared, she thumbed through Carl's drawers. She pulled a file from under his pants, gathered credit card receipts from the desk, then took the credit cards from the coffee can in the kitchen. Heart pounding, she packed them in her bag and zipped it shut. Checking to make sure the two men hadn't returned, Stephanie carefully hid the suitcase in her car and then, with an oversized handbag, she walked to Vern's apartment. She tried the master key she'd taken from Carl. It didn't work. Vern didn't trust anyone, she thought wryly.

Uncertain, Stephanie stood looking at the locked door. Hesitantly she walked to the back and then looked for any witnesses. For a long time she contemplated breaking a window. She even picked up a large piece of concrete that had broken from the road. She didn't have the courage. She'd take what she had from Carl. That would have to be enough. She wasn't motivated enough to break in. Disappointed in her own lack of courage, she slowly walked to the front of the building and then across the parking lot that was already hot in the sun. Here she let the concrete rock drop and, using a different set of keys, opened her car door.

At the bus station she abandoned that car and bought a ticket to Utah with a credit card obtained with someone else's identity. With a determination only slightly diminished by her failure to get Vern's private files, Stephanie retraced her steps of two and a half years ago. And when Ann opened the door, she was surprised to see that Stephanie had returned to the adoption agency.

CHAPTER 25

"I'm just here to ease the transition," Kathy said soothingly when Laura refused her entrance. "I really do have your best interests at heart."

"I doubt they're really coming anyway," Laura said, refusing to move from in front of the door. "Please go away." Her eyes were puffy. She'd slept little. She'd started crying when the lawyer had said there was nothing he could do to stop the exchange. She'd been crying ever since.

"Given time," Bill Climbs, a family-law attorney, had said, "I can maybe prove the parents unfit. But legally, right now, you don't have much of a case. I can do my best for what's right for the kids. I've been working with family disputes for a long time, but we have to work within the law. We can see if there is anything that indicates neglect, but right now I have no documentation to disagree with the advice of the state agency."

"They are unfit," Laura had sobbed. For nearly ten minutes, Laura told why Carl couldn't be a father and how Stephanie didn't know how to be a mother as long as Carl was around.

Patiently the attorney listened. "I understand," he finally said, "but nothing has been documented and the state's number-one objective is to keep biological families together."

"That's stupid," Laura was adamant.

"What about the trauma of suddenly being taken from his home?" Michael asked.

"That's why they send a social worker. But you have to also recognize that disruptions happen to a lot of children—divorce, deaths, foster situations. When these things happen, we spend a lot of time talking about how resilient kids are. And in some ways they are. Look at him."

They all watched as Ryan pushed a red car around a carpet that was painted to depict city streets. Realizing he was being talked about, the little boy looked up and smiled. The smile faded when he saw their sober faces. He left his car and came to hug Laura's knees.

"Which social worker has your file?" the attorney had asked.

"Kathy MacKenzie." Laura unconsciously rubbed the back of her neck.

"Kathy is head of the department," Mr. Climbs said. "She's good."

"Good? She hasn't helped us at all," Laura protested.

"She cares about kids," Mr. Climbs said, "but she has to work within the laws. She didn't write the law. Her job is to place kids within the structure of a series of laws that were established for the benefit of children. Granted, most of these laws were written by people who know very little about adoption issues. Your social worker has spent considerable effort petitioning the legislature for legal changes."

"She hates us," Laura said.

"She's doing her job, which is to try and reunite children with their parents."

"We just won't be there when they come," Laura said childishly.

"Don't run," Mr. Climbs advised. "Then you become the hunted. Don't do that to yourselves or to Ryan. Let me do some background checks and see what I can find out about these parents."

"Will you come tomorrow?" Michael asked.

Bill groaned inwardly. He didn't have time. "Ten o'clock? I'll try."

They gave him their address. They left to spend a night praying, crying, and holding a confused little boy.

Now the morning was here. Kathy was here. A policeman was parked across the street. Sister Steele and Gail had come, but the lawyer hadn't.

Carl drove slowly down the street, easily finding the address. He was alone. Vern was shopping at the mall. The two made a point to be less identifiable by not being together for business. The father stopped the car and stared at the front door. A strange nervousness developed in the pit of his stomach.

For a long moment, he realized that maybe this was one possession he didn't really want. Before the thought had completely formed, he saw a form peering from the picture window. *Showtime,* Carl thought. He smiled and parked, glad Vern had suggested purchasing a stuffed teddy bear and an expensive car seat now strapped in the middle of the wide backseat.

Kathy MacKenzie watched from the porch. Sister Steele watched from the living room windows as Carl stepped unabashedly from his car. When he ascended the stairs, Laura grabbed Ryan. Michael held her and waited stoically for the knock.

He was suspiciously kind, this absent father suddenly returned. Kathy introduced herself. Carl thanked them all for taking care of the little boy. He expressed hope that the care would remain as good. He told them how Stephanie had decided to quit work in order to stay home with Ryan.

"Where is Stephanie?" Laura demanded.

"She couldn't face you. She's so embarrassed. She is, however, very impatient to see her son. She was going out to buy a crib when I left."

"He hates cribs," Laura said. "He's too big for a crib now."

"Then we'll take it back," Carl said, suddenly impatient to leave.

"You never got him one before," Laura said. "He slept in that stupid carrier."

Carl nodded understandingly. "We weren't very understanding of a baby's needs. On the phone Kathy suggested we take some classes about how to raise a kid. We plan to do that immediately. Now can I see my son? I haven't even had the chance."

Michael's jaw tightened painfully when Carl took Ryan from Laura. The father awkwardly held his son and spoke kind things to the little boy's face. Michael felt that only he recognized how the other man was acting a part for the benefit of the crowd. Only Michael knew that Carl was more sensitive to the group's reaction than he was to what the child was feeling. Suddenly detaching himself for his own protection, he watched the actions play out before him—the scenes unfolding like a choppy film reel. Ryan's actions were what registered with Laura. She watched the little boy pull back and then turn to watch Laura and Michael for their response.

"I think he's okay," Carl said.

Kathy suggested that Carl take the little guy directly to Stephanie. "He'll know his mother."

Laura kept asking Kathy if anyone would check on Ryan. Kathy kept telling her that he was with his parents now.

Laura kept saying Carl needed to stay and let Ryan get used to him. Carl said he needed to get going, that Stephanie would be expecting him. Laura insisted they not leave until Mr. Climbs came. When Carl realized who Mr. Climbs was, he became even more determined to go.

Laura sobbed as Ryan tried to go back to her. Sister Steele tried to comfort Laura. Michael tried to think. Should he call Mr. Climbs? Should he just let Ryan go? He was ready to suggest Carl sit down and they'd explain to him about Ryan's eating and sleeping habits when Gail burst in screaming. She had relapsed recently, but Michael had been assured that she was doing better. This did not look like better.

"Connor told me you were coming this morning, but you can't take him! He needs to stay!" She attacked Carl, hitting his face and yelling that he didn't really care for his son if he didn't leave him where he was. She grabbed Ryan and shoved him back into Michael's arms. Then she turned to yell at Carl, periodically hitting him in the chest. Carl fended off Gail's attack. Gail turned to talk with Ryan. "Don't let him take you, tough guy. This is your home right here. You scream and holler and let your position be known." Kathy stepped outside and motioned to the police officer, who came in and tried to subdue the girl who had started a new tirade about two kinds of fathers. Every time Carl tried to reach for Ryan, Gail swatted him off, telling Ryan to let the absent father have it. "You don't need that guy. You need the dad that cares for you."

The officer and Sister Steele tried to convince Gail to let Sister Steele take her home. Gail continued to lecture Carl and Ryan about how they didn't belong together. "I'll be back," Sister Steele told Michael as she tried to lead a screaming Gail out to the porch. Gail wrenched free, grabbed Ryan, and started down the stairs with him. Everyone followed. Ryan was terrified. Gail turned and handed him back to Michael and continued talking about who was willing to help Ryan regardless of what happened in the future. "Certainly not someone like you," she yelled at Carl.

Kathy insisted that the confusion and crying were detrimental to the child and suggested Carl remove Ryan immediately. Laura told Michael to do something. Didn't he care? Carl forcibly took Ryan and headed for the car. Ryan's eyes were desperate and deepened to confusion and pain when Carl placed him in the car seat. The boy then did something he had never done before. He screamed, "No! No! No!" His little legs churned. Kicking and panting, he fought. As Carl tried to buckle the straps over his shoulders, the boy twisted and screamed. He batted at the hands that were becoming increasingly rough.

Michael slipped into the other side of the car and sat by the terri-fied child. "It's okay," he said, soothingly running a gentle hand over the small head. "I'm right here."

Ryan stopped kicking, and Carl awkwardly finished buckling the confusing straps. He stood up, closed the door, and climbed in front. Michael stayed in the car.

"You don't know what he eats. You can't change his diapers. He'll scream all the way to Las Vegas. Leave him here until Stephanie can come and bond with him. This is too traumatic for a child."

Kathy pulled open the front passenger door and climbed into the car. "How's he doing?" she asked.

Michael answered, "He's scared. He needs more time to get used to leaving. This isn't the right way."

No one spoke for a while. Carl planned to slap the kid if he started crying again.

"Often the smoothest transitions," Kathy started a professional lecture, "are those where a familiar adult goes with the child to the strange location."

"Okay, I'll go," Michael said with no hesitation. He closed the door on his side. "Tell Laura to pack me a bag. I'll be back when Ryan feels comfortable."

"You don't need no bag," Carl growled. "Stephanie can take care of him."

"Then I'll stay with him until then," Michael said calmly.

"Good. Good," Kathy said. "This is a settlement which demon-strates that you both appreciate Ryan's concerns and are willing to set aside your own considerations. This is a sensible arrangement for Michael to help transition the boy."

There was more confusion. Gail allowed Sister Steele to lead her away. Laura finally brought a bag with a change of clothes for Michael. She brought Ryan clothes, diapers, and his old white blanket. She stuck the bundle through the window. Kathy gave professional instructions to both men sitting silently in the car. Finally she got out. She didn't like what was revealed about Carl as he sped away, barely pausing at a stop sign before screeching up the road.

"We'll make certain there are follow-up services," Kathy assured Laura.

The young woman continued to watch the spot where the car had just disappeared. A blue van turned the corner and pulled up beside the watching women.

"What the heck?" Laura said when she recognized Stephanie. "What are you doing here?" Laura moved toward the absent mother. "I thought you were out buying a crib."

"Have they already gone?" Stephanie asked.

"Why are you here?" Laura demanded.

"My name is Ann. I'm with an adoption agency. Where is the baby?"

Laura ignored her and the question; instead she addressed Stephanie for the second time. "Talk!"

"First," Ann said, "where is the baby?"

Kathy clarified what had happened.

"Michael went with them?" Stephanie asked.

"Carl," Laura said, spitting out the name, "was having trouble handling a baby by himself."

"He was alone?" Stephanie asked. Then she murmured, "Of course he is. They're less identifiable not going places together." She quoted what she'd heard them say on numerous occasions as they opened new accounts or cashed stolen checks.

"Who was supposed to be with him?" Laura asked bitterly.

Stephanie took a deep breath as she began to shake. "I'm sorry," she said. "I'm sorry for all the trouble." Then she started to cry. "I'm sorry. I wanted to get here in time to stop Carl from taking Ryan."

"As long as Carl is the father," Kathy said primly, "he has rights to his son."

"Not if he's in jail," Ann said.

"Is there reason to believe he may have committed a crime deserving incarceration?" Kathy asked doubtfully.

"There is," Stephanie said quietly.

"Maybe we shouldn't have let that child go," Kathy said.

"Ya think?" Laura asked.

* * *

Vern was eating a ham-and-cheese sandwich when Carl pulled into the mall parking lot. He raised one eye at Michael, examined the baby a little more closely, and then climbed in. "You hire a nanny?" he asked, jabbing a thumb at Michael.

"You got anything else to eat?" Carl asked, pointing to the Arby's sack. Vern handed him a foil-wrapped sandwich. "Did you get my purchases returned?"

"Yes," Vern said, frowning.

Carl laughed a little. "How much cash we got?"

"Enough to get home," Vern said, irritated that Carl insisted on talking in front of Michael.

"You got enough to get home?" Carl asked Michael. He looked at Michael in the rearview mirror and laughed. Unwrapping his sandwich, he laughed again and pulled onto I-15 heading south. For several miles no one spoke. Michael held Ryan's hand and tried to smile at him. The little boy watched Michael's every move and clung tightly to his finger. The sun poured in through the sunroof, nearly blinding Ryan since he'd leaned so far back in the poorly installed car seat. Michael took the blanket and tried to make a shade by hooking the material to the inside dome light.

"What are you doing?" Carl snapped.

"The sun's in his eyes," Michael explained, his voice calm.

"Tell him to close them. I don't want that rag hanging up in here."

Michael lowered the blanket and then tried to adjust the seat so it sat up more. "Would you like to know about your son? What he eats. His schedule?"

"Stephanie will know," Carl said.

"Actually, he's changed quite a bit. He might not even remember her. Very likely he will continue to cry when she takes him."

"He'll learn," Carl said.

Michael tried to understand Carl's motive for coming this far for Ryan. If he could understand the motive maybe he could effect a change.

"How are you going to get home?" Carl asked conversationally.

"Probably bus," Michael said. He recognized the edge to Carl's voice. Michael had lived with his father's brand of bland sarcasm.

"You got enough money?" Carl asked politely. "I hear you've had some financial problems."

Vern warned the driver with a look that he ignored.

"Hope you got cash," Carl said impersonally. "Doubt anyone will take your checks."

Michael caught Vern's next warning look. *They took the money,* Michael thought, fear and anger pouring through him. After telling Laura to leave her purse, Carl had never taken them out to eat, he remembered. *They're crooks. Could Mr. Climbs prove that? Would Kathy MacKenzie see this as reason enough to approve adoption, or would she place Ryan with Stephanie and assign someone to teach her parenting skills? How involved was Stephanie?*

"I've got money," Michael said into the prolonged silence, curbing his rage with a renewed sense of hope, his tone casual even to his ears. Unlocking his seatbelt, he leaned forward. "I've never met your partner here." He stretched his right hand to shake awkwardly over the seat. "I'm Michael Ross. Your name is?" The emphasis on the word *partner* alarmed Vern as he weakly shook Michael's hand. Michael's cheerfulness alarmed Carl.

"And what do you do?" Michael asked Vern.

Vern told him the truth. He managed the apartments where Carl lived. Despite Michael's suspicions, nothing about Vern's dress belied his story. The Wranglers were old, the checkered, short-sleeved shirt stained.

Self-doubt flooded Michael. He smiled bigger. Maybe the two in the front seat were thieves, but maybe not.

As he leaned back again, Michael could see his reflection in the rearview mirror. Surprised, Michael moved forward slightly and looked again at his own cheerful face. One dimple dominated the right cheek. Nothing on that face indicated the fear he felt pushing on his chest. The eyes that gazed back saw his own father. Michael remembered his father smiling, his father laughing, his father shaking hands with the health inspector or the zoning commissioner. His father shook hands and smiled at customers, telling them he'd see them next week when their route came through again.

Had his father been scared? Had his smile also covered fear? Had his father been afraid of being alone? Failing? In the whole of his life,

Michael had never wondered. Had Joseph Ross covered fear with a convincing smile? Without a God to turn to, had Joseph hated himself so much that he couldn't love others? Without a Savior to turn to for strength, did fear turn mean?

Riding in the back of a gray sedan with two possible criminals in the front and a fearful child in the back, Michael bowed his head and offered a prayer of gratitude for his knowledge of Jesus Christ. Then, for the first time, he prayed for his father, that somehow he could accept the truth and the love of Christ. The car passed Springville and then Spanish Fork while Michael petitioned the Lord for his father, then for Ryan's safety, and then for wisdom.

When Ryan started whining softly, Michael asked Carl to stop so that they could feed him. "You don't have a bottle or something?" the man grumbled.

"He's too old for a bottle. We need some soup. Maybe mashed potatoes," Michael insisted.

They passed several restaurants outside of Beaver, and Michael calmly suggested that Kathy would be interested in any treatment that constituted neglect. Ignored nutritional needs would fall into that category. Michael amused himself by using Kathy's professional jargon. Carl wasn't quite sure what Michael was talking about, but he stopped at a market outside of a small town. "We can buy something here," Carl muttered.

Michael got Ryan unhooked from the car seat and carried him into the service station. Holding the boy by the hand, they slowly toured the store, finally choosing a yogurt, a hot dog without the bun, and a large Sprite. Michael told the cashier that Carl would pay, and then sat at one of the red plastic booths. Sitting Ryan to the side of him, Michael slowly cut up the hot dog and started to spoon yogurt into the little boy's mouth.

Carl strode forcefully out to the car. "I will not be told what I can and cannot do with my own kid. Nobody tells me where to stop." Carl's anger mounted as he realized how he had been manipulated into having Michael in the car. Now Michael was manipulating the duration of the stop.

"I'm the one who says when and where we stop," Carl said to no one in particular, then he slammed back through the doors where

Michael was nonchalantly teasing Ryan about having ketchup on his chin. The two companionably shared the pop until the straw sucked air off the bottom of the ice-filled cup. Ryan giggled and took the straw to suck again. "We're leaving," Carl demanded. Ryan's face went sober.

Michael smiled, got up, and reloaded Ryan.

CHAPTER 26

Laura stopped pacing back and forth in the police station and stood in front of the phone. Her mother would be glad Ryan was gone. Ryan complicated things. Her mother hated complications. She liked neat boxes and spaces for things and people. Ryan was complicated.

Her dad, Laura thought, *would help.*

You don't have much time, an inner voice said. *Planes are fast.* A panic seized the girl. She dialed. Her father listened. "We all came immediately down to the police station so Stephanie could tell the cops. She's in there right now telling them about everything. About stolen credit cards and false IDs. Apparently there's another man with Carl. They're the ones that took our money. Got all the information they needed out of my purse. The police have called in a special agent of something. Kathy says she made a real mistake and she's trying to get some emergency service for Ryan, and the cops are supposed to be watching for the car. The police won't give me any information, though. I keep asking if the car has been spotted and they won't tell me."

Laura listened for a moment. "Michael went willingly, so they have no jurisdiction to get him."

Lance asked what time Michael and Ryan had left. He concluded that the car had probably already crossed the Nevada border. "Are the Nevada police watching?"

"I . . . I don't think so," Laura said uncertainly. "I don't know. Maybe. You'd think that both states would be informed."

"If Stephanie was so concerned about Ryan being taken, how come she showed up so late?" her father asked.

Laura had wondered too and asked as much. "What happened was that Stephanie and a friend of Stephanie's had gone to social services where they were going to tell Kathy about Carl's crimes and get a restraining order. They waited there for her, but Kathy was at our house."

Laura's father said he'd fly down. "If you haven't heard from Michael or the police by the time I get there, we'll fly to Las Vegas and get him and Ryan."

"Can you hurry?"

"Your mom's not here. I'll leave her a note and come right now."

"Mom won't approve," Laura said hastily.

"She needs time to think about things, then she opens up more. But I'll be there."

* * *

After Ryan's lunch break, the car was mostly quiet. Michael talked softly to Ryan, discussing the passing scenery, tickling him on the kneecap. "We could use a little more air back here," Michael suggested kindly. "Ryan is really sweating." With a scowl into the rearview mirror, Carl flipped the air conditioner on high. Later Michael told him it was a little too cold. With another scowl, Carl flipped the switch lower. Twice Michael suggested that they close the sunroof for shade, that Ryan was having trouble seeing. Carl closed the shade. It was about then that Michael offered to teach Carl one of Ryan's favorite bedtime songs.

"Listen close. You can watch the actions through the rearview mirror. Where is thumbkin? Where is thumbkin?" Michael sang, his hands behind his back. The right thumb appeared as he continued, "Here I am." The other thumb appeared. "Here I am." The thumbs wiggled at each other as he sang, "How are you today, sir? Very well, I thank you. Run away. Run away." Ryan laughed, and Michael continued, "Where is pointer? Where is pointer? Here I am—" Carl cut them off.

"I understand. No more singing."

"If you have a pen and paper, I'll make a list of his favorite foods," Michael said. Without waiting for a reply he started to list the foods.

"He loves bananas, but after he's had enough he starts smashing them and rubbing them on the high chair and all over his hair. That's really a mess to cleanup. Then, of course, he really likes cherries, but you have to take the pits out. That's sort of a time-consuming kind of thing. Tomato soup is a favorite, but you have to take his shirt off if you don't want it stained. A bib won't work. When you use a bib, you just end up with two things to wash, so we just take the whole shirt off. Sometimes we just feed him in his diaper and then bathe him right after supper. That seems to work best. For breakfast he likes eggs, mostly scrambled, but don't get them too done. He doesn't like cheese in them. He usually likes juice before he goes—"

"Would you mind?" Carl cut in. "Stephanie's going to take care of the kid."

"Well, that's good. Of course, when I talked to her, she didn't want to care for him either. And since she left him for half of his life, I assumed that he wasn't her top priority."

"Things have changed."

"You can't just push the pause button on kids and come back and get them when you want to."

"You haven't figured something out yet, have you?" Carl said. "He's not your kid. He's mine."

"Then you need to care for him," Michael said. "I'm just trying to help you. Now at night he doesn't much like a crib."

"Shut up," Carl snarled. "Just shut up."

Michael refused to be intimidated. "Actually, he needs to be cared for right now. I think we need a rest break."

"What the — for?"

"He needs a diaper change."

"Doesn't he use the toilet?" Carl yelled.

"We've been working on that," Michael said calmly. "We try to reward him with M&Ms when he goes, so you might want to get . . ."

Carl stomped on the brake and pulled to the shoulder. A car passed, honking in irritation at Carl's sudden stop. "Change the diaper," Carl snarled. "Change it."

"We could have waited until a rest area," Michael said agreeably, "but okay." His hands shook slightly as he unhooked Ryan and got the diaper bag. Laying the little boy on the seat, Michael tickled him.

Ryan didn't respond. This new situation frightened him. Michael dropped the soiled diaper next to the car and put a new one on Ryan. Pulling shorts up around the little boy's waist, Michael stood Ryan up and hugged him.

"Get him back in that seat," Carl commanded.

Michael strapped the child into the car seat and then asked pleasantly, "Do you want to pop the trunk and I'll put this diaper in the back?"

"No. What I want," Carl said as he slowly turned in his seat, "is for you to get out."

The gun he was holding was the same one Laura had found almost a year and a half ago.

"What are you doing?" Vern asked, horrified.

"He needs to know who's boss," Carl said, jabbing the gun toward Michael, who was standing with his right foot on the side of the road, his left foot in the car. "Now get out."

Michael faced the gun with a mixture of shock and acceptance. Unfortunately he'd been right about this man all along—this man's need to control knew no bounds. "No," Michael said without moving. "I'll leave when Ryan's back with Stephanie."

"You'll leave now," Carl threatened. "Get out."

Everyone knows I left with them. There are witnesses . . . He wouldn't dare shoot! This was Michael's last thought as Carl shot one bullet over Michael's shoulder and then accelerated. The car lurched ahead and Michael's left foot caught as the back door swung against it. His back hit the pavement first, then his head bounced twice. The door pinned his left foot into the car and Michael was dragged; his hair and T-shirt scraped away, then his skin. For ten feet his body gathered tar and rock particles before his ankle broke, then he fell away from the vehicle. The momentum rolled him into the rocks bordering the highway.

"What are you doing, man? You're crazy!" Vern yelled.

Carl kept accelerating.

"Stop! You—" Vern was mad, but his raised voice could hardly be heard over Ryan's terrified screams.

"Carl!" Vern yelled. "Go back! You've gone crazy! What is your problem? You just killed a guy!" Vern started to yell obscenities mixed with threats and declarations about Carl's lack of sense.

Ryan's howls continued until Carl yelled, "Shut up. Shut up!" He swung a fist toward the car seat, missing the child by several inches, but Ryan was instantly quieted. He clutched his blanket and whimpered. Vern didn't shut up. "You've killed a man. He'll be found. They know he was with us. You can't kill people."

"He was driving me crazy."

"Tell that to a jury."

"I'll say he tried to take my son. I had to save my son. I'll tell them that he had been plotting since we left to take my son. You'll back me up."

"You can't kill a guy. Pull over in St. George. Call the police. Tell them to look for him. If he doesn't show up, you'll be investigated. I'm getting out. I don't want to be seen with you. I won't testify for you. No one even knows I was with you."

"Stephanie knows."

Vern swore. He threatened. He finally talked Carl into calling the police from a phone booth outside of St. George.

The phone call was so illogical the dispatcher almost didn't send a patrol car to look. She didn't associate the call with a dispatch sitting on her desk about stopping a car with three men and a toddler. Instead she called a patrol car and relayed as best she could the essence of the phone call. "Some guy said he had a passenger that tried to take the driver's son. Said it scared him so bad that he took off and the passenger got knocked away from the car. Somewhere north of St. George on the west lane. Said he was so scared he doesn't really remember where. Said he didn't want the guy hurt, just wanted him out of his life. Said that about ten times."

A police car rolled along the highway looking for a stranded man and found nothing.

About the time Laura finished talking to her father and started to pray for her husband and son, two bikers found Michael. They were on their last leg of a fifty-mile ride from Cedar City to St. George when one of them, wiping sweat from an upper lip as he got ready to drink, glanced toward the freeway.

"I don't want to be a hero if it involves blood or risk," he said calmly to his companion. "So you go over there and see who that guy is."

"What guy?" his companion asked, fatigued and more than a little tired of his friend's brand of humor.

"The one that appears to be bleeding on the side of the road."

In the end, both would-be rescuers left the trail and headed toward the freeway. While the one with an aversion to blood waved down Bobbi, a housewife from Cedar City, his companion ignored the risk of disease and tried to stop the bleeding from Michael's head wounds. In response to Bobbi's cell phone call, an ambulance screamed out of St. George.

* * *

Heat poured through the sunroof. Ryan's forehead formed beads of perspiration where the rays hit the white blanket. He kept the material over his face, refusing to look at the men in front of him, refusing to acknowledge that Michael had left him. Yet Ryan knew the men were there; he could hear their arguing.

Vern's anger was high-pitched and accusing. Carl drove fast. Rather than find another way home, Vern decided to stay with Carl just until they got to Vegas. From then on, they were parting company. Carl was too explosive and unpredictable for a game that should be played methodically and carefully.

"Why did you have to get this kid anyway?" Vern asked. "You couldn't leave well enough alone."

"He's my son," Carl said.

"You don't even like him," Vern snarled, and then fell silent. Mentally, he started shutting down his operation. He knew which files he needed to destroy. He'd clear out, start somewhere else. There would probably be an investigation. He told that much to Carl, warning him to destroy all evidence of stolen identities.

"Stop worrying," Carl said. "They'll find Michael. I'll explain I was scared. This'll blow over."

Heat waves shimmered off the pavement as Carl turned into the apartment parking lot. "Where the—?" Carl then let loose a long string of angry curses. Stephanie's car was not in its assigned spot. "Where is that woman? She needs to take care of this kid."

"It's your problem," Vern said, getting out and motioning for Carl to open the trunk. He lifted out an overnight case. "I'd suggest you destroy any evidence."

Carl muttered something about how he wasn't going to act paranoid and where was that woman. With his own overnight case, Carl entered the empty apartment. Silence. Nothing moved. Carl felt apprehensive as he looked around. She was gone. Had she left for good? Carl checked the coffee can first. Empty. He checked the drawers, and then he screamed, cursed, and called her names. After banging one fist on the table, he rushed to Vern's apartment. A truce was called as they gathered incriminating evidence to destroy.

CHAPTER 27

Gail's mother smiled when Leslie Steele brought Gail into the living room. "Well?" she asked.

"They took him," Gail said in disgust. "But I created such a ruckus Michael had to go just to calm the child."

"You what?" Leslie hit Gail lightly on the arm. "That was an act?"

"It was no act," Gail said, rubbing her arm. "I meant everything I said. But everyone's been too calm. Didn't get any results. Only us crazies can get away with acting like that."

"Gail," said Leslie, a formal reprimand in her voice, "that is horrible. How will we know if you're okay if you go around putting on an act?"

"I'll know," Gail's mother said.

Leslie smiled faintly. She understood.

Leslie was still preoccupied when she returned to Laura and Michael's home. *Mothers could tell,* she thought, and Gail had accomplished one thing. Ryan at least had Michael for the transition period.

No one answered her knock. "Laura," she called pushing the door open. "You won't believe what Gail did." Still no answer. "Laura?"

No one in the bedroom. The phone rang just as she turned to check in the back.

"Yes, this is his residence," she answered the caller. "No, his wife isn't. What's wrong?" Leslie listened. "I'll come," she told the hospital spokesman.

Conrad Steele left his office as he spoke to his wife on the cell phone. He ran across the parking lot as he listened to her describe how Michael had left with Carl and now had been found nearly dead.

"What kind of car?"

"I don't remember," Leslie said helplessly.

"What time?"

"I don't know. I left to take Gail home while Laura was packing Michael a bag."

"How's Laura?"

"I haven't found her. I don't think she knows."

"Did the hospital call the police?" Conrad's questions were terse.

"I don't know. I didn't ask."

"I will."

Conrad was still interrogating the police when he picked his wife up six minutes later. "Get hold of the police in Vegas," he said into his small phone. "And arrest these men for something more than white-collar theft. I think they tried to kill my son."

Flipping his phone closed, Conrad took a deep breath and then tried to concentrate on traffic. He didn't speak until they were speeding south on I-15.

"Stephanie came and reported this guy, Carl, for stealing identities." Conrad Steele explained what he'd learned to his wife. "The cops were supposed to stop him. They haven't yet. According to the detective I finally spoke with, Stephanie, Laura, and an officer flew to Vegas. I'm assuming Laura called her dad to fly them. The police let Stephanie go to identify another accomplice. The officer went to keep tabs on Stephanie, who's been arrested for her part in identity theft. They had no idea about Michael. If something happens to that boy, I'll make sure the state presses murder charges. I swear I will."

* * *

"There's the car," Laura said. She was in the back of a squad car from the Las Vegas Police Department. Her father sat on one side, Stephanie on the other. A Provo policeman sat in front with the officer who had met them at the airport. Laura climbed out quickly and rushed past the Buick toward the apartments. Turning to look over her shoulder, she asked Stephanie, "Which apartment?" The blanket caught her eye. Pale against the black upholstery, a little knee, a foot held perfectly still.

He's in there. Oh, no. Oh, Father in Heaven, please! The girl rushed around the car, yanking at door handles. They were locked. Twice she hit a window with a fist. The officer ran to his car for a door-release kit. Laura didn't wait. She grabbed the piece of concrete Stephanie had dropped less than forty-eight hours earlier and slammed it against the side window. Glass spattered. The impact bruised her hand. The glass cut her arm when she reached in to open the door.

Ryan was limp. His sweat had long since dried up. The officer took one look and rushed back to his car to call an ambulance. Laura held the small body. Her tears cooled only small patches of the pale skin.

Guilt-driven adrenaline pierced Vern and Carl when the siren screamed into the parking lot. They peeked from the window. The ambulance siren died near the small knot of people surrounding Carl's car. A small body was laid on the gurney.

"Oh no," Vern whispered when he saw Stephanie lay a hand on the boy's arm.

Carl didn't speak.

Laura watched the paramedics pull clothing off Ryan's pale, limp body. She watched them pour alcohol on his arms. "Where's Michael?" Laura asked, looking wildly around. "Michael wouldn't have left Ryan like this." She climbed into the ambulance after Ryan.

As Lance approached the officer, police departments in two states were sharing information. The on-site officer was listening to a bulletin reporting that Michael had been picked up outside of St. George, descriptions of the men who had knocked him off the roadway, and a list of the men's alleged crimes. The officer reported Ryan's condition, called it child endangerment, and requested backup that was already en route. When the second set of sirens entered the apartment parking lot, Vern and Carl were still hiding behind curtains. Vern wanted Carl to go over to the ambulance and cry over his son. Carl thought they should both flee. The officers spoke briefly, and Stephanie pointed to Vern's apartment. Seeing the police approaching, Carl rushed through the door, ranting about how he couldn't believe he'd possibly forgotten his son in the car, thanking them for finding the little boy, attempting to cry as he asked the boy's condition, and suggesting that he had only been gone for a few minutes.

"I can't believe I forgot him. I was so worried about Stephanie. I'm glad you're here, Stephanie. Is the little boy okay? Oh, thank you for finding him," he blubbered unconvincingly.

"Where's Michael?" Laura yelled as she blocked the ambulance door, refusing to allow Carl in to see his son.

"He tried to take the baby," Carl explained sadly. "We dropped him off outside of St. George."

Laura pictured her husband walking along the freeway in the dreadful heat. Before she could voice her anger, the officer handcuffed Carl and read him his rights.

Vern cussed in resignation and then fell silent as he was led to a separate squad car.

Laura saw none of the arrests. She watched as a catheter was inserted into Ryan's small vein for the IV. A paramedic radioed an estimated time of arrival to the nearest emergency room. The ambulance door slammed, and Laura braced herself as they rolled swiftly toward the open street.

* * *

Michael didn't know who was with him. He didn't know where he was. The pain was pounding in a head filled with black. He tried to open his eyes. The effort, although heroic, was unsuccessful, and he faded into the darkness. Leslie Steele had not noticed the eyelids flutter; she was listening intently to the two men. "We had no idea he was this bad," Lance Keeyes said, watching his son-in-law. Conrad Steele had explained that the initial CT scan indicated a major intracranial mass. The boy had arrived at the St. George hospital semiconscious, but had deteriorated rapidly because of swelling within the brain. Surgery had been advised. Now every bodily function was being monitored on the injured young man: motor response, blood pressure, body temperature, respiratory rate, even intracranial pressure. Two nurses were present. One frowned and indicated they needed to leave. She ushered the three out of the intensive-care unit, then hurried back to her patient.

The three stood awkwardly around the sterile waiting area. Leslie and Conrad Steele listened grimly as Lance explained how he had gone with an officer to the hospital where they'd taken Ryan. Laura had been watching helplessly as a team of nurses cleaned vomit from Ryan's pale, quiet face. A doctor had assured both Laura and Lance that vomiting was a normal response to heat stress.

"The officer told Laura that his communiqué with the Utah police indicated that Michael was in the hospital with a broken ankle. I'm not sure the officer really knew that Michael had a concussion, or if he was just trying to spare Laura because she was so worried about Ryan. Laura knew you were here with him. She wanted me to fly up here, help you give Michael a blessing, and then when he was strong enough, fly him down there."

"She needs to know," Conrad said

"Has Ryan been awake much?" Leslie asked.

"He sort of woke once, right after I got there, but then he had a convulsion and they medicated him."

"Are convulsions normal too?" Leslie asked, quietly feeling Laura's pain at Ryan's suffering.

"In severe cases."

"How severe is this case?"

"No one was saying. We can expect anything from a full recovery to heart problems, kidney failure, brain damage. I don't know."

"Is Stephanie with him?" Conrad asked.

"They arrested her. I offered to post bail. She refused. Said Ryan was better off with Laura."

"Laura's needed here," Conrad suggested.

"This will tear her apart," Leslie murmured.

"Maybe we shouldn't tell her for a while," Conrad offered, feeling for Laura's sanity.

"I promised I'd call as soon as I had talked to Michael," Lance admitted.

"Well, you haven't talked to him."

"Yes, but the surgery went well. There may need to be skin grafts on his back later. I've got to call Laura."

"You can't tell her on the phone," Leslie quietly begged.

For several moments they debated over what they should do. They prayed. Finally Leslie weighed in. "I'll call Gail. Ryan knows her. He likes her. You can pick her up in Provo and fly her down to Vegas. Laura could leave Ryan if Gail were there. Gail could use being of service. Michael could use Laura."

CHAPTER 28

For the next two weeks Mandy Keeyes complained extensively about how absent her husband had been. "Where are you now?" she asked one day.

"St. George," Lance replied, leaning back on his hotel bed. "Michael had a skin graft on his back. We wanted to be there when he came out of recovery. He's been conscious a lot more. He's been able to help make decisions about his care."

The next day the father and daughter called from Las Vegas to say that Ryan was unconscious again. His kidneys still weren't functioning properly. That same afternoon they were back in St. George saying that Michael had talked to Laura for over an hour.

When they called from Las Vegas that night to say Ryan had been awake for a few minutes, Mandy announced that they were crazy. "How many miles are you putting on that old plane? How much in gas and hotel rooms is this costing? If Ryan's mostly unconscious, it doesn't really matter who's with him."

Lance didn't answer his wife. He pictured Laura talking softly to the unresponsive boy, asking Gail about how his vital signs had been, cornering the hurried doctor. Lance pictured how cheerful Laura was in front of Michael. How encouraging and brave she'd been talking to her husband about Ryan's condition and that prayers mattered most right now. "You would be proud of our girl," Lance finally said. "She's demonstrated more strength than either of us thought she had."

"She needs to—" Mandy stopped. She didn't really know what her daughter needed to do.

"Laura suggested that Ryan be moved to St. George," Lance explained to his wife. "But if he's moved anywhere, they want him transported to Primary Children's Hospital in Salt Lake. Right now, though, they feel he should remain where he is. Michael is progressing well, and no one will even think about jeopardizing his recovery by moving him. Laura tries to schedule being with both her boys. Gail has been staying here with Ryan."

"Maybe Laura should concentrate on helping her husband get well," Mandy said.

"Laura's doing what she can."

* * *

Ann approached the door quietly, watching the scene for a moment. Gail's easychair was in the reclined position, her right arm shielding her closed eyes from the light that streamed in with the late afternoon sun. Laura sat next to Ryan, alternately watching the IV drip slowly into the snakelike tubing and watching Ryan's motionless face. She lay her head against the sheet and closed her eyes.

"Knock, knock," Ann said softly. Laura jumped slightly. Gail remained motionless. "Are you still here?" Ann asked as she leaned against the wall. Laura sat up straight.

"Uh, yeah." She was so tired that several seconds passed before she recognized the adoption worker. "I just wanted him to have someone familiar here when he wakes up again."

"How's he doing?"

Laura rubbed his little arm. His hand lay limp. The long lashes never moved. He looked like a plastic doll.

"The electrolytes are better," Laura said. "The doctor feels he'll be strong enough to transport soon. They feel Primary Children's would be the best for him. Maybe they can figure out why his kidneys still aren't functioning very well."

"How's Michael?"

"He's better," Laura said, suddenly weary. "Brother Steele left a few days ago, but Sister Steele has gotten a hotel room and sees him every day."

"You've been able to talk to him?"

"He's tired a lot. He's glad when I come, but then tells me to come back here and make sure Ryan's okay."

Ann motioned to Gail and spoke quietly, "Are we bothering her?"

Laura shook her head. "Gail's a friend of ours. She stays with Ryan when I'm not here. She's gotten really good at sleeping in that chair."

Ann asked about Lance and where he stayed. "A hotel. He's resting. He's probably going to call my mom."

"Your dad has been extremely helpful, hasn't he?"

Laura nodded. Although she had tried, Laura knew she would never be able to adequately thank her father.

In the silence that followed, both women alternately watched the IV-drip and the little boy's motionless face. Finally, Laura bluntly asked, "Why are you here?"

Ann knew this would be uncomfortable. "Stephanie signed guardianship of Ryan over to me."

Tears threatened Laura's eyes. They wouldn't be the first tears she'd cried in the last two weeks, but they were the first to be cried in front of anyone besides her father. She fought the tears and said nothing.

"Stephanie and I talked for a long time," Ann continued. "She loves her son, and she does want to do what's best for him. She'll spend time in jail now—probably not much since she's providing so much information for the police, and then she'll be on probation. She'll have trouble finding any kind of employment. She can't support her son. She would like to see Ryan placed in a good home for adoption.

"She would like you to adopt Ryan," Ann continued quickly. "She knows what kind of mother you've been for him. She's extremely grateful. But we decided that for right now placing him in my guardianship would be best. Having guardianship allows me to make arrangements for financial aid to pay these medical bills. Some will come from the state, some from Carl if there's anything left after paying off his victims. Stephanie also knows that Ryan may never fully recover. If he doesn't, she recognizes that you might no longer want to adopt him. She felt that signing guardianship over to me would take a lot of pressure off if you decided you didn't want to adopt a child with problems. She felt that if I was guardian, then you could wait and see how he's doing before you make a decision."

Ann paused for a long time. Laura sat still, watching Ryan's face.

"Michael's going to take some time to heal," she finally continued. "His injuries and medical bills are going to be a setback. You've got a lot to consider. You've already done a lot for this little boy, and I'm sure you'll want to help him adjust to any changes. If you decide to adopt, I'll help with home study and legal requirements." Ann paused. "But you don't have to make any decisions right now. Wait. Think things over very carefully. See how Ryan's chances for full recovery are. Make sure there won't be any emotional or physical delays in his development."

"That's stupid," Gail said, pushing the recliner down with a pop that startled both Ann and Laura. Gail was a silhouette against the fierce sunlight. Her voice just as fierce.

"You don't shop for kids, rejecting those less than perfect, sending back anything you don't like. When you're pregnant, you pray for healthy, well-adjusted children, and then you accept what God gives you. You take the child God gives you and say this child is for me to raise. It's not my child, it's God's child, sent to me for help, for love. My job is to help this child. And sometimes the person that gives birth isn't the one who has that responsibility. Sometimes the responsibility was meant for someone else. But the responsibility is the same. You don't always get a perfect kid. You don't always get convenience. You get what God sends. If you can't take Ryan with problems, you have no right to him. What if he overcomes this and then becomes sick ten years from now? You going to send him back? I don't think so. Plan to help him, come what may. If you and Michael can't carry the weight, you ask God to make you stronger or you find help for your load, but you don't dump a human being that's still willing to be helped. My mom didn't. As long as I let her, she helps me."

Gail left the window, left the room. When she passed in front of the other two women, she didn't seem as fierce as when she'd been a voice from the light.

EPILOGUE

Delicate flowers decorated the silver lace vine that twisted along the porch railing. A two-man pup tent was pushed next to the vine, making a perfect child's campsite.

Laura had wanted the tent taken down, but she'd been outvoted. "It's our wilderness camp," her oldest son exclaimed. "Our camping," his two younger brothers echoed. The tent was crowded with books and blankets and bread crusts.

"The problem here," Laura had said sternly, "is that I'm outnumbered."

"Then let's work on getting us a girl," Michael proposed.

"Eeeew," the boys spoke in unison. "No girls."

"I'd like a girl," Laura had said.

Michael remembered the conversation as he passed the tent and opened the front door to his home. *Another year and Seth will have to find someone new to smell his newt colony. We'll be able to afford something bigger,* Michael thought. The living room was unusually clean; no toys cluttered the carpet and the windows were shining. Laura was alone in a warm and fragrant kitchen. She had just hung up the phone.

"That was Gail. She can't be here for the baptism. Her husband has to work, but they'll come by this evening," Laura said, carefully lifting cookies from a baking sheet. "I thought you were going to get home early."

"Kyle called from Salt Lake. I'd sent him and two other guys up there this morning to work on a solarium we're maintaining. They were supposed to hang some new plants and check emitters on an automatic sprinkler system. One of the crew got upset when they were removing the dead plants."

"Why?" Laura asked, curious despite her irritation that these things always happened when she wanted Michael home.

"I don't know," Michael said, taking off his cap and tossing it on a shelf. "I never did figure that out, but he did a few inappropriate things."

Laura could see the scars on the back of Michael's head. They only showed if the hair was moved by a hat. Today she felt an unusual tightening in her stomach as she saw the thick white dents across his scalp. "Is Connor on that crew?"

"No. He's been rewiring a pump in one of the greenhouses."

"And these inappropriate things in Salt Lake, did they cost us any money?"

"Not this time."

"Did it cost you a contract?"

"No, the owner has an aunt who's mentally ill. Your parents get here?"

"About noon. Mom brought you a present. She said it was for her favorite son-in-law. Of course, you're her only son-in-law. Now they're out with the boys buying everyone matching ties. Dad went to help with crowd control and make sure the ties weren't really ugly. He hated those plaid ones she got three years ago for the baby's blessing."

Michael took a cookie, studied it, then took a bite. "How many kinds have you made?" he asked, motioning to the plastic containers.

"Four or five. I'm not sure."

"A bit excessive, babe?"

"No," she said, snapping the lid onto a full bowl. "Can you please take down that tent? It looks trashy."

"No one's coming to inspect the house." Michael moved to the sink and began to scrub cookie sheets. "They're coming for a baptism. The rest doesn't matter." He rinsed the sheets and set them in a dish drainer. Laura was sweeping energetically at the floor when he spoke again. "I ran by and saw Stephanie today."

Laura stood motionless, then slowly turned to look at him. "Why?"

"Invited her to the baptism. He's her son too, Laura. I wanted her to know that we were thinking of her on this special day. I wanted her to know he was excited and that she was welcome to come."

Laura took a deep breath. "Is she going to come?"

"I don't think so. I told her if she didn't come, I'd bring her a picture."

"Why don't we just buy her a dress that matches mine and make it a real family affair?"

Michael narrowed his brow at the sarcasm, recognized his wife's pain, and pulled her against his chest. For a moment she resisted, then lay against him. "I guess I should have called her," Laura said into his shoulder. "I haven't talked to her since she was here for his birthday. Did she want to come tonight?"

"I'm not sure. She still doesn't feel she belongs in church, but she's better. She wanted to talk about Ryan though."

"What did you tell her?"

"That his tent was still on the porch. That he plans to play soccer again next year. I told her we might drive to Las Vegas this fall to see Mom and Dad. I suggested she might want to come."

"That does sound lovely," Laura said, the sarcasm back as she looked up at her husband. "A nice little family vacation."

"We don't have to," Michael said. "The other day you thought it was a good idea."

"That was one of my good days," Laura said.

"What's wrong today?" Michael asked quietly.

Laura lay her head back against his chest. "Nothing really," Laura sighed without looking up at Michael. "It's just, during these kind of milestone days, I start wondering if I've done enough for Ryan. I mean, six years ago, when we didn't know whether he'd ever be . . . be . . . totally healthy again, I decided God wanted him to be my responsibility. And I thought that was really magnanimous back then. But I didn't know how I'd feel about Ryan in the future. I was afraid I would think of him as a burden maybe. Well, now I know how I feel about Ryan. I know how much I love him. I know how intense my belief is that he was meant to be in our home. I know that the Lord sent him to us for a reason. But I don't know if he feels that—if I've done enough to help him feel that. When he's fifteen, will he feel our love? When he's seventeen, will he feel that he belongs? When he's thirty, will he wonder if his life would have been better elsewhere? I don't feel threatened anymore because I doubt my own feelings—I doubt his. I mean, when Ryan first stayed with us, and then when we first decided to adopt him, I wondered if I'd love him enough." Now she looked up at her husband. "I wondered if I would love him as much as the children I gave birth to. I know now that I do. But will *he* know that? If he knows my love is as strong for him as for the others, then I don't care if he is curious about Stephanie or even Carl. I don't care if he has a relationship with them and brings something good to their lives. As long as he doesn't do it because he doubts our love or . . . is insecure about his place in this family. And I'm scared because I don't want him running to them because someday he might think our standards for him are too high."

Michael didn't give false promises. He knew there might come a time when Ryan would wonder about his role in their family. He knew there might come a time when he might use his biological parents as an excuse for making poor choices. Michael held his wife for just a moment more before their three sons burst into the kitchen. The eager brothers shoved packages at their parents, rehearsing in detail how their grandpa refused to wear a tie with Daffy Duck on it.

"So we bought ties with ferns on them because they look like Dad's greenhouse," Ryan announced. "We'll look just alike," the boy said proudly, holding up a strip of fabric that to Michael looked like a solarium with too few water sprinklers and too many dead plants.

While the others clambered for a cookie, Laura knelt down next to Ryan. "I love you," she said.

"I know," he said agreeably.

"You're doing the right thing by choosing to be baptized."

"I know." He nodded solemnly and then reached over her shoulder and took a cookie from his little brother's hand. The younger child screamed.

"Ryan, don't take your brother's . . ." Laura started to reprimand, but Ryan was gone, chattering something about seeing if his white shirt was the same as Dad's.

About the Author

ViAnn Prestwich has degrees from Brigham Young University and Southern Utah University. She spent nearly ten years teaching high school. During that time, she often worked with students who had behavioral disorders and learning disabilities. She has written for various trade magazines as well as taught as an adjunct professor. She and her husband currently live in Washington state with their five children, some of whom joined their family through adoption.

60S 3.10   33
32:08 3m

35   3.29
       640
  32:20

(
3 60
2 80